THROUGH THESE DARK GATES

a novel

BROOKLYN K. BIEGEL

ALBERTA, CANADA
FOUR SEASONS NORTH PUBLISHING

THROUGH THESE DARK GATES

All Scripture quotations and paraphrases are taken from the King James Version (KJV) of the Bible, public domain.

This is a work of fiction. Apart from well-known people, events, and locales that figure into the narrative, all names, characters, places, and incidents are either products of the author's imagination or are used fictitiously.

Published in Canada by FOUR SEASONS NORTH PUBLISHING

Library and Archives Canada Cataloguing in Publication
Names: Biegel, Brooklyn K., author.
Title: Through These Dark Gates / Brooklyn K. Biegel. Description: First edition.
Grovedale, Alberta : Four Seasons North, [2022]
ISBN 978-1-7780610-0-4 (softcover)
ISBN 978-1-7780610-1-1 (hardcover)
ISBN 978-1-7780610-2-8 (ebook)

Printed and bound in Canada by Friesens Corporation
2022

To Dad and Mom—

who first taught me the fear of Yahweh.

"Yea, though I walk through the valley of the shadow of death,

I will fear no evil: for thou art with me."

Psalms 23:4

AUTHOR'S NOTE

As an explanatory note to modern readers, I wish to address the usage of some sensitive language within the manuscript. This is an historical novel, and as such the term *Negro* is used exclusively by me within the text on account of the vocable being a standard and non-inflammatory one used in the nineteenth-century lexicon of speech to denote black ancestry. As an apology I wish to reference other works of historical literature in which the vocable has also been used—one example being the still hotly controversial abolitionist novel *Uncle Tom's Cabin* by Harriet Beecher Stowe, published in 1852. In addition, I have chosen to lowercase the terms *black* and *white* for the same reason—these terms were not historically capitalized in literature of the time and were used in the nineteenth-century lexicon of speech to denote heritage ancestry.

CONTENTS

PROLOGUE

THE MISTS OF DARKNESS

Off the Coast of Ireland
March 1845

Lord God Almighty seems angry… angry at me. Dark clouds look like demon faces jeerin' at me from a nightmare, an' the shriekin' wind lashes the icy salt spray of the Atlantic intae my eyes, addin' tae the sting of my tears. My heart—I see half of it bleedin' on them bonnie green shores while Ireland slips away, swallowed by fog as the clipper Narcissus dashes westward.

My petticoats freeze tae my legs an' ankles. I shiver. Through the dark mists a tall hatless shape paces the starboard deck. He looks at them black waves that churn the hull, an' he curses. They look back at him, an' they laugh. He walks, but he walks in a cage.

Am I Jonah, or is he?

The vessel lurches on a roarin' breaker. I clutch the iron railin' but my hands slip. I tear off my plaid shawl an' lay it 'cross the iron tae get a grip, an' I tell my heart that the cold don't matter when the pain's so great.

Yet guilt is a vulture. It sweeps down an' snatches me. I struggle. I tell myself I wasnae cruel; I had nae choice but tae leave. Just a common, unmarried midwife. Och! How could the Lord 'spect a body like me tae care for the wee bairns of an adulteress?

But my conscience fashes me still, an' each rush of black water stabs the pain down. My thoughts go four years back—

back tae the Magdalene Asylum. There I stood afore the gates beneath her window, my face pressed against them icy bars, listenin' helpless tae her cries of pain in childbirth. Only minutes afore the wee lass had stood afore me on the other side of the iron fence. For nine months she'd been locked in there—an' 'twas hell. Nothin' was left of her poor wee body. Her wee face—blanched like death! Her bonnie flaxen locks—matted an' tangled! Her chill, raw-boned hands clutchin' mine as she pressed her weddin' ring intae my palm.

"They would take it from me and sell it for money if they knew I'd kept it!" she had whispered, in tears. "Och! Take it now—hide it for me—and if I die ye must give it tae my wee bairn!" She pressed her swollen belly.

Lookin' past her tortured face, I seen two dark shapes stalkin' up behind her through the gloom.

The nuns, comin' tae take her away. An' she kept cryin'.

"He won't forgive me! Och! My dear, precious Johnny won't forgive me! I beg him! I beg, beg, beg. And the dirty nappies of other women's bairns I wash, and wash, and wash until my hands are raw and my heart is sick to death… But it's not good enough for him! Not good enough for Johnny! It will never be good enough! Never good enough for him!" Bowin' against the fence, she sobbed, scarce able to draw breath. "I love him still! I love him still… I do! I never thought he'd learn of it. Oh! But now I'm sorry. Sorry! Oh so sorry because I sinned against him and against heaven! God forgive me! O gracious God… forgive me!" She gripped my hands through the bars as though she knew the nuns were stalkin' her. I felt the strength of a contraction shudder through her body, an' she gasped, sayin' desperately against the pangs, "Pray tae God for my poor wee bairns. God in heaven hears ye when ye pray—I know he does—an' he knows my wee bairns need ye now. Och! Won't ye help tae save them from this hell?"

Tears burned my eyes an' I nodded. I took the wee gold ring an' slipped it intae my dress pocket.

The women came. One clamped her steely hand 'round my lassie's spare arm, then wrenched her back as my lass cried out.

"Who are you?" the woman snarled at me.

"A servant of the lassie's family; a midwife, ma'am," said I. "This woman is in labour, she ain't well. Ow, please, ma'am, please! Allow me tae come in an' help her!"

The second woman stepped close tae the fence, blocked my view. Her look was dirty. "We know how to deliver children here," she said, then turned an' walked away, draggin' my lassie with them till they disappeared inside the dark walls of the asylum.

'Twas the last time I saw her face.

Five hours I had stood there. Midnight, an' the whimper of a wee babe from the window told the child came safe from God. But the next day my lassie was gone. They say she bled tae death.

Four years rolled by. Each Monday I passed those gates on my way home from market. My heart prayed an' my eyes searched for the wee face of the bairn I knew would look jist like my lassie—aye, they said the babe was a lass, an' told me her name. Then one day I saw her. She was playin' with her ball outside in the stark brown yard with three others, all stick-thin, too. I went tae the part of the fence shaded by a spreadin' ash tree, an' with my basket on my arm I beckoned the lass. She saw me an' came near.

"Can ye keep a secret, lass?" said I, stealin' the ring from my pocket.

She blinked her cornflower-blue eyes an' nodded.

"Don't tell naebody, ye hear? It's from yer own mother, lass. 'Tis her weddin' ring. Hide it safe—there in yer stockin', see? Never tell a soul, promise?"

She gaped at me, then at the ring glitterin' in the sun. "In my stockin'?" she whispered, leanin' closer.

"Aye, lass, for now," said I, then turned. If I tarried, 'twould be danger. "Run along now, lass. Aye, run!"

I hastened up the street, with one glance back. She was playin' with the other children. But she watched me, too, like she wished tae follow.

It happened scarce two weeks ago, but weeks turn tae years for me now. My lassie's face—her words, tears, cold hands, an' my promise tae nae leave her bairns in that hellish place—aye, how an empty promise will turn tormentor!

"Lord God Almighty! Mercy! Mercy! Mercy!" Sweat an' tears stream down my face. "Rattle the cage, O God! Rattle the cage!"

Can he hear me? Can he see?

I lift my voice an' scream intae the chill blast. "Ye're the first an' the last! Ye were dead, but now ye live! Ye hide from us, an' yet ye know the thoughts of men! Ye hold the keys tae hell an' death! The body of Jesus Christ was sacrificed once for all—I know it! I know it, an' I thank thee! I thank thee! Now help us, Lord! Oh, help us tae understand it an' believe ye will turn this evil for the good! O God, my God! Ye say ye give good things tae them who ask! Ye say ye open doors tae them who knock, an' I'm knockin' now! Och! I'm knockin' knockin' knockin' like I nae have knocked afore! Hear prayer, O Lord! Hear prayer! Hear prayer!"

I bow over the railin', bawlin' fit tae die. But somethin' draws me through the tempest.

I will go before thee, and make the crooked places straight: I will break in pieces the gates of brass, and cut in sunder the bars of iron.

I look behind me. My russet hair snaps my cheeks, lances my eyes… I'm alone. But that voice I know like I know the beat of my own pulse. I lift my face intae the rain an' taste sweet an' bitter waters. "Och! Then, Lord God, look! Look down from heaven upon these sparrows! Alone, alone, alone! Draw them tae ye! Their poor mother died in that cage… I know ye forgave her, but— Och! Break the fowler's snare! Make it so these precious bairns may escape it, an' make them a testimony for Jesus!"

The ship tosses on a long wave. It roars. It peaks. It seems tae hang from a noose. Shadow waters swirl below. I feel sick. Then… then… Is it a touch on my shoulder? Aye, a warm touch… a hand? I strain my eyes but cannae see— jist that dizziness stirrin' everythin' 'round intae a midden.

Then I'm fallin': down, down, down. All I see is black, black, black, an' nae more.

PART ONE

— CHAPTER I —

THE SIXTH COMMANDMENT

Magdalene Asylum, Dublin, Ireland
Late April 1851

"*Mea culpa, mea culpa, mea maxima culpa*!"

Striking a chapped, bony fist against the flat of her bosom, Kate Fletcher repeated the Latin words in acknowledgment of her guilt, just as she had done every day through Lent and for the past two weeks leading up to the Sunday of her First Communion. She could not get Thaddy Murray out of her mind. Nor could she banish the sinful motivation to wear her white linen Communion dress and veil for him rather than for God.

Kneeling on the cold floorboards in the centre of the large orphanage bedroom, with her simple linen veil cast aside and her uncovered head bent in painful contrition, Kate could still see her reflection looking back at her from the window glass, for she had stood in front of it only moments before, gazing upon herself in a cloud of vain delight, feeling as beautiful as a princess and thinking only of him…

Thaddy Murray, the handsome altar boy. The boy she wanted to marry.

But now that she had committed the sin of vanity, she could not escape the terrorizing sensation that her soul was dangling over the pit of hell. And all on the day of her First Communion. The day that was supposed to be the most important one of her whole life.

"Katie! Kat-*ie!* What's takin' so darn long?" The shrill, childish voice rang through the stairwell, accompanied by the drumming of little feet dashing up the steps. "Everyone's outside waitin' for ya!" Just then a small, wiry girl in a plain smock burst into the room, panting. "*What?* An' ya ain't even got yar shoes on yet? Sister Emma-Margaret is gonna be mad as *hops* atcha!"

"I'm coming!" Kate scrambled to her feet as she tucked an olive-wood rosary into her pocket. Sister Emma-Margaret had gifted it to her that morning for her First Holy Communion. It made her feel very special and grown-up.

"C'mon, Katie!"

Kate rolled her eyes. "I know, Collette!" She slipped on her donated white Communion shoes. They were ugly and had scuff marks on the toes, and when she tried to walk, they were so big that she needed to scrunch her toes together to keep her feet from coming out. She would rather go barefoot, but Sister Emma-Margaret would never hear of *that.*

Collette scratched her tousled golden curls and frowned. "If ya had a second pair of stockin's, ya could put 'em on an' it might help a bit."

"Well, since I *ain't* got more stockings, this'll have to do. 'Sides, they *are* the nicest shoes I've ever had. C'mon, let's go."

The girls dashed down the narrow wooden staircase and out the front door into the damp April air. A group of about twenty girls, all between the ages of ten and fourteen, huddled and shivered in the muddy front yard of the Magdalene Asylum. Each girl wore a pinafore over a dull-white shift along with a small veil over tightly braided hair.

Involuntarily, Kate reached up and touched her head. Soft braids rippled under her fingertips. "My veil! I left it on the floor!"

"Aw, don't worry, Katie, here!" With a smirk Collette whipped out the veil and a wilted flower chaplet and shoved them into Kate's hand. "Ain't ya glad we's sisters, even if we ain't got no ma an' pa, 'cause least we can look out for each other, hmm?"

Kate swallowed hard. "That's right, Collette," she said, taking the articles.

But she knew it was not right. They were not really sisters after all, and that was the trouble. She had lied to Collette—said her family name was Clayton, too—just to make the younger girl feel better—happier—but now she would have to undeceive her as soon as possible.

"Next time, child…" A woman's threatening voice made Kate's skin crawl. "Next time you will be the first one out here instead of the last. Understood?"

Kate peered up into steely eyes as the shadow of Sister Emma-Margaret closed over her like a storm cloud.

"Next time, child." The woman wagged her scraggy finger at Kate. "Next time."

But by Sister Emma-Margaret's tone, Kate doubted there would ever be a next time for a bad girl like her, for by then hell would surely have swallowed her up alive.

Throwing a withering glance at Kate, Sister Emma-Margaret moved back up the line, handing out a wax taper to each of the communicants. Meanwhile, Kate fought tears as she struggled to pin her veil and the chaplet of flowers on her head. It did not matter that the pink flowers were half-dead or that the veil was torn in one place and had a yellowish stain in the middle. What mattered was that they would cover up all her beautiful hair—all of it.

Sister Emma-Margaret had reached the end of the line. Her stiff, veiny hand held out the last wax taper in front of Kate. Kate took it gingerly.

"Be careful with it, child," said Sister Emma-Margaret, then glided back to the front of the line.

Kate swallowed, ashamed of her trembling hands. "I won't have a *stitch* of sausage at dinner. I *won't*!" she said as the procession of girls began the march down the dreary street toward the church. "And I'll only have *half* of a boiled egg, too!" But her stomach did not agree. It rolled with hunger when she thought of the two foods she loved best. So she pressed her lips together till they puckered, vowing not to be tempted, but her vow could not vanquish the enormous spread of delicacies her imagination summoned up when she thought of the celebration dinner to be given later that day. It did not count that she hadn't eaten since dinner the day before. Fasting from food and water from midnight until the reception of First Communion was simply a part of the sacred ritual—it would be sacrilegious not to. Eating no sausage and only half of a boiled egg was simply her own punishment for being late.

Just then she felt a nudge at her side.

"I saved this for ya, Katie," Collette whispered as she pushed a small package into Kate's hand.

"What's this?"

"Jist my oatcake from breakfast." Collette glanced around nervously. "Don't tell anyone, but I saved it for ya 'cause I knew you'd be *starvin'*."

Kate felt faint. She knew Collette only wanted to ease her struggle, but the light, nutty aroma of the oatcake swirling into her greedy nostrils only made the pit in her stomach feel hollower than before. "No." She shoved away the soft, round package.

"But Katie?"

"Don't tempt me!" She quickened her pace as they approached the grey limestone church. If St. Catherine of Siena had the strength to live solely on the Sacrament at times, then Kate Fletcher could have that strength, too.

The painful knowledge that she had hurt her friend could not outweigh the punishment awaiting her should she succumb to the temptation to disobey orders and eat the oatcake. She wished she could somehow make Collette understand how complicated it was, but Collette was only ten years old.

Kate fixed her eyes on the grey steeple that narrowed into a triangular point against the cloudy sky. A rose window was imprinted in the centre of the front façade. She hoped the sunshine would break through those sad clouds during Mass because it always made the stained glass inside so pretty. The church bell in the gable above the rose window was tolling now, speaking out in deep, solemn, haunting reverberations.

"… six… seven… eight," she said aloud.

And then the bell stopped. It was only one more hour before she would receive the Real Presence—before she would receive Jesus Christ himself, the Creator of heaven and earth, through her mouth in the Blessed Sacrament.

Kate wiped the cold perspiration on her brow. "Holy Mary, Mother of God, pray for us sinners..."

But her faults of that day, and of all the days previous, grew heavier and heavier with every step—with every breath, every word.

They ascended the wet stone steps and passed through the faded-red double-leaf wooden doors and into the warm entrance hall, where a low humming issued from the small knots of poor families gathered just outside the sanctuary. A few local labourers and their children, all silent and withdrawn, were already lined up next to the confessional box.

Collette tugged on Kate's sleeve. "Ya nervous?"

Kate's gaze darted toward the sanctuary, where tall wax candles flickered on the altar beneath the crucifix. She steeled herself. "No, I ain't nervous." She was, but Collette needn't know that.

"Well, if I was you, I'd be *awful* nervous!"

Kate squeezed her eyes closed to shut out the beautiful vision of the bright orange promised to all the First Communion girls. She would give hers to Collette as an apology for lying to her.

"Ya look like a bride in that dress, Katie!" Collette surveyed her friend with a look of approval, then glanced down at her own rough grey smock. She tugged on the frayed blue ribbon of her ugly bonnet before pointing at Kate's chaplet. "Those pink an' yellow an' green flowers make yar eyes look even bigger an' greener! I think ya'r the prettiest girl here—an' yer my own big sister! But why cover up yar long brown braids? They're so shiny an' thick—the others *must* see them!"

"Hush, Collette!" Kate said in a harsh whisper when she saw two girls look back at them and frown. "Don't say that!"

"What's wrong? I'm jist sayin' the honest truth."

"There're plenty of other girls here, an' we all look the same."

"No ya don't."

"Yes we do."

"No ya *don't*!"

"Stop it!" Kate snapped. "See! Those girls are looking at us now."

"They're *jealous* of ya 'cause I said that."

"Then don't say things if it's gonna make someone else jealous!"

Collette wrinkled her nose. "But it ain't yar fault—an' God ain't gonna change yar looks for *them*!"

Kate noticed Sister Emma-Margaret looking at them, and she pressed her hand on Collette's arm to silence her.

"Fall in line for confession, Katherine," said Sister Emma-Margaret icily. Her back was like a plank as she leaned her hard face down and forward. "Remember, the Father Confessor is *in persona Christi*. Do what he taught you and do not fail to confess to him every sin of thought or action, for Jesus the Father has no pity upon those who make a bad confession."

Kate's heart thudded against her chest as she recalled the previous night, which had been spent in an agonizing examination of her conscience. "Sister Emma-Margaret, I, I… Well… What if I can't 'member everything? I mean, keep them organized? Every sin, I mean, that I might tell the Father Confessor?"

"No excuses, Katherine. You know the catechism by heart, don't you? Of course you do, child. Therefore, there is no reason why your memory should not be able to recall every sin you have committed that you might recite each one individually to the priest. Have you not prayed to the Blessed Virgin Mary to help you make a good confession? It is the Mother of God alone who will help you do it right, and so curb the wrath of her son Jesus."

"I have asked the Blessed Virgin," Kate said as she remembered the story of the girl who grew blood-sucking leeches on her tongue because she failed to tell the Father Confessor every wrong thought and deed she had committed in a week. But today, the terror of imperfection and failure in the confessional seemed one hundred times more dreadful than other days, for this time she must unveil every part of her ugly black soul to the Father Confessor, and once he discovered it, he could forbid her to partake of the most Blessed Sacrament—or, worse still, his power could damn her soul to a miserable fate in hell.

Sister Emma-Margaret walked away. Kate went to the large basin containing the holy water and dipped her fingers into it. Then, quivering from head to foot as she held her taper close to her body, she slipped into the lineup assembled before the hand-carved oak confessional box. When at last her turn came, she stepped into the dimly lit box and pulled the red-velvet curtain closed behind her. Inside it was warm and stuffy, almost suffocating, and she became dizzy as a sweet, pungent smell wafted to her nose. She knelt before the covered metal screen and presently heard the small door slide open. Under a shaven head, beady eyes inside a fleshy red face leered at her from the shadows on the opposite side of the grate.

"What is your name, my child?" came the smooth, slurring voice of Father Andrew.

"Katherine Fletcher, Reverend Father." She rushed through the preparatory prayer, then froze, mute with terror.

"Have you been a good girl, my child?"

Kate choked back a sob. "Reverend Father, I have n-not. I, I accuse myself of the sins of vanity, lyin', an'… an' selfishness."

"Vanity, lying, and selfishness, my child? And in what way have you pleased the devil by committing these sins?"

"I was vain 'bout my looks and I lied to my friend."

"Hmm… You also referenced the sin of selfishness, my child. In what way were you selfish?"

Kate's courage flagged, but she nerved herself. "I was selfish 'cause I wanted to marry Thaddy Murray."

"And do you no longer *want* to marry Thaddy Murray, my child?"

Kate's cheeks burned when the priest said his name. "No—I, I mean yes. Or, well, I s'pose I, I don't really know for sure, for he ain't asked me yet."

"And if Thaddy Murray kissed you, what would you do then, my child?"

Kate's legs went limp. *If Thaddy kissed me…* She hadn't even thought about him kissing her, let alone what she would do if he ever tried, but it seemed like a wonderful possibility. Yet even as the suggestion swirled around in her mind, giving her a hazy taste of pleasure, she felt guilty. Would it be *right* for them to kiss? Only married people kissed, and she wasn't nearly ready to become a married woman yet. She was scarcely twelve years old.

Finally, though the heat of shame still burned her cheeks, Kate set her jaw and answered, "I'd only let Thaddy kiss me if we were married."

A muffled chuckle issued from behind the screen.

Kate hoped she hadn't said something wrong. "Reverend Father, please forgive me and bless me! I promise to be better this week, and not even *look* at Thaddy or any other boy in that way ever again if that is what you want!"

The priest hemmed. "And what about your sin of lying, my child? You said that you lied to your friend. What lie was this?"

"Reverend Father, I told her we were sisters."

"But there are no sisters at the asylum, my child. Only orphans."

"Yes, but I knew *she* wanted a sister, Reverend Father, so I, I lied to make her happy—I told her my family name was Clayton, too, like hers."

Again, the priest hemmed. "Happiness is not holiness, my child, nor does pleasure gender purity of heart. To imagine something that is not true, and then to teach an innocent child to believe it, is a terrible sin."

"But Reverend Father, w-why?"

"Worldly happiness and bodily pleasures of any kind, my child, feed the flesh, and they must not be indulged. In fact, they must be actively opposed if one is to receive the commendation of God. Activities such as singing, and clapping, and dancing, and smiling and laughing, and even reading are snares particularly dangerous for children. You ought to remember that the devil does not waste his precious time on men and women and poor little children who are deceived by such things."

"But—Why, Reverend Father? Why does Satan not waste time on people like that?"

"My child"—the priest's eyes widened as his brows drew together and he lay notable emphasis on the words—"it is because people such as them are already *his slaves.*" He paused and cleared his throat, and a stagnant odour issued forth like steam on the trail of his damp breath. "My child, do you wish to be the devil's slave?"

A chill crept up the back of her neck and she felt suddenly faint. She shuddered. "Oh, no! No, Father Andrew, I do not!" She almost wept with fright. "Indeed I do *not*! Forgive me, Reverend Father. Please forgive me for all my sins, and for lying to Collette. Please, Reverend Father? Oh! I promise not to tell a lie ever again. Please, forgive me! Forgive me, please!"

"My child, you must go to your friend and tell her that you are not sisters. Indeed, you are both the children of wicked and sinful women who broke the sixth commandment."

A rush of heat spread over her body as she racked her brain to recall the order of the ten commandments in her catechism. "Please, Reverend Father," she stammered, embarrassed for her ignorance, "does the sixth commandment say not to murder?"

"No, child. The sixth commandment says, 'Thou shalt not commit adultery.'"

Kate almost sighed with relief. Murder was like heresy, and certainly more sinful than adultery—or was it? "But… what's *adult'ry*, Reverend Father?"

Again, the priest cleared his throat, and his mouth issued forth the stagnant flow of steam. "Adultery is when a married person touches someone who is not their spouse."

The sudden change in his tone made Kate's blood run cold as she imagined what he meant. "You mean… *my* mother did that?"

"It is why you are at the asylum, my child. It is where your mother worked out her penance and board until she died, removed from the reach of society, because of her mortal sin. It is not an uncommon thing for the children produced by these unholy unions to also maintain work at the asylums to atone for the sins of their mothers and shorten their time in the purifying fires of purgatory."

Suddenly her life took on new meaning: the long days toiling in the asylum year after year with little food and no pay and no friendship returned except between herself and Collette;

the miserable women who lived, worked, and died there; the ragged children who made up the asylum's sad population. Now—yes, *now*—she understood an unspoken language! Now she was undeceived! Now she understood why! Of course her life was not meant to be happy, or even easy. And neither was Collette's. Their lives were meant to be penance—penance for the sins of their mothers.

"And so you see, my child, how God hates sinners?"

Kate nodded slowly. "Yes, Reverend Father."

"And do you know that the Church of Rome alone has the power to forgive such sinners?"

"Yes."

"My child, do you also see how easy it is for sin to be committed by the body—that is, the flesh?"

"I, I think so."

"Then you must learn to see your body as God's enemy, and you must punish it, mortify it, deprive and debase it in order to bring it into total subjection and unquestioning obedience."

"Reverend Father..." Kate gulped. "I mean, how do I d-do that?"

"By securing God's favour in offering your mind and body to the Mother Church through suffering as Jesus did."

"Suffering as Jesus did? But I don't know if I could ever suffer like that... Reverend Father, he was tortured so awful bad, I—"

"Nevertheless, you must. That is," he added, "if you, a wretched sinner, seek true acceptance before God."

"But how do I do it?" Kate ventured, hardly daring to raise her voice above a whisper.

"Are you not an orphan, my child?"

"I am, Reverend Father."

"Well, who has taken care of you for all these years?"

"The Sisters of Mercy at the asylum, Reverend Father."

"And do you not think that you owe a very large debt of gratitude to those kind women for giving you shelter and comfort in your time of need?"

Guilt clawed at her heart. Lately she hadn't been feeling all that grateful to the Sisters, but it would be a good idea to repay them if she could. "If I could pay 'em back, Reverend Father, I would—God knows I would. But I ain't got nothing to give."

"That is not true, my child."

"It ain't?"

"You have a body that can serve, is that not true?"

Kate nodded.

"And did you not say only a moment ago that if you could repay the Holy Sisters for their kindness, then you would?"

"Yes, Reverend Father, I did say that," she whispered, hanging her head.

"Then to emulate the example of the Holy Sisters and offer your own life up to God as they have done would not be impossible for you. Correct?"

A hard, dry lump gathered in her throat. She had admired the Holy Sisters, but she had never thought of becoming one. Her dream was to become a beautiful bride dressed in white linen, with hair wreathed in baby's breath and yellow daffodils and with a pretty ring on her finger. And she would very much like a few children of her own... She still wanted to marry Thaddy, and if she became a Sister she would not be able to do that.

"Reverend Father, how could I know if— Well..."

"Yes?"

"More than anything else in the whole world I wish to please God and do his will. But how can I know what his will *is*?"

"Begorra, such a question!" He stopped himself short and cleared his throat. "Katherine Fletcher, you must realize that it is always God's will that a young girl offer herself willingly upon the altar of service to the Church of Rome."

Kate wondered if she heard a prick of impatience in his voice—of edginess—for his sudden exclamation had made her feel exposed. "I'm sorry, Reverend Father, for my questions..."

But he did not seem to hear.

"When girls such as yourself offer themselves to God—that is, to the Pope of Rome and his establishment, the Mother Church," he went on, "they take vows of crucial poverty. They also make a pledge to never marry. They remain virgins by offering themselves as the spouse of Jesus Christ. He is their Heavenly Bridegroom. These particularly special girls"—he laid simpering emphasis on the words—"are given the opportunity not only to gain God's favour by giving up all earthly treasures to serve and pray for lost humanity, but they can also atone for the iniquity of their mothers and save even their most wicked and vile immediate family members from prolonged misery in the purifying fires of purgatory."

"But Reverend Father, I don't know who my family members are, or even if they were vile and wicked."

"No doubt they were, child, for you would not be in the asylum if it had not been your family's sins that put you there. And your family members are begging you to free them now, Katherine. They are screaming in the pain and anguish of their torment, waiting for you to see the fires that burn them, and to lessen the days of their suffering. And do you know, child, that if you do not resolve to be obedient to the Pope and his Church, and offer your mind, body, and soul in service to it, then you make yourself an heir to the sins of your family, and a companion in their misery?"

"You mean," Kate gasped, trying not to cry as she felt for her rosary and clung to it, "that if I don't give up my whole entire life to the Church now, I might never get into… into…" She could not finish, for in that moment heaven seemed to close its gates upon her, and God to turn his back, and her dead relatives to wail and gnash their teeth in the fiery chasm as they blamed their agony upon her.

"I know, my child, how every little girl like you wishes to be married, and wear a beautiful wedding garment, and wear a pretty wedding ring… no?"

A chill crept over her. "Yes, Reverend Father," she said, unable to dike the flow of tears.

"Well, I promise you that the special girls who choose to marry Jesus will certainly have all three. But for now, my child," he continued, ignoring her tears, "you must reflect upon your pathetic state as a sinful creature and feel utter aversion for your flesh. Only by the merciful aid of the Blessed Virgin Mary may your penance bring you forgiveness, for the wrath of Jesus is softened only by her pity and intercession on our behalf." He clapped his hands together. "And now for your penance. You will say five Hail Marys, two Glory Bes, and one Our Father; and to atone for your sin of lying, you shall choose one act of self-mortification."

"Yes, Reverend Father."

"I hereby absolve your sins, my child." The priest made the sign of the cross in front of the metal grill. "*In nomine Patris et Filii et Spiritus Sancti.* Amen."

Biting her lip to repress a sob, Kate rose to her feet. She parted the velvet curtain and slipped out into the hall with her head down, breathing the free air outside the curtains and blinking as her eyes adjusted to the light. She made her way to a solitary place in a side wing of the church and knelt before the white marble statue of the Virgin Mary. A halo of twelve yellow stars encircled her head, and a painted blue robe swaddled her flawless infant. Kate had often wished she could be that child and have a mother as beautiful and pure, but now as she gazed upon the stony features, the motionless limbs, the fixed eyes, and the plastered smiles, she felt as alienated from the Madonna and her divine child as if her own limbs—even her own heart—had been turned to stone like them. She, Katherine Fletcher, was a worse sinner than she had even imagined. Her mother had broken the sixth commandment; and unless Kate could atone for such an unspeakable act, she would never reach the ideal of piety, purity, and grace demonstrated by the sinless Mother of God.

Sick with shame, she placed her taper on the floor next to her, then fumbled for her rosary, wrapped it twice around her right hand, and crossed herself. She fell to her knees and crushed her burning lips against the cold marble feet, spilling her tears upon them before she finally drew back, clasped her hands, squeezed her eyes shut, and began her first Hail Mary.

Once she had completed the recitations, she picked up the taper and joined the other First Communion girls as they gathered in a group just outside the doors of the sanctuary. To the left of the altar, the small church choir was singing "Ave Maria," accompanied by the pipe organ.

Presently a Sister with a lighted taper came up to the group of girls, smiling graciously at them. "You ought all to be grateful for such elegance," she said in a low voice as she lit their tapers. "Such candles are costly, and because of your unfortunate circumstances, you ought to feel much indebted to the Church for such a luxury."

"Do we have to hold them for the whole time?" one of the girls asked.

"Better be careful we don't trip with it," added another in an anxious whisper, "or tip it too far to one side or we could set our dresses on fire!"

Kate glanced nervously at the bright flame dancing in front of her face, its heat almost pressing against her skin. How would she walk with it all the way down to the front pew without setting fire to the whole church? Suddenly she saw herself accidentally dropping the taper, its flames shooting out and spreading wildly across the dry wooden floorboards and sweeping up the pews and walls and ceilings. She could hear the shrieks of the women and children, the shouts of the firefighters. No one would be able to escape as the church went up in flames and crashed to the ground. Then she, Kate Fletcher, would be bound with cords and led to the city square, scoffed at and ridiculed as her head was drenched with pitch and her body lashed to a stake from which she could not escape.

Heretics were burned that way—she had heard stories—and surely murderers would be, too.

"Look!" exclaimed another girl.

Kate turned and caught sight of Father Andrew coming up behind them, plumed in finery.

"Oh look! His robes! Aren't they *beautiful*!" came a chorus of feminine voices.

Wide-eyed, Kate gazed at the sweeping gold, white, and scarlet robes draped over the priest's corpulent form. She had never seen such costly fabrics in her life, and she wondered where he got the money to buy them. Her own used dress seemed less than common compared to the clothes he wore. But her wonderings were quickly dismissed when she concluded that Father Andrew probably deserved the richness, for with a heart as holy as his, he could surely afford to cloak his body in wealth.

He was accompanied by a deacon and three white-robed altar boys; one bore the torch, another the thurible, and the third a tall golden crucifix.

Thaddy… Kate's heart skipped a beat as the boy with the neatly combed wavy russet hair bore the shining cross in front of him as he walked. He did not look at her—it was as if he did not know she existed. But she still felt proud of him and knew he had never looked so handsome. One day, Thaddy would be a real, grown-up gentleman, and he would wear a starched cravat, and smooth trousers, and coattails, and say lovely things—perhaps to her.

"Look, there's Brigid O'Sullivan! See the lace on her dress!" one of the girls squeal delightedly.

Looking in the general direction, Kate saw her, too, and a lump in her throat made her swallow hard against envy as she watched her smile at Thaddy, then Thaddy smile at her.

Brigid was a sweet red-haired girl of Kate's own age, who always came to church with her parents and little sister and two brothers. She was always prettily dressed in pinks and yellows and blues and lace. With skin as fair and plump as apple blossoms, eyes as bright as stars, lips as red as cherries, and a family name like O'Sullivan, Kate did not doubt why Thaddy looked at Brigid but ignored her. Her heart stopped for an instant.

Were Thaddy and Brigid the perfect match? When they grew up, would *they* get married and have the perfect life? Would *they* be supremely happy?

Kate swallowed again. If that happened, then Kate Fletcher—the skinny orphan who Brigid and the other girls called Poker-Face—would need to be as happy for Brigid as she would be if she herself were to be Thaddy's bride.

The thunder of the organ announced that the procession was to start down the aisle. The girls, led by Thaddy and the two other boys behind him, were instructed to walk in pairs down the middle of the nave toward the altar, then bow in reverence before it prior to assuming their places in the front pew.

Trying to maintain measured strides, Kate followed the others, not daring to take her eyes off her burning taper. As they entered, a general rush of sound went up as the solemn congregation rose to their feet to honour the procession. From one corner of her eye, Kate thought she saw Collette waving to her in the crowd.

When Kate reached her seat in the front pew, she watched Father Andrew approach the altar. Her gaze fell involuntarily on the pyramid stamped into the front of the grey-and-red marble structure. In the centre of the pyramid was a single engraved eye surrounded by shafts of light. She had imagined it to be the Pope's eye, but Sister Emma-Margaret said the eye belonged to Providence. Later, when Kate had attempted to explain the meaning to Collette, Collette declared Sister Emma-Margaret a liar. One-eyed creatures, Collette asserted, were gigantic man-eating monsters, so Kate gave up the lesson immediately, concluding that Collette's head was so full of fairy tales that she would only misunderstand explanations.

Back at the altar, Father Andrew bowed low and ascended the three steps onto the platform. His pudgy white hands made the sign of the cross before his inflexible voice led the obedient congregation in a tedious recitation of the *Kyrie eleison.* He then made them wait as he performed a solo vocal performance in honour of the juvenile communicants. Although she tried to listen to his singing with the rapture she knew she ought, Kate's ears would not obey. They *would* hear his singing and cringe at the faulty intonation of each note. They *would* hear the frog in his throat, and they *could* not respect that Father Andrew loved the sound of his voice more than they did.

But her eyes were worse.

As the congregation obediently performed the recitation that followed, those rebellious organs interrupted to ask why God had given Father Andrew such a thick, bulging, disfigured nose that turned bright red every Sunday morning, as though it had just endured a night of severe pinching. They hated the yellow whites of his eyes, comparing them to a bowl of rotten eggs. In fact, her own eyes could not even be grateful that Father Andrew had eyes at all, for they were so beady, peering out of such shallow, fleshy, browless sockets as they scanned the congregation with a leer, it was impossible for her not to imagine that he knew something everyone else did not.

Following the Introductory Rites came the laborious Collect Prayer, various readings, and a Psalm. Kate wished she could understand the words, but everything was performed in Latin.

"Someday I'll know what it means," she said to herself. "If I become a Sister, then I can learn Latin."

The Liturgy of the Eucharist began as haunting Gregorian chant was sung and the altar was prepared with the sacred vessels. The thin discs of unleavened bread and the wine were brought forth and the missal opened. One of the altar boys held a golden basin of holy water while Thaddy stood next to Father Andrew, a rectangle of snowy-white linen draped over his arm. Then Father Andrew, while curling and flexing his fingers by turn, drew near with squinted eyes, reached forth his hands, dipped them into the water, and washed.

When he stepped away from the basin, Father Andrew dried his hands and next approached the centre of the elaborately prepared altar. He made a wide, spanning motion with one arm, saying, "Rise," which was followed by a somewhat lethargic general stir as the congregation stood. With everyone on their feet, Father Andrew reached forth his hands and hovered them over the gifts as he pronounced the five mysterious Latin words, "*Hoc est enim corpus meum.*"

Through the mirage of sounds, Kate hears again the voice of Sister Emma-Margaret speaking to her about *Bon Dieu*…

"By this prayer the priest performs the miracle of transubstantiation, turning the sacramental bread into the Holy Body of Jesus Christ God, and the wine into Holy Blood."

"And we havta *eat* it?" Kate says with a shudder.

"You mean *him*, not 'it,' child," Sister Emma-Margaret corrects. "Yes, Jesus Christ himself: his body, blood, soul, and divinity."

"But why must we, Sister Emma-Margaret?" asks Kate—for she does not wish to eat a human, even if he *does* look just like a little flat cake.

"Do you seek full possession of the Saviour, child? Do you wish for your soul to receive its necessary food? If you do, the only way to get it is through partaking of *Bon Dieu*—which is the wafer-god."

"But Sister Emma-Margaret? I don't understand. How will the priest make the wafer an' wine turn into God?"

"Don't be silly, child. The priest has the power to perform miracles."

"But Sister Emma-Margaret, how many times must Jesus die like that?"

"Child, you know the regularity of the Mass."

"Yes, but doesn't it hurt him?... Jesus, I mean? Doesn't it hurt Jesus?"

"Be quiet, child. You sin when you imagine such things. Your attention must be upon obedience to the Pope, not these foolish questions."

Kate shook herself, blinking away the thoughts smearing her vision.

The priest was turning his back to the congregation now, facing the crucifix as he elevated the thin, disc-shaped Eucharist above his head and chanted the *Anaphora* in a low, solemn voice. The *Sanctus* bells rang three times as thick clouds of incense burned around the altar, folding the crucifix in a blue shroud of sweet-smelling smoke. Flames seemed to be licking at the edges of the wafer as morning sunlight poured like wine through the eastern ruby-stained-glass window that depicted the exquisite Madonna and Child. Kate told her mind to be quiet, but when she glanced at the window and then back at the grim crucifix, it wondered first who nailed Jesus on the tree and then asked how the Virgin Mary could be the mother of Jesus at the same time as Jesus was Kate's "father" and Mary was Kate's "mother." For if they were "father" and "mother," her mind insisted, it seemed they ought to be married.

"Don't question... Don't question! Don't question!" she repeated under her breath, forcing her eyes back on her taper's wavering flame. A drip of wax scalded the back of her hand and she winced against the pain, then adjusted the taper's position and scolded herself for her clumsiness. She could just make out the priest's movements as he lowered the Eucharist and placed it on the altar. Her eyes wandered away from the taper as Father Andrew again recited something in Latin, then took the golden chalice of wine in his hands and elevated it above his head just as he had done while consecrating the Host. The *Sanctus* bells rang again three times as he lowered the cup and placed it on the altar, bowing low before it.

Kate exhaled, feeling that she ought to thank God that Father Andrew had not accidentally spilt any of Jesus's innocent blood on his fine robes, for blood would certainly stain worse than the wine might have.

The congregation recited the *Pater Noster* followed by the *Agnus Dei.* Father Andrew then took the silver-gilt ciborium, in which resided the consecrated Hosts, while the deacon took the chalice, and together they presented the transformed gifts to the people as they joined in singing the Amen.

With eyes that glinted—almost grinned—Father Andrew pinched the thin white wafer, placed it on his tongue as his neck and cheeks crimsoned, and closed his lips lightly as he paused, as though, with meditative pleasure, he savoured the taste of the suffering victim.

Tears rolled down Kate's cheeks as she watched, but she could not wipe the tears away because both her hands gripped the flaming taper. She shuddered as she imagined again the warning voice of Sister Emma-Margaret in her ear: "Remember the boy who was told never to chew the Host?"

Yes, she remembered. The bad little boy had chewed the Host and blood had spurted out.

Now Father Andrew was lifting the chalice to his fat lips. He drank deeply, then sighed as he wiped his mouth.

Kate trembled as disgust mingled with anxiety. She shut her eyes against the sight. "Oh… the blood of Christ himself!" she whispered, hardly suppressing the inner agony that broke out in a muffled sob.

A moment passed and she dared to re-open her eyes.

Dizziness made her sway. Usually the strong smell of the incense didn't distract her, but now her stomach churned and curdled. She wondered what hour it was… How long before dinner time? She dreaded when her turn should come to eat the Host, but she felt so hungry that all she could think about was how that little piece of bread would ease the worm gnawing at the walls of her stomach. She wished she could have a sip from that cup, too—she had never felt so thirsty before. But only Father Andrew and the deacon were holy enough to drink from it.

The priest beckoned to the communicant children to approach the altar. A group of Sisters stood nearby, ready to hold each child's taper before they went up. The girls filed out of the pew one by one and relinquished their candles. They knelt in a row in front of the altar and then a long strip of spotless white linen was draped over their outstretched hands; none but the priest's hand was permitted to touch the Host. Kate, near the end of the line, waited for the priest to descend from the platform.

At last, Father Andrew stepped down, holding the glittering silver-gilt ciborium. One of the altar boys followed him, carrying the shiny gold paten.

Thaddy.

Kate tore her eyes away even as her heart raced. She remembered her promise to the priest to never look at him again, but now Thaddy was coming her way, carefully guiding the paten beneath the priest's hand and to the chin of each communicant girl while she received the Eucharist. Soon it would be her turn… soon Thaddy would be standing right next to her, almost touching her. She squeezed her eyes shut.

"*Corpus Domini nostri Iesu Christi custodiat animam tuam in vitam aeternam.* Amen."

It was Father Andrew's voice, slurring as usual. Kate opened her eyes. His bloated form was inches from her face as he leaned slightly forward and held out the Host.

There in front of her, too, was Thaddy. And he was looking at her.

Kate could hardly think. The priest was standing there, waiting for her to open her mouth, but her nerves and limbs were paralyzed.

"*Corpus Domini nostri lesu Christi custodiat animam tuam in vitam aeternam.* Amen," Father Andrew repeated, this time with greater emphasis; and Kate could feel the terrible eye of Collette's man-eating monster upon her.

Shaking herself, Kate shut her eyes and extended her tongue. She felt the wafer touch it. It was so light, almost airy. First salty and then sweet. She let the wafer slowly dissolve, but as it did, her stomach twisted, and she remembered her former hunger.

It seemed even worse than before.

❧

"So, how d'ya feel?" Collette asked, piercing Kate with her sharp cornflower eyes as they walked side by side along the muddy dirt road lined by low rubble walls on their way back to the asylum.

Keeping her gaze fixed on the slippery ascent before them, Kate said, "Fine." She felt any other opinion risked being hypocritical.

"But I mean, do ya feel any *different*?"

"Different?"

"Like it'll be easier for ya to be good now?"

"To be good?"

"Yeah. 'Cause ya ate Jesus."

Collette had a way of making the holy Sacrament sound gruesome.

"I, I s'pose so, but—" Kate halted, tossed her hands up, then walked on in silence.

"Know what I seen?" asked Collette.

"No."

"Thaddy Murray lookin' atcha."

"Oh."

"Do ya think he likes ya, Katie?"

"Don't be silly. Thaddy looks at other girls, too."

"But do ya *feel* anythin'?"

"What do you mean?"

"Ya know—anythin' like love?"

Kate bit her lip. "Collette, I don't even know what that

feels like, so how do you expect me to tell you?"

"Well, *I'd* know if it happened to *me*!"

She raised her eyebrows. "Really?"

"Yeah, 'cause whenever I smile at Art an' he smiles back at me, I feel warm an' cozy inside. I think that's what should happen to *you*."

"Feelings are only half the sum—or less."

"Huh?"

"First of all, you ain't supposed to be smiling at boys like that."

Collette halted on the side of the mud road and planted her skinny hands on her skinny hips. "Now that ain't fair!"

"It ain't?" Kate turned around to face her. "Who says so?"

"Who says *smilin'* is *sinnin*?"

"It ain't right for a girl to flirt with a boy."

Collette's ears turned crimson. "Ya callin' me a flirt?"

"Don't sass me." Kate set her lips together, turned, and trudged up the rutted hill. She heard Collette's footsteps behind her, sloshing through the puddle she had just avoided.

"Ya know what *else* I seen?" Collette bellowed.

Kate tossed her braids and kept walking.

"A mouse."

Kate cringed. "A mouse?"

"Yeah… A real cute one, too. He was peekin' out from under the altar at Mass. I named him Perky."

"At Mass?" She wondered if Collette would ever learn to pay attention in church.

"Katie, I don't think God is really in the Host."

Her throat constricted and she stopped short, facing Collette. "Of course he is. Don't even talk like that."

"But that's what I *think*."

Kate narrowed her eyes into slits. "And just what makes you *think* that God ain't in the Host?"

"'Cause."

She rolled her eyes. "*'Cause* ain't an answer."

Collette squinted back and said threateningly, "The mouse ate it."

"Ate it?"

"Yeah, it *ate* the Host."

"Y-you saw the mouse *eat* the *Host*?"

"With my own two eyes, I did! When Father Andrew walked to those steps with his fancy bowl of wafers, one fluttered to the ground an' Perky scuttled out from under the altar, snatched it, an' shot back under the altar, where he munched it like nobody's business. An' *that's* how come I think God *ain't* in the Host, 'cause if he *was*, a mouse couldn't eat him like he ate that darn wafer."

"Collette, you better not be lying to me! Liars don't get into heaven."

"I ain't lyin'!" She threw her arms outward to lay physical accents on her words. "Honest to God, I ain't!"

"And stop swearin', you sound like a heathen!"

"I ain't swearin'! It's all true—all of it!"

"If you don't stop this, I'll tell Sister Emma-Margaret on you!" Kate whirled around and stalked up the road, grinding her teeth together.

"Fine!" Collette shouted back.

The company of girls reached the front yard of the asylum and passed through the rusty iron gate. Marching up the long flight of stairs to the front doors, they entered the inner porch and removed their grey wool jackets.

The smell of frying sausages and potatoes wafted to Kate's nostrils. Her stomach turned over. She was famished, but the smell nauseated her.

"Phew! I'm hungry—and that sausage smells like heaven!" exclaimed Collette as she hung her coat on its peg. "Ya must be starved, Katie—ya ain't had a bite of food since yesterday afternoon!"

Kate remembered how the Host had stuck to the roof of her mouth, remembered how she had swallowed it. She groaned now as bile gathered in the back of her throat, its bitterness making her gag.

"Why, Katie! You've gone all white! What's wrong?"

Kate could not answer. Her head was spinning, her stomach had turned into a sickening knot, and she could hardly repress the urge to heave. Clasping her hands tightly over her mouth, she bolted out the front doors and flew down the steps into the open air. Hardly had she reached the eastern corner of the building before a powerful wave of nausea swept over her senses, and she bent over, vomiting violently onto a patch of bare ground. A succession of dry heaves followed, inducing a cold sweat.

"Are ya all right, Katie?"

It was Collette's voice.

Kate swayed and reached one arm out, trying to steady herself against the rough bricks of the building. "I'm fine… I'm fine," she gasped, kneading her stomach while acid burned her mouth and throat. Hanging her head, she slowly opened and shut her eyes in an attempt to refocus her cloudy vision. She caught sight of the foul-smelling green-and-brown puddle of mucus and bile gathered at her feet. Tears rushed to her eyes and her mind raced with panic, then a cry broke from her lips.

There, with its matted grey head stooping low over the unsightly puddle, was a dog. And it was licking up the steaming refuse.

Kate's heart filled with horror as the truth of what had happened—and the sin it entailed—rushed upon her mind.

God would not forgive her this time. She had vomited up Jesus. There could be no sacrilege greater or more heinous than that.

— CHAPTER II —

HUNGRY

Condensation leaked from the top right corner of the rotted-out windowpane and dripped into the three half-full bowls that Kate had set beneath it two hours earlier. All the orphans had been sent to bed a quarter of an hour before, but Kate, barefoot and clad in her thin cotton nightgown, stood alone in front of the long, narrow window at the back of the room that served as a bedroom for fifteen girls. She looked out over the dusky hills and misty valleys beyond the town. There was no fireplace in the room, and the chill made her shiver.

The sun had long since set. A navy darkness cloaked the lowest part of the dome and spread itself upward. A few scattered stars looked down from it—looked down at her—and twinkled through the leaves of the lonely apple tree outside the window. A nest of six baby sparrows was nestled on the biggest branch of that apple tree. They had hatched yesterday…

Now some of the stars were forming the Big Dipper.

"What are stars?" Kate whispered.

It wasn't often that she felt reluctant to go to sleep, but tonight the dawn of the next day seemed to drag away for many more miles than the shadowy hills, and she wondered again if she had chosen too hard a penance to atone for her sin. She had never slept on the bare floor before, nor had she seen other girls do it—but she was a worse sinner than other girls. She was a liar.

Her eyes wandered to her bed—the blanket, the pillow. She coveted them. With neither of the room's windows sealing properly for months and almost every wall having at least two cracks, the draft was creeping in—she felt its cold tongue licking her ankles.

But it did not matter. She must suffer.

Kate shifted, then moved away from the window. Perhaps she could delay her self-inflicted punishment a little longer by sitting down at the desk at the foot of her bed, where a stubby tallow candle flickered its red nose at her.

She went over to the candle and carefully cupped her cold raw fingers around the tiny flame. It sputtered and stank, for it was old, but at least it was better than the rushlights they used to have. Next to the candle she saw her rosary and catechism. Her hands were warm now and the stiff muscles had relaxed—perhaps she could stay awake a bit longer and read. Reaching for the little book, she sat in the chair and strained to see the familiar pages—every word on those crinkled pages was already drilled into her memory, and she felt sick of seeing them, but it wouldn't hurt to tire her eyes for sleep in making out the faded small typeset.

"Kate, I'm hungry—so hungry… Do ya hear me?"

Kate pressed her lips together. "Stop hissing at me, Collette. Go to sleep," she said, trying to ignore the hollowness of her own stomach.

Collette threw the covers forward and sat bolt upright in her bed. "But I can't sleep 'cause my belly's rumblin'!"

"You had my orange, so stop complaining."

"Yeah, but that was such a darn skimpy thing, it don't even count worth nothin'."

"Then why didn't you ask for more potatoes at dinner if you were still hungry?"

"But I *did* ask! An' Cook, she scolded me somethin' awful, called me a selfish lil' sauce box an' said I had no business askin' for more when there's thousands of starvin' children the world over. But Katie, Cook don't even know what it's like to be starvin' 'cause she gets all the food she wants an' is fatter than the big ol' pig stuffin' our dinner sausages!"

"Hold your tongue, Collette!"

"Make me!"

"Make you what?"

"Make me not say what I *wanna* say! The spoiled rich girls at church say what *they* wanna say. They even call me Stringbean an' you Poker-Face! So if Cook is as big an' fat as a pig, then I'm gonna say so!"

Kate pushed the catechism aside and went to sit on the edge of Collette's bed. "Are you jealous of those girls?"

"Jealous?" Collette wrinkled her freckled nose. "'Course I'm jealous. Ain't *you*? With all their pretty bonnets an' airs, 'course I'm gonna be jealous as *hops* at 'em!" She sniffed back tears and ejected her pink tongue, licking the hazy stream running from her nose into her mouth.

Kate handed her a stray handkerchief. "Collette, jealousy is a sin. Did you know that?"

Collette snatched the handkerchief and blew her nose until it vibrated. "Yeah, but what good does it do *knowin'* a sin's a sin?" She sniffled. "It don't help me *do* it no less."

"Did you ask the Virgin Mary to help you?"

"No."

"Why not?"

"'Cause she can't hear me."

"Yes, she can, Collette. The Virgin Mary is in heaven."

"No she ain't. Someone made her into a stone statue, an' stones ain't got ears."

Kate rolled her eyes, stood up, and walked away. "Then just go to bed," she said, plunking herself back down at her desk and resuming the catechism. But no sooner had she read a sentence than Collette's whiny voice interrupted her.

"Whatcha readin'?"

Kate tried not to sound as annoyed as she felt. "The catechism."

"Ain't that borin'?"

"No."

"Ain't it 'bout worn out by now? You must've read it 'bout twenty times yesterday. Why do ya read it?"

"Because I… I love it," she said—but even that was a half-lie.

"Why? What good does it do ya?"

Kate leaned back against the hard wooden chair, determined to maintain control of a simmering impatience. After all, love was supposed to suffer long and be kind, and she must be a mature example for Collette and make good on her promise to Sister Emma-Margaret. "Collette, I want to tell you something," she said in calm, measured tones. "Come here."

Collette slipped out from under the coverlets and slid over the corner of the bed, revealing painfully stick-like legs as her nightdress pulled up toward her knees. She padded lightly toward the desk.

"When I grow up"—Kate clasped Collette's spindly fingers—"I'm to become a nun."

Collette's eyes widened. "A *nun*? Like Sister *Emma-Margaret*?"

Kate nodded solemnly.

Collette wrenched her fingers from Kate's grasp. "I *hate* Sister Emma-Margaret!" Her eyes shot daggers as she took a firm step back and crossed her skinny arms across her chest. "She's simply *vicious*!"

"Collette! You must not say such horrible things! Don't you know it's wrong to speak disrespectfully of your elders—especially of the Holy Sisters?"

"Yeah, but I don't care!" Collette stomped her foot, then marched back to her bed and climbed in with a loud huff. Reaching under the coverlets, she extracted two faceless rag dolls with hair of brown and grey wool, then frowned at each one by turns. One doll was dressed as a male in a faded red-and-white gingham shirt and threadbare overalls, while the other wore a discoloured white dress with a blue apron and straw sunbonnet. Kate watched as Collette began impersonating the voices of the two dolls.

"Pa, I'm hungry. *So* hungry!" she said in a squeaky voice, waving the female-dressed doll furiously back and forth. Then she lowered her voice, imitating a fatherly bass tone as the male-dressed doll replied, "Be patient, lass, dinner's cookin'. Can'tcha smell it?" Collette inhaled deeply, then exhaled with pleasure. "Oh yes, Pa!" she squeaked. "An' it smells *so* good!"

Pushing her catechism aside, Kate rotated on her chair so she faced Collette. "Collette, look at me."

Collette looked up. Were her eyes watery?

"If you wish to be a *good* woman when you grow up, then you must learn to obey."

Collette slammed down her dolls and stuck out her chin. "Obey? But I don't love any of the Holy Sisters, nor the priests—they're so cold and stern! At any rate, why ought I to obey those I can't even love?"

"'Cause God says you must."

The blood rushed to Collette's cheeks. "Then I don't love *God* either!"

"Collette!"

"What? And anyway, I don't think God is really there!"

"How can you say such horrible things?"

"'Cause if he *was* there then he wouldn't let me go hungry and he'd give my papa back to me!" she shouted.

A black silence followed, and Kate glanced around. Several bodies stirred beneath the thin wool blankets. A groan issued from beneath one, an incoherent voice from another. A few tense moments elapsed, but there were no complaints. Kate pressed her lips together and glowered at Collette, then stood up quickly, plunged to the bed, and clamped her hand over Collette's mouth.

"Shush!" she hissed, feeling the wet of tears on her palm. "You'll wake the whole house and then we'll *both* be doing penance!" She grabbed Collette's arm and dragged her off the bed, forcing her into a sitting position against the wooden bed frame. A corner of the wool blanket was dangling off the side of the bed, and she pulled it over their heads. "Oh, Collette! You can't even be decent, can you?" she said, her voice muffled by the weight of the blanket. "Every single day I try to help you be a good girl, but you don't even try to help me back—*ever!* You're proud and stubborn like a stupid old mule!"

"But I hate always tryin' to be good, Katie! I *hate* it!"

"I said *shush*!" Kate hissed, raising her hand and performing the gag action.

The inky blackness blotted out Collette's face, but her fierce sniffs and blubbering told that she was furious. "All right, all right!" she hissed back. "But Katie, I mean that no matter how hard I try *not* to lie or make fun of Father Andrew, or look at boys, or be jealous of pretty girls in church, I can't never *do* it. I've been tryin' to be good for my whole *life* but it never, *ever* works!"

"Oh, come on, Collette! You're only ten years old—not a hundred! You haven't been trying for *that* long!"

"Well, I'd rather be a bad girl *forever* an' get punished for it rather than try to be a good girl an' have no fun at all!"

"Collette!" Kate dashed away a stream of tears running down her own face. "I don't want Father Andrew to unlock hell and send your soul there in the end. Can't you see I'm trying to *help* you? But if you keep going on like this, an' shutting others out, you'll be sorry *forever*!"

"But Katie..." Collette's voice softened. "I ain't shuttin' *you* out. I love you. I really do!"

Kate felt thin arms wrap around her shoulders and a cheek lie against her arm. She sniffed back her own tears. "Collette, please understand me—all I want to do is what's right. We are all alone in this wide, wide world... but we *do* have each other." She wiped her wet face on her threadbare sleeve and forced a smile into her voice. "Now, will you promise me you will grow up to become a good and obedient woman like I'm trying to be? It would break my heart more than anything else if you left me 'cause you didn't want to be good."

"But... good, Katie?" Collette's face contorted. "What do ya mean, '*good*'?"

"Good, like... like..." Kate began, trying to think of something, then she recalled the Madonna and Child. "Good like the Virgin Mary," she concluded.

Silence pressed between them. Collette hemmed but did not answer.

"Katie... Why do ya wanna become a nun?" she finally said.

That morning's confession crashed in upon her: the humid odour of the confessional box; the sticky flake of wafer pressed against the roof of her mouth; the stench of her own vomit steaming from the frozen ground. The dog eating it...

"'Cause..." she said.

"Ya said *'Cause* ain't an answer—'member?"

Kate remembered. Summoning her grown-up tone, she replied, "I want to be like the Virgin Mary. She never sinned."

"Did you ever meet her?"

"Of course not."

"Then how come ya know she ain't sinned?"

"Because that is what we have been taught. Now, stop asking silly questions."

"*I* think the Virgin Mary was just a plain girl," Collette said. "Plain—like me an' you. An' ya know what, Katie?"

"What?"

She hemmed again. "We've *sinned.*"

Kate groaned. "I know that. But Mary wasn't *like* us."

"So," Collette ventured after a short pause, "is that the *real* reason why ya wanna become a nun—to be like Mary?"

"I must offer something back to God and the Mother Church for all the good they've done for me. I think I'll become a Nursing Sister. That way I can help sick people get better, like Jesus did."

There was a muffled exclamation before Collette thrust the blanket from their heads and squinted at Kate through the dim candlelight. "Do ya feel bad?"

"Feel *bad*?" She involuntarily lifted her hand to itch a dry spot on her scalp.

"Yeah, bad. *Guilty* bad, I mean."

"I, I don't know…"

Collette pushed out her blistered lower lip. "I thought ya wanted to marry Thaddy Murray an' have babies, though. If ya become a nun, that can't happen 'cause nuns can't get married."

"Nuns get married to God," Kate said.

"But they don't get married to *a man* an' have babies an' do things like *love.*"

"It's much holier for a woman to get married to God than to a man, I think."

"Well," Collette sighed, "I'd still rather marry a *real* man than, well, ya know… a *god.*"

"But it's almost the same thing. We'll even get a wedding ceremony, and a beautiful wedding garment, and a pretty wedding ring. Don't you want those things?"

"I don't like *things*, Katie. 'Sides, the wedding dress might have stains on it."

"You'll change your mind when you grow up." She tried to sound casual, but a certain fear weighed down her heart. If

Collette did not become a Sister, then that would mean they would one day be separated…

"My mind ain't changin', Katie. I won't marry Jesus."

"Why not?"

"'Cause I don't like that he's skinny and dead. Do you?"

"I… I… well…" Kate fumbled with her words as she considered Collette's interpretation of the Heavenly Bridegroom. It was not an attractive image of the Christ, but it still felt sinful to not wish to marry him.

"An' ya know somethin', Katie?" she added, a mischievous smile arching her voice.

"What?"

Collette dove her hand into her stocking and groped about, then stopped short. "If I tell, then promise me to never breathe it to a soul… Promise?"

"I promise."

Collette's face was solemn but her blue eyes danced. "'Member, Katie, don't lie. Liars don't get into heaven, right?"

Kate swallowed and pursed her lips. "I know."

Collette pulled her hand back out of the stocking. In between her fingers hung a thin gold necklace, on which dangled a delicate, glittering gold band.

Kate gasped. "What's that?"

"A ring, silly—don'tcha have eyes?" She held the gold band up to the candlelight.

Kate looked more closely, then reached out and touched it. Three letters were engraved on the inside of the ring in scrolling calligraphy: *C, F,* and *D*. "Collette! You… you little stealer!" she exclaimed.

"Liar!"—snatching the ring closer to her bosom—"I did *not* steal it."

"Then where'd you get it?"

Collette smiled—it was a taunting smile. "Guess."

"Don't be stubborn. We ain't supposed to have fancy stuff here. It's the rules."

"But I don't like rules," Collette whined. "An' Katie, don't tell, right? You *promised*."

"I know, but—"

"'Buts' ain't allowed in promises. You ain't gonna tell a *soul* 'bout it. It's *our* secret."

"We ain't allowed to keep secrets from the Holy Sisters."

"But Katie!... The woman told me not to tell!"

"Woman? What woman?"

"The woman with the red hair who gave it to me. She said it's my ma's weddin' ring an' I'm s'posed to keep it safe."

Kate's mouth dropped open.

"But," Collette added, "I'm gonna share it with *you,* Katie, 'cause we are sisters, an' sisters share things, right? We'll keep it under my bed frame—see? I keep it safe here most of the time. An' ya know what I'm gonna do with it when I grow up?"

Kate shook her head, fear petrifying her limbs.

"I'm gonna find the man who gave this ring to our ma."

There it was. The lie—again. Haunting her. A chill fingered itself up the back of Kate's neck as she looked at her friend—at the clenched little fist, turned red and white, that gripped the stupid piece of gold.

"Collette…" She swallowed hard. "There's something I must tell you."

"'Bout what?"

"About all that, you know, what you said… I mean, well, about our being sisters and orphans and all."

"So?"

Kate twitched her lip, wondering if there were a way to say it gently. "We ain't really sisters," she blurted.

For a terrible instant Collette gaped, then a smile flashed across her face. "Liar again!"

A cold shudder passed through Kate's body. "I ain't— I mean *I'm not*—lying, Collette. I promise."

"What do ya mean, 'We ain't sisters'?" Collette laughed. "'Course we are, ya always told me so."

"I did say that, but it is not true."

The smile on Collette's face froze, and she tipped her head to one side. "Why'd ya say it, then, if it ain't the honest truth?"

Kate still remembered the day she first told the lie to Collette: it was Collette's fourth birthday, and Collette had cried because she didn't have any mas, or pas, or sisters, or brothers; and so she had invented the lie.

"I wanted to make you happy that at least we have each other for family… right?"

Collette rubbed the back of her sleeve beneath her dribbling nose and gave a violent sniff. "Why'd ya say a lie to make me happy, Katie? I don't like lies."

Kate glanced furtively into Collette's watery eyes. Finding them fixed on her face, she looked away with the sickening sense that she must already be the devil's slave.

"Who told ya we ain't sisters?"

"I've known it all along"

"Then why ya tellin' me now an' not before?"

"Father Andrew told me I must confess to you… he said that happiness ain't holiness and that the devil doesn't waste his time on poor little children that smile and dance and laugh because they're already his slaves. You see… my name is really Katherine *Fletcher*, and *yours* is Collette Clayton. And… Collette?" She gulped back a stiff lump in her throat. "Father Andrew said both our mas were wicked an' sinful women who broke the sixth commandment."

"What's number six?"

"Adultery."

"Huh?"

Kate's ears burned and her mouth wouldn't open, and she squirmed beneath Collette's wide-eyed, innocent gaze.

"I said *huh?*" Collette leaned on the last syllable as her eyes scrutinized Kate's face.

"Fine—our mas kissed men they weren't married to and…" Kate's tongue felt suddenly parched.

"An' what?"

"And… that made *us*."

Collette tipped her head sideways and squinted, squeezing tears out onto her wan cheeks.

Kate tried to ignore her and said with feverish haste, "We live here 'cause we need to do penance for our mas so they get out of purgatory sooner."

Collette pressed her lips together and buried her face in the wool blanket just in time to muffle a succession of sobs.

"Collette, why are you crying now?"

A blubbering noise issued from within the blanket.

Kate made another attempt. "What is it?"

Collette's face, red and damp, came up for a moment, and a long sniff was the only answer she gave before plunging it back into the covers.

"Collette, you must speak clearly."

The damp red face surfaced again, accompanied by a hard, almost lifeless gaze. "Ya *lied* to me!" Up came the blanket and down went Collette's contorted face, burrowing into it again.

Kate clenched her jaw, pressing away the guilt that felt like a millstone hanging around her neck. "I'll explain."

The blanket replied with two blubbering syllables. Kate tugged at it, and Collette's face, streaming with tears, looked up at her with a forceful, "Huh?"

"Collette, the Mother Church is our family now, and you're too young to even think of leaving it.'" She paused, then tried to finish with a gentler tone. "Now, let's set this misunderstanding aside."

Collette pouted. "It ain't a misunderstandin'. It's *a lie.*"

Kate squeezed her eyes closed to keep from rolling them in exasperation. "All right, then. Let's set this *lie* aside and forgive each other and get back to normal. Now, can you promise to be good?"

For a moment Collette was thoughtful, almost penitent.

Kate gave her a nudge. "What is it?"

"I don't like makin' promises I can't keep."

"What do you mean? Of course you can keep a promise about being good. It's the only way you'll get into heaven."

Collette's matted golden curls wagged from side to side. "Then I prob'ly won't get in at all, Katie, 'cause I'll never be good enough."

"Never mind that. I'll help you." Though she tried to mask it, Kate's breath caught in her lungs as she watched Collette's lips slowly coming together to form a reply.

"Well…" Collette toyed with her ring, pushing it onto her thumb and twisting it around and around. "I'm 'fraid I might not do as well as you."

"Don't compare yourself to me." Kate scrambled to her feet. "At any rate, you're younger than me. By the time you're my age, being good will be *far* easier for you."

"Honest?"

Collette's distrustful tone made Kate fidget. "Of course I am. It's always easier for grown-ups to be good."

Collette did not answer; she just took turns sliding her ring on and off each of her fingers in a pensive, ritualistic fashion.

"Don't worry, Collette. All right?"

"I ain't worryin,' Katie, I'm jist… confused."

"I think you're tired. And you know we always start feeling confused when we're tired."

"But it ain't that, I know it—" Collette began, but Kate cut her short.

"You really ought to go to bed now."

The stubby candle had burned itself out, but shafts of moonlight filtering through the limbs of the bare apple tree outside the window made a puddle of silvery light on the floor. Smothering a yawn, Collette crawled up into her bed and lay down as Kate spread the wool blanket over her. She bent and kissed Collette's thin cheek. "Good night, Collette. Sweet dreams."

Collette kissed her back. "Night," she said, and cuddled down.

Kate stood over her, watching until Collette's eyes drifted closed, then she tiptoed to the desk. Taking her rosary from where it lay next to the catechism, she moved to the window and stood in the centre of the cold puddle of silver light flooding in. The stars of the Big Dipper were winking at her now.

Kneeling on the hardwood floor, she folded her hands. For all the Sisters and priests, she still wanted a father—just like Collette wanted one.

"Dear God… Please send me a pa," she said, not wanting to cry but feeling the tears and words come together. "Could you?"

The bedclothes whooshed.

"Katie, do you wanna pa more than ya wanna be a nun?"

Kate sucked her lips in to keep herself from shouting. "Eavesdropper," she groaned. "You're supposed to be sleeping."

"Yeah, but *do* you?"

"It don't matter."

"Yes it does."

"No, it don't."

"Yes it *does*!"

"Well, *fine*," said Kate, sulking. "I guess I want a pa more, but I'm still gonna become a nun. Now go to sleep, will you?"

"Fine."

A rolling and swishing accompanied Collette as she pulled the blanket soundly over her head.

Kate crossed herself hastily. "*In nomine Patris, et Filii, et Spiritus Sancti.* Amen." With a final covetous look in the direction of her empty bed, she held her breath and cast herself on the floor, laying her back flat against the wooden boards. It was harder, and colder, than she had expected.

The blanket was just over there… and the small pillow… no one would know…

"Lying is a sin," she whispered. "Besides, St. Catherine of Siena's bed was a plank and her pillow only a log." She tightened her grip on the cross of her rosary, pressing it against her flat, bony chest.

Five minutes crawled by. Blankets rustled overhead again, followed by a snicker, and she groaned inwardly.

Collette's head peered at her over the edge of the bed. "Whatcha doin' down there, silly?"

"Sleepin'."

"Sleepin'?" Collette snickered again. "Naw! Y'ain't sleepin', 'cause ya heard me talk!"

"Well, maybe I *would* be sleeping if you hadn't woke me up!"

"Why down there? Ain'tcha cold with no blankets?"

"I'm doing penance," Kate said dryly.

"Penance? For what?"

"For my sin. Now lie down."

"What sin, Katie? I already forgave ya for lyin' to me."

Kate tried to think fast. "For my sin of, of *vanity*," she said quickly. It was a half-truth, so she wasn't actually lying *again*—or was she?

"But ya ain't vain, Katie. Who told ya ya'r vain?" Collette propped herself up on her pillow.

"I did. I told Father Andrew I was vain about my looks, and he said I must choose one act of self-mortification if I want to be forgiven."

"But *he's* vain as a rooster about all *his* robes!"

"Oh, shush. What he does is his business, not ours. Go to sleep."

She heard Collette roll back and rearrange herself in bed. Two minutes passed.

"I still think ya'r silly to sleep on the floor like that," Collette said. "What if ya get a sore throat?"

Kate ignored her.

"Katie?"

"I don't care what you think. I'm going to do my penance."

Another two minutes passed.

"Katie?"

Kate moaned and rolled her eyes. "What's wrong now?"

"I can't sleep."

"Why not?"

"Now *yar* stomach's rumblin' too loud!"

Though embarrassed, Kate could not shut her mind to the truth that her belly was hollow, her ribs were like washboards, and her jagged wrist and knee bones stuck out like a skeleton's.

"Plug your ears, then, an' stop whining." If she could endure the gnawing of the hunger worm, Catherine of Siena would look down from heaven and smile on her suffering.

"I hate how skinny I am, too, Katie!" Collette whispered, leaning over the edge of the bed. "I stick my fingers in my ribs every night and count each one, but it's no use—I never get any fatter!"

Kate knew she was thinking of the pretty dimpled girls at church.

"Katie, can I jist say *one* more thing?"

"Fine. Say it."

"Since I've been vain 'bout my looks lots of times, I could sleep on the floor with ya an' bring my blanket to keep us warm."

"That wouldn't be penance, then."

"It wouldn't?"

"No. You better stay in your bed tonight."

"But I can't sleep knowin' ya'r freezin' down there!"

"Well, you'll have to, because I ain't budging."

Collette sighed dramatically, then muttered, "I wonder who's more stubborn—me or you."

"Go to bed. Now."

Convinced that she had silenced Collette at last, Kate lay on the hard floor, painfully conscious of the biting draft creeping like a snake from outside and stiffening her limbs.

Bracing herself against an uncontrollable inclination to shiver, she clenched her teeth and squeezed her eyes shut, remembering the poor baby sparrows outside who would be cold and wet in their nest. But there were six of them—at least they could huddle together to keep warm.

Kate could not huddle.

What would she like to eat for breakfast? She would like steaming oatcakes and summer butter very much. She would like a big glass of fresh milk. She would also like an egg… and an orange… and a warm fire to sit by… and a blanket, and a pillow…

After what seemed like hours, she turned to lay on her left side. Several minutes passed, then she turned onto her right, then on her back again, but it was useless. The floor was the floor. Sleep refused to visit her, and dawn seemed like an eternity away.

⁂

Lively chirruping startled Kate from her sleep, and her eyes flew open. Morning sunshine was bursting over the windowsill and wreathing the dusty, cob-web encrusted rafters in the vaulted ceiling above her head, turning them to silver. An unusual pain in her lower back reminded her where she was, and she sighed with relief. Her night of nocturnal penance was finally over—and it hadn't been quite as difficult as she had expected. Pushing herself up on her elbows, she rubbed the sand from her eyes and looked around.

Her heart sank. A wool blanket was lying over her body, and her head had been resting on a pillow. Had she sleepwalked and brought her things onto the floor with her?

She looked over at her bed. Her own blanket and pillow were still in their usual place, spread out perfectly without a wrinkle. She fixed her eyes on Collette's bed. It was empty. And it had neither blanket nor pillow.

Her ears pricked to the sound of low, steady breathing, and with mounting dismay, she looked over to see Collette curled up beside her.

She was sound asleep.

— CHAPTER III —

STILL HUNGRY

St. Agnes Mercy Convent, Ireland
October 1859

Letters, sums, and diagrams blurred together as Kate tried to refocus her eyes on the medical textbook. She pressed her hand against her forehead: the words seemed to enjoy giving her a headache. A groan escaped her lips, her body fidgeted, and the cilice of rough goat's hair beneath her habit pricked her hive-swollen skin. Moving increased the pain; she stiffened, then held her breath against the reoccurring urge to scratch.

Shudders passed from scalp to toes as drips of icy sweat trickled down her chest beneath the hairshirt. To undress—to tear the undergarment off her body and cast it off, to mop the clammy moisture from her skin—was all she wanted.

She wanted to eat, too. As much as she schooled herself to fast more days in the week than she ate, the smell of apple pie still deceived her senses.

"Herbs… a drink of water, some bread," she said, closing her textbook and her eyes. Her patron saint had done with less.

She pushed the heavy textbook aside. It collided with the catechism and the self-flagellation whip that waited on the tabletop. Clenching her palms on the rough edges of the desk, she stood up. Her chapped knuckles stung. She looked at them. They were bleeding.

Ah, but they had served well—her knees and eyes also, for six hours yesterday, crawling and straining with her to scour the stains and scuff marks from the cold stone flags of the convent halls till they reflected her image. Though the task itself was merely penance received from the priest, the Mother Superior had thanked her. But Kate hadn't slept that night: such gratitude harrowed her conscience; if she had forgotten to mop the farthest corner of that hall, then the fault would certainly betray her body's lack of self-mastery and its inability to obey what her mind knew could have been her very best effort to render the floor spotless.

No man's eyes could see the filthy, unconquered thoughts and emotions that usurped her will; no man's eyes could follow the ungodly tangents, or gluttonous censures, or judgmental criticisms of the faults of others that were continuously galloping through her mind, leaving her exhausted.

Three solitary chimes echoed through the courtyard, summoning the inhabitants of the convent to gather in the chapel for the evening prayer.

"Five minutes… and will Collette be there on time?"

With quick, shallow breaths, Kate smoothed the front of her habit and tucked a stray lock of frizzy hair beneath her white veil. She hated how dry and brittle her hair had become. Her once healthy nut-brown mane, which she had fancied to be prettier than even Collette's thick golden tresses, was still an object of secret pride, especially when she recalled how some girls had coveted it.

"But what does beauty matter now?" Her wedding ceremony of first vows was but a week away and the Mother Superior's shears would lop off all her ugly, weed-like hair.

Going to the cell door, she slipped out into the dim passageway, which was already lined with over a hundred black-robed Sisters and novitiates gliding in noiseless single file toward the chapel. Kate knew none of them, for making friends in the convent was strictly forbidden.

With her head bent, gaze on the floor, and hands concealed within her heavy black linen sleeves to mirror the other girls, Kate pushed her vanity aside by reminding herself that she would be so closely occupied with her nursing and the preparations for her final vows in three years that she would not have time to be vain about her appearance.

As she passed by Collette's cell, her eyes darted to the closed door, almost willing it to open. But it did not open, and she dared not pause to wait.

Was she depressed again? Depression had overcome Collette every year in winter for the past three years since they had been admitted to St. Agnes. It estranged them from each other. But perhaps Collette had simply forgotten about their agreement? Perhaps she was already in the chapel, waiting for her?

The procession stepped outside into the cool autumn evening. The air brimmed with the musty smell of rotting leaves, and Kate could not resist the urge to breathe deeply and enjoy it; the fragrance was like a drink of cool water, quenching her tired brain. The convent's peaceful lawns and gardens spread before her, studded by high ash, dogwood, and oak trees and enclosed by mossy stone walls; and the old grey facades, turrets, and towers and vine-clad green archways stood out like frowning giants against twilight clouds stained pink. As they walked, the floor-length habits of the Sisters rustled the dead and half-dead brown and gold and crimson leaves scattered over the courtyard's grey cobblestones, sweeping them aside like the whispering wind blowing through the rusty leaves of the primeval oak shadowing the chapel.

At the northeast end of the enclosure, they passed beneath the cloistered walk leading to the heavy panelled oak door. Kate paused at the threshold to steal a glance over the silent fields and the dark mass of woodland stretching below the convent. All was wrapped in a gauzy purple haze. The full harvest moon hung suspended halfway between the horizon and the zenith of a pale, cloudless sky, washing the courtyard in silvery waves of light. A winding red path led to clusters of elegantly pruned shrubs that encircled the lofty white marble statue of the Virgin Mary, and away to the southeast loomed the massive gates forged of polished black iron. Though shrouded now by the gathering dusk, she knew three pots of yellow daffodils kept watch like little sentinels on the right side of those gates.

Kate followed the other novitiates as they passed through the door, entering the narthex on the western end of the chapel. Inside, flickering candlelight mingled with the moon rays filtering through the ocean-blue, and blood-red, and rich emerald, and white-gold pieces of stained-glass that painted the windows along the aisle walls. The voiceless procession of young girls padded along the nave in the direction of the altar, where towering wax candles in polished brass candlesticks burned brightly beneath the feet of the crucifix. Kate peered out from behind her veil, hoping to catch a glimpse of Collette's tall, shapely figure somewhere in the chapel, but it was nowhere to be seen.

The novitiates glided to the foot of the altar and knelt before it, lifting their eyes to the Eucharist exposed in the glittering monstrance. With reverent exactness each girl made the customary sign of the cross before slipping into her usual pew, folding her hands, and bowing her head to wait in motionless expectation as she listened for the priest to begin the evening rites.

Mechanically, Kate followed the example of the other girls, maintaining an exterior of faultless attention as she listened to the priest's Latin repetitions, sang with the others the Latin hymns none of them understood, and let the strange text roll off her tongue without making her ears listen to it.

Where was Collette?

At the close of the prayer service each novitiate received her benediction from the priest, then filed out of the shadowy chapel and outside into the courtyard, now dark and still and solemn. Though she tried to steady her breathing, every step along the main passageway and down her wing of cells induced a steady tightening in Kate's stomach. It was mandatory that each novice be in her private cell by the time the bell announced the ninth hour, at which time each girl was to lock her own cell from the inside. Loitering, or visiting, or entering the cells of fellow novitiates was strictly forbidden. But as Kate drew near the corner of the passage that ran past Collette's cell, a strange, gut-wrenching sensation arrested her and she stopped short, as though held back by an invisible hand. Without a second thought she slipped out from the line of novitiates, pressed her body close to the rough, iron-bound door, and placed her hand on the cold latch. She dared not knock or wait to be invited—she only hoped the door was not locked.

Breathlessly she turned the latch. It gave way. She opened the door just enough to sidle through, then closed it soundly behind her. The air was black as pitch inside the small square cell. Only a shred of dim, silhouetted moonlight wrestled with the shadows as it descended from the window that stared down from a high point in the wall. All the cell windows were like that—just high enough that it made it impossible to look outside into the yard.

Satisfied that her escape was unobserved, Kate whispered, "Collette? Are you in here?"

There was no answer. She shuffled forward through the blackness with arms outstretched, intent upon crossing the floor to where she knew a rickety wooden desk stood. There she would surely find a tallow candle, but would Collette have a box of lucifer matches on her desk?

Three steps forward and her foot struck against something soft. Her ears pricked to a guttural, rasping sound and she froze mid-stride, uttering a muffled exclamation. She crouched and reached into the shadows until her trembling fingertips brushed against a warm mass gathered in a heap on the floor in front of her. She felt the curve of a shoulder. Grasping it, she shook it violently. "Collette? What's going on? What's happened to you? Get up! Get up!"

A sudden spasmodic gasp preceded a slight stirring, followed by words spoken in strange, unearthly syllables: "Let… me… die!"

"You're choking! What's happened to you?"

A tortured silence answered.

"Light! I need light!" Heart pounding and hands shaking, Kate fumbled around in the darkness until she found the desk, where her hands groped along, touching fabric, then a book, then a key, until they closed upon a matchbox. Shaking hands tore the box open; she smelled juniper wood. As she struck the match tip against the sandpaper, a garlic-like odour wafted to her nostrils as the stick ignited and her trembling fingers laid it against the rush wick. The flame took hold of the rush and ate up shadows. Her eyes darted about. A short white cambric veil lay across the desk next to a thick leather-bound book.

Then—a faint stirring behind her—she spun around. There! A yard or two away, Collette's figure, a limp heap on the floorboards! And there, above her, a twisted bedsheet dangling from the rafters. And there— What? Another bedsheet? Snarled through Collette's abundant hair and ending in a tight knot at her bare white throat?

A deep, guttural sound shivered the cold silence in answer, and horror seized Kate.

She shot forward and fell to her knees at Collette's side, sweat gathering on her forehead as she tore at the noose. "Oh!... God! Don't let her die! Don't let her die!"

At last her nails dug the cloth loose. There was coughing and sputtering and gasping as Kate heaved Collette into a sitting posture and began desperately to slap and rub her hot face and back.

"Why… didn't he… let them… stone her, Katie? Why?"

"Who? What do you mean?" Cold sweat dripped down Kate's back and chest, drenching her habit, making it cling to her skin, making her shudder. Somewhere, the low, resounding echo of the church bell began to warn of the ninth hour.

One… two… three…

Kate made a move to stand, but Collette caught her wrist in a steel grip and with renewed energy yanked her close, riveting her glowing eyes on Kate's face while her voice trembled with pride and passion as she said, "They say 'God is love'—"

Six… seven… eight…

"But Kate!... They tortured my mother to death for her sins!"

… Nine.

And the chime died away, leaving the silence to threaten her.

"Kate…! If the Jesus—the Jesus of the Romish Church—is the same Jesus of the Bible, then why, why—" Collette's voice broke in a succession of sputtering coughs that lasted several minutes and culminated in a final heave as her hands went to her chest and pressed against it as she struggled to regain oxygen. "Why… Why didn't these nuns and priests forgive my mother, Kate? Like Jesus forgave the adulteress woman?" She drew air again with quick, palpitating breaths as she continued. "He told the scribes and Pharisees, 'Ye who are without sin cast the first stone.' But could they do it? No! Why? Because their own secret sins and their disgusting partiality blacked their conscience and condemned them to the fate they had planned for *her*!" Tears scourged her marble-white cheeks as she thrust a crumpled piece of thin paper at Kate.

Startled, Kate took the paper and searched it.

"You see, there! There!" She coughed again. "In the eighth chapter of St. John! It says it in plain English!" Collette pointed wildly to a place on the page, her rasping voice regaining its momentum through the strength of feeling that possessed her. "Caught, red-handed! 'In the very act,' it says—she was caught in the *very act of adultery*! Jesus had every right to have her stoned—to stone her himself! She deserved torture and death and hell, just like they all said she did, but Jesus let her go without so much as a scratch! Will the priest explain that for me, Kate? Will he? And what about the man she was with—where is *he*? Feasting in his house? Rubbing his hands together as he waits to see the woman suffer for his half of their sin? It takes two people to commit adultery, Kate! *Two* people! Who will give him the stoning *he* deserves? Who will repair the false balance? Ha!" she cried exultingly. "Have the priest explain *that* to me!"

Kate glanced behind her to the door, imagining she heard footsteps outside. "You're confused," she said in a low voice. "This writing is confusing you! You already know the rule that scripture must only be read with the interpretation of a priest! Where did you find this?"

"If I tell you, you will hate me the more—for I stole it! Yes! I stole it!" she shrieked, pushing herself away from Kate. "Stole that Bible there on the table from the library of forbidden catalogues that no one is permitted to touch except the priest who hides it there, calling it 'dangerous,' and snickering at all of us because we are so stupid and blind to believe him! I ripped this page out, intending to take it with me when I should hang myself and die and go to hell!"

Kate shuddered as Collette's brazen face and fiery eyes bore into her. "How could you dare do such a thing? Surely the priest would burn that book if he found it in your possession!"

A terrifying grin flashed across Collette's face. "Then let him come and burn me with it!" she cried. "They're thieves and robbers—all of them! If ever I thought I would leave the priest's confessional box more holy than when I first stepped into it, I was wrong! Oh! So utterly wrong!" A flame of crimson blazed across her face as her voice swelled with passion. "What warped ideas, what dark secrets, what doubts have opened to my imagination through the questions the priest asks of me when we are alone together! Oh yes! That sniggering priest sniffs out my weaknesses! His tongue poisons my conscience! Look at his ears! They itch to hear the sick details of all my wicked thoughts! And his fat belly? Yes! It gloats over my shame! Oh!" She almost shrieked and wept with disgust. "His sick, perverted appetite drools over my innocence and lusts over my virgin mind! Oh! My childhood was stolen by him—stolen! Stolen, I tell you! And, oh! If any fearful, shamed, deluded woman ever hated the man who abused her then *I*—yes!—*I* hate *him*!"

Her voice lowered to a simmer, and she stepped closer. "But Kate, listen! Listen to me! Before you judge me, tell me that *you* have never sat before that tiny screen door separating you from a man who has vowed celibacy and never wondered how he can escape the lures of his flesh when a poor innocent girl is spilling her innermost thoughts to him in such a way as to provoke his fleshly lusts to reel with desire? Oh, Kate! Kate, no! You cannot say it hasn't happened to you!"

Kate recoiled at the sickening image. "You lie, Collette! You lie! The Father Confessor has the Holy Spirit and represents him to us; you must not curse and derail him who has been given such a divine office in our lives!"

"You mean Father Andrew?... Meant to represent the Holy Spirit? The only spirit I know that old frog has is the one that comes from the wine bottle he sucks on every day!"

Kate froze but could say nothing, for she recalled the reek of liquor on the priest's breath that very morning.

"Katie, all I want is freedom. Freedom!" she went on wildly. "Freedom from that snakepit which is the confessional! And if it comes through suicide, so be it, for I can abide a living death no longer!" With a focused effort she struggled to her feet, her face livid, her eyes glinting even in the darkness with a chilling mixture of fury and derision, her glossy tresses like liquid fire flying about in all directions as she towered over Kate. "Ah! You condemn me, don't you, Kate?" She laughed sharply. "No matter! I scorn people's contempt of me; nay, I laugh at it—*laugh*! Yes! Because I see how the fear of man has enslaved your conscience, and the conscience of so many others, and beaten them to a pulp; and I see, too, how this perpetrated and unquestioning subjection to the Mother Church is nothing more than veiled idolatry!"

Collette's defiance filled the room, and Kate knew its strength was no match for her. "You're tired and sick, Collette," she said, wondering at the same time if Collette was really going mad. "You must go to bed and get some rest. You'll feel differently in the morning; I'm sure you will."

Collette's eyes were drawn daggers. "That's a lie! A darn lie, I tell you—and I'm sick of lies! Lies! Lies! Lies! That's all I ever hear! You've listened to lies so much, Katie, you think they're the truth! 'Collette, you're tired,' you always say—well, I am tired now!" she cried. "Sick and tired of being *duped*! 'It will be easier to be good when we're grown-up,' you said. Well, it's not true—and you know it isn't! It's harder now—harder than ever!

"And I feel like a perfect hypocrite," she continued, "living every day painted in all the right colours, making all the right motions, saying all the right prayers, but doing it all with a mind as perverted as a heathen and a spirit as heavy as a bag of dead men's bones! I spent enough days in my childhood dreaming up a hoard of false sins to confess to the priest just so I'd receive his favour for my excessive honesty and penitence. But oh! Never did I think that lying about sins I did not commit could be a worse crime than confessing merely that I had made fun of Sister Emma-Margaret, stolen a piece of bread from the kitchen, and been jealous of a girl because a pretty boy smiled at her. Kate, didn't you once tell me that liars don't get into heaven? Well," she exclaimed bitterly, "aren't hypocrites and liars the same thing?"

She paused, then said in a lower tone, "Kate, there are two

ways for me to silence the demons in my head. The first is to kill myself—for demons cannot torment a dead person. The second is to leave this place, offer myself up as a feast to the bottomless appetite of sin, and find what momentary pleasure I can in it."

Suddenly, she seized her white novitiate's veil from the desk and shook it at Kate. "For you see this hateful piece of fabric, Kate? You see it? Look! They have given it to me as a symbol of my shame and condemnation, as a way to test my obedience and subjection to that miserly old Pope, but I cannot wear it—I cannot. Kate, do not look at me that way with eyes of terror. I may go if I wish to, can I not? I am still a novitiate—have you forgotten? I have taken no vows! Sealed no promise! And since I cannot bow my spirit to the grievous burden they wish to lay on my back, and since I have failed to end my own life, I will leave. But I warn you, Kate: do not attempt to persuade me otherwise. It won't work. And as for your beloved priest," she added contemptuously, "you may tell him that if he pursues me like the disgusting brigand he is"—she flung the veil aside as though it were a menstruous cloth—"he must prepare to cross swords with a *free* woman!"

Still kneeling on the floor, Kate gaped up at Collette. "You cannot do it, Collette! You promised me you'd stay here in the convent! You promised me we would stay together always! You owe your life to the Church—to your poor mother who is crying and suffering in purgatory! Don't you realize? Oh, please! Please! You promised! You promised!"

Compassion flitted across Collette's face, but then her hand plunged inside the bosom of her uniform and withdrew a gold necklace threaded through a gold ring. "Kate," she said, dropping her voice to a whisper as she crouched down, "when I was a child I made a vow that I would one day search for my pa—the man who gave this ring to my mother." Her words trembled with conviction as she cradled the golden ring between her slender white fingers. "*That* is the vow I will keep."

Rebellion branded that ring. It had been a fanged viper since childhood, and one which Collette had been expected to shake off when she became a novitiate.

"What! That ring again?" Kate cried, clawing wildly for it. "Give it to me, Collette. Give it to me now—*now*!"

"No!" Collette tore herself away and dashed into the far corner of the cell, clasping the viper to her bosom.

"You were supposed to have given that up—you told me you would!" Kate scuffled to her feet. "Have you any idea the sin it is to secretly possess any object that brings back memories of your past life?"

"Of course I know it! But I lied—just like all the rest of you lie, so it makes us equal!" Collette laughed outright. "But what do I care? I want the truth, and I *will* find it!"

"But what if your father is dead?"

"Kate!" Heat surged into her cheeks. "*I* am dead so long as I stay here! Hungry, thirsty, naked, ignorant—I can no longer tolerate myself being a shackled slave to a religion of lies!"

"But this is just the beginning, can't you see? It will get better, I promise! Now," she added, making quickly for Collette's desk, "throw that book away—the writing in it confused you, and look—look what is happening!"

"You think my own mind can't understand plain English?" Collette hissed, plunging in front of Kate with her arm outstretched, grasping the Bible before Kate could. "I know what I read!"

"Then forget about it, Collette!" Kate pleaded. "Forget! That is what we are expected to do! Forget the past, and those struggles you experience now will disappear next week when we take our vows. Be patient!"

Collette looked her straight in the eye. "That's another lie you believe, Katie," she said. "The lie that things will get better when they are really getting worse! You say you want to be the Bride of Christ—but I know you don't really mean that! You can't! No living woman with red blood flowing through her veins is going to make me believe she has no appetite for male attention and no desire for a man to make love to her!"

"Stop it, Collette," said Kate, grasping Collette's forearm and shaking it. "Stop it now! Our body is the enemy of God! Do you hear me? The *enemy* of God! It molests us, just as our superiors teach! We must deny it—*kill* it—or be damned!"

Collette yanked her arm from Kate's grasp and stood there, defiant. "Then what is wrong with suicide? I was about to kill my body just now, but you stopped me. Why?"

"We use our body to *serve* others, and thereby mortify our flesh!"

"Ah! Of course! Of course! How stupid of me not to think of that!" Collette laughed as her chin elevated and her head tilted back, making way for a brilliant smile to reveal a stunning row of white teeth behind a curled red lip. "Serve… yes! A servant!... Yes, yes! *Now* I understand! A servant! A slave—*to Rome*!" she cried as her voice suddenly rose and hardened at once. "And a very *sick* one, too—sick enough that it must grovel to its master for food, but alive enough to still serve him. Right? Just the way a bad doctor likes it!" As she spoke, she dove her fingers into the abundant waves of her hair and combed through the heavy tresses along her scalp. "And Kate," she added, shaking her head and assuming a simpering pout as her hands came to her sides and she began to pace the room, "once I am reduced to a heartless machine without senses and feelings, what about my soul? Where will it go? Do they have a bottle for it, like they have for the ashes?"

She stopped speaking, staring at Kate, waiting.

Kate stared back at her, her hands gripped into fists at her sides. Oh, how she wished for a pair of shears with which she might shave the rebellion showering those waves of gold from Collette's pate, sending her to damnation! But look! There, on the desk, the key to this very cell—could she not take it away with her and return later with shears in her hands while Collette slept?

"You sick woman!" she burst out. "Sick and deluded to ask such ignorant questions! You already know, Collette! You already know! Heaven, or purgatory, or hell—you decide *now* by the actions you perform here, on earth, and if you give yourself wholly to God's service, *then*, Collette! *Then* you will certainly secure eternal peace for your soul! Don't you understand? Don't you *want* that?"

Collette snorted. "Kate, who is this 'Heavenly Bridegroom'—this invisible lover you fantasize about?"

"Christ—Christ Jesus!"

"I don't believe you."

Kate jerked her head back. "What do you mean?"

Collette tossed her tangled curls and laughed. "Look at the crucifix, Kate! 'Jesus' looks like a dead corpse on a tree—a dead god for dead people to bow down to, is it not? And because of that strange, pharisaic dilemma, your superiors carefully explain to you that a certain living 'representative' will need to take his place—*in persona Christi,* no? But then, on account of your too-honest eyesight, you ask—as any sensible person who still possesses a partially unadulterated intelligence would ask—just who *is* this '*in persona Christi*'? The priest of Rome, you say? Ah, yes! Of course, of course! you cry in amazement. But then you stop—oh? You say. Pardon my insubordinate questions, but—do I actually wish to *marry* him?" A smirk toyed with the corners of her full mouth, and her eyebrows lifted as she nodded slowly, deliberately.

Mockingly.

"Quiet you—*you*!" Kate screamed, her mouth and lips stiff with fury. "You are scandalous!"

"You are right," Collette returned calmly. "Utterly scandalous. But at least I'm honest, no?"

Kate glowered back, her freezing hands again contracting into fists at her sides as Collette continued.

"Wouldn't Father Andrew be furious?" she hissed in a taunting whisper, beginning to pace. "Wouldn't he, Kate? Furious that his dirty secret has got out? Furious that his cheap litter of little nuns-turned-harlots might not wish any longer to be shackled to a polygamous 'Heavenly Bridegroom'—hmm?" Collette clasped her hands behind her and threw her head back as she continued pacing. "I like to think, Kate; I like to *imagine*... to imagine what things might really be like beneath the glitter... things like pretty girls becoming 'brides' with dresses and rings, and then everyone asking, Well! What about the poor little boys? Who will *they* marry? Is there a 'Heavenly Bridegroom' for *them*?" Her eyes flashed with triumph and contempt. "Either our superiors are partial to the bodies of women or they are grossly perverted—or perhaps both?" She stopped short and turned around. "Kate," she said suddenly, her voice lowered and trembling with intensity, "How do you even know God is really there?"

"By his power," said Kate, her forehead knitted as she motioned with her hand." You see it in the Church, through the Pope, you feel him through the Sacraments—Christ is present, his body, blood, soul, and divinity in the Eucharist, and you know him there, when you partake of it. Collette, you know all that!"

"But that is just the trouble!" exclaimed Collette, "I do *not* know! I see the pomp and the so-called miracles, yes, but I do not *feel* them—I do not believe them, for they do not change me!" She continued pacing up and down the room, hands held behind her back. "I'll tell you what I shall do, Kate," she said, stopping abruptly. "I will test God. I will find out who he is. I will find out if he loves me. I will find out if he sees me, and if he cares. I will know if his Word existed in the beginning—if it truly was made flesh and dwelt among us, or if we are merely worshipping a blaspheming deity clad in chasuble and pallium who shakes his fake keys in our faces and makes women and girls abuse and sacrifice their bodies to appease his wrathful lust! What do you think?"

"Collette! Think! Think! You have absolutely no money! What will you do? How will you survive?"

"I will find a suitable job for a young lady," Collette said staunchly. "Probably as a seamstress in Dublin. And I will make my way fair and straight all the way to Paris—just like any other woman might."

Kate laughed suddenly. "You? A seamstress?" she cried. "You can hardly sew a straight seam, let alone display tact enough to advertise yourself for a job that requires at least minimal skills with a needle and thread! All you can do is scrub floors, change diapers, and wash laundry, and if I know you, you will pickpocket your way to Paris before you become a seamstress!"

"Oh, really? You think I am that inept, Kate? Truly?"

"You are the product of a fallen woman's infidelity," said Kate desperately. "When people find out what you are, you will be a scorned and ridiculed member of society, and no respectable business will dare to hire you."

"Oh? So you scorn me, too, then, do you Kate? You label me and condemn me to failure on account of what my mother was? And you think that's fair? But don't bother to explain." Collette gave a short laugh as she made a sudden movement toward the bed. "I'll just prove you wrong."

In an instant Kate rushed forward and took hold of her shoulders, yanking her back. "No, you will not go!" she cried. "Certainly you will not! There are wolves out there, Collette! Men and women who care nothing for you—who would take advantage of you and deceive you!"

"Wolves, you say?" Collette spat. "And what about wolves in sheep's clothing making their lair right inside these walls? Are these less vicious, do you think?"

"Hold your tongue!"

"I once told you I hated them." Collette gave her a withering look. "That feeling has not changed."

Kate had never slapped someone before, but now, fuelled suddenly with rage, she dashed forward and her hand struck a sudden sharp blow across Collette's face. The sting in the slap was like a razor across Kate's palm. "How dare you speak against them after all they've done for you," she cried out. "You spoilt, ungrateful girl!"

The words vibrated through the cell.

Kate drew back—back against the desk, her palms pressing against the rough wood edges.

The slap had branded a bright scarlet spot into the soft white flesh of Collette's cheek, but she had not flinched. "You're afraid, aren't you, Kate?" Her voice was measured and cool.

Kate tried to hide her tottering resolve by forcing a short laugh—the key was behind her; she could grab it now. "Afraid?" As her eyes secretly measured the lengths of hair streaming down Collette's shoulders and bosom, her fingers crawled backward, found the iron key, and closed upon it, and her mind planned the scheme that would force Collette to stay.

"Yes." Collette's eyes welled with startling softness. "That's why you starve yourself, and vomit up your food, and flagellate yourself, and cut yourself with razors until the blood oozes from the wounds, leaving those dark spots on your habit, plastering it to your skin. You think God sees those wounds and smiles on them, don't you? You think that if you didn't have them, he'd send you weeping to the devil's hell. But what kind of love feeds on suffering like a vulture feeds on a dead carcass?"

She shook her head regretfully, then, to Kate's surprise, reached out and seemed as though she would take Kate's hand—the hand that held the key.

Kate shrank back. "My home is here—here," she said, sidling away from the desk and then backing away from Collette, step by step, toward the door as she secreted the key in her pocket, knowing that when Collette could not find it, her unpredictable nature and disdain for convent rules would allow her to go to bed without a second thought of locking her cell. "Do not torture me further—do not make me choose between it and you!"

"Katie, no… Katie, please?" She was walking toward her now, emotion quivering in her voice, tears bathing the red spot on her cheek. "I'm not saying you must choose. I'm simply saying that I love you—that you are my sister and my friend, and always will be."

A rising in Kate's stomach made her groan, and she stumbled back, snatching herself away from Collette's touch. Infection was inevitable now from a woman as sick as Collette, for if the heretical ideas that had conquered Collette should conquer her also, then what must be the eternal punishment and shame impending such a life?

"Collette," she said, hardening her tone, "I no longer want your friendship. I want God. I want to give myself up to his service for the sake of my mother and my family. I am their hope—their salvation, their chance to escape prolonged suffering. But you… you! You vain, empty thing!" She gnawed her lower lip against the tears. "You seek to sow doubt in my mind and turn me against them! But I will not listen—no, I will not! Next week my first vows will sever the emotional cords that have bound us to each other. I shall die to you, to myself, to everything I have ever known. I will receive my own ring! I will be wedded to the Heavenly Bridegroom. I will shave my head *bare* for him, which is something you, with all your stubbornness and conceit could *never* do!" She shook her trembling finger at Collette's flying hair and lifted her chin against tears as she added, "If you like you may scorn that I will one day seal my final vows with my own blood, but know this—know that *blood* is the only way!"

The colour drained from Collette's face. "But… Kate," she said at last, and took a faltering step closer, "is this what you truly want?"

Kate lifted her hand to ward off Collette's advance. "Oh! It is what I *need*!" she burst out, and her whole form shook with the violence of the feeling that possessed her.

A cold, impenetrable hush fell about them. They stood there, struck dumb by the force of their opposing convictions.

"Then goodbye…" Water filled Collette's eyes till it spilled over again; she took a deliberate step forward, ignoring Kate's resistance as she stretched forth her hand. "Katie?"

Kate darted to the door. The latch was hardly discernible through the spots that flashed in her vision and made the room lurch from side to side.

"Katie?" There was an unusual quaver in her voice. "Please… Promise to remember that no matter how far I go, I will always love you, and I will always call you my sister."

The final word shocked the air.

Sister.

Kate clenched her hands into fists until her nails dug into the soft flesh of her palms. Collette's promise was nothing less than a Judas kiss.

"I am not your sister," she said in a voice she did not recognize. Her fingers crushed the cold latch as she laid her quivering body against the door, pushing it open.

Tears scorched her eyes as she fled down the cold, dark, deserted hallway, chased by an army of skeletal spectres that threatened to devour her sanity. Finally, she reached her cell and burst into the blackened room, shuddering as she bolted the door behind her. She leaned her back against it, clutching at her chest that heaved with her palpitating heart, lurching with irregular pulses, trying to choke her. It was dark, but she knew her vision was clouding—a shroud was closing in over her head, smothering her, pressing against her fevered brain until she feared to breathe.

"She won't go—she can't!" she gasped, groping desperately for the key in her pocket, seizing it, ripping it out. "I will make her stay—indeed! I will make her—for she will not leave if her hair is short and ugly!"

Engulfed by a terrible silence, she sensed an icy, emaciated hand reaching through the darkness—reaching for her body just as her hand had reached for that key. It grasped her throat, and squeezed. She flinched—the key fell from her stiff fingers, clanging to the floor like a gong while she pressed her fist over her lips to keep herself from screaming. But she could see the spirits before her—and there, too, the self-flagellation whip with its seven cords lying next to the two books on the table, calling to her, commanding her to take it up in her own hands, and raise it against her body, and torture the flesh she hated—to shred it with pleasure and spill out its blood on the floor for the sake of her dead family, and herself, and for the girl she had once called her friend.

Her hand fell from her mouth as a moan of agony escaped her quivering lips. Like a bruised reed, she wavered in the tempest. At last overcome, her knees collapsed beneath her, and she fell on the cold stone floor, and wept.

— CHAPTER IV —

IN WASHINGTON

April 15, 1861

John Dallington had seen the advertisements posted up all over the town. Eye-catching and bold with wide print beneath the spanning Roman eagle and banner, they fluttered on innumerable fences and billboards and decorated the shop windows and doors of the fledgling city, boldly crying:

Save our Union!!! Come to the Rescue!
Wanted: 75,000 Able-Bodied Men!
TO ARMS! TO ARMS!!
God and your country call!

Just then a group of high-strung schoolboys came marching down a side street, waving newspapers and banners while singing "Yankee Doodle" with more conviction than if the song had been a Sunday hymn.

"A new idol," John muttered, eyes squinted as he noted the red, white, and blue flutter against the bustle of the street. "With thirty-three brilliant stars to bow down to."

His black Morgan gelding tensed underneath him, increasing his gait to an edgy prance. John drew the bit slightly backward. "Easy. Easy, Skipper boy." He loosened his grip on the clammy reins and stretched his tense fingers.

Civil war was inevitable. For months he had been expecting it, long before the rumours or the shelling of Fort Sumter had begun. Now it was reality, and the whole country rose on a wave of patriotic enthusiasm and expectation as President Lincoln sought loyal troops to squelch the rebellion and restore strength and peace to the Union.

John rounded the northeast corner of Pennsylvania Avenue and guided his horse into the crowds along the wide muck-sodden, puddle-ridden street swarming with adults and urchins and beasts of all kinds. All of them appeared to be swimming—swimming, as it were, in the wake of a mud-flood over which the now recently dismembered and fire-hazardous green copper-covered wood dome of the sandstone Capitol building, along with its almost perfectly aligned though partial obelisk, may have watched for a mysterious span of uncharted years. They loomed alongside their imposing Greco-Roman and Gothic sister-architectural wonders known as the Patent Office Building, the General Post Office, and the Smithsonian Institution, whose thundering voices of unspeakable magnificence rose from that infamous, mosquito-infested swamp upon which the city of the District of Columbia had been established.

To the left, the porch of the National Hotel hosted tight knots of smoking businessmen and a handful of dirt-smudged farmers. No doubt Confederate sympathizers—all of them, attempting to be fashionable.

Farther down the street opposite the National Hotel stood Harvey's General Store, distinguished by its singular sagging front veranda and yellow-green siding. The political views of the store's owner, along with his customers, was betrayed without apology by the throng of tall-standing Negroes and robust white farmers spanning youth to middle age, surrounded by white men in black Hardee hats, dark-blue kepis, Prussian blue coats, and sky-blue trousers with the variants of double gold strips or piping along the leg.

Among the voices, John heard the clear, powerfully enunciated tones of Dr. Robert Hall, and he saw above the crowd a familiar pair of sinewy arms emphasizing with forceful gesticulations the doctor's vocalized opinions respecting what was printed on the front page of the press release held in his hand.

John drew up his mount to the hitching post in front of Harvey's and called out, "Robert! Hello, Robert!"

The doctor's demonstrations continued floating with his voice above the general clamour of townspeople, all of whom proved their eagerness to snatch the juicy morsels of news and conspiracies on the war by chattering loudly, and pressing forward, and listening attentively, and cheering patriotically.

"Hall! I say"—a little louder, a little more urgently—"*Doctor* Hall!"

Instantly, Hall's face turned. His eyes, quick as an eagle's, scanned the street as though searching for an emergency. When he noticed John, his face relaxed and beamed with recognition, and instantly he swam through the mass, shook off the residue, and came forward onto the sun-soaked boardwalk. "John—son of a gun!" he cried.

"Hoots, man!" said John as the thirty-five-year-old doctor strode to the side of his horse, rolling the newspaper into a funnel and slapping one of his palms with it as a grin spread across his angular face shaded by two days worth of whiskers. "Excitement follows you, my friend. What's the latest conspiracy in modern history you're lecturing on now?"

The doctor grinned. "As Sir Francis Bacon and his Knights of the Helmet would like it—'All the world's a stage, and all the men and women merely players.' I anticipate the entrance of the mitred tyrant sometime soon, but, in the meantime, it's easy to see that the Freemasons are chuckling quite contentedly as they watch the masses worship their infantile scheme of Darwinian Evolution which will reduce the laymen's wits to jelly for more than a century after the effects of this war are realized. Ah, you see?... Look behind you." He jerked his chin forward as he tapped the roll against his palm repeatedly. "Recruitment offices—sprouting up on every major corner in this town."

John made a half turn in the saddle and looked back. A long lineup of men stood before yet another recruiting station. "Aye, fishers of men," he muttered. "The adage is becoming propaganda."

"I take a shift performing physical exams in the back of that office tomorrow," said the doctor. "Reckon you'll be signing the enlistment roll yourself?"

Denying a sudden tightening in his chest, John forced his gaze to rove again down the avenue to where it climaxed in the stunning architectural expanse crowning Capitol Hill.

He studied the open vault of the sprawling white building's cast-iron dome. Though decked by cranes and scaffolds, it seemed proud to boast the architectural design of its solar inspiration—an inspiration that only pagan Roman architecture could supply. It was idolatry, and he despised it.

"I'm an Irishman, Hall. Not a patriot."

"Ah! But sentiments like that won't help free the black slaves, will they, John? Second Rome or not, at least DC has a president willing to take a crack at breaking the chain of ignorance and injustice on this continent."

At that moment they were interrupted by a shrill, soprano-like voice coming down the avenue.

"Sirs? Sirs! May I have the pleasure of interviewing you, sir, on the recent happenings at Fort Sumter on Friday, sir?"

It was a frenzied press reporter in a grey cap and oversized breeches, and he was running up to the hitching post, looking at John. And Hall was laughing.

"Not a patriot?" the doctor remarked in a low tone as he watched the advance of the desperate street wanderer. "You'll have a tasty line or two for the reporting spree, then." His eyebrows were wiggling and moustache twitching as he glanced up at John and crossed his arms over his broad chest, leaning back slightly as though preparing himself to enjoy a favourite scene in a theatrical production.

The reporter came to a full stop in front of the hitching rail, his eyes looking as though they were about to burst their sockets and jump through his spectacles as he flourished his pencil and notebook, ready to begin the report.

John grimaced and tugged at the cuff of his buckskin jacket. "Not Fort Sumter today, lad," he said flatly. "We already know that Lincoln asked Davis to free the slaves and then presented Davis with a Bible and a gun—and that Davis picked up the gun."

"Per-perhaps something else, then, sir?" suggested the reporter with a desperate smile that revealed a line of misaligned teeth jarred mercilessly between the corners of a narrow jaw. "Immigration perhaps, sir? You're speech is Irish. Perhaps you wish to speak to the notable influence our Irish and German immigrants may have in the future of this war?"

"Immigration? That's grand," said John with a smirk. "Then you have a noble job ahead of you, with that pen and paper of yours, lad. Ready?"

The reporter nodded and fixed his eyes on the page.

"First of all," John began, "warn the Union to beware the treacherous fingers of the Democratic press that drip with the blood carried over from the hand of its Roman Catholic friend, Pope Pius IX. The Pope enjoys flattering Davis—who, in return for his education by the charitable Dominicans, can't help but turn a sympathetic ear toward the vendetta the Romish Church fosters against the honest President of the Union who has always preferred to hold the Bible in his hand. It's obvious the leftists have already adopted Rome's prejudice against Lincoln on account of his brilliant court defense of the French-Canadian priest, Charles Chiniquy, in '56." John paused, watching for an expression on the reporter's face that might betray a subjective opinion on the contentious topic. "Lad, have you heard of it?"

The reporter, still scribbling, nodded quickly. "The man was most insubordinate, sir, was he not? Later suspended, and then excommunicated, too? Perhaps one might call him an apostate, sir?"

"Perhaps. The unsigned excommunication was a sham on the part of the lily-livered Bishop and his drunken priests who nailed it to the church door—not that 'excommunication' mattered to Chiniquy—but the rash act certainly exposed the yellow face of his jealous opponent."

"But this Chiniquy was a rather nasty fellow; he was, uh... very uncooperative, it would seem, with the Bishop of Chicago, I believe?" the reporter feebly ventured.

"Ah—then you see my point. The Papacy makes no bones about ruining the reputation of anyone who defies it, and using pen and paper to do it."

Again, the reporter nodded quickly and scribbled furiously.

"Remember: yours is a noble task, lad—you, too, have pen and paper, and can speak the truth using those humble, unassuming tools to do it."

"Yes, sir."

And John continued. "Lincoln was the best lawyer and most honest man in Springfield at the time. Thank God for him. And for the press, and the Irish boys who waved those papers around the country and eventually got the attention of the intelligent Miss Moffat, whose direct testimony proved Chiniquy's innocence against the slander and perjury he endured at court by LeBelle and Bishop O' Reagan. The villains perjured themselves in the end—got slammed so hard they didn't know what hit them—and they fled Urbana, tail between their legs. Rome knows the power of words on paper— Write that line in the report, lad," said John, pointing his forefinger at the scribbling reporter, "and then say that since the court case, the Democratic press has echoed Darwinism by calling Lincoln more than just an ape and a bloody monster. Tell the Union to pray, too, like Lincoln's mother taught him to pray. Her Honest Abe didn't earn his name by chance, you see, and Chiniquy knew that and sought Lincoln out for that reason. Our rail-splitter has been in Rome's crosshairs ever since they lost the case to him—it's what Chiniquy feared would happen—and Union sympathizers should never imagine that the Pope isn't still plotting his revenge on Lincoln. In fact, if assassination attempts on President Lincoln's life begin to unfold, the public would do well to assume that it's the underhanded efforts of the Vatican to martyr a saint."

The reporter's pen halted and seemed to shudder, and his spectacles seemed to float uncertainly above the mass of letters to reveal a pair of round, blinking eyes. "Is this still a… a topic on immigration, sir?"

"I'm coming to that, young man." John rubbed the wiry thickness of his beard between his fingertips. "It all begins with politics and religion, though—control what people hear, control what people think. The old saying still holds true, doesn't it?"

The reporter hemmed as his eyes ascended and his pen paused. "I'm sorry, sir… what's that, sir?"

"That all roads lead to Rome." John paused, noting the reporter's pen was still not moving. "You got that down?"

The reporter's eyes reverted back to the page and glued themselves there, and he nodded, scribbled, and nodded, and John continued.

"I'm an Irishman. Such a heritage comes with a past heated with Catholic and Protestant debate. And now"—he flexed his legs by standing up in the stirrups—"let's talk about the United States Constitution."

"And, uh, sir..." the reporter began gingerly, adding a mild, awkward hem to soften his interruption. "How does that relate to immigration, sir?"

John laughed lightly and sat back down on the saddle. "My point is that the Romish Church blatantly contradicts the Declaration of Independence. With Rome's laws and teachings against equality, liberty of conscience, the right to serve God as the conscience dictates, and her hatred against religious and governmental independence outside of her supreme authority, she declares herself this country's most deadly foe. Despite the inevitable infiltration of Masonic traditions in the ceremonies and architectural designs in the map, rest assured that your founding fathers stood up for you, lad, when, in the 1776 Congress, they asserted the self-evident truths that 'all men are created equal, that they are endowed by their Creator with certain unalienable Rights, that among these are Life, Liberty and the pursuit of Happiness.' But show me which of Rome's mad dogmas—aricular confession, the priestly vows of celibacy, and the infallibility of the Popes, just to name a few—actually support the fundamental ideals of the Republic? And then observe that the majority of Irish immigrants are devout Roman Catholics—trained in Catholic Schools and nunneries just like the majority of our Confederate neighbours to the South have been trained—and accustomed from infancy to revere Rome's tyranny with the obedience of a machine. If Lincoln is to succeed, common sense dictates that the Union must be aware of the discrepancy during their enlistment examinations." He looked toward the recruitment office and motioned past the jangling streetcars, impatient riders, ponderous omnibuses, swaying wagons, and noisy pedestrians

"Oh, yes, sir, over there. Of course, sir," returned the reporter.

With his eyes scanning the crowd of men still gathered outside the recruitment office, John suddenly noticed a familiar dark-haired, broad-shouldered, tall young man step out of the door. His stride was resolute. Resolve carved itself in the expression of his high forehead.

"Paul!" John called over the din as he recognized the twenty-five-year-old blacksmith's son.

A smile overspread Paul Weston's bearded face and he lifted his hand in salute. "Mr. Dallington!" He waded through the congested street to the hitching post and stood next to the doctor, who levied a good-natured punch to the young man's shoulder.

"Physical examination—passed," the doctor reported officially. "He's solid as a plank."

"Good day, Dr. Hall!" said Paul, grasping the doctor's hand in a vigorous handshake.

"They reeled you in, did they, Paul?" John said with a half smile as the two men found comfortable standing positions, leaning forward with one or both elbows resting against the hitching rail in an attitude of supervision.

"Did so," Paul asserted. "Figured I might not have my chance if I waited too long."

"Militia?"

"Yes, sir. Are you enlisting?"

John hesitated. "We'll see after the three-month term is up."

"You don't think three months is enough time?"

"It's optimistic, but unrealistic." John adjusted the burgundy silk handkerchief at his neck and scanned the swarm of crowds. "Still, if they're loyal to Lincoln that's one step in the right direction. But these men are citizens, not soldiers. They're greener than grass."

Paul pushed his sweat-stained beige hat back on his head. "Like in the Revolution."

"This'll be the second of those on our soil."

"Second Revolution?"

"Sure."

"Couldn't be that great—could it?"

"Greater, in comparison. At least three years—not months—judging from the two wars at hand."

"Two wars?" Paul repeated, half laughing.

"Sure—Doc knows it, too, right, Hall?"

The doctor nodded as he selected a cigar from the front pocket of his dark-green vest and inserted it between his lips. "Sure thing," he said, and struck a match across the hitching rail. The match flared and he laid it to the cigar. "Two sets of slaves, two wars to fight."

A sudden hem and "Gentlemen?" reminded John that the reporter was still there.

"Aye, lad?"

"Gentlemen, may I add this to the report?" he asked less feebly than before, addressing both the doctor and John. "It is an interesting perspective for the paper."

"Of course."

And the reporter scribbled on.

"Two sets of slaves?" Paul continued, his expression slackening.

A wagonload of goods was, at that moment, driving past them in the opposite direction.

"You see that driver, Paul?" said John, pointing to the hunched, sad-faced mulatto man in a slouched hat who held the reins to a team of heavy mules. "You see his leering, well-dressed white master beside him?"

"Poor Negroes—they need help bad."

"Sure they do. The cause to free the slaves from perishing like animals on Southern plantations can't be argued. But Jefferson Davis and his Democrats hate our old rail-splitter for more than just throwing a wrench into their plans because he advocates the emancipation of the blacks. They hate him because he opposes the Jesuits, advocates freedom of conscience amongst all men—black and white—and won't stand by to see either race oppressed by the power of tyranny—physical or moral."

"But racism and religion are two entirely different arguments," said Paul, shifting the position of his elbow on the hitching rail. "To say that white slave owners here and the Pope thousands of miles across the ocean are two sides of the same coin seems somewhat far-fetched to me."

"But not for the skilled tyrant. Both systems are a mere chess game to him, and ignorance is the checkmate scheme by which he intends to outwit his opponent."

"Catholics are good, moral folks, Mr. Dallington—at least the ones I know," Paul insisted. "And for years their religious orders have aided the less fortunate. The Sisters of Charity and the Sisters of Mercy are excellent examples."

Irritation quickened John's pulse. "Can the leopard change his spots? I'm a Protestant Irishman who loves this free country, but when I see my poor, ignorant Roman Catholic neighbours flocking to this free soil, stalked by legions of nuns and priests and bishops, what else am I to conclude but that the immigration movement is a prelude to a war which has been engineered by the Papacy to infect a free land with ready-made moral slaves and their cassock-robed taskmasters?"

"Gentleman, ahem!" interjected the reporter, his pen alighting from the paper as his hand went up to adjust the crooked lean of his spectacles as though his professional decorum depended upon their perfected position across his nose. "A most *interesting* point, gentlemen, to be sure. And, uh, if I may, sir,"—looking at John while his pen tapped the air inquisitively—"if I may ask you, Mr., uh, Mr. *Dallington,* sir, with respect to your opinions on immigration, if you believe, sir, that adhering to personal religious prejudices in times like these will promote unity or tension in the North, sir?"

"It's obvious," returned John, "that Catholic dogma abounds in the South. Irish immigrants—at least by majority—are already Rome's slaves. Theoretically, then, an Irish Catholic would be the most easily 'Confederatized' and, therefore, the Union's most likely turncoat."

The reporter squinted. "But, uh, with due respect, sir, you are Irish, sir. It appears that your view is a personal criticism, sir?"

"I am Irish, yes. But I am not Roman Catholic. Neither am I a senseless Protestant who denies that popery today is as treacherous as it was during the Inquisition of the Dark Ages. The *pet* technique used by infallible popes to secure the service of their slave-peasants was to convince them that they were too dumb to understand the Bible, and then to conveniently withdraw the slave's accesses to the written word that might, allegedly, 'confuse' him. Now look to the enslaved blacks.

It is, you know, a most dangerous things for the black man to possess the rare talent of literacy."

A tremendous laugh broke from Dr. Hall as he threw his head back and pushed himself away from the hitching rail. "Precisely, my friend!" he cried. "Precisely! The Confederate master keeps his poor Negroes chained to cotton stalks and sugar cane the same way Rome turns her male slaves into effeminates and keeps them chained to papyrus scrolls practising their calligraphy."

The reporter looked up from his scroll, his pink lip protruding, his spectacles slipping. "Does that conclude your opinion on immigration, sir?" he said with a less feeble though modest hem.

"Yes, lad. It does. You've done a grand job."

The reporter attempted a brave smile. "Many thanks, sir—gentlemen." He nodded to Paul and the doctor as he retreated down the avenue.

"We'll be watching for your report in the paper tomorrow, young man!" Dr. Hall called after him, then resumed his lean against the hitching rail with a chuckle. "A juicy line or two, indeed, John. You think his head was spinning?"

"A wee bit, perhaps," said John. "I'll be surprised, though, if less than half of his report makes its way into the paper." He turned to Paul. "Coming up to the house this afternoon? Peter and Priscilla haven't seen you for a week. They'll beg a visit before you leave for the army. Ellen will have tea set."

"Thank you kindly," Paul said, his studied calm attempting to eclipse a more enthusiastic internal emotion that was betrayed by a deepening of the ruddy colour in his cheeks. "I'll get my horse," he added, retracing his steps toward the recruitment office.

"Meet you there." John then turned to Hall. "And you? Does another lonely bachelor fancy a taste of Ellen's biscuits today?"

"Not today, sir," the doctor replied with a half chuckle. "Other engagements."

"Aye, other engagements?" John repeated. "Found yourself a lass, then, have you?"

"No, no," returned the doctor with a laugh and a somewhat bitter note edging his tone as he resorted to the former tapping of the old newspaper roll against his palm. "This bachelor has wasted enough time trying to hunt down a respectable one."

"Ah, perhaps you lack assistance in the matter—have matchmakers made themselves scarce to you?"

"On the contrary, sir. They seem to grow more numerous with the years, which renders their well-meaning efforts the more detestable. Therefore, after much consideration, and having resolved that a single day with his ideal is better than a lifetime with the average, the lonely bachelor has confirmed his bachelor state as being more to his taste than pledging his love to one among a slew of desperately available females."

"Well, Doc, can't blame a man for being a mite head-shy if he's tasted a bad apple or two," said John, nudging his mount's flank. "I know the feeling myself. Just don't let it bitter you against the right one." He turned the gelding's head and raised his arm in farewell. "Watch for that paper, Doc. I'll meet you at Harvey's tomorrow, noon, to get the lowdown."

— CHAPTER V —

THE MISTS DEEPEN

Standing unobserved in the shadow of the parlour entrance of the family's farmhouse, John watched his daughter at the piano. Her graceful figure was clad in delicate white muslin, girdled at the waist with blue satin. Gently puffed short sleeves decorated rounded white arms with dimpled elbows while hands of small, soft, and shapely proportions coaxed a soothing strain from the keys. Her voice, clear and strong, sang out her favourite hymn. But her cheeks bore the traces of tears.

"Just as I am, though tossed about
With many a conflict, many a doubt,
Fightings and fears within, without,
O Lamb of God, I come, I come."

The scene was paradoxical. And as he watched, the words and music pricked an offence he could not reconcile. Priscilla was the morning dew; the sun in a stainless summer sky; the sweet song of the robin. Conflicts, doubt, fears of any kind were unknown to her. How could she sing as though having known them? Of hardships and poverty she could not complain, nor of discomfort, hunger, or lack of privilege or opportunity. All was hers; she had but to name her desire and, be it within his human power, he would move heaven and earth to bring her joy.

Then what had inspired the tears? Did she sense something lacking? Did her heart question him, or speak to her of secrets he could never reveal to her? Was the undercurrent of his past rising like foam upon the cresting, windblown waves?

Had he let something slip?

His eyes roved about the room; he noticed Ellen, and his scalp prickled. Seated in her rocking chair and knitting, she did not see him. But she appeared weary, preoccupied. The crow's feet around her eyes were deep; her complexion was an unwatered plant; the grey threading her rusty hair expressed more than just years. And that brooding look—it seemed the talebearer of a conscience that pleaded with her will as she listened to Priscilla's singing.

John drew his mouth into a straight line and bit his lip. Ellen knew what silence she must maintain. The Scottish woman offered the maternal support his children needed in the absence of a mother, and she held a valued place in the family—a place that rivalled the position of a blood relation. But she was still a servant who received an honest wage. A servant who had promised him to keep family affairs exactly what they were.

But Ellen Kelly was a woman, with a woman's sensibilities and a woman's weaknesses—a woman who would never cease to berate him and criticize his alleged lack of compassion.

"Mr. Dallington!" she had said that night ten years before. "Och! I've seen many bairns safely intae the world—I've caught twins, sir—but my eyes have nae seen what they see now. I cannae do more! Please, sir, send for the doc!"

Suddenly he was back on the Fairfax County road, plunging his spurs into the flank of his black Morgan gelding, squinting against the driving rain…

The moon is full; it glances nervously out from behind jagged black clouds that scar the unsettled face of the sky; it trembles as it uncovers the nakedness of the bare countryside.

Usually, the winding dirt road is a bowl of dust, but tonight the rain has turned it to marbles and grease. A yellow shaft of lightning severs the darkness for an instant, making the precarious trail look hideous—like the dirty face of a wailing woman.

Mud flies up in all directions as Skipper's hooves sink into the mire with steady, trampling thuds, accenting the deep thunder rumbling overhead. Aye, how the sound reminds him of the jeers and sneers and mockery still rising against him from his father's parish—all the shattered dreams and tainted ideals he eternally endures because of her.

He spits out a chunk of clay, feels its gritty residue between his teeth. It is still two miles—two long, treacherous miles—before he reaches the doctor's house in Falls Church. Two miles—they seem no less than twenty.

He tries to blink away the bits of wet dirt shooting into his eyes, but he is blind.

"She ruined me!" He drives the spurs deeper. "Spoilt, selfish, ungrateful woman—to grind my unsullied reputation into that mud and wreck the life I wanted!"

He spits again, but this time with contempt, and he curses through his teeth as though the studied Calvinism and Reformed theology he has sweated over for decades is nothing but chaff in the wind.

They are trotting on a slippery descent now, clattering over the old wooden bridge that spans the swollen brown waters of a tributary off Tripps Run. The unpredictable rivulet is higher this year—water is licking away at the low, sandy banks, threatening to wash out the bridge before he and Dr. Hall are back across.

They reach the outskirts of Falls Church. The scant, dingy town is dead. Skipper's hooves mash through the thick sludge before Weston's Blacksmith Shop, then slosh across the slippery, mud-plastered boardwalk in front of the dusty old shack that serves as the town bank. Turning off the main avenue, they enter a side street lined by houses on one side. Through the rain John scarcely distinguishes a glimmer of lamplight peering out from a lonely window.

A little farther forward, a few more houses passed, they stop in front of a whitewashed structure with two gable windows and a dilapidated veranda—the doctor's place.

John purses his lips. "No lights," he says.

He swings down from the saddle, leaving Skipper's reins dangling in the mire as he bounds up the front stairs and strikes several blows across the front door.

He waits, huffing, trying to catch his breath. Rainwater drips over the wide brim of his black felt beaver hat. There is no answer. He strikes another set of harder blows—still no reply.

The rain pours down in silver sheets. Skipper nickers, paws at a puddle, and tosses his sopping head. A sharp thunderclap, followed instantly by a glaring lightning bolt, make both John and horse jump.

"Eejit!" John growls, striking his hand across his sodden thigh. He hasn't even tried the door. Its iron knob is cold as ice when he tries to turn it, but it is locked from the inside.

A raw shudder passes over him, and he snatches his hand away as though from a red-hot branding iron.

She is still behind that door—in his mind—and to his ears, those sheets are still moaning.

"Dr. Hall! Dr. Hall! Open your door, man!" he bellows, beating the door with both fists tightly clenched, choking on a lump of emotion tightening his throat. "In God's name, open your door!"

He deals more blows, but the door is unyielding; it is laughing at his skinned, bleeding knuckles as though it knows they have bled before—often, and a hundred times worse than now. Wood splinters had once lodged beneath his skin and dug into his fingernails, but he had welcomed the pain—even sought it—wishing that at least for once the physical pain would drown out the truth that drew the blood, making more white scars.

"What in tarnation?" comes a man's voice from behind him. "Who's there?"

John whirls around. A young man in a dark oilskin overcoat and hat is standing in the rain at the bottom of the stairs, his hand grasping a black leather medical bag.

"Doc! Hoots, man, where've you been?" John leaps down the stairs, sloshing into a puddle of rainwater beneath the overflowing eaves.

"Over in Washington—at the Richardson's place. The missus just gave birth to number seven—a healthy girl, strong as all get-out." Dr. Hall's wet charcoal moustache twitches. "Why? What's the matter?"

"Robert, can you ride to my place tonight? My wife's in labour. Ellen says something's wrong—no progress."

"Great Scott—nothing like full moons and babies! How

long have you been waiting here?"

"Ten minutes." John seizes his horse's reins and springs into the wet, squeaking saddle.

"Son of a gun," Dr. Hall mutters, jogging briskly toward the small whitewashed barn on the south side of the house. "Wait a minute," he calls back. "I'll throw the leather on old Mustard." He disappears inside. A minute later he reappears, this time posting atop his sleek palomino gelding.

Skipper chomps at the bit, paws the puddle again, nickers.

"Right behind you, John!" the doctor shouts, lowering his hat over his forehead—a shield against the wet onslaught.

John reins his horse into a sharp turn and spurs him forward onto the road going west. Riding abreast with the doctor, they keep up an alternating canter and gallop along the treacherous road, then cross the tributary's bridge. But John feels hardly eased when they finally canter along the long avenue lined with tall maple and beech trees leading up to Dallington House. The long, naked branches, tossed and torn by wind and winter frosts, stretch themselves upward and outward, making eerie, shifting imprints against the stormy sky. John forces his eyes to lock on the steady light of an oil lamp in the kitchen window of the Colonial-style red-brick farmhouse; he catches sight of his twelve-year-old daughter standing there, looking out.

"Priscilla…" he whispers. She is waiting for him.

The men dismount in front of the arboured entrance framed with shrivelled brown vines. The heavy breathing of the horses accent the atmospheric tension; their flanks quiver; their middle hindquarters billow white with shivering foam. Looping Skipper's reins over the hitching rail, John rushes into the warm, dim entryway, then kicks off his mud-spattered black leather boots and flings his hat and coat across the rough oak bench, leaving a trail of stocking-shaped gumbo footprints behind him. Dr. Hall follows close.

Priscilla comes to meet them, her face white as a sheet.

"Papa! You're back! I'm praying that Jesus will make the storm stop, too. It's such a *terrible* storm, Papa! Almost like the one in Mr. Longfellow's poem!"

"Ah, *The Wreck of the Hesperus*?" he remarks absently—they

had read it together the night before. "The doctor's here, Prissy—he knows what to do."

Dr. Hall holds out a brown paper bag to Prissy. "Peppermints?" His voice seems to quaver—is it nerves? "For you, miss—two," he is saying, throwing his hat and coat on a peg, attempting a casual air.

"Jesus will help you, Mr. Hall," Priscilla is saying as she receives the bag. "Won't he?"

John wants to tell Prissy that this is no time for questions, but instead he clears his throat. "I suppose he will help, darling," he says aloud despite knowing that Doc Hall, though a closet historian and skeptic, is not a churchgoing man. "Only one peppermint, Prissy—save one for me," he calls back as he makes for the long corridor. "Doc?... This way."

They approach the bedroom on the northwest side of the house. The door is partly ajar; a shaft of lamplight glints along the oak floorboards. John pushes the door open. There is Ellen—her short, healthy figure leaning over the edge of the bed as she bathes his wife's forehead. Mary is partially sitting, propped up by several feather pillows. Her eyes are squeezed shut, her strained, small face almost grey, her lips turned a pale purple and held firmly together by her now inflexible jaw.

"How is she, Ellen?"

"Mr. Dallington, I wouldnae lie tae ye." Her look is strained; a damp tendril of her rusty-coloured hair has escaped the diminutive knot at the nape of her neck and clings desperately to the side of her blanched cheek. "The lass ain't good right now, Lord help us—she willnae eat nor drink naethin'."

John makes a halting step toward the bed. He places his hand on his wife's head; strokes her damp, jet-black hair.

Mary's eyes open and she looks up at him wearily. "Darling?" A weak sigh follows, and her eyelids droop again.

He hears the splash of water in the ironstone washbasin.

"Soap?"

Ellen is handing the doctor a bar of brown lye soap.

"What's the story?" asks the doctor as he washes.

"Babe's sideways, sir—willnae budge—an' she's swollen worse than I've ever seen. She's too weak tae get up an' walk—

we did for hours yesterday an' today, but lassie's worn out now. I gave her two tablespoons castor oil—a good remedy I've always used with success, Doc—then later sweet raspberry-leaf tea, an' last a tonic of lemon an' orange, salt an' honey, an' a pinch of soda that she wouldnae take—said it tasted bad. I've caught many babes in my time—but och! This wee lass is past thirty-five years old, Doc, an'—" But she could not finish for emotion.

The doctor was observing Mary, calmly asking details of Ellen as he mopped his arms with a linen towel.

"She's less than halfway there now, Doc—an hour ago she was better, but when I told her gently that the doc was comin' tae help, an' she heard ye comin' in, it upset her."

"Ah. Water broke when?"

"Yesterday night."

"Strong labour but no progress," he muttered to himself as he shook his head. "And pushing for how long?"

"Five hours."

The doctor rests the back of his hand on Mary's brow, then his own. "No high fever—just warm," he says. "Brown or green waters?"

"No, sir."

"Any bleeding?"

"Aye, lots a few minutes ago. 'Twas bright red, sir. Scared me tae death, it did."

"Hmm."

Just then a squeaking door hinge draws John's attention. He looks around. It is Priscilla, peering into the room.

"Papa? Is Mama all right?" she whispers, wide-eyed.

"Out, Prissy—out," he says. "I'll come." He steps away from the bed, leaves the room, closes the door. Priscilla stands in the hallway, shivering.

"Papa, I'm so worried," she says. "Something feels wrong."

John scoops her up in his arms—light as a feather, she is. "Nothing's wrong."

"But are you certain God won't let anything terrible happen to Mama or the new baby?"

"I'm certain. Doc and Ellen know what to do."

"And Ellen knows all about babies, too, doesn't she? She helped lots of mamas give birth back in Scotland and Ireland—she told me so. But how does Mr. Hall know what to do? Didn't he just get out of medical school?"

"Yes—Harvard. He's a good doctor, Prissy. Listen, Mrs. Richardson just had a strong baby girl tonight, and Doc was helping. We have nothing to worry about here."

"Oh, Mrs. Richardson had a baby girl! I hope Mama has a baby girl, too! You know how I've always wanted a sister, Papa!"

The doorlatch clicks behind them; John jerks around. The doctor stands on the threshold, his face studiedly calm.

"Mr. Dallington," he says, wiping his hands. "Baby's transverse, and the fresh bleeding tells that the situation is life-threatening on both accounts. The only chance is to get that baby out by Caesarean section."

"But the risks, Doc—how high?"

"Might as well ask how high they are if we don't do it. Both are the same. Problem is, your wife's weak and swollen from pushing too hard too soon—she's exhausted. Severe contortion of the pelvis tells me that the baby won't pass through the birth canal. If we don't operate now, the child could die."

John's eyes sting; his jaw clenches against the cold trembling sensation that grips him. His eyes fog over as his mind looks upon Mary's wan face, willing her to talk to him. But she is too incoherent to speak—to tell him what she wants.

To leave her and the baby in this condition would be as inhumane as to subject Mary's body to the mercy of the surgeon's knife. She had once told him how afraid she was of childbirth… of dying. The first three months of bedrest had roused those fears tenfold for her—and gendered in himself a guilt he could not shake.

That guilt returns now, like a familiar demon, sucking vitality. If Mary dies, he will be guilty. If the baby dies, he will be guilty. But if he forbids the doctor to operate, two lives may be lost, and he will be guilty of the crime of doing nothing.

His throat constricts; his hand runs deliberately down the front of his rough beard to stifle the vague consent he knows he must give in saying, "Do what you think best, Doc."

The doctor nods, retreats into the room, and closes the door.

"Oh look, Papa, you're so wet!" Priscilla is pointing to a damp spot darkening her lilac calico dress. "You really ought to dry off before you catch your death!"

"Now you're sounding like Ellen," he says, pushing aside a sickening sense of presentiment constricting his chest. He looks down and sees rainwater dripping from his clothes and making dark patches on the floorboards. "Well, come, then," he says, setting Priscilla down. "Let's go into the kitchen and I'll dry off by the stove."

They make their way into the kitchen, where a low fire crackles in the black cookstove. A brass kettle hums on the stovetop, a crescendo of steam shooting from its shapely spout. John stretches his hands over the warmth while Priscilla climbs into his big oak armchair.

Her little arms yank the red wool blanket from the back of the chair, then she scrambles to stand on top of the thick hide of the bison robe spread over the seat. "Papa, here! Dry off with this," she says, holding out the blanket to him.

Carelessly he takes it and drapes it over his shoulders. How intently she watches him!

"There," he says, "how's that?"

"Papa," she says suddenly, tears starting to her eyes. "I'm still afraid for Mama—are you?"

He takes her in his arms, holds her close, and feels her small frame shudder against his chest. "No," he says.

But he is afraid, wondering that this little child can trust him as she does, for his shadowed conscience never allows him to forget the old life he left on the shores of Ireland, though years, like the waves of the boundless ocean, have washed away the passionate wake of past actions.

"You know what, Papa?"

"What, darling?"

"I feel ever so sad for all the little boys and girls in the world who *don't* have mamas and papas like I do… Papa?"

"Hmm?"

"If I was *them,* I just know I'd feel so terribly jealous of *me.*"

John shifts her in his arms and clears his throat. "Ah! But you are *not* one of them, right, Prissy? You are my little Miss Priscilla Dallington, with nothing to worry about and nothing to fear." He presses his lips into her rich nut-brown curls. "Will you remember that, sweetheart?"

She sighs. "Yes, I'll remember… if you want me to."

"I want you to."

She draws her head up and searches his face. John hopes she is not mistrusting him. He can paste on an easy smile, but will her honest eyes detect the lie in his?

Before she can question him, he sets her down briskly. "Well!" he says, feigning enthusiasm. "Shall we stoke the fire and put the coffee on?"

He moves to the woodbox and seizes two pieces of dry oak, shoving them roughly into the stove with a loud clangour. The wood crackles and hisses on top of the hot orange embers.

"Here's the coffee, Papa." Priscilla is holding out the stubby dovetailed pinewood and cast-iron coffee grinder. "I ground the beans when you were gone because I knew you would want some when you came back."

"Good girl, thank you," he says, taking the box of fragrant grounds.

"The tin cups are in the warming oven—four of them—and here's the cream and white sugar on the table. Oh, and Papa?"

John raises his eyebrows as he dumps spoonful after spoonful of the fresh grounds into the coffee pot.

"Do you want your peppermint from Dr. Hall?"

"Peppermint?" All he wants is an extra-strong cup of coffee. Or maybe two, or three. "You have it, Prissy."

"But you said I could have only *one*, Papa—remember?"

John cringes at his absent-mindedness, and he adds another spoonful of grounds. "Then, uh, save it for tomorrow."

"Or can I give it to Mama after the baby comes?"

"Yes, if you wish."

"Oh! Papa! Isn't that too much coffee? Look! You've emptied the whole thing!"

John glances at the empty box. "Aye, it'll be good and dark, won't it?" he says, ignoring her astonishment and his own as he tosses the coffee grinder and metal spoon on the table.

Confounded clatter!

He wipes his forehead on the back of his sleeve. His eyes burn as he takes the brass kettle and pours the boiling water into the coffee pot, then places the coffee pot on the hottest part of the stovetop. He tries to blink away the irritation like he tried to blink away the bits of dirt out on the muddy road, but it makes no difference.

"Papa? Why are your eyes so red?"

"Red?"

Just then they hear slow footsteps approaching the kitchen entrance. Ellen appears in the doorway, cradling a tiny bundle wrapped in a patchwork quilt.

"Oh, it's the baby! The baby! The baby!" Priscilla springs to Ellen's side and peers into the colourful folds. "Oh, Ellen, is it a girl? May I hold it now? *Please*?"

"Ye've a bonnie wee laddie, Mr. Dallington." Ellen is looking at him now—but why are her eyes so swollen? Why so red? Why are her thin, parched lips held so limp and unsealed?

Another step sounds outside the kitchen—this one quick and heavy. Dr. Hall appears. Blood sullies his shirt; the dark hair of his forearms seems plastered to his skin.

John makes a halting step forward. "Hall?"

Why is the man wiping his hands mechanically on that stupid red towel? Why is Ellen's face intentionally averted? An iron fist clamps his gut. "What is it… Hall?" His confounded voice quivers like a child's. "How is Mary?"

"You have a fine new son…" falters the doctor.

"I can see that. But how is my wife?"

The baby begins to cry.

"Shh, shh, my wee bairn," coos Ellen, rocking the infant in her arms.

"Ellen, why is he crying?" asks Priscilla.

Ellen does not answer.

The doctor is looking at the floor. "I'm sorry." The words break from his lips like a thunderclap.

In two strides John passes Ellen and reaches the doctor,

his hands seizing the man's shirt collar, elevating him from the ground, shaking him violently. "Robert! My wife!" he shouts. "How is she?"

"I'm sorry, John… I, I could not save her."

John feels himself totter; blankness covers him as he stares into the doctor's face. Each dreaded fear, fresh with venom, fresh with spite, coils tighter and tighter around his heart while it jeers at his crippled faith.

"Oh, God, no…"

His hands lose their grip on the shirt collar; they fall limply to his sides. He pushes past the doctor and runs into the hall, scarcely aware of the sputter and sizzle of the coffee as it boils over on the stove.

"Mary?" he calls through the house. "*Mary*!"

But the echo mocks him.

He reaches the bedroom and throws the door open. There on the bed, buried amid the soiled sheets that encompassed her like some bloody shroud, lay the corpse of his wife. Her lips are parched and colourless, her once-rosy complexion petrified to stone. Her emotionless eyes stare unblinking at the ceiling as if, under some unearthly spell, they contemplate some strange, ghostlike image.

He rushes forward, propelled to his knees at the side of the bed. A second look into the soulless face, and his heart turns numb. He clasps the lifeless body in his arms and buries his face in the cold, cold bosom. His heart craves nearness, but God has never seemed so far away.

Suddenly, as though his thoughts burst their bounds of reason and reality, a gigantic cataract of memories and pains crashes in on him, dashing his deflated spirit like a storm-tossed ship driven against the hard, bitter reef of some deserted shore. Tangled in straggling seaweed, dripping with ocean water and tears, he looks around at the bleak landscape, at the sand that stretches for endless miles beyond the craggy rocks with no green tree, no water spring, no friendly shelter in sight.

That reef is his home now. Those rocks that had shattered his hapless hull are his new companions. He may be the son of a staunch Protestant minister from England who inherited the faith of his ancestors, and all the Biblical knowledge, and all the flawless eloquence; his father may have been a member of the Orangemen; John himself may have the Westminster Confession to boast of in defense of his religion. But when despair enters, none of it can save him.

His Norman's Woe has come, and his life is the wreck upon it.

— CHAPTER VI —

A SUITOR

"Oh, Papa! You're home!"

Priscilla's song came to an abrupt stop. She sprang from the piano and rushed forward, arms outstretched to welcome him.

John pasted a smile. "Prissy, your playing is lovely, as always," he said, kissing her forehead as he embraced her.

"Oh, and I see Paul has come with you," she said, her green eyes brightening as Paul, who had been tending to his gelding in the barn, made his appearance. The young man far outdid the handfuls of suitors who had quickly—and others not so quickly—passed in and out of Priscilla's consideration; and her unreserved reception of him now made obvious the fact.

"Aye, we rode together from town, sweetheart." John watched the two young people exchange glances. "He'll stay for tea. Is it brewed?"

But Priscilla was not listening. She was watching as Paul removed his hat and smiled at her.

"Hello, Miss Dallington."

"Hello, Paul." Her feminine response was quiet, accompanied by a dainty lowering of her head and a clasping of her hands in front of her.

"Tea, Priscilla?" John said, interrupting.

Priscilla's blush deepened. "Oh yes—certainly, Papa. It's nearly ready. Ellen and I will fetch it."

She turned to Ellen, who, with an approving eye and a half smile, was observing the scene over round rims of wire-framed spectacles.

"Aye, my biscuits and white rolls will be done by now," she said as she set her knitting aside and bustled toward the door.

John watched her discreetly. Indeed, Ellen Kelly's tendencies to compassion made it all the more reasonable for him to suspect that her influence might one day damage the polished enamel he had applied to the surface of his two children's lives.

"You got coffee on, too, Prissy?" he said loudly. "I'll have it instead of tea."

"Yes, Papa."

John turned to his guest. "Coffee or tea?"

"Tea for me, please. Thank you."

Priscilla dipped a curtsy and went tripping out of the room close on Ellen's heels. Her petticoats swished like ocean waves; her wide hoop skirts undulated like sails in the wind. Did she remember that she had once sailed aboard a clipper ship in a storm?

The melancholy was coming again to plague him. Drawing his hand across his forehead, he walked briskly across the room, stepped onto the autumn-coloured paisley-patterned wool rug in its centre, and eased into his large oak chair. He made an easy motion for the young man to take a seat on the upholstered settee opposite. "Paul, make yourself at home."

A well-worn gold-gilt volume of *Uncle Tom's Cabin* lay open on the low carved-mahogany tea table in front of them. The book offered a reasonable topic of diversion. John picked it up and leafed through the pages. "'Vicious propaganda' the critics call this one, inspired to be written by a mother of seven on account of her conscience rebelling against the Fugitive Slave Act passed in '50—sold over three hundred thousand copies its first year in print. It's still a hot topic—could be for centuries. You like reading, don't you?"

"Reading? When I have the time," Paul returned, glancing sheepishly at the tall bookshelves filled with more gold-gilt volumes. "But time is something I don't get enough of to spare. Work's been uncommonly busy."

"Burning the candle on both ends these days, are you?" John commented, scanning the pages and looking at Paul by turns.

"Might say that."

He offered a nod of approval as he slapped the book closed. "The word of God says it is good that a man should bear the yoke in his youth. Now that you've enlisted you'll be bringing in a fair salary—fifteen dollars a month on average, I'd say. Your father will take over the shop, I suppose?"

"With my younger brother."

"Lew's between the hay and the grass by now; must be fourteen?"

"That's right. He's learning the trade well. Father's proud of him."

"Well, he's got a good example to look up to." John stroked his coarse beard as he studied Paul's face, which had grown sober. "You got any plans in the making once the war's ended?"

Paul laced his fingers together. "I got my eye on a small plot of land northwest of here about fifteen miles. It's a nice, fertile piece with plenty of timber on it but enough open sod to plant a good hay crop and garden. The price is fair, so with my savings from blacksmithing I'll buy it before I leave, then with whatever I earn in the service I figure that—if God grants me mercy—I'll come back, haul me some logs, and have a cabin built on my land within a year."

"Sounds like you've got it all thought out," said John after a brief pause in which it appeared Paul was struggling to say something more. "Reckon you'll be looking for a little wife to go along with all that?"

Paul's eyes sought the paisley rug. "Reckon so. Time's moving along."

"You got someone special in mind?" He cleared his throat and took out his penknife, noting the red flush that crept over the young man's cheeks and extended quickly to his neck and ears in a brilliant tide. John whittled his fingernails in silence, satisfied that he had finally struck the gold.

"Matter of fact," Paul began, avoiding eye contact, "I was hoping to talk to you about that before I leave." Unlacing his calloused thick fingers, he planted his hands firmly on patched knees and forced his gaze to meet John's. "I'd like to ask your permission to court your daughter, sir."

John protruded his lower lip, nodded gravely, and resorted to Paul's example of studying the paisley rug while his mind revolved. It was what he had suspected, and he was glad that Paul had finally put the assumption into words. A moment passed, and he leaned back in his chair, crossed his right leg over his left, and whittled away with the penknife, making no effort to bring the awkward silence to a premature end.

"Of course," Paul went on, taking in a generous breath as though having held it for some time, "since I'll be away for a spell, I'd only be able to write to her—if that suited you both?"

"Well, you're an honest man, Paul." He nodded slowly as he made eye contact with the blacksmith's son. "As far as I know, you're impeccable in work ethic, unmatched by other men your age. I've watched you for several years. You may not be aware that you are quite popular among your unmarried female acquaintances and the subject of some very impatient speculation among Washington's reservoir of single young ladies and their mothers." Paul's face reddened, causing John to doubt that the young man was wholly oblivious to the secret—and sometimes not so secret—admiration that his masculine personage had excited amongst the fairer sex. "And precisely what," John added briefly, confining his eyes to the whittling effects of the penknife on his fingernails as though he had not noticed Paul's blush, "is it that attracts you to my daughter?"

A polite nod, a swallow as though of nerves, and a "She is God-fearing, sir, and beautiful" comprised the suitor's modest reply.

"Well, you will have to talk to Prissy, see how she feels about it." John lay the penknife aside as he examined his fingernails. "But seems to me," he continued, looking up, "a good proposition that the two of you should keep up acquaintances while you're away."

Two vertical furrows that had been pushed up between Paul's thick eyebrows smoothed, and he inclined his head in a polite nod. "Well, I, I thank you very much, Mr. Dallington."

Just then Priscilla and Ellen entered the room, their arms laden with teapot, coffeepot, milk pitcher, and a sweetly fragrant basket of baked goods.

"Mmm, that smells good!" John slapped his hand across his thigh as the two women tastefully arranged the tea table with rolls, biscuits, and gingerbread. Spying the latter, he clicked his tongue brightly. "Ellen," he asked, feigning humorous skepticism, "are those your famous gingerbreads?"

"Aye, ye's right there, Mr. Dallington," she returned, her face beaming. "'Twas my dear mother's own recipe back in the Highlands. I owe it tae her."

"Aye, dear Miss Kelly, you shouldn't have!" John tossed her a wink, then reached for a gingerbread as Priscilla poured the steaming tea and coffee and passed him a cup.

"White gold, Prissy?" he said, noticing that the tray lacked refined cane sugar.

She looked at him with a sweet half smile. "No, Papa—there is beet sugar, however, which I can fetch, if you wish?" she said, about to make for the door.

Not surprised, though partially irritated at her unspoken zeal toward the abolitionist movement—for Lucretia Motts's influence of abstinence had touched even the conscience of his privileged daughter—he waved his hand and said, "Never mind, I'll take mine black."

Priscilla's view knew neither exception nor mercy when it came to enforcing the personal law that anything touched by slave labour would not be touched by her. The mantra had reached into the privacy of her wardrobe, showing itself in her exclusive use of silks, linens, and wools—and had extended to the recesses of the kitchen pantry. It was a wonder the house even contained coffee. The teapot itself had known only the herbs that produced Priscilla's "liberty tea."

"Delicious rolls, Miss Kelly," remarked Paul as he politely enjoyed the repast, sipping his creamy, unsweetened currant and raspberry-leaf tea with the utmost relish.

"Peter must not be back from school yet, Priscilla?" John asked. "He'll want his gingerbread, too—yes, delicious, Ellen." He took a generous bite of the spicy cookie.

"Ellen uses only beet sugar in her baking—we call it 'free sugar,'" Priscilla pointed out as she selected a white roll. "Peter shall likely be home in a few minutes."

They spent a quarter of an hour in light, pleasant discussion before the conversation turned into a current of great interest to Priscilla: Paul was asking her about Mrs. Stowe's book.

"Mrs. Stowe is an exceptional authoress," she said eagerly.

"Good fiction and poetry are meant, like music, to touch the soul's depths, and Mrs. Stowe's book has certainly succeeded in this, and at the same time has put a face on the injustice of black slavery and its system like no other American novel has ever done. It quickly became a sensation in England and received notice from Charles Dickens, Queen Victoria, and even the great Russian novelist, Leo Tolstoy." She took a sip of tea, then her white forehead knitted delicately while she suspended her teacup between her little white fingers. "How can those Southern slaveowners claim to be disciples of Christ when they treat their fellow humans like worthless chattel? It is most infuriating." She took another sip of tea. "To enslave men who are created in the image of God, to strip them of their rights as humans, and then treat them like animals—indeed, worse than animals—is not only wholly unchristian but a blatant insult to basic humanity—it's the worship of Darwinism, in my opinion. Our country would do well to take an example from the heroic efforts of men such as John Newton and William Wilberforce. They truly did their duty as Christian men and fought for those who could not fight for themselves. We must do the same here, in our country."

A wide smile burst over John's face as he listened to his daughter's animated delivery, her conviction stirring in his memory the lines of Hannah More, which Priscilla had often recited to him. Meeting her gaze, he tried to quote it:

"*Disperse her shades of intellectual night,*
Repeat thy high behest—Let there be light!"

He paused, raising his chin and eyebrows expectantly. "Prissy, will you finish it?"

Priscilla's cherry lips turned up at the corners; they parted; her eyes glowed, her cheeks warmed, and she finished quoting as he joined in for the final line:

"Bring each benighted soul, great God, to thee,
And with thy wide Salvation make them free!"

At that moment the loud noise of tramping feet in the hallway outside the parlour interrupted the equilibrium, and the door burst open while the *clink-click* of a swinging empty tin lunch bucket accompanied Peter Dallington's advent into the room.

"Howdy-ho! Howdy-ho, everybody!"

The lad's left thumb was hooked in his overall strap; his straw hat sat lopsided on one side of his tousled head; a healthful ruddiness born of spring sunshine and open meadows burst from his freckled face.

"Peter! How was school today, son?" asked John as the boy sauntered in, eyeing the spread of dainties with growing interest.

"Are those *gingerbreads*?"

"And how was school, son?"

"It was good, thanks, Pa! Ellen, may I have one of *those*?" he said, pointing significantly.

"Aye, ye may," she said. "But first, laddie, ye go an' wash up yer hands an' take off yer hat, like a gentleman ought."

"Yes, Ellen!" Peter bolted from the room and was back in less than a minute.

"Aye! Hair even combed!" John said approvingly, noting the slicked back dark hair.

Peter plopped down on the settee next to their visitor. "Howdy, Paul!" He grinned as he received his prize from Ellen, who followed the delivery with a glassful of milk.

"Were you good to your teacher today, son?"

"I think so!" came the combined reply of munching words and gingerbread. "I won the spelling bee, anyhow. But Miss Lavendula, she was terrible fussy today for some reason. Nick Carson said she might be worrying about her folks down in South Carolina 'cause of all those rumours 'bout the shooting on Friday. Seemed none of our cursive was 'flowy' enough, Miss Lavendula said, for grade-fivers like us who'd been practising for a year already. And some of the girls' fountain pens were leaking on their dresses, which made 'em cry like babies… Pa, you should've seen them cry!... Ellen, can I have another one?"

"Please?" Priscilla interjected with a hem of correction.

"*Please*?"

Ellen offered him a second gingerbread. "Aye, but drink yer milk, too, laddie!"

"Oh I will, Ellen!"

John tilted his face downward and looked across at Peter. "You just keep up your cursive there, son. And your spelling, too. A man never knows when he'll need the weapons of paper and pen to make war against the enemy."

"Huh?" said Peter, only half-attentively. "Writing is for girls, Pa—boys hardly *ever* use writing. Boys need to know how to shoot a gun… Pa, I was thinking 'bout that—I want to get me a gun and do me some coon hunting this summer. Nick Carson has a gun. How much money is a gun, Pa?"

John suppressed a laugh. "You just eat your gingerbread, son," he said with a humorous wag of his forefinger. "We'll discuss that another time."

Peter shovelled another gingerbread into his mouth and chased it down with a gulp of milk.

"Papa," said Priscilla presently, "did you hear more on the rumours of Fort Sumter that were circulating after church yesterday?"

"I did," he returned, preparing an answer that would avoid alarming her more than was needful. "Our garrison surrendered to the Confederates after thirty-four hours of burning and no food but pork left for the men to eat. Despite the surrender, though, Major Anderson remains patriotic—so said the drums and the fifty-gun salute for his flag that went up as he finally evacuated the fort."

Peter's mouth, half full of partially chewed gingerbread, dropped open.

"Peter, laddie"—Ellen frowned over her spectacles at him—"mouth closed?"

Priscilla set aside her half-eaten white roll. "Papa?" She clasped her hands in her lap. "What is being said now?"

"President Lincoln's calling for a militia to cut down the rebellion."

"Gol-*ly*! A militia, Pa?" Peter swallowed a last bite and squirmed to the edge of his seat. "How many men, Pa?"

"About seventy-five thousand."

Priscilla tilted her head sideways, her delicate eyebrows slanting. "Seventy-five thousand?" Her eyes glistened, then pooled; they stared without seeing.

"Not for you to fret about, Priscilla. Listen, no fretting, all right? All will be well."

Did she hear him? Her gaze had fixed upon Paul.

The young man was leaning forward, elbows resting on his knees as he rubbed his hands together. "I've enlisted," he said quietly.

A vocal tremor escaped on a shaky "Oh!" that accompanied Priscilla's fingers as they petted the folds of her muslin skirt.

Peter bounded from his seat, eyes alight. "Enlisted! Paul's enlisted in the army? Oh boy, Pa!... Paul! You're gonna be a soldier in the army! You'll get your own uniform and sash and sword belt, too—and a gun! Pa, I wanna go, too—may I? May I, Pa? We'll take on them Rebels like nobody's business!"

"Whoa, whoa!" said John, laughing outright. "Hold your horses, Peter, the war's hardly started and you're talking like lock, stock, and barrel is ours before we've even smelled powder!" He stopped short when he saw Priscilla's face change again, this time to a look of enforced resignation.

"Then the war has started?" she said, rising to her feet and ignoring Peter's jabber, which diminished only partially through Ellen's hushed reprimands. She walked to the long bay window overlooking the pink and white of the budding apple orchard. "But all will be well, won't it? All will be well… Then surely it cannot last long… surely not. Right, Papa?"

"A man can't say for certain—things like war are never certain. You take them as they come, and do your best to keep your head above the waters."

"Papa?" Her voice was shaking, but her quivering chin was lifted, head tilted back, lips sealed firmly. "Are you going?"

All eyes were on him now, provoking him with the same question, criticizing him. He must make good his response, for, in the presence of a potential son-in-law whose own courage to join the army had been displayed already, it would not be difficult for his personal views against the idolatry of patriotism to be misunderstood as cowardice. "Well," he said—it seemed the thickness of the silence thickened further in anticipation of his answer—and he added a careless wave of his hand, "if the upheaval in the political arena continues at the rate it's going now, then, Prissy"—taking in an easy breath, an attempt at casualness—"yes, I reckon I'll be joining the army." He stood up and stretched mildly in an attempt to alleviate the tension.

Paul followed the example and rose from his seat. "I, uh—I reckon I should be getting on by now," he said. "Thank you kindly for the tea, Miss Kelly. Thank you, Priscilla. I guess I'll be seeing you around, soon… I hope."

She was nodding and smiling at him, but tears were rolling down her cheeks.

"Goodbye, Mr. Paul—Lord bless ye," said Ellen, lifting a handkerchief as she waved after him.

Escorting Paul to the front door and down to the barn where his horse, unsaddled and tied, was resting, John bade farewell to the young man and walked leisurely back up to the house. When he reached the garden, he noticed Priscilla walking up the avenue, her head and shoulders wrapped in one of Ellen's green plaid wool shawls—armour against a sharp westerly wind that had lately arisen, introducing an angular mass of slate-grey clouds that foretold a spring rain. It was inevitable that Paul, mounted on his chestnut gelding, would pass her on his way down the drive to the main road.

At the arboured entrance, John paused beneath the cover of vines and looked back. He watched as the young suitor reached his daughter's side, reined in his horse and dismounted, and removed his wide-brimmed hat. He could not hear what they said, for they were too distant, but he noted the manner in which they parted, and the energy in Paul's posting as his horse trotted southward, and the buoyancy in Priscilla's step as she made her way up the drive toward the house.

— CHAPTER VII —

THE SOUND OF GUNS

Dallington House, Fairfax County
July 21, 1861

The deep, dull rumblings of cannons and musketry shattered the tranquility of the Sunday evening. A single crimson slash bled a foreshadow above black silhouettes massed along the horizon. High expectation and terrible urgency rivalled eternally for supremacy over an eerie, unsettled stillness.

From his position at the high gable window of the spare room, John looked southwest over the fruit-laden apple orchard toward Manassas, observing the lurid glow of flashing artillery that reflected off the sombre canopy of slate-grey clouds over the battlefield of Bull Run.

Opening the ball from either side had been unnecessary to convince the majority of Northern sympathizers that the Union had already won the battle. But to John, the optimism was vanity. After their three months of service, Federal soldiers were just homesick.

Still, such sentiments had obviously rubbed off on Northern circles, for flocks of optimists with plumed hats and shiny buggies had gathered on the hilltop at Centreville, ready to watch the victory in full-out party fashion—and have a nice little picnic on the side. John had declined a personal invitation for his family to join their lunch baskets with those of the excursioners, arguing that overconfidence was not simply foolish—it was a tasty recipe for disaster.

Now the crimson slash disappeared. The black mass seemed

to eat it up, like death. Somehow, a moon was rising out of it. And as John's eyes scanned the stain of false twilight that remained, the pit in his stomach told him that the Potomac would be a Nile turned red with blood and all of Pharaoh's magicians would not quench the thirst of Egypt.

And soon, too, would white feathers be brandished by women and maidens in the streets and byways of the infantile capital, ready to deck the men too yellow and sweaty to sleep under canvas. He would not be among those cowards, though he despised American patriotism, for the sound of those distant drum rolls was the goading voice of ego that warned him not to turn himself into a laughingstock and lose the respect of a daughter and son by refusing to rest a Springfield rifle on his own shoulder.

"Papa?"

Priscilla's light footsteps padded through the dim room, accompanied by the flicker of candlelight, and reached his side. He turned and looked at her. A pink-and-white eyelet dressing gown curtained her frame; the thick braid draping down her right shoulder shimmered like rich-brown taffeta in the moonlight. She was beautiful, but her presence exuded questions and uncertainty. He knew what she feared—he feared it, too, but she need not know it.

Gently drawing her to himself as she came near, he guided her head to rest against his chest.

"He's out there, Papa, isn't he?"

"He is."

"What if he doesn't come back?"

"He'll come back."

Paul was a crack shot and, by now, would be a skilled soldier. For the past three months his letters had arrived each week with faithful regularity. And after tonight, they would continue to arrive.

"You and Ellen were making sandwiches for the army relief tomorrow?" John asked as a diversion. "Sewing shirts and bandages, too, right?"

"Yes, we were."

"We'll take the wagon to Washington tomorrow about noon. There will be plenty of men needing food and coffee after today." He felt Priscilla's shoulders shake as she struggled against an impending sob. "You are tired, aren't you, Prissy?"

"I cannot sleep, Papa… I am impatient—so impatient. And terribly afraid." She was quiet for several minutes, but he sensed that she wished to say something, so he waited. "Papa?" Her voice did not exceed a whisper. "If our God is a God of love, then why does he allow suffering and heartache to take place in the world?"

Like salt on an open wound, Priscilla's words stung his memory. They brought him back to Ireland—back to the door that was locked from the inside. A legion of emotions spiralled through the quicksands of thought, and the fear of blundering through an impending explanation of the consequences of sin as it began in Eden struck him dumb. But then, somewhere in the recesses of his mind, when thought and prayer and painful desperation mingled to form one strong, silent appeal, his lips began to move. "Man reaps the fruit of his own actions, Priscilla. God cannot be blamed for the consequences man endures because of his own choices. But it is the Almighty's design that his mercy build a purpose out of man's suffering when man decides to trust God with the rubble of his past."

"How does a man trust God, and know that God hears him—especially when that man is in pain?"

Old feelings rose like smoking flax before him. And, eager for a renewed flame, half-dead coals shimmered and leapt up as though stirred and poked by a sword. Yet he must reply—even if he disbelieved the truth of his own words. "Priscilla, will you believe me when I tell you this?"

"I will try."

"Pain is a part of life. Every man feels it, and every man must live through it. Either it will soften him or it will embitter him. It is his own choice. But the sovereignty of God can turn evil for good when we put our trust in Christ's mercy and redemptive power. And so must you do, sweetheart." He patted her arm and released her. "Pray for Paul, and trust the Lord about him. That is all—and it is the best—that you can do."

Priscilla drew back and focused her gaze upon his face. "It makes me wonder what lies around the corner… I confess,

Papa, that I am afraid to suffer and do not have peace because I worry so. My stomach is in knots, and my mind frets when it ought to be still. But your strength makes me feel safe." She nestled her head against his shoulder again. "I will ask God to help me trust him the way you do."

Instead of balm, her words were the smiting rod that chastised his conscience for his hypocrisy. The words of his own tongue seemed to turn on him, transformed into the fateful witnesses judging his own heart's unbelief. Time itself—solemn, haunting—stood afar, waiting for him to prove the faith he lacked to see God's hand in a past he could not reconcile.

The false twilight finally faded as the moon rose into the sky. The sounds of the distant battle died away into a silence pierced only by the bittersweet cry of a mockingbird in the orchard below. The air was silent, but it was not quiet. No, it was alive, and dangerous, creeping with unrest and betrayal—he felt it. If the war continued, it would be folly to imagine that Priscilla and Peter could be safe so close to the front lines. Virginia was crawling with slaveholders and Confederates. And if he was to enlist in the Federal army, he must send his children and Ellen away posthaste.

Priscilla bade him goodnight and retired to her room, but John, restless and preoccupied, paced the room, then lounged—sleepless—in a chair, and at last returned to the window and stood there as the sad aspect of the grey-faced dawn peered over the horizon's rim, meeting the leaden sky that shed fitful tears along blood-sodden fields.

Bleary-eyed and drowsy, he descended the narrow wooden staircase and retreated to the dim, hushed kitchen at the east end of the house, where a gloomy drizzle spattered the outside of the foggy windowpanes. The grandfather clock in the parlour struck out the fifth hour. Ellen would not be up and around until six, and he was coveting a strong cup of coffee to dispel his sleep-deprived lethargy.

He placed his hand on the cast-iron stovetop. It was cold. He went to the kindling box. It was empty.

"Peter, that boy—forgetting his chores again," he muttered as he seized the rough wooden box and thrust open the back door, his mind forming the reprimand that would ensure his son would never neglect the kindling box again.

Outside, the air was heavy with moisture. He retrieved a log of dry poplar from the woodbox beneath the eaves and went to the chopping block. He yanked out the hatchet wedged into its corner, then made quick work of the log. He gathered up the splinters scattered across the damp, trampled grass around the chipped-up old block and was about to step back inside the kitchen when he was arrested by the distant splash and crunch of hooves that sounded along the gravel drive.

Glancing back, he made out the dark shape of a man on horseback coming up the road toward the house. John strode to the edge of the house and stared through the feeble light. The horse walked with a mild limp. It's bare-headed rider slumped forward so heavily that it seemed the saddle's broad, high pommel was the only thing keeping his body from keeling over and falling into a sorry heap on the side of the road. The reins drooped in the rider's sagging right hand; the left hand dangled at his side, lifeless. As the man drew closer John distinguished the blue cape and trousers of a Union soldier.

"Hello!" John shouted, then waited as his voice trailed through the still, misty air. A vague lift of the rider's head, a weary scan of the yard, and a return to the slumped posture was the only answer.

Tossing the bundle of kindling into a dew-drenched bed of marigolds, John broke into a full run, clearing a bed of feverfew and lavender in a single bound as he dashed across the lawn and down the road.

"Whoa," he said, slackening his pace as he caught the reins of the horse with one hand and placed the other on the animal's sweaty shoulder, bringing it to a stop. The soldier's tight-fitting Prussian blue coat was torn, smoke-stained, and rancid with fumes. There was no insignia on the arm—the man was a private. A dirty haversack was slung over his back, and a long Union rifle, with the bayonet still affixed, rested broadside across the front of the saddle. The rider's head was shrouded by a bloody bandage, his face black with cartridge powder and spattered with mud. The soldier looked up, his face pale as death.

"Paul!" cried John.

The young man uttered a groan, a sob. Sudden tears carved muddy rivers down his face.

"Paul"—John grasped the young man's limp shoulder—"are you hurt, Paul? What's going on?"

"The Greybacks whipped the tar out of us!" Paul's voice cracked with hoarseness; it broke with feeling as he shook his head over and over. "McDowell made a full retreat across the Potomac—we didn't re-form our lines. I came to warn you—in two days or less, the Rebs plan to sack Washington."

John's stomach tensed.

"Fairfax is a daredevil place for your family, sir," Paul sobbed. His hand lifted, but it was too uncoordinated to wipe the tears and mucus sludging down his mouth and jaw. "I'm sorry I'm crying, sir, but I'm scared—scared for your family, sir, and Priscilla. Everyone else is running crazed into Washington, but the Rebs might torch it... You'd better get out of here quick, Mr. Dallington! You better get out real quick. The Rebs'll be after us, like hell."

"Come up to the house, Paul—come, you're hurting bad. Where are you wounded?"

"I'll be all right... just a couple cracked ribs, I think's all, and that beastly Rebel yell blasting my ears out. Some rest and water'll do the trick. I'm thirsty something fierce."

The grey drizzle was turning into a full-fledged downpour. John led the horse up to the back door and tied it to the hitching post, then aided Paul in sliding down from the saddle. A sharp outcry as his feet hit the ground told his suffering. Carefully, John draped the young man's arm over his own shoulder, supported his swaying frame into the kitchen, and lowered him into a chair. The soldier passed out of consciousness and collapsed forward onto the table.

"Ellen! Priscilla!" John shouted through the house.

The pattering of feet overhead and down the staircase preceded the breathless entrance of both women in their nightgowns.

Ellen—a mushroom in her frilly, puffed, polka-dotted nightcap—exclaimed, "Lord God! Mercy! It's Mr. Paul!" and bustled forward in haste.

Priscilla froze in the entrance. "Paul?" Her hands flew to her mouth. "It's Paul!"

With careful, swift motions, Ellen removed his coat.

"A couple broken ribs, he figured," John said, observing the action.

Ellen unwrapped the head bandage, revealing a wide gash across Paul's high forehead. "Warm water, Prissy," she ordered. "Haste!"

Priscilla bolted to the stove.

"Stove's cold, Prissy," John said, remembering the bundle of dry wood he had cast into the wet garden. "Here; I'll fire it up."

Priscilla snatched the wooden pail beside the washstand. "I will fetch water." Bare-headed and barefoot, she flew into the rain, splashing heedlessly through a puddle before she reached the green iron water pump between the house and barn.

John followed her outside, frowning and smiling by turns as he watched her whirlwind movements with the pump handle. "That lass," he muttered, shaking his head as her arm flew up and down, up and down as though her life depended on it. She apparently had no perception of the wet cold, for as the rain soaked her hair and drenched her eyelet dressing gown now hemmed with mud, it appeared that she could turn any misfortune into a cheerful inconvenience where a beloved was concerned.

John walked to the marigold bed, but when he eyed the unfortunate kindling sprawled across the sopping foliage, he elected a fresh start, resolved to teach Peter the necessity of being faithful with his chores. He went to the woodbox, and he then caught sight of Priscilla. Her hand was still flying with the pump handle despite the river gushing over the sides of the bucket.

"It's full, Prissy! Full!" he shouted, laughing at her blind enthusiasm. "That's enough!"

Breathlessly, Priscilla brought her arm to a halt and grabbed the handle of the bucket, lugging it with her toward the house.

"Next time you put on a coat and hat," he cautioned as she passed him. "You'll catch your death, remember?"

"Oh!" she exclaimed, pushing aside the wet tendrils plastered to the sides of her face as she reached the top of the two steps before the door. "I'm sorry—I will next time!" she said, then disappeared into the house.

"And be a mite calmer next time, lass," he added to himself, shaking his head. "The sky isn't falling just yet."

John finished splitting the wood and went inside. Within five minutes fire blazed and crackled in the cookstove and soon water steamed in the kettle.

Ellen damped a cotton cloth, which she used to soften the dry blood crusted over Paul's forehead. "He needs tae lie down—I can check his ribs then," she said, looking at John. "Shall we move him tae the bedroom?"

"Sure. Prissy, come."

Carefully, they moved the unconscious Paul to the room adjacent the kitchen and laid him down on the bed. Priscilla tenderly arranged a generous supply of feather pillows about his head while Ellen slipped the suspenders off his shoulders and removed his dirty, sweat-stained shirt.

Ellen examined his ribs. "Four broke is what I feel—three on the right side an' one on the left. Need's the knit-bone."

"Have to wrap him up good, and just let him be till he comes to," John said. "'Knit-bone'—that's your remedy?"

"Aye. Comfrey will do it, sir."

"Oh!" exclaimed Priscilla. "The plant you brought from Ireland! Shall I fetch some from the garden now?"

"Aye, lass, ye do that."

"Ah-ah, put on a coat and take your umbrella this time," John called after her as she swept out of the room. "It's raining cats and dogs out there."

At seven o' clock, John woke Peter and brought him downstairs, prepared him a breakfast of scrambled eggs and hash browns, and then allowed him to view the wounded hero before sending him off, albeit reluctantly, to feed the chickens, collect the eggs, and stock the infamous kindling box.

The remainder of the morning was anxiously spent as Ellen nursed Paul and Priscilla waited for him to emerge from unconsciousness. At eleven o' clock he awoke.

"I'll hitch up the horses," John said to Priscilla, who was carefully spoon-feeding Paul a repast of bone broth. The rain shower had retreated momentarily into heavy cloud cover.

"Regardless of what those Rebs plan to do to Washington in the next day or two, our hungry boys will be retreating there today, and Prissy has sandwiches ready for them—right, Prissy, with the coffee? Supplies boxed and ready to go?"

"Yes, they're in my wicker basket by the front door. Peter already put the box of bandages and shirts in the wagon, Papa."

"When are we leavin', Pa?" asked Peter, close on John's heels when they reached the back door.

John pulled on his high leather boots. "Less than an hour, son," he said, and grabbed his hat from a wooden peg. "I want to talk to Paul first and get a lowdown."

After he had hitched the horses to the long box wagon, John returned to Paul's room. He leaned against the doorframe, watching the threesome gape at the now highly sensational storyteller and his stories.

"And how many Greybacks are headed to Washington?" asked Peter from his perch on the edge of Paul's bed.

"Seventeen thousand is what we heard."

"Gol-*ly*! That's a lot!" Peter leaned forward. "Are you gonna go back to the army soon, Paul?"

"Once these ribs heal up, I sure am." He looked squarely at Peter with serious humour. "Can't light out just 'cause we've been whipped, can we?"

Peter's enthusiasm answered with an elevated chin and a definitive "Nope!"

"The Federal army won't go down that easy," Paul continued. "There'll be a call for more recruits soon as the dust settles."

Peter cast a glance out the window and his face brightened. "Then this rain's perfect for that!" He pointed to a mud puddle two yards away from the eaves. "That dust out there'll be settled real good by now, so the army'll be able to get back at it Lickety-split!"

John glanced over at Priscilla. A telltale muscle in her face flinched. Paul met her gaze, and then her face reddened, her lips parted, and she looked at her hands twisted in her lap.

"In light of all Paul's been telling you," John said, coming forward as all eyes turned in his direction, "it's not safe here for women and children. As Paul knows, Fairfax is a dangerous county now, and will become more so. Homestead raids by famished soldiers will be the next scene in the drama. Our unpopular views on slavery and secession have already garnered us enough threats from the neighbours. I think it best we plan a trip to New York."

"New York?" Priscilla blinked.

"Yes. I'll arrange passages for you there."

Peter scratched his mop of hair. "*Passages?* What passages, Pa?"

"To Ireland, son. You will stay with my sister, your Aunt Augusta."

"Aunt Augusta? But I thought"—Peter wrinkled his nose—"we didn't like her?"

"It's been donkey's years since I saw her, but Augusta has been living on the family's Irish homestead ever since I immigrated. She keeps it maintained, at least. And that homestead is the securest, most practical place for you to stay at this time."

Peter contorted his freckled face. "Aunt Augusta is an old maid, right, Pa?"

"She's unmarried, yes, son," John returned. But he remembered his feeling of helplessness the day he watched Augusta, perched like the little peasant queen of Ireland in the high seat of the curricle, drive away from the homestead because her vanity had been tickled by the smooth promises of a womanizer. "Aunt Augusta will take good care of you two and Ellen. I know that."

Priscilla's inquisitive though innocent expression foretold that she wished to speak. "But… did you not have a falling out with each other?" she ventured. "Is that not why she has been estranged from us all these years?"

Aye… a falling out. Indeed. He could still hear the shrill tones of her voice…

"I'm the fella's Colleen now, John!" Augusta cries. "And London! London, the city of my dreams! Mr. Renwick promises me money and privilege there—surely ye won't hold me back from this chance to have what I've always wanted!"

John stands at the white wicket gate in front of the old Irish homestead, a young man seething with rage. And there is his giddy, plump, apple-faced sister—with her pansy. Her charming, white-suited, bow-tied, slicked-haired English *pansy*. He stands five foot four inches from the dirt, but thirty-four years have not wilted his noxious charms, nor his talent for swooning women.

The odour of the pansy's orange-blossom cologne gags him; the greedy look in those black eyes that are shaded by long, curling eyelashes gags him, too, for they glint like a hungry wolf while they devour the figure of his virgin sister.

"John?" she says. "Someday ye'll understand—ye'll feel true love, and know—yes, ye'll know, John! Something good will come of this—something good always comes of bad, right? All ye see now is yerself and yer dream to be a minister in this parish, like Pa was. But I promise, John, I promise, for all the pain I cause ye now, that one day I'll do ye a favour ye'll not be able to repay. It may take donkey's years for me to do it, but I will repay ye, I will. I will!"

But first the pansy had dumped Augusta; and then, in tears, she had returned to Ireland; and then John had immigrated; and at last the little peasant queen had reclaimed her solitary throne on the family homestead. In his absence, and her destitution, John had felt it incumbent upon him to provide for her, which sentiment manifested in a routine, every-six-months' allowance with which she was able to maintain the old thatched-roof cottage and garden, in addition to a very modest purse of spending money dedicated to herself and the welfare and innocent diversion of her beloved cat, Rufus.

"Papa?" Priscilla was nudging him.

"People have their differences, let's keep it at that," John said, drawing a quick breath as he pulled himself from thought. "My sister Augusta owes me a debt, and I believe this is her opportunity to repay it."

"But Papa—what about you?"

"Priscilla…" He looked at her solemnly. "I will be enlisting."

Priscilla's hand went to her mouth, a self-imposed muzzle against remonstrances, and the room grew silent.

"I will be dispatching a letter to my sister this afternoon."

So saying, John retreated to the parlour. He listened for voices behind him that might report that the young folk contradicted his decision, but he heard none. As he entered the parlour, he paused in the doorway, his gaze roving along the rich wood of the wall panelling to the full-size oil-on-canvas painting of Caspar David's *Wanderer Above the Sea Fog.* As he contemplated it, his secret fascination for it returned, reminding him of the reason he had kept the magnificent piece of art hanging in the same place above the mantlepiece for nearly a decade. Caspar David had made an enlightened suggestion with his brush, a metaphorical masterpiece to the unspoken reality in the soul of conflicted man. A painted man on a painted precipice who looked down into a painted sea of rock, and shadow, and mist. This painted man was master over his destiny. This painted man was the ambiguous expression of John Dallington, who wandered amidst a clouded ocean of secrets that no man knew but himself.

He sat down at his writing desk and began scrawling a letter. But for the faint, rapid scratching of the pen nib across the page and the persistent tick of the grandfather clock, ten minutes passed in silence. Then he stroked his signature and folded the letter. He placed it firmly into an addressed envelope. Movement outside the door made him look up.

"Aye? Who's there?" he said.

A dark mop of hair bobbed behind the doorframe.

"Son, what are you doing?" He made a short laugh before sealing the letter and going into the hall. There was Peter, standing with his shoulders thrown back and his head held high in an attitude of brave exultation.

"Can't I go with you to the war, Pa? Can't I—please?"

"Not this time, Peter," he said, patting the lad's wavy hair. "You're not old enough. For now you must practise being a brave, trustworthy soldier and look after your sister while I'm gone. It is a great responsibility, you know that?"

"It is?"

"Aye, son. To be a woman's protector is a noble task. Indeed, it's a man's God-given duty on behalf of the weaker vessel."

"But Pa! Prissy is older than me, and she ain't weak, neither—just ask her!"

John smiled and bent forward with his hands on his knees, looking into his son's eyes. "But Priscilla is precious—precious like a goblet made of crystal. A treasure that must be handled with the utmost care, lest it shatter. If a man can do that, then one day he will make a real soldier. Do you think you can do it, son?"

"Well, Pa… sure. I don't really *want* to, but I will 'cause I wanna make you happy. But Pa?" His tone was pleading, expectant.

"Yes, son?"

"Does that mean I can stay up till nine o' clock?"

"Now, now, Peter—a growing young man like you must get proper rest," John said, and chuckled. "Eight o' clock it is and eight o' clock it shall be until you turn fourteen, like we agreed, remember?" John looked up as Ellen and Priscilla came out of Paul's room and down the hall toward them. "And if you do not heed, Peter, then Ellen will lay the law down—aye, Ellen?"

"Aye, that I shall do, Mr. Dallington," she said as she drew up. "These wee bairns are my joy. Ain't naethin' I love more." She dabbed her eyes with her white embroidered handkerchief in her hand. "But Lord God love ye, Mr. Dallington—please, sir, take good care of yerself!"

Priscilla came and stood at his elbow. "Papa, when we leave, what will happen to the house—the farm and our animals?"

"Frankly, Priscilla, I don't know," John said, lowering his tone. "If our area is invaded, it could turn into a hospital or a battleground—if it isn't torched by the Rebels first."

He noticed Priscilla's delicate frame quiver. She embraced him, resting her head against his shoulder. He wished he could smooth away her fears the way he smoothed her silky brunette hair, but he feared that if he spoke, his words would form a hackneyed phrase that would mock her feelings.

Peter stepped up. A sob caught in his throat. “Oh, Pa, I don’t want you to go! I don’t, Pa!” He flung his arms around both of them, his body shaking with tears as he began to cry.

John bit his lip against a surge of emotion and tilted his head back. Moisture pooled in his eyes, then spilled. He stroked Peter’s head, drew him close, and kissed both his children.

“You two are all I have now,” he said, and drew them closer still.

— CHAPTER VIII —

THE WHITE KID GLOVE

Union Army Training Station
November 1861

"Suh, oh suh! Letta, suh!"

John stepped out of the canvas Sibley tent into the mild evening air as a barefooted contraband boy pulled a cream-coloured envelope out of the mail bag slung over his shoulder.

"For you, suh!" the husky lad repeated cheerily. Fine white teeth set in a sturdy, well-developed jaw contrasted with the lad's rich-brown skin tone as his high cheekbones rose in a brilliant smile.

John took the envelope. "Thanks, son." Priscilla's flawless Spencerian script detailed the front. He patted the boy's coarse mop of curly black hair and smiled. Ever since the Negro orphan had been welcomed into the regiment after narrowly escaping recapture by his Southern master, John's liking for him increased by the day.

The boy dashed off to the main tent while John sauntered to the campfire. A handful of soldiers were assembled around it for the evening's review of the day, each man finding his separate diversion in smoking pipes or cigars, gambling, or draining black coffee from tin mugs. Despite the usual jokes and ribald laughter, a general feeling of exhaustion told that the boys were feeling the effects of another day's rigorous training.

Spying a vacant log a few paces from the fire, John sat down. He studied the envelope. It was the first letter he had received from Priscilla since their departure for Ireland, and he had waited weeks to receive it. He ran his fingers across the oval-based, obviously American *de facto* penmanship style; it was the closest possible thing to holding his daughter's hand in his. He retrieved his penknife and broke the seal, and as he unfolded the letter, a fragrant shower of dried rose petals fell from the soft pages.

September 14, 1861

My dearest Papa,

We have arrived safely. Our voyage was smooth and uneventful, and we thank God for that, as I know you will, too. What a charming place Ireland is! The snug little stone cottage with its garden and mossy rock hedges is delightful. I wonder why our family ever left it.

Yesterday noon Aunt Augusta met us with her horse and buggy at the Blue Boar Inn near the dockyard in Queenstown. As we picked our way through the throng, her salt-and-pepper hair (which she does not bother to cover with a hat when she goes out, much to Ellen's disapproval) and her generous, fluffy-like figure instantly reminded me of our dark Brahmapootra hens. What a singular woman Auntie is! And 'Rufus' (her fat orange cat whom she treats like a child) is horribly spoiled. Auntie's moods are a pendulum, changing from one extreme to another from hour to hour, and sometimes from minute to minute, and she's as critical as a Doomsday judge. When I asked when we may visit Dublin, she said we weren't cut from the right cloth to fit into that *society.*

"Dublin is a prickle bush," she said with a cluck. "Romanism is its plague, and prejudice will sniff out any folks who don't carry a rosary or cross themselves when they pray. It's been that way for donkey's years. If ye want Protestant sympathy, my dear," she added, "choose Belfast."

Fiction and purgatory make her squawk more than a hen after she's laid her egg.

"Priscilla," she said from her nest (which is the rocking chair), "I hope ye're not spoiling yer head reading those trashy romance novels they're selling these days?"

I assured her that "trashy romances" do not interest me, and that, in fact, I was reading John Milton's epic poem.

Rufus sat curled up in her lap—as usual on all the evenings—and she petted him while she criticized me and wondered aloud if Milton was "that Italian fellow who wrote that book called, The Divine Joke, *or something such? I've heard it's dreadful—especially the rhymes about hell."*

I knew she meant The Divine Comedy, *but I told her simply that I hadn't read Dante's famous cantos yet.*

"Yet, Priscilla?" she squawked. "Promise me ye'll never touch that Divine Joke *book, or whatever they call it, with yer pinkie finger. That Danto bloke was a full-blown Catholic from the Dark Ages, and his* Purgatory *is as much fiction as romance trash is. Rosicrucian propaganda belches from it, I doubt not, and who knows what else that's connected to the secret societies that are all the rage these days." She petted poor Rufus so hard that he protested with a painful mew. "Yer father wouldn't approve the rubbish, mark my words, lass!"*

It never works to ruffle her feathers by disagreeing, so I assented—and explained that my book, Paradise Lost, *was a gift from you. That's when the cross-examination began and Milton's conversion from Catholicism to Protestantism stood on the witness stand. Satisfied that Milton could be trusted, she said I could go back to "*Eden Lost,*" then she ordered Peter to fetch a bedtime snack of fresh cream for Rufus. But by that time I was quite worn out and went to bed.*

Upstairs I went to the big bedroom that Ellen and I share on the northeast side of the cottage. It was yours and Mama's bedroom, she told me. Peter slept across the hall in the small bedroom where two beautiful handmade cradles are. I asked if you made them—like you made yours and Mama's beautiful oak bedstead—but she said the potatoes would burn if she didn't check them right away.

But back to Peter. Well, Peter being Peter, he hated being inside even for one night when he knew there was an old straw pallet in the barn loft where he could sleep instead (he also protested the fact of being made to sleep on the floor in a "baby's room.") Thirty times today he begged Ellen to allow him to sleep in the hayloft. Ellen consented on the condition that he ask Aunt Augusta, and

Auntie's condition was that he repair the damage done to the west wall of the loft. The wall has been horribly broken up. Something seems to have smashed through the centre of it, leaving splintered, gaping holes in the timber that the wind wails through. Auntie despises untidiness, even in an old hayloft out back. I asked her how the hole got there, but she didn't know. I told her you might, but she turned to me with a curious expression and clucked, "Your pa is like a puzzle I can't find all the pieces to, that's what!"

At any rate, Peter appears to enjoy carpentry, and I said you'd be proud of his work since you like things to be neat as a pin.

I hear Auntie calling for dinner now, so shall bid you farewell. I love you, and pray you are well and safe. May God grant you wisdom.

With all my heart, I remain your most loving and affectionate daughter,

Priscilla Dallington

P.S: I have heard rumours of an abolitionist—a Miss Clara Barton who worked some time as a clerk in the Patent Office—who is now doing charity work for the Union after witnessing the heartbreaking retreat of Bull Run. I am greatly inspired by her example, Papa, and because I know the many needs of the war relief effort—and because I myself long to assist it, though it be by a very small contribution—I am sewing more linen shirts, which I will box and send to you with my next letter, for distribution among the army.

With his arms resting on his dusty, smoke-stained knees, John blindly folded the letter. "A puzzle she can't find all the pieces to," he repeated to himself, his stomach twisting into hard knots as he contemplated the analogy.

He dreaded that Priscilla might soon learn that those ugly holes in the hayloft matched the ugly scars across her papa's knuckles. But worse still was his fear of Ellen. And those cradles—he had forgotten about them. They were like bait to draw it all out of her. One slip of her tongue could dash Priscilla's world to pieces, and he would not be there to shield her. He would not be there to explain, or adjust the truth, or help her forgive it.

He pushed himself upright and lifted his face to the night sky. From a break in the motionless canopy of treetops, silver stars twinkled like diamonds tossed across a navy velvet curtain. He shoved the letter back into the daintily addressed envelope and slipped it into the inside breast pocket of his dirty blue Union jacket. The low voices of two privates drew his attention. They sat before the campfire across from him, chortling at some crude joke. He could see their dirty faces, smell the sweet, intoxicating aroma of their cigar smoke. It reminded him of Geoffrey…

Geoffrey's visit is more than unanticipated. Recently returned from Lancashire where he had spent the past six months visiting kinfolk, he was making his call—as was his former custom—late into the night.

"Where is Aggie?"

The dashing fair-haired young man sprawls out his tall, athletic frame across the family's heirloom settee in front of the stone fireplace. "I expected to see her here tonight."

John pauses. "Aggie is gone," he says.

"Gone? Well, when will she be back?"

John leans against the mantel and stares into the dancing flames. "She left, Geoff."

"She left? What do you mean? For good?"

"For good."

"Well!" Geoffrey slaps his hand across his soft, creamy thigh and spouts a curse. "What for?"

Cringing, John runs his fingers through his hair. He hates Geoffrey's swearing. "For a man," he says.

Geoffrey's frame jolts upright. "Augusta Dallington left for *a man*?" He plants his hands on his knees. "And all this time I thought Cupid's arrow had met its match in her! Who is the lucky bloke?"

"The bloke is an English pansy."

"Name?"

"A Mr. Darcy Renwick."

Geoffrey whistles while a simper toys with the corners of his graceful mouth. He produces a cigar from his vest pocket, strikes a match on the heel of his shiny black boot. "Well, tell me: where have they gone? Not to London, surely?"

"They have gone to London."

One thin, reddish eyebrow arches like the back of a cat. "She always gets her way, but I never thought she was capable of drawing *that* lucky of a card with fortune."

Fortune indeed. "It's blind stupidity that drew that card, Geoff."

"And you'll never forgive her, right?"

John clamps his lips together and shoots him a fierce glance to assure him he never will.

"She'll certainly get her life of wealth and privilege!"

"The man's a lying sleeveen."

"Is he?"

"I smelled the sulphur on him. He'll wring her out and toss her."

"Chances are nine out of ten, correct?"

"Ten out of ten."

"How can you be sure?"

"I feel it."

Geoffrey plucks the cigar from his lips, throws his head back, roars with laughter.

But there is nothing amusing to John. "Since when did you start smoking?"

"Smoking?" Geoffrey crosses his legs and balances the smouldering cigar nimbly between soft white fingers. "Oh-hoh, let's say, about four months ago?"

A stick of firewood—John notices it suddenly, for it's the last one in the woodbox, and the fire is dwindling. He grabs the piece and tosses it onto the glowing orange cinders, evoking sharp cracklings and billows of sparks.

"Oh, come now, Your Holiness, relax, relax!" cries Geoffrey. "It's great craic—even relieves stress. Here, try one." He is reaching into the vest pocket of his embroidered silk vest, extracting a fat cigar.

"No, thanks."

Geoffrey makes a face and places the rejected cigar back into his vest pocket, then puts his own between his thin, wet lips. He inhales deeply. He exhales. He blows three smoke rings with careless effort, then smirks. "Well, my friend, enlighten me as to what your plans are for the next… let's say, twelvemonth?"

Is Geoffrey laughing at him? He has no plans—at least, none that are still in one piece. "You've changed, Geoff. What is it?"

Evidently, John's bluntness is a surprise. "Me? Changed? Well… possibly." The athletic shoulders shrug and the long legs spawl. "But I'd say you need some fireworks in your life. You're so boring now, it's no wonder you're getting old before your time!"

"And you have a suggestion?"

"A suggestion?"

John wishes he had kept his gob shut, but it is too late.

"Why, John boy! I'm so glad you asked, for I certainly do have a suggestion, and it is exactly what I put to you over two years ago—only then you were too conceited to hear it. Get yourself a lassie, John boy, get yourself a lass! Now, now, Your Holiness—don't give me that famous look of yours, like you know better!" He springs from the settee, strolls to the fireplace, and places his hand on John's shoulder while he leans inward and says, "Now, I know you insist on keeping Colleens out of your life until you've reached the mid-twenties and have your little parish neat as a pin, but come now! If you want my advice—"

"I don't believe I do."

"Nonsense! Stop putting the long finger on marriage—you're not doing yourself or our eligible lassies any favours by it! What about that pretty, shy, little blonde-haired Venice that couldn't take her eyes off you at the shearing festival last year—is she still unwed? A lad would've been blind not to notice her."

John senses his face beginning to burn; he shifts on his feet and leans his forearm against the mantlepiece. She is pretty—that shy little blonde-haired lass.

Geoffrey simpers. "Sure, her folks don't sympathize with your religious views, but that's grand. And she's not the only lass, either: there're scores more who've got their eyes and hearts set on *you.* Why not get down off your high horse now, John boy, look at courting, and give it a lash?"

"It only takes one, Geoff. I'm determined to wait it out for her sake."

"But John! If you're eternally shy around females, how will you find the lass you want?"

"God will bring her to me."

A bellowing laugh follows. "It baffles me, how you do it—honestly! Me? I'd go stark crazy!" He shakes his head, smiling to himself, then adds, "Find a wife sooner than later, my friend, and in five years have a family of your own and be the minister of the country parish. It's what your pa wanted, right?"

"My pa wanted me to wait till I was twenty-five."

"Reason?"

"Maturity."

"Maturity? *Pshaw*!" Geoffrey waves his hand. "You're just in denial of what you *really* want—admit it!"

John grits his teeth together. He will never live in denial of anything, and as the only son of Peter Dallington, he will do his best to honour his father's wishes.

"And you're determined to waste six years of your life digging through dusty two- and three-inch-thick theology books just to appease a dead man? What, you think he's looking down from heaven ready to cast you down with bolts of lightning if you get married too soon?"

"No, Peter Dallington is not looking. But God is."

"God—watching *you*?" Geoff laughs and swears at once. "That's the most half-witted sermon I've heard you preach yet!"

John tenses. "Stop slagging, Geoff. Or do you want a box?"

"Oh-hoh! Meant no offence, Your Holiness," he says with sarcastic droll, relaxing back in the settee. "So, sure, your minister father is dead. But let's talk common sense now. Unless you study pagan superstition like you study religion, you don't essentially believe Peter Dallington would turn in his grave if you forgot his famous dictum, correct?"

A searing look against the side of his face makes John shift his arm on the mantel.

"Who's going to help you care for the farm? The animals?"

Irksome persuasion indeed, but John cannot ignore it.

"Your sister abandoned you, and a man needs a woman to cook and clean while he's out shearing and bringing in the crops. If your old man knew of the strait you're in now, he'd desist. And remember, John boy—there's a dearie out there, waiting for you… her name?"

A fluttering sensation, then a half-hearted effort to control the unruly thoughts, the whirlwind fantasies, but John is already induced with desire. His helpless will dwells longer and longer upon her sweet memory… No, it is not forbidden fruit, for he will need a wife someday, just as Geoffrey says.

He meets his friend's probing gaze; his heart freezes. What lurks behind the manner in which Geoffrey's wetted lips mouth her beautiful name? What sound rolls off the untamed tongue, and makes him shudder?

Staring into the dwindling orange and red remains of the campfire, John could still see the glittering eyes; and his mind chastised himself for his ignorance. Geoffrey's eyes had often glittered—but they glittered more when she entered their company.

John lifted his gaze, traced the constellation of Ursa Major with his eyes, breathed in the brisk taste of the forest evening. He could still smell the fragrance of her hair—it was on every harvest wind; he could still see her violet eyes—they were in the depths of every evening sky; he could still feel her soft hand resting in his palm, even now. But like an evil spirit, Geoffrey was always there with them, watching from somewhere in the background. And like a famished hyena, his ghost still fed upon the heart he had stalked and ripped to shreds all those years ago.

The two privates laughed again in tones unsettled and perverse—tones that summoned a sleeping giant from its lair. Sneering from the midst of the shimmering ashes, John saw Geoffrey's face, and it taunted him like a laughing Judas.

John stood up and stretched his stiffened legs. "Night, boys," he said to the two soldiers as he walked past them and through the wooded bluff toward the tent. Dead leaves and twigs crunched beneath his feet. He could scarcely make out the tent's white, twelve-foot-tall triangular shape standing out against the thickening darkness; the stove pipe that rose from the centre of the tent was completely invisible amidst the camouflage of the shrubs, trees, and other bushes that surrounded the army encampment.

When he reached the tent, he caught hold of its rough canvas flap and threw it over his head. Warm air, heavy with the smell of oilskin and the rank odours of sweat and decaying breath, surged from the opening, accompanied by the regular deep breathing and snores and grunts of eleven dirty soldiers. He stepped inside, weighted by the prospect of a cold, empty bed and another morning on which he would awake to find her closeness nothing more than fantasy.

He fumbled to the left side of the tent until his hands fastened on the edge of his cot. He kicked off his boots, unbuttoned his coat, unhitched his trousers, and threw everything into a heap on the dirt floor. Stretching himself out on the narrow cot, he pulled the sheet and thin wool blanket over his chest. Then he closed his eyes and waited. Minutes passed. The haze of unconsciousness settled softly over his brain. His breathing slowed. There—above his head he began to see the crossbeams of the old vaulted hayloft…

His knuckles begin to throb. He looks down at them. The calloused skin is peeled back. Wood splinters stick out of them like porcupine quills. They are wet and sticky with his own blood. He looks up. There is the hole—the terrible gaping black hole that he has punched in the barn wall, imagining in his fury that it was the face of the man he thought was his friend. But just when he thinks he has pounded that face to a pulp, the empty hole becomes many holes, each with another replica of that face, puncturing the entire wall until the shredded wood panels and dilapidated frame creak and sway and shudder in the cold, changeful winds sweeping through it from the glowering west.

Somehow, even after each beating, nothing changes inside him. His mind is still tormented. He still burns with unquenchable rage. The pattern continues unabated, night after night, beating after beating. His enemy is alive, haunting the world, and with each changeful wind the hideous face returns…

Geoffrey's face. The face that kills but will never die.

Tonight Geoffrey's demon eyes glitter red with passion. His form swells larger, more terrible, grinning with savage delight while his presence and power swallow up the scarred opening and press in upon John, scorning his despair, laughing at his everlasting pain. Through the darkness his long, slender hands appear, uncoiling and slithering toward John like a serpent. One hand is naked, the other wears a soft white kid glove. It is a leprous finger. It points straight at John's heart.

Throttled by a sense of dread, John searches a vast, desolate, windswept plain for her beautiful fleeting form. His hands ache to touch her, to hold and caress her, but she has fled beneath a ghastly crimsoned sky.

A demon's laugh peels through the death-like stillness. In despair John looks down, expecting to see his throbbing hands pierced with wood splinters and sullied with blood. But they are changed. They are no longer thick and calloused and muscular. No longer bloody and scarred. Instead he sees that they have grown long and slender, like a serpent.

One hand is naked. The other wears a white kid glove.

— CHAPTER IX —

A POSTPONMENT

St. Agnes Mercy Convent, Ireland
July 1862

Kate harboured a secret trepidation of the venerable foundress and superior of the mother house, Mother Cecelia Doyle. The formidable sixty-year-old matron, with her sharp mind and emperor's bearing, struck a fear into Kate that no priest's prying questions could equal. Mother Cecelia was meant to replace her own mother; Mother Cecelia's virtue ranked second only to that of the Virgin Mary—indeed, Mother Cecelia was a virgin herself. Still, the admiration Kate was expected to feel toward the older woman could not squelch the fear of ever incurring the bad opinion of so revered and respected a person.

It was this fear that gripped Kate one morning in July.

She was working in the surgical ward, putting away the clean instruments lately used in that morning's gallbladder operation, when one of the Sisters entered.

"Sister Kate, Mother Cecelia would like to see you in her room at one o' clock," she said.

Hardness gripped Kate's stomach. It sounded like a death sentence. Younger Sisters were summoned by the Mother in only the most extreme cases, and personal interviews with her often involved a transgression.

As Kate removed her little gold wedding ring and washed it in the warm soapy water and then shined its smooth gold surface with a corner of the black wool serge of her veil, she wrestled to find what she could have done—or failed to do—to draw the unwanted attention. She reviewed the events of the last four days. She had been completing her nurse's requirements by working in St. Agnes Hospital not far from the mother house, assisting the interim doctor in the surgical ward…

Had she forgotten to administer a prescribed dosage? Had she overdosed an ill patient? Had the doctor found her clumsy or inept in yesterday's gouty foot amputation? Or perhaps Mother Cecelia had observed a manifestation of sinful pride in her own abilities as a nurse and decided it was time to deal out a warning that would humble her back to an acceptable mindset of servitude and obedience?

She slipped the ring back on—it glided on easily, since it was slightly too large. Then she flexed her fingers and nerved herself for a cold reprimand. Only three weeks separated her from the day of her final vows: the vows that would subject her entirely and completely to God. Oh, the good she could do with her life! The relief she could give her poor, unknown family! And how she longed to do it because she was the only one who could.

At one o' clock Kate walked with leaden steps along the corridor toward Mother Cecelia's room. Her eyes distinguished the foot-deep indent of the office's door in the grey stone wall. Four yards away. Two yards. Three steps… She was there, holding her breath, lifting her hand to knock. Three light taps on the rough wooden door and it opened into the shadowy room.

A Sister, round and kind-eyed, stood in the open doorway. She was dressed just like Kate in the long black wool serge habit with long, wide sleeves; the heavy black veil that draped over her head and shoulders and fell past her belted waist; the snowy-white linen coif, pique dimity, and guimp that carefully concealed the flesh of her neck, ears, and forehead; and, depending from the left side of the thick black leather cincture, the black rosary with its singular large ebony-and-white Mercy Cross, its distinguishing feature being that it lacked a corpus.

"Come in, Sister Kate," she said in a thin voice. "Mother Cecelia is expecting you." She bent her head and stepped aside as Kate entered.

Lustrous rays of summer sun filtered through the chestnut-and-yellow stained-glass windows at the back of the office, illuminating an emaciated, thorn-crowned image of the Christ stretched out upon the crucifix. As she looked upon the corpse, Kate became conscious of the ring on her finger; somehow she had not become used to wearing it yet, though it had been three years since her wedding day when the Bishop had placed it there.

But it did not matter if she was used to the ring, or even if it were loose. She was a married woman, and the ring and her veil both said so.

The rasp of a chair sliding across the polished floor proceeded the dark shape of Mother Cecelia as she rose from behind a massive carved desk. "Thank you, Sister. You may leave us now."

Kate shuddered at the measured, chilling tone. Her eye caught a final glimpse of the other Sister as she bowed and exited the room, and then the door closed with a vacant click, and Kate was left alone.

With her hands concealed behind her scapular, Mother Cecelia glided around the desk, then extended one hand in the customary greeting, her eyes strained and squinted by a smile that wilted Kate's courage. "Welcome, my child," she said, and arched what might once have been eyebrows but were now two hairless ridges that crested the area above her paper-thin, purpled-veined eyelids.

Kate approached, trying to ignore the locking in her knees as she knelt at the woman's feet, remembering the last time she had done so. It had been on the day of first vows, just after the wedding ceremony, and the Mother Superior had gripped the heavy pair of garden shears and shaved Kate's head bare. Oh, how ugly it had made her look! How monstrous! And then how grateful Kate had been to receive the cumbersome headgear that was meant to replace her former vanity. She could still see the idolized nut-brown lengths swirled in a heap on the floor. She had stolen a coveting glance at the pile of tresses, but Mother Cecelia had swept them up in a dustpan and discarded them. Alone that night in her cold cell, Kate had pulled on her rough nightdress and retreated under the bedclothes, but without her long hair she still felt naked, and for hours she had wept for shame, listening to the eternal *swish-swishing* of the metal shears ringing in her ears like a rebuke for her cruelty—recalling a night long before… recalling the shears she had gripped in her own hands, and of the abundant mass of gold spilling through her fingers and falling to the ground… while Collette slept.

"My child?"

It was Mother Cecelia's voice, croaking. Quickly pulling herself back to the present, Kate took the proffered hand in her own and pressed it to her lips, holding her breath against the putrid stench that issued from the copious folds of the older woman's garment.

No—it did not stink, Kate told herself. She simply was not used to the personal smell of an elderly woman.

Daring to lift her gaze for the first time, Kate noted the horizontal lines in Mother Cecelia's high forehead, which seemed as deep and dusty as harrowed furrows in dry, barren soil. Thin lines etched the corners of her mouth and creased the wan, unsoftened tissue of her colourless lips.

"Please, sit down, my child." Again, the shrivelling smile. Again, the arching ridges. With an air of superiority, Mother Cecelia glided back to her seat behind the desk before indicating a lower straight-back, hard-bottom chair opposite her own.

Kate slipped into the chair, swabbing her clammy palms against the rough serge of her habit.

Mother Cecelia rested her folded hands on the desk as her keen lashless eyes fixed upon Kate's face. Such eyes could not fail to read the critical thoughts of others, and for this reason Kate wished she could be blind to Mother Cecelia's long, beak-like nose; her monstrous nostrils that flared with unsightly emphasis and even hissed softly when she breathed; the small pink-and-white growth planted in the oily crevice between nose and sallow cheek; and the embarrassing prickle bush of chin hair.

"Are you well, my child?"

Kate started. Her mouth went dry. "I, I'm fine, thank you," she stammered.

"Good." The shrivelling smile curled up the withered lips.

A torturous silence settled between them as Kate waited for the reprimand.

"Perhaps you are wondering why I have called you here, my child?"

Kate's mind was benumbed to every response except a dumb nod and an almost inaudible "Yes."

"Sister Kate," Mother Cecelia began, her voice coming out with a croak. With a dignified "Ahem," she cleared the croak and sighed. "I have received a letter of urgency that requires immediate attention." She reached across the desk for a folded sheet of paper.

Kate followed the movement, convinced that the letter was from the interim surgeon and contained both his bad opinion of her and his declaration of her ultimate failure as a nurse.

Unfolding the letter, Mother Cecelia scanned it as she said, "It is from the United States War Department, written by one of the ward mistresses of the establishment, a Mercy Sister by the name of Sister Bernice. It is signed by her as well as a certain Dr. Robert Hall, the head surgeon of the Hall General Hospital in Washington, DC."

Kate resisted her need for breath, reminding herself that the blow would still come.

"This establishment of the said Dr. Hall is currently being aided by our Mercy Sisters, who have been serving in the United States for many years, as you know, and have offered their services in war hospitals across the country. It is apparent by their communication"—she tipped the letter toward Kate—"that, despite anti-Catholic views held by the North, the officers and Cabinet members of the Union are willing to forego the general prejudice in order to secure the extraordinary abilities demonstrated by the nursing community of religious Sisters. The military is desperate for good nurses. The unwholesome combination of convalescent men nursing other convalescent men is far less than ideal, and their Sanitary Commissions and Relief Society knows this. Many of the medical establishments, particularly those nearest the battlefields but even the general hospitals in removed cities and towns, are overcrowded and understaffed, and doctors and nurses everywhere are seeking additional medical assistance. In this letter"—she gestured again with the missive and looked pointedly at Kate—"contains a plea that we send a division of our medically trained Nursing Sisters to assist them—at least eight nurses. The Pope approves such activities," she added, "for he knows how our work of charity in these vulnerable circumstances can only have a positive influence upon the leverage of the Holy See."

Kate's legs twitched beneath her habit; she sat rigid, distractedly twisting the wedding ring on her finger. A war across the ocean had nothing to do with her; indeed, she could be dismissed straightaway.

"Sister Kate, it is with immense satisfaction that I have observed the strict standard by which you have modelled your conduct. Your life displays wisdom and constancy, an obligation of service to God which you fulfill without excuse. Furthermore, you are faithful to report the misconduct of other Sisters, and subsequently incurred the favour and trust of your superiors. Indeed, you have proven yourself a worthy candidate." Mother Cecelia paused deliberately, as though anticipating a reaction. "A candidate who is a skilled and competent nurse, which, my child, brings me to the point of our meeting."

Kate felt her body go completely still. A single nod attempted a modest acknowledgement of the compliment, but confusion made her brain fevered and her eyes unseeing.

"Sister Kate, in the spirit of our founder, the Venerable Mother Catherine McAuley, we must not only devote our lives to prayer and silence but also to the service of the poor, needy, and ignorant. You are eager for God, my child. You are eager to pray and be silent before him. But are you as eager to serve his children?"

Kate had not disappointed the surgeon, nor performed a misdiagnosis, nor even fallen prey to conceit of her talents, yet impending judgment shadowed her soul more darkly now than ever.

"My child, I do not feel that you are yet ready to partake of your solemn perpetual vows."

A shock, a lurch of the heart against the bosom, and Kate smothered a gasp.

"There is a steamship sailing tomorrow for the United States, and there is a need on that continent that requires eight Nursing Sisters. You, Sister Kate, are the best of the seven that our mother house is able to send."

Leaning forward, Kate clutched the edge of the desk. "But Mother Cecelia," she stammered, "what about my, my ceremony? I, I do not wish to leave this place... I love it here, and there is no telling how much longer the war might last. Please—can't you find someone else to go in my place?"

"There is no one else, Sister Kate, with a body as young and strong as yours." Mother Cecelia's tone was flinty, her face unmoved by emotion, and yet somehow the wrinkled mouth did not forget its shrivelling smile. "Your ceremony will be postponed until your return. Father Andrew will be accompanying you on your voyage and will be assuming his regular responsibilities in either a hospital or on a battlefield. Sister Kate," she added with squinted eyes and reproachful emphasis, "just because something is not easy does not mean it is not good. Have you forgotten your vows?"

Kate could never forget them. "Poverty, chastity, obedience, and... service," she recited meekly.

"Ah yes, *service*, my child. It is what distinguishes us from other orders. And as a Mercy Sister you must live faithfully in such a spirit. But tell me, how will *you* display such a spirit?"

Kate recalled her catechism. "I will despise all personal desires, and..." She felt instinctively for the smooth, four-and-a-half-inch tall ebony Mercy Cross of her rosary dangling at her hip. She held it in her palm and looked long and steadily at it, remembering how she had promised Mother Cecelia that she would never part with it till the day she died—for the venerated item would certainly be passed down to another Mercy Sister just as it had been passed down to her. She finally said, "And to be myself the corpus of Jesus which our Mercy Cross does not have, for the sake of the Body of Christ."

"And we know that the Body of Christ is what, my child?" The shrivelled mouth twitched.

"It is the Holy Mother Church."

"My child, as I observe your reaction, I think it right for you to take personally for your motto the words of the Virgin Mary to the angel Gabriel. Will you tell me what they were?"

"'Behold the handmaid of the Lord,'" Kate recited, hot tears blistering her eyes, "'be it unto me according to thy word.'"

Mother Cecelia nodded with pleasure. "And, Sister Kate, I know without asking that you wish to emulate such a perfect example of unquestioning obedience."

But Kate could not keep back the gush of tears that gave way like a faulty dike beneath the influence of angry waters.

"Ah," said Mother Cecelia, "but perhaps you feel our decision is unfair?"

Unable to bring herself to reply, Kate sunk her teeth into the soft flesh of her cheek and gnawed it till her eyes watered with pain.

"Sister Kate, you must recognize your sin of pride and self-love. You must learn to submit your self-will to the authority of the Church and receive this verdict of indefinite absence from the mother house as a test of your humility."

Kate could not restrain herself. "But dear Mother Cecelia!" she cried, rising from her seat. "I beg of you! I do not want to go! I—"

"Sister Kate!" The woman's eyes flashed and she raised her hand, commanding silence. "You have taken a vow of obedience."

Kate dropped her gaze and forced herself back into the hard-bottomed chair, shamed by her inability to strangle her emotions. "Yes, Mother Cecelia. I will go." Though her mind raved and disputed, her voice was hardened, lifeless. Every nerve in her body vibrated; her will rebelled; her soul wept for her poor mother; and her heart hammered so violently against her bosom that she thought it would burst its confines and leave her limp and lifeless on the floor.

"You will do well to remember, my child," said Mother Cecelia as triumph flickered across her face, "that it is circumstances such as these that prove to us the most self-disciplined and flawless candidates of our order." Rising from her seat with an imperial bearing, she walked around the desk and approached Kate.

Kate bent her neck and bowed her head as she knelt before the older woman.

"My child, you are a living representation of the crucified

Lord. I adjure you to use your time of absence to work in yourself a more complete understanding of self-sacrifice and inner perfection. Remember that in this work of service you perform an act of great charity and sacrifice. Rest in the knowledge that you embark upon a most blessed work. May Jesus, Mary, and Joseph bless and help you."

Kate felt a chill, heavy hand rest upon her head in an act of benediction. The words *In nomine Patris, et Filii, et Spiritus Sancti. Amen* were pronounced over her as a wrinkled thumb touched her forehead and made the sign of the cross.

Squeezing her eyes shut, Kate gave in to her impulse and clasped the outstretched hand, pressing the palm to her cheek and holding it there, wishing it could ease the inner struggle. Numberless tears streamed down her face as burdened conscience lashed nervous brain and chastised thoughts cursed a broken though unyielding heart.

Suddenly possessed with an ability to perform that from which her will shrank so utterly, Kate constrained it all for a single instant, hastily drew the clammy, withered hand to her lips, and, weeping, kissed it.

PART TWO

— CHAPTER X —

A STRANGE COMPANION

New York Harbour
September 1862

Kate stood on the slippery deck of the SS *North Star* as the steamship approached the crowded, drizzle-draped harbour of New York. Through the low, wispy white and grey clouds, the dark shape of land looked like a sleeping mammoth. She shivered, then reached her hand beneath her raincoat, feeling for the reassurance of the metal and wood crucifix that was tightly secured at an angle in its front waist pouch of the leather cincture. Although she was relatively dry beneath her oversized raincoat and black umbrella, the bone-chilling dampness had inched its way into her limbs and stiffened them like a plank. It did not ease her discomfort that she had hardly slept during the nearly five-week-long voyage. Taxed and overtired, her nerves strained raw as she contemplated the bleak unknown that lay before her.

As they entered the harbour, the dank smell of fish grew thick like a stale, half-decaying blanket. The Irish, French, and German immigrants onboard didn't seem to notice, for their angular faces shone with renewed eagerness as they huddled about the railing with their skinny, rag-clad children, some chattering, others praying, and a few making grateful demonstrations of the sign of the cross upon the appearance of the long-awaited shores that promised them new hopes, new homes, and overwhelming abundance. But Kate would not sympathize; this New World would be a tomb before it could ever be a home.

A muffled shout went up from a group of rowdy Germans near the bow as the vessel was moored to the dock, assisted to its resting place by several brawny sailors. One had a patch on his eye, another boasted a gaudy pair of diamond earrings dangling from overstretched earlobes, and a third didn't seem to care that when he grinned everyone saw the unsightly gap left by a vacated front tooth.

"Come with us," said a low voice at Kate's shoulder. It was one of the Sisters of their company. "We'll wait over there together until the summon to leave."

Kate followed her to a far corner of the steamship where a circle of Sisters, shaded by Father Andrew in his priest's black cassock, stood voicelessly together. Father Andrew's leer was upon her as she joined the group of Sisters, so she avoided him.

The crash of jostling luggage and the scuttle of feet accompanied a band of coarse seamen as they hauled trunks and bags from the vessel's hull and deposited them on the swaying wharf, where the goods waited to be taken to wagons and omnibuses parked along the shoreline and along the high road. A loud general summons from a blue-jacketed soldier began the transfer of mulling passengers from deck to gangplank to loud, confused dockyard.

Kate fell in line as the group of Sisters moved in single file toward the gangplank. A fleshy sailor with the weight of a massive travel trunk bulging his bare arms passed in front of her, his fierce, sniggering eyes poking out at her from beneath a mop of straggling black hair. He stopped and scanned her figure with a casualness and a toothless simper that made her feel sick. She focused her eyes ahead and pressed forward, wishing the Sister in front of her would speed up her pace.

"Shy, are we?" the man sneered as she stepped onto the slimy gangplank.

Though it seemed the precarious walkway might give way beneath her, Kate hurried away, but the sailor's cackle followed until the bustle of the seaport closed in around her.

The prolonged deluge had left a sea of mud and disarray in its wake. The docks were swamped with people and sailors unloading cargo from the clippers and steamships arriving in the harbour. Several yards from the main wharf, six or seven fishing boats tugged at stubborn moorings. Scowling fishermen with leathery skin and bristly beards like dehydrated seaweed slouched against crumbling boats and blew smoke rings from crusted-out pipes. Midshipmen barked orders to their crews while the cries of salesmen competed with the yells of newsboys who wildly waved the day's paper above their heads.

"Oysters! Crab! Lobster! Fish of all kinds! All for a bully bargain you can't refuse!"

Frantic shouts a few yards inland caught Kate's attention, and she looked to see a stocky, red-faced, red-haired, white-aproned seafood peddler gesticulating from the corner of his stand. People hustled by with as much regard for his enthusiasm and wares as though he impersonated an irritating circus clown. Some even laughed at him.

Kate balanced on the mud-caked crates and fractured boards that made a ramshackle bridge across the worst part of the sludge and up the miry bank. With a final backward glance at the peddler, she watched him wipe his face with a handkerchief, then blow his nose as his shoulders slumped downward. Did he have a family to feed? Even though seafood was the sacred food reserved for Fridays, if she had money of her own she would buy the poor salesman's oysters just to cheer him up.

Three Union soldiers conducted the company across the dockyard and up a boggish trail to where a heavily built stagecoach and an open wagon were parked along the high road. An angular man dressed in black robes came forward to greet them as they reached the top of the incline.

"Greetings, Brother and Sisters," he said, introducing himself to Father Andrew as the priest of the order, sent from the New York parish to organize their journey to the capital city. "We had expected to offer your company a comfortable ride to Washington by locomotive, but, most regretfully, train travel is most unsafe due to recent sabotages by the Confederates. And even if there were no such dangers, the troops being conveyed for the next several days have made such transportation unavailable. We have therefore arranged a stagecoach to conduct you to the capital. A convalescing Union Private will be driving the stagecoach, and your luggage will be hauled on that wagon by its driver." He motioned to a large open wagon with a faded-red frame and green box drawn by four weary-looking dappled mules, next to which stood a towering, thick-shouldered black man.

Kate had never before seen a black man, and what little she had heard was that the Africans were mostly illiterate jungle pagans, with unfeeling spirits in comparison to the Anglo-Saxon race, and the majority of whom were best suited to labour under the supervision of upper-class citizens of prosperous Southern plantations.

Slowly, they passed the black man. Kate glanced into his face, and questioned herself. A kind expression shone from his large, soft, dark-brown eyes. He appeared to be fully human—certainly not less human than herself.

Father Andrew stepped into the stagecoach first, grunting as he heaved his flabby, effeminate form up onto the step and inside. Once seated he panted for breath as though he had just run a mile, his double-chin doubling and his red nose reddening from the bodily exertion. Kate could not forget Collette's comparison of him to an old frog.

The oldest Sister of the seven was next in line, followed by the others in order of age. Kate, being the youngest, was left to the last.

"I was told there's room for six—seven if you press together," remarked the parish priest, peering inside the dim interior of the coach. Four of the Sisters pressed nervously together on one bench. The two thinnest sat opposite, squeezed into the opening not plugged by Father Andrew's bloated shape.

"Ahem." The parish priest ran his forefinger along the edge of his starched white collar as he glanced at Kate. "Someone may need to sit, uh, there—up top." His gaze travelled to the high seat of the stagecoach.

"I can take that seat," Kate said. "The open air will be pleasant."

His expression relaxed. "Very well, then," he said, and closed the door of the coach.

Kate moved to the front of the vehicle and glanced up at

the lofty pinnacle, then down at her long habit. Indeed, Mother Cecelia would certainly disapprove of her lifting her skirt and climbing up the side of that stagecoach.

But Mother Cecelia was not there.

Drawing breath, she hoisted her skirt halfway up her calves and grasped the rough top edge of the wagon wheel, preparing for the first step.

"Sista, may I help?"

It was a man's deep voice, sweetened with an accent she did not recognize. Halting, she turned around. The tall black man was hasting toward her, removing his straw hat from a crop of coarse, tightly curled black hair that resembled sheep's wool. A kind smile lit his face as he held out his pale-palmed hand.

"Oh…" said Kate, shying as she looked at the hand, then back into the man's smiling face, then back at the hand. What would Father Andrew think—would he disapprove? She had never held a man's hand before, let alone a black man's hand.

"I don't want ya takin' a tumble, Sista," he said kindly. "It's okay."

Kate breathed more easily. Father Andrew was not there to see—he was dozing inside the stagecoach and would never know of the incident. Immediately, Kate took the hand and allowed the black man to help her into the high seat.

"Ya comfy up dere, miss?"

Kate adjusted her position, straightened her skirt, and glanced around. She could see everything—even behind the coach to where several soldiers and sailors were shoving trunks and carpet bags inside the box of the mule-drawn wagon.

"Yes, very much," she said, daring to smile.

The black man tipped his hat. "Lor' bless ya, Sista."

There was no barbarism in this man. He was as gentle as a child, with a countenance that brimmed with a deep warmth and beauty of soul, as well as a sensitive intelligence that lauded him a more reasonable and honest man than any white-skinned sailor at the docks.

A gangly young man in cowhide boots approached and slapped the black man good-naturedly on the shoulder. "Hey! Ready to go, Sam?" He hooked his thumbs in the belt of bullets that cinched his buckskin breeches and then surveyed the loaded wagon. "Quite the load."

Kate shrank from notice, but with a quick glance from her vantage point, she quickly made out the characteristic details of the newcomer. He was about twenty years of age. An army revolver hung on his left hip, and a weather-beaten leather hat, rippled around the crown with a rim of sweat, fit his head in a way that suggested he had been born wearing it.

"Ready, suh!" said the black man, and he was gone.

"Take up the rear, hey?" the youth of the cowhide boots shouted after him. "Davy rides shotgun—he's with you."

The lanky youth made the coach sway as he stepped on a wheel and swung himself into the driver's box. When he saw Kate he halted, and his plain, smallpox-scarred face bent with a half grin. "Why, howdy, marm!" He hastily lifted his hat to reveal dusty, sunburned ears and a dense mop of tawny hair. "Guess there weren't enough room in the coach for ya, hey?"

Kate shook her head, her face growing warm as he sat beside her on the long wooden bench.

The honeyed, musty odour of horse sweat and sod wafted from his homespun jacket. He leaned forward with a leisurely air, his elbows resting on his bony knees as he pulled leather driving lines out from beneath the seat and balanced them loosely in his smudged palms. His hands were spindly but enormous. His first finger turned into a stub at the first knuckle, and his rough fingernails were so yellowed, and the fibre of his calloused skin so stained, that Kate doubted if the harshest soap or most rigorous scrubbing could ever make them clean again.

He twisted around as though his torso had been a spring winding up, then called, "Ready to move?"

"Suh!" came the reply.

The spring unwound. He let off the brake and then made a kissing sound. "Giddy-up!" he said, slapping the reins across the backs of the horses. The harnesses jangled and the stagecoach jarred and creaked and swayed, then pitched suddenly forward over a high rut as it began a slow advance into the slippery road.

As the stagecoach ascended the hill, Kate glanced at the road behind them. The mule-drawn baggage wagon was close in the rear, driven by Sam. A coloured youth sat next to him, grasping a long-barrelled shotgun. Kate assumed this must be the aforementioned Davy, "riding shotgun."

In the harbour below, the outlines of tall ships with towering masts stood out against the horizon, eclipsing small, brow-beaten fishing boats that swayed in the undulating waters near the quay. Beyond stretched the endless expanse of ocean: the miles of water that separated her from the sacred walls that had once kept her beyond the reach of temptation. How long would it be before she would be safe behind them again?

She could hear Mother Cecelia's parting words. "Remember," she had instructed, "as a Nursing Sister, you will be expected to serve men of all ages, ranks, and religions. Be circumspect. You are a woman of the cloth, and men are dangerous creatures. Curiosity about them only leads to sin."

Despite Kate's resolution to squelch curiosity, the test that lay between her and her ceremony of final vows presented itself as the most gruelling of all. Closing her eyes, she forced her hands quiet by knotting them tightly together in her lap. Still her lips could not prevent a sigh.

"Homesick, marm?"

The inquiring voice pulled Kate from her thoughts; her eyes flew open to find the driver's gaze fastened on her.

He grinned, revealing a straight row of teeth that looked like they had been fermented in tobacco juice. "Homesick, marm?" he repeated, scratching the crop of scruffy brown whiskers sprouting across his heavy jaw.

"No. No, I am not homesick at all, sir," she lied, adjusting her position on the bench to facilitate a more decent cushion of space between them.

"Huh! Really?" He tugged at the faded-red cotton handkerchief around his thick neck. His protruding Adam's apple bobbed, and he turned his eyes back on the road. Then, leaning slightly to the right of the stagecoach as though to take aim at a rut in the road, he craned sideways, pursed his lips, and ejected a speedy stream of dark tobacco water. "Nice sub for a spittoon," he said, wiping his mouth on his grimy sleeve.

Kate blinked, fascinated and appalled by his crassness. Only the devil's slave would dare do such a thing—and the devil's slave had no business asking if she were homesick.

Half an hour passed as they travelled along the high road in a southwesterly direction. The persistent drizzle had generally abated, and in the west, pure beams of light severed the veil of leaden clouds and poured like waterfloods over their craggy ledges.

The stagecoach rumbled over a wooden bridge and down a road lined by a well-weathered wooden fence. On one side, rolling hills and dense forests stretched for miles, while on the other a multitude of canvas tents studded green pastures with striking precision. A moving mass of organized foot soldiers panelled one end of the field, their rhythmic march vibrating through the stillness. It sounded like an alarm—persistent, unceasing. The strict order reminded her of the convent.

In the centre of an adjacent field another company awaited orders from their commander. Suddenly, the loud shout of an army drill instructor boomed through the air, paired almost instantly with the sharp, deafening discharge of many guns. Kate flinched and clapped her hands over her ears.

"Target practisin' is what them's doin'," the wagoner commented without looking.

Kate dropped her hands into her lap, continuing to observe the training procedure as though she hadn't heard him until the stagecoach turned a curve in the road and the army encampment disappeared.

"You a-feered of anythin', marm?" asked the driver casually. "Guns, maybe?"

"No," she said.

"Soldiers, p'rhaps?" He offered another demonstration of the notorious tobacco juice.

Kate feigned a cough, but her unruly hands would fidget without permission.

He glanced at her and gave a satisfied grunt. "Must apologize, marm, fer all the chewin' and spittin'." His face contorted with honest distress. "Ol' habits die hard. I've been workin' on this one fer a coon's age, but it won't lay off. I ain't no drinker, but since fourteen, chewin' tobacco's been my fix, and now I know that once a feller starts, he might be dragged to the dickens before beatin' the dern thing."

Indeed, it was a wretched practice, and Kate wondered what his mother thought of it, for chewing tobacco was certainly a sin equal to breaking one of the ten commandments.

"Never seen a nun this close up before," he said, pushing his hat farther back on his forehead and scratching his tawny hair. "Heck!" he exclaimed with a half chuckle, "always did kinder wonder what they looked like but never thought one could be so dern pertty. What'er they doin' anyhow—lockin' ya up away from the real world, Miss… uh… er?..."

Kate stiffened. "My name is Sister Kate, sir," she said coolly.

"Well then…" He paused, and the Adam's apple bobbed sympathetically. "Sister Kate, I meant no disrespect by sayin' ye'r pertty," he said, but Kate caught a trace of contradicting humour dancing in his blue eyes. "The name's Jack Gunderson, and I'm a good ol' down-home, pie-eaten' Yankee from Springfield, Illinois. Same town as Honest Abe is from, and I'm right proud of it!"

Kate acknowledged the exclamation with a single businesslike nod.

"Well, now we're acquainted—that ain't so hard, hey?"

Kate did not answer. She preferred to create an awkward pause by twisting the ring on her finger instead.

"So," he said presently, "ye're married?"

Kate's back turned into a plank. He had noticed her ring. Instantly, she forced her hands to still and her palms to press against her knees. How her mind raced! How her mouth went dry! If she said no, she would be lying. If she said yes, he might ask her husband's name. And if she told him that she was married to God, well—what would he say then?

"It's… uh… none of your business, sir," she blurted, then squeezed her eyes shut against his look.

The rhythmic tramp of the horses' hooves and the groaning and bumping of the wagon's wheels over the sodden road absorbed the awkward silence of several long minutes while Kate convinced herself that she would rather have lain in a coffin for nine hours than sit for one on the edge of that stagecoach bench.

"Do ya like our president?"

Kate cleared her throat. At least he was making some effort at changing the conversation. "Which one is yours?" she returned feebly.

"Abe Lincoln. Jeff Davis is president of the Confederacy, but he's a Copperhead."

"Forgive me," Kate said, "but politics is not something I follow closely."

"Aw, nothin' to apologize fer, marm. But ya should educate yerself sometime—through the grapevine, marm, like I do. You'll either love or hate Uncle Abe. That's how it is with folks 'round these parts. Them Jesuit assassins are after him steady—with more gunpowder than you can shake a stick at."

"Jesuits? You must be mistaken. The Jesuits are a highly revered religious congregation of scholarly and evangelistic men of the Mother Church."

"That's right—they take oaths, too. Extreme ones, with naked daggers pointed at their hearts—'least, that's what ol' Sawbones says."

"Ah," Kate said. "Was that through the grapevine?"

"Sure thing, marm. All Protestants are damned—that's the Jesuit's opinion—and they swear to do away with any they can get their hands on."

"And, uh…" Kate hemmed. "What has that to do with your president?"

"No offence, marm"—Jack wiggled his thick eyebrows—"but I heard that the Confederates have an underhand deal with yer Pope."

"Oh? May I ask what religious denomination Mr. Lincoln is a member of?"

"He ain't a member of no demon-nation—"

"Denomination," Kate quickly corrected.

"Yeah. Uncle Abe's jest a good 'ol gospel-livin', Good Book–believin' man. Tall as a church steeple and swell as a saint. But them Jesuits—they got a heck of a grudge against him."

"You seem to be fond of conspiracies," said Kate, hoping he would stop talking about them.

Jack grinned. "If ya wanna call truth a conspiracy, I'll say ya nailed it."

"Brother Gunderson, may I ask what brings you to transport a stagecoach of Nursing Sisters?" said Kate, diverting the subject.

He spat, and then he grinned. "It ain't 'cause I'm yeller, marm, that's for sure. No sir. I seen the elephant before I came here, sure thing. Fact is, I was at Port Republic— Ho! What a row! Them Greybacks fought like Killkenny cats, and meantime I got a mini ball rip right through the ol' leg. Hurt like the dickens, it did. But I figured it was my rightful pun'shment fer breakin' the sixth commandment."

Kate started, his reference to the sixth commandment transporting her into the dark, stuffy, incensed confines of the confessional. She knew exactly what the sixth commandment was. Her own mother had broken it. But now she was in the presence of a man who not only chewed and spat tobacco but had broken that very same commandment—and confessed the sin with as much ease as though it had been a regular and even natural occurrence. She wanted to jump out of the stagecoach and run for her life.

"That's the dangdest part of bein' in a war, ya know—breakin' the sixth commandment all the time," Jack went on loudly, tugging again at the red handkerchief. "Awfulest feelin' in the world, takin' a man's life when ya have no choice but to. Only way I can just-fy it is knowin' that all 'em poor black folks would havta live forever in slav'ry if we didn't fight and kill off a few Rebs to free 'em."

Kate frowned. "I'm afraid you misunderstand, sir. The fifth commandment, not the sixth, is 'Thou shalt not kill.'"

Jack frowned back. "No, marm, I ain't misunderstandin' nothin'. The parson in our regiment preached lots of sermons on number sixth. He made sure us fellers knew 'xactly the order *and* how to remember 'em by. I keep track of it bein' the sixth commandment by countin' my five fingers on one hand and stoppin' on the chopped-off pointer of t'other hand—

see—and that's how come I know it's the sixth command and not the fifth."

Kate involuntarily felt for her catechism in her pocket, intending to prove him wrong, but the catechism was not there. She glanced behind them at the mule-drawn luggage wagon lurching over the road several yards behind them. "Brother Gunderson, my volume is in the luggage wagon. But I can tell you that the catechism says it is certainly the *fifth* commandment."

"Hmm.... maybe that's how come our sums don't match. My parson, he don't use no catches-him—"

"Catechism."

"—he jest uses the plain ol' Good Book." He gave her a sidelong glance. "Ya know what that is, hey?"

"No, I do not."

"It's the Bible, marm," he stated, and twitched the reins over the backs of the horses, which urged them out of a sluggish walk.

"Perhaps your parson has not asked the assistance of a Roman Catholic priest in presenting his interpretation of the passage?"

Jack raised his eyebrows. "Huh?"

"There are many dangerous opinions propagated by common laypeople who do not understand the Holy Scriptures, and who go about construing much erroneous propaganda, much to the confusion and detriment of souls."

Jack's confusion showed itself in the deepening lines of his dusty brow and the widening of his eyes. "Oh, well... anyhow," he said, blinking as he simultaneously lifted his overgrown right foot and rested it against the front ledge of the vehicle, "gettin' back to this here leg— Ya wanna know the rest?"

There was nothing better to do, and since the former subject had grown rigid and uncomfortable, Kate consented.

"I got transferred to Hall's General in Washington—used to be a hotel," Jack resumed. "Got the dern leg near sawed off—and had diarrhea and the shakes on top of that. Thanks be I'm near fit as a fiddle now, so ol' Sawbones sent me to fetch you gals before Wednesday next, when I'll head back yonder to join my regiment. So ya see, marm," he added, "I ain't no hospital rat, like ya maybe thought, hey?"

"I was thinking no such thing, Brother Gunderson."

Jack turned a laugh into a loud hem. "No need to 'Brother' me, neither. I ain't no holy man like…" He jerked his head in the direction of the stagecoach, then winked. "You'll be a nurse workin' 'longside 'ol Sawbones, hey, marm?" He dug into his coat pocket and retrieved a piece of chewing tobacco, tossed it into his mouth, and chomped. "He's capital. A hard case to crack but straight as a die. Got a bully sense of humour, too, 'specially when he's a bit wallpapered."

He tossed her a significant wink, but she could not hide her confusion.

"Ya know what I'm sayin', hey? 'Wallpapered'?"

Kate shook her head.

"Well, now, marm." He paused. "What I mean is when he's been into the *whiskey*."

"I see, Brother Gunderson."

"Hey— What's that? I ain't yer 'Brother' nohow." He shook his rangy finger at her playfully. "Mind that." He swirled his tongue over his front teeth, then gave her a crooked grin that made him look nothing less than the veritable impersonation of a scarecrow.

Kate looked away, wondering if his mental abilities were just slightly unsound.

Her manner only seemed to amuse Jack further. "Back at the hospitals, good nurses are gettin' scarce as hens' teeth."

"Are there no volunteers?"

"Oh, there's plenty of those—they jest keep dyin' of the shakes."

"Oh, I'm very sorry…"

"Yeah, well, that's nice of ya. Sister Teresa-Marie passed away last week. She did amputations with Sawbones. But the Good Lord left us a couple of the best. Take Bernie—ol' Sister nurse at the Hall General. She calls the shots."

Kate blinked at the irreverence. "You call our Sister *Bernie*?"

"Only when she ain't listenin'." Jack grinned. "It's cuter than *Bernice*— Don't look too concerned there, marm. Bernie's sweeter'n cherry pie. Strict, too. Keeps track of everythin' in her little brown book. Nothin's gonna get past her. There's a few more, but I don't make a habit to remember the names: Sister Maria this, Sister Mary that—up, down, backward, forward—it's all the same to me. But heck, can they cook!" He whistled, then his face puckered. "But I guess anything beats them wormy sheet iron crackers, desecrated vegetables, and goobers we'd been livin' on in camp… But back to yer situation, marm. After all that talk of shakes and Sawbones, seems yer feelin' a few nerves yerself—wonderin' maybe if ya've got what it takes to last?"

It was true. Jack's colourful descriptions startled her, but she was reluctant for him to see her true feelings.

"Brother, uh—" She began, but then corrected herself with a hasty sniff, confused as how to continue.

"Ya ain't owin' to answer, marm," he said with an approving smile as the coach rattled on. "But how 'bout I give ya my personal opinion?"

Kate couldn't decide if she wanted his opinion or not, but when minutes passed and she lifted her eyes, she caught him looking at her in a way that suggested he was drawing up his observations into an orderly mental sum.

"You'll last, sure thing," he finally said, craning his neck to accommodate a final spit into a gaping pothole before granting a firm nod of approval. "Sure as I'm a sinner, I reckon you'll last a while."

— CHAPTER XI —

A NILE OF BLOOD

Two days after The Battle of Antietam
Friday, September 19, 1862

It was seven days before the stagecoach arrived on the outskirts of Washington. The side roads near Philadelphia and Baltimore had been riddled with Southern sympathizers, causing "Shotgun Davy," as he became affectionately known, to be on full-time alert and Jack to keep his .44 Colt Army revolver loaded in his holster, ready to be cocked at a moment's notice.

Not long after the onset of their journey, Jack had delivered his personal view of the map.

"It's a ley line to follow," he had told Kate, "from New York, Philadelphia, Baltimore, Washington—one straight line on the flat map, specially designed, says Sawbones, by secret societies to hook up to Stonehenge and the Great Pyramid for magical powers." He had dug out his tattered map and let her study it until they began jolting along the pothole-ridden Washington and Baltimore Turnpike Road.

That was the day the stagecoach suffered a broken axle, which set their travel back a full day and a half. Exposure to two mornings and afternoons of inclement weather and one night of sleeping on the hard ground under the open sky with wolves howling in the distance had left Kate comparing convent penance to real life in untamed, war-torn America. Everything was worse than she had expected. And they had not even arrived at the hospital yet.

Despite the delays, Jack had contended that they would drive into Washington by three o' clock on Friday. He was right. The stagecoach jostled into the fledgling capital at half-past two from the northwest, travelling along the Bladensburg Turnpike Road. A host of other traffic flooded behind them—a muddy, sad, agitated tide. Union soldiers patrolled the military forts on the outskirts of the city, clad in dark-blue jackets and blue-grey trousers and kepis, with glittering muskets thrown over their shoulders.

Since the elder Sisters had declined the high seat next to the driver, the spot was irrevocably confirmed to Kate. Jack's tide of words did not recede, but she was surprised to realize she was actually tolerating it.

"Major General McClellan bucked up this town 'gainst Lee's Rebs," he said as they entered the city. "That's how come our Yankee boys are here. But even brains like McClellan can't keep out the odd Judas. Southern sympathizers show up in this town like snakes in the grass."

In the distance an imposing stone monument rose through the grey mist, towering over the mass of three-story buildings stretching out beneath it in all directions.

"Ya see that thing—away over yonder?" said Jack, pointing.

"What is it?"

"The start of an obelisk—in memory of George Washington. Wait till we get closer."

They mashed and jangled through an overgrown cow trail that served as a side street turning southwest, at last ushering them into a wide rutted street that Jack introduced as Pennsylvania Avenue. Shouting war contractors and government workers thronged the streets, and military recruiters bellowed for more enlisters to join the Federal army. Droves of loaded army ambulances rumbled along the thoroughfare, accompanied by the weeping of women and wailing of children that rose like smoke from the city square. Bright flags fluttered everywhere. Marching drums beat successively, bugles blared, and carts rumbled and rattled along, never resting.

Jack nodded toward a group of black men lounging near one of the small grocery shops. "Them darkies'll be lookin' fer a job."

"More contrabands?"

"Yep. They wanted freedom so bad, but when they get it

most Negroes don't have a clue what to do with it. Some'll likely enlist. One darkie told me he'd enlisted 'cause he banked on gettin' a bullet in the brains of his Virginny master." Jack protruded his lower lip and shook his head. "There's rumours everywhere now that Lincoln's gonna make an Emancipation Proclamation first of January—grant all slaves in any State their freedom forever. Most of the poor black folks've been treated worse'n animals, but the Good Lord gave 'em a mind to think jest like me and you. Look at ol' Sam. Ain't nobody gonna beak off and tell me that jest 'cause his skin's a few hues darker'n mine he ain't equal to a white man any day. But try tellin' *that* to some uppity white folks—there's a whole shebang of 'em are stuffin' their heads so full of those new monkey-to-man human evil-u-tion shenanigans that they're startin' to disbelieve that every man is made in the image of God. You agree, marm?"

"I believe God puts men and women where his Providence appoints them. There are times when certain human beings are put under the authority of others who hold higher standards or have greater influence for purposes we may not understand."

Jack's eyebrows rose as he uttered a half laugh, half hem. "Ya don't think slavery's downright wrong?"

"The subject of authority versus slaveholding are two different things."

"Slaveholding is authority abused. It ain't equality."

"It depends on the slaveholder. Is he cruel or kind? God-fearing or atheist?"

"Any man what puts his brother in irons, then sells or buys him like cattle at auction is cruel and atheist, plain and simple."

"I beg your pardon?"

"Makin' a man a slave ain't lovin' yer neighbour as yerself—and lovin's Biblical."

Just then a group of rowdy, poorly dressed boys romped past the stagecoach, waving their hats and flags above their heads, wildly singing,

"Mine eyes have seen the glory of the coming of the Lord;
He is trampling out the vintage where the grapes of wrath are stored;

He hath loosed the fateful lightning of His terrible swift sword:
His truth is marching on.
Glory, glory, hallelujah!
Glory, glory, hallelujah!
Glory, glory, hallelujah!
His truth is marching on!"

Jack turned to look at Kate. "Ever heard 'Battle Hymn of the Republic'? Folks sing it regular 'round these parts."

He reined in the horses to make way for a white-canvas-covered ambulance wagon pulling away from a two-story building, into which dozens of empty stretchers had been carried.

"Hey, mister!" Jack yelled out to the ambulance driver. "What's the news?"

"We've halted the Rebs' advance!" the man shouted over the din. "It's been at a hellish price, though, and we're swimmin' in a Nile of blood 'cause we ain't seen no bloodier battlefield than that cornfield and no bloodier day than Antietam!"

The ambulance rumbled away.

"Well doggie!" exclaimed Jack. "God bless our boys—we won!" He flicked the reins and resumed the pace as he tossed a piece of celebratory tobacco into his mouth.

A loud honking hubbub to the left drew Kate's attention, and she looked to see a flock of geese paddling about in murky puddles and potholes. Nearby a massive sow wallowed in a hole of stinking mire and feces, eating leftover waste from the city and grunting with satisfaction as she trained her litter of piglets to do the same. Kate suppressed the urge to gag, pressing her hand to her stomach. She would never eat pork again.

"Way back there is the Navy Yard," Jack said. "Fishermen and homeless folks live in them coves over the wharves."

Even from a distance the stench of stagnant waters, fish, and algae rose from the feebly lapping waters of the bay.

"Lookee to the west—a first-rate view of the to-be obelisk; and the Capitol opposite, in the east; and the Big House that way, to the north—yeah, that snow-white house with thick columns. See?"

They were a good deal closer to it now. Though the massive

four-sided pillar made of many stones was still under construction, the incomplete obelisk peered down at them like a giant rising from the wastelands of antiquity.

"Looks like somethin' from Egypt, don't it?"

"Egypt?" Kate wrinkled her nose, noting the homely herd of cattle dotting the pasture at the monument's base. "I've not studied Egyptian architecture."

"Me neither—jest the grapevine. I guess it was Mills's idea to copy Baal's shaft. It's pointin' right toward that gaping dome—see? Lucifer an' the roamin' demons of all them sleepin' giants have a hay-day when the rays of the sun hit that shaft an' dome jest right."

"What exactly"—Kate hemmed and straightened her posture—"do you mean?"

"Well, marm," he hemmed back modestly, "all ya gotta do is put two and two together and know that what them stone masons an' Luciferians are sayin' is too bad a picture to spell out in plain language. The whole shebang is a satanic ritual. An *a-boma-nation* of the heathens, as the Good Book puts it. When it's done, they'll cap that shaft with an Egyptian pyramid like the star on their Christmas trees. They shows it on the great seal. Only diff'rence bein' it might not have an eye in the middle of it—like the seal's got."

"Oh? An eye… in a pyramid?"

"Yeah." Jack grinned. "Ya know?"

"It is a religious symbol, known as the Eye of Providence. It's on the altar in the church."

"Hmm," he said, shrugging. "Sawbones says the Freemasons put it there. Underneath it says"—and he hemmed impressively—"NOVUS ORDO SECLORUM."

When he turned to look at her, pausing with an expectant grin, Kate realized that he must be waiting for a response, and she cleared her throat. "And, uh—the translation?" she ventured.

"It's Latin, marm," he said, looking instantly awkward. "I thought Latin was yer church language?"

"It is, but I cannot translate it."

A sideways grin disfigured his face. "Yer bluffin', right?"

"No."

Honest concern crossed his face. "If ya can't translate, how do ya know what ye're sayin' 'Yes' and 'No' and 'Amen' to in church?"

"I… don't. The priest interprets."

"Aw, well, I can't translate Latin neither, but them words mean 'New Order of the Ages.' It's a secret code of the *Illuminati*."

Kate did not have the courage to ask what that was.

His mouth twitched. "Wanna change the subject?"

Kate was straining her gaze ahead, observing the obelisk and, directly west of it, the half-dome that coronated a massive sparkling white Greco-Roman structure.

"That's the Capitol," Jack pointed out.

"The model seems reminiscent of St. Peter's Square in Rome," said Kate, noticing how the monument seemed coincidentally positioned on a straight line across from the Capitol building.

"Been to the Vatican, marm?"

"I've seen diagrams and heard first-hand accounts from Father Andrew, my priest who has travelled there himself to visit our Pope and kiss his ring."

Jack drew his head back as his eyebrows rose incredulously, and he exclaimed, "Well doggie!" with a soaring whistle. "Ya know, some call Washington the second Rome. The District and Vatican City are like twins separated by the pond, so yer… uh… priest"—he cleared his throat—"should feel right at home over here." He smirked as he contemplated the half-finished cast-iron dome and the glittering white sandstone cladding the brick of the incomplete building. "There's a makeshift army camp right inside there, if ya can believe it. Lookee—ya see them Greek-like temples yonder, and that there castle? Sawbones swears that any brick laid in this town that has any serious weight to it was laid by the Freemasons—or maybe some prehistoric folk livin' here before us—and we're doomed to firestorms."

"Firestorms?"

"Sure thing—conspiracies. They're written all over this town, marm, in the map plans, street plans, building plans—the biggest one bein' the question of how all this hefty Masonic architecture came to be hauled in and built up by us tiny folk on top of a zodiac-map in the middle of a soggy swamp—and what all of it has to do with the honest Pilgrims of the

Mayflower. Can ya tell me how'd those good Christian folks come to know 'bout these signs and symbols, and match their maps with the constellations and legends of Atlantis?"

"Atlantis?"

"Yeah. Noah's flood sunk it, so Bacon and his Freemasons are remakin' it in America. The Tower of Babel in Shinar didn't work as far as lingo goes, so thanks to that Shaker-of-the-Spear, Bacon gots his own plays, language, and stage to act out his new world with."

Kate fidgeted. "How do you know that?"

"Ya wanna know?"

Kate thought again and shook her head, knowing that Jack's questionable influence must certainly be coming, once again, through the grapevine of the notorious "ol' Sawbones."

Jack smirked. "Lookee yonder." He pointed to a magnificent red sandstone building with towering Gothic spires, turrets, and battlements. "The Smithsonian Institution there is known as The Castle. Once this war's over I reckon their scientists will commence diggin' up the bones of them giants—wouldn't surprise me none if they hid 'em on us, too."

Kate blinked. "Giants?"

"Yeah."

Kate remembered Collette's fairy tales and her childish talk of the one-eyed man-eating Cyclopes, and she hardly repressed a shudder. "You mean you… you believe in…?"

Jack threw his head back and laughed. "'Course—their mounds riddle this country."

"Mounds?"

"Sure, *mounds*—giant tombs," he said impressively. "Uncle Abe says the species of extinct giants even gazed on Niagara Falls, like we do. Ya believe in them, too, marm?"

Kate swallowed hard. "I don't… think so."

"Well, ya might change yer mind once ya hear the stories—like when the Anasazi Indians were eaten by 'em."

Kate cleared her throat as she clasped her hands more tightly in her lap. "I am sure those are merely fairy tales."

Jack shrugged. "How do we know fer sure?" he said. He kissed to the horses, whose pace had slackened, then looked ahead as though something had distracted him. "Hey! Up there, yonder's the President's House. Strikin', ain't it?"

To the north, beyond the surrounding houses and several other looming edifices, Kate caught sight of the President's House. The pillars of the white building glittered in a shaft of sunlight breaking through the canopy of clouds. A grey marsh slumped below, and beyond stood the banks that diked a great river surging along the southwest border of the town, where several anchored steamboats and sailing vessels swayed.

"Down there's Tiber Creek, the marsh," said Jack. "A space north of the President's House there's liable to be a goat's head stuck in the street plans. And that's the Potomac. And that's the Long Bridge down there—see—it crosses over into Virginny. Them steamers are carryin' wounded boys 'cause the ambulance ride hurts 'em like heck."

They passed an ugly, dilapidated saloon. From within, a loud riot of confused accordion and piano music clashed with the wild voices of drunken men. Two brazen-faced women with tangled hair, half-dressed in thin red and purple satins and straggling black lace, lolled on the front porch, casting their eyes wantonly toward the wagon as it ambled by. They looked like leeches ready to suck blood at the slightest invitation.

Kate glanced over at Jack to see if he had noticed them. The reins were gripped in his dirty, calloused hands; his hat's brim was pulled firmly, almost fiercely, over his forehead.

"They oughtta keep their eyes to themselves," he muttered under his breath. The hard-set jaw and the grim firmness that had settled over his countenance told that he would not make a second glance in the direction of the prostitutes to save his life.

"If yer out gettin' a breath o' fresh air, marm," he said once they had passed the saloon, "watch out fer them pickpockets—they're like fleas." He motioned to a knot of hungry-looking street urchins with dark rings under their eyes. "Orphans, most of 'em. Ya'll lose yer greenbacks before ya know they've got a thumb and finger in yer pocket."

"I have no money to lose," she said, looking at the huddle of miserable children. Again she felt the gnawing of the worm that had eaten her stomach by day and kept her awake by night in the cold orphanage room as a child. "But if I did," she added, "I would buy each of those children something good to eat."

Jack glanced at her, then back at the children. "Yeah," he said, jutting out his lower lip, "I bet ya would."

At last the stagecoach pulled up directly across the street from the entrance of a massive three-story-high brick structure, and the baggage wagon lumbered up behind.

"Golly!" Jack exclaimed. "Looks like we've arrived with all the excitement!"

Thirty ambulance wagons were being unloaded in front of the hospital. More surged forward. A long train of stretchers and crutches and comrades carried bodies that either writhed or stilled with deathless pain. The agonized groans of the wounded entreated the unmerciful rumble and hustle of the streets while exhausted soldiers clad in grimy tatters—their heads, arms, and legs wrapped in bandages crusted with blood—hobbled up a wide stone staircase to where several Nursing Sisters bustled about in the entrance of what looked to be a former hotel.

"Poor kid," Kate heard Jack say. She looked in the direction of his gaze and noticed a young soldier—surely no more than eighteen or nineteen years old—whose leg, amputated beneath the hip, still oozed with blood that soaked through the dirt-stained bandage covering the ghastly stump. Two comrades supported him under the arms as they made their way gradually up the hospital stairs. "Reckon it could be me someday," he muttered.

Jack stowed the driving lines beneath the seat, then leapt onto the street corner. "You gals'll have yer hands full before ya have time to catch yer breath. Lookee—Sister Bernie—at the top. Here—stay put, hey?" he said, tying the lead team to the hitching rail. "I'll talk to her."

He sprang across the street, dodging his way through the slow-moving mass of wounded, then bounded over the boardwalk and took the hospital steps three at a time. How he managed to keep his ungainly limbs from getting tied up in knots through the ordeal was a mystery, but once at the top, he successfully balanced himself and doffed his hat as he stepped toward a Nursing Sister who was giving directions to a coloured attendant. The Sister smiled a kindly welcome at him, they made their exchange, and presently Jack returned to the wagon.

"You gals follow me," he said. "Bernie says it's all hands on deck."

Kate climbed down from the high driver's bench and was tottering on the wagon wheel when she noticed the green slime below. The wagon wheels were submerged at least several inches in it.

Jack stepped up. "Need a hand?"

It would not do to vacillate now—it would only be a quick touch. She grasped his calloused hand and jumped from her perch.

"Careful," he cautioned when she released her grip and swayed unsteadily on the brink of the treacherous slime.

She dusted the front of her habit, ignoring him.

He threw open the door of the stagecoach, and the Sisters climbed stiffly out, followed by Father Andrew, who rubbed the sleep from his eyes as he wobbled precariously along the mud-plastered boardwalk.

Jack marshalled the company across the road and overcrowded sidewalk, then up the stone steps to the massive oak door. Once in the main hall of the hospital, he halted and his overgrown arms suddenly sprouted above the mob, imitating the motions of a windmill.

No sooner had he completed the demonstration when a short woman of about fifty years old appeared before them. She was dressed in a black habit and long starched white apron, and the Mercy Cross attached to the black beads of her rosary swayed from the left side of her moderate waist. She did not keep her hands concealed beneath the folds of her sleeves as was customary: her sleeves were rolled up to the elbow and her hands gesticulated freely while she spoke.

"That's Bernie," Jack whispered in Kate's ear.

"Thank you for coming, my Sisters, Father," the Sister was saying, adding a warm smile to her address. "Fresh volunteers are a welcome sight. We've been understaffed for weeks, and our fatigued Sisters here have been no match for the sea of casualties arriving from the fields of Antietam. News is that upward of nine thousand Union soldiers alone were numbered wounded on the field. I regret that I cannot be spared to show you to your quarters at the moment. I trust you are willing to set to work at once?"

A general assent was made.

"Excellent. Your trunks will be brought upstairs. You may follow me." She smiled again, causing her small eyes to disappear inside the creases of her eyelids and the uplifting of her high cheekbones, which resembled little ripe apples.

"See what I mean?" Jack whispered close to Kate's ear as they followed the older Sister. "She's nice as punch, ain't she?"

Kate felt like glaring up at him but bit her lip instead. She was trying to hear what Sister Bernice was saying and he was distracting her—and "punch" was certainly not a decent comparison for a Sister.

"You will find that we are far behind in several areas," Sister Bernice went on. "Dr. Hall has been working around the clock to keep up with the surgeries and amputations. Wounds must be washed and dressed, men undressed and properly bathed—not to mention the laundry, which is in a wretched state. Two or three of you can take over laundry while a few redress wounds and write letters. Most of the men cannot write, but it eases their minds to send letters home to their loved ones. One of you is skilled with surgeries, I understand?" Kate shifted, but Sister Bernice did not wait for a response. "Whoever that is should prepare to assist the doctor. Now, come this way, please."

Casualties were still being delivered on stretchers, but the main ward was full, and they were being packed along the walls and corners of the hallway, making it necessary for the company to walk single file down the corridor until they reached the threshold of what appeared to be the main ward.

The dense stench of waste and infection hung everywhere, and as Kate peered through the open doorway of the ward, she stifled the urge to cover her nose. The long, dim, cobweb-vaulted room was lined with occupied beds, and the dusty wooden floor was swamped with mangled bodies. Black mobs of flies swarmed and hissed above the soiled bandages strewn carelessly across the room. Some men swore, some prayed, and some cried out with voices cracked with thirst and tears, while others lay completely pale and silent as though willing themselves to be swallowed up by the blackness of their agony. Among them glided two Sisters, passing between beds, administering care, giving instructions to coloured attendants who milled about the room.

Just then, a shriek severed the air, followed by the harsh rhythmic rasping of a bone saw.

"The operating room," said Sister Bernice, pointing to the open door of a side room. A stream of blood trickled down the floorboards toward the entrance. "Dr. Hall is performing amputations. He has not had a break since he began at five o' clock this morning."

Through the open door, Kate glimpsed what looked to be two convalescent men, one white boy, and a Nursing Sister, all standing around the operating table. They were assisting the surgeon—a moderately tall, sinewy man in his thirties whose raven hair was stiff with grease. He bent over the operating table, a bone saw gripped in one hand and a bloody knife clenched between his teeth. Discoloured sleeves were shoved up past the elbow; blood lathered into the dark hair of his hands and forearms as he deftly performed a leg amputation.

The leg was quickly sawed through, and as it was caught by the assisting white boy and deposited on a growing pile of various other limbs, the surgeon straightened up and tossed the bone saw and the knife on a nearby table. Briskly wiping his soiled hands over the front of his bloodstained apron, he turned and spied the group of Sisters standing in the hall. One eyebrow arched and he clicked his tongue. He spoke a discreet word to the Sister attending him. She nodded and withdrew, and the surgeon carved his fingers through his dirty, uncombed hair as though to rid himself of thought. Then all at once he began to whistle. Kate recognized his tune as the chorus sung by the group of boys in the street. He took several quick strides forward, which brought him through the doorway and to a stop in front of them. There the whistling stopped. His scuffed, sweat-glistening high forehead contracted. He looked at Sister Bernice, then at the Sisters, then at Jack with a critical air of inspection.

"Jack! Son of a gun, you made it!" he exclaimed in a voice tinted by a southern accent.

"Howdy, Doc!" said Jack, grinning from ear to ear as he stuck out his gangly arm and wrung the doctor's hand. He didn't seem to notice that the surgeon's palm and fingernails were crusted over with days of layered uncleanliness.

"And brought our flock of Nightingales, too?" the doctor went on, rubbing his jaw of shady whiskers as Jack stepped aside to allow him to resume his inspection. "Son of a gun," he muttered with a wry smile. "Are they ready to work eighteen hours out of twenty-four?"

"Yes, Dr. Hall, these are our Nursing Sisters come from Ireland," said Sister Bernice with perfect equanimity.

Dr. Hall nodded curtly and cracked his knuckles, looking amused when he elicited a slight response of shock from the taciturn women, and then he took one step closer and scanned them. "Much obliged, Sister. I'll learn their names later. How many of you? Five, six— Ah, seven! The holy number, eh? Well, it'll take all the able hands in this establishment to succour this pathetic mob." He tossed his head in a gesture of aloofness, crossed his arms over his chest, and regarded the Sisters with a disparaging air. The rank smell of his body sweat drifted on the already-reeking air. He seemed proud of it, just as he seemed proud of his filthy hands and blood-smeared clothes and apron. Meanwhile, assistants were ushering stretchers in and out of the operating room as the next patient was prepared for surgery. "Well, who's the surgeon?" His bleared, bloodshot hazel eyes glinted and the untrimmed moustache fringing his upper lip twitched with sarcasm.

Kate was careful to avoid his judging gaze as he searched their faces. No one was answering, but she knew they were all awaiting her response.

The surgeon tapped his foot and huffed impatiently. He uncrossed his arms. "Shy, are we? Get over it. I need another assistant for a foot amputation over here. Now." He turned on his heel and walked away.

"Sister Kate?" Sister Bernice addressed her. "I have been informed that you are well-trained in assisting with surgeries?"

"Yes," Kate said. But for the first time in her life she wished despairingly that she would have studied instead to be a teacher, or a cook, or a gardener—anything but a nurse.

"Very well. Will you assist the doctor." It was an order, not a question, and she dared not resist.

"Of course. Yes."

"You may follow him into the operating room."

Kate drew breath and nodded.

"Buck up your courage, marm. Ye'll get through."

Kate looked up. Jack was smiling down at her. His voice sounded soft and kind after the doctor's grating sarcasm, and suddenly his homely, pockmarked face was something she no longer wanted to turn away from. She decided she would much rather suffer another ten-day ride in a bumpy wagon listening to his endless chatter and jarring slang than a single day working alongside a man as incalculable as Dr. Robert Hall.

"Guess I'll see ya 'round, marm." He tipped his hat to her with a sidelong glance, then turned and sauntered down the corridor.

Kate watched his lanky frame disappear through the front door. Something about him made her wish that he could stay. "Well, but there is nothing else to be done, is there?" she said to herself, then turned her face forward again, drew in a fast breath, and resolved that, should it be her scaffold of execution, she would march toward that operating room and do her duty.

Entering the operating room, she glanced around. It was illuminated by shafts of afternoon sun streaming through two cobweb-encrusted windows on the west side. In the centre of the floor, the next intended patient lay on a breast-high flat table. Around him were gathered the white boy assistant and the two convalescent men whose naked torsos and arms glistened with sweat and blood while their foreheads creased with stress above eyes that turned attentively to the doctor, watching for his direction. But the doctor ignored them as he selected several bloody knives laid out on the rough, dirty table before him.

Kate went to the table. A tattered copy of *A Manual of Military Surgery* lay open upon it. The doctor was scanning the pages of the book as he simultaneously selected his instruments.

When Kate approached, he glanced up.

"Ah, so you're the new surgeon?" He quickly looked her up and down as though determining her strength. "Looks no more than twenty-five. How's the constitution? Better not faint at the sight of blood like some of them do." He picked up a rumpled, dirty white apron and tossed it to Kate.

The fabric stank with dried blood and grime. Her stomach churned in protest, but she squeezed her eyes against it, tied the stiff apron around her waist, and vowed to launder it at the first opportunity.

"Chloroform." The doctor's voice sounded mechanical. He moved to a maple apothecary chest. The lid was thrown open, revealing an array of tinted glass bottles, cans, and tins of medicine. He retrieved a glass bottle and unceremoniously thrust it at Kate, taking a step nearer to her as he did so, and her pulse quickened as she smelled liquor on his breath. "This way," he said, seizing a single-edged amputation knife and moving briskly to the side of the operating table, muttering to the air as she followed close at his heels. "Almost surprised they let you in, Sister. But you can thank your habit for that. Superintendent Dix scours the Union for nurses, but you'd fail examination for her nursing corps—too young, too pretty, and definitely too Catholic."

A low, bitter groan from the patient on the operating table proceeded a sudden cry, followed closely by a frantic repetition of "Can you do something, Doc? For the pain? Something… Doc!"

The patient was only a boy. He had chestnut hair and freckles, and soft, dark-brown eyes.

"He's had morphine already," the doctor remarked, shaking his head. "Sonny," he said loudly as he stood over the boy, scanning his rigid body as though it were a piece of damaged furniture he was about to repair, "you're a soldier. Hold the line now."

The boy did not reply, but beads of perspiration broke out on his forehead and his pale face contorted with suffering.

Dr. Hall stepped to the edge of the table and grasped the boy's mangled foot, ignoring the boy's grimace as he deftly unbound the soiled bandage and tossed the odorous wrapping aside to reveal the grisly foot injury. "We'll make this quick work," he remarked casually as he flourished one of the knives and prepared to make the first incision.

Kate looked at him blankly, shocked by his apparent lack of concern.

He caught her expression. "You'll get used to this way, too, soon enough, little girl." A flicker of humour danced in his eyes for an instant. Then his dogged, pragmatic air returned as he turned his eyes back on his work. First instructing Kate to administer the chloroform and then ordering one of the convalescing men to hold the lad still, he struck up the whistling chorus and began the operating procedure.

— CHAPTER XII —

DEATH, AND HELL FOLLOWED WITH HIM

Near Fisher's Hill, Virginia
September 21, 1864

John squinted against the brightness of the September morning, trying to discern the delicate features of his daughter's face as he opened the polished-mahogany miniature containing her portrait. But the sunlight glared against the glass, making it impossible to discern her features. He needed to look at Priscilla, to see her eyes, her warm smile, just one more time to dispel the chill that told him he would die that day.

Snapping the miniature shut, he grasped the reins of the second lieutenant's horse and led the animal away from the group of soldiers awaiting Major General Sheridan's command to march. He stopped the mount beneath the cool shade of a mighty spreading oak tree on the side of the road. Stepping over one of the gnarled roots, he leaned up against the tree trunk, then opened the miniature. Ah, Priscilla's face… her large almond-shaped green eyes gazed back at him with a simplicity and peace that his restless heart envied.

"Howdy, Sarge! That yer sweetheart?"

John looked up as Private Gunderson swaggered up to him, a sideways grin disfiguring his ruddy, scarred face. He was chewing his tobacco cud again.

"My daughter, actually," he replied curtly. Gunderson always seemed to start his rambling at the most inopportune moments, and this was one of them.

Gunderson hemmed. “Ya got family back home, Sarge?”

“Two children. They’re away for the time being.”

Gunderson reached out and scratched the thick forelock of the lieutenant’s gelding. “Where’s that?”

“Ireland.”

“Golly—from ’cross the pond, hey?” He glanced at the new stripes on John’s sleeve. “Done pertty dern well in the army, Sarge, must say. I owe my congratulations to ya for yer promotion at Third Winchester. Bet my brass buttons ye’ll be a captain by the end of this war.”

John recalled the action of the lieutenant who, following the battle, had emerged from the smoke with a black grin, brandished his knife, and cut the stripes from the uniform of a dead sergeant, then handed them to John.

“Better you get it than that nutcase over there,” the lieutenant had said with a laugh as he jerked his chin at Gunderson. “He’s trusty, but illiteracy will keep him from rising to more than just a higher rank.”

John hoped the prestige of his new position would soon wear off the annoyance he felt at being compared to an eejit like Private Gunderson.

Gunderson’s piercing pale-blue eyes found the miniature. “Mighty pertty gal.” He leaned in. “So, when did ya immigrate?”

“About twenty years ago.”

“Live ’round these parts?”

“We homestead in Fairfax.”

Gunderson hemmed again with an interest that irritated John like an itch he could not scratch.

“What’s yer daughter’s name?”

John turned a sharp eye on him as he shut the miniature with a sound click. “You’ve got some neck, Private,” he warned. “My daughter is already spoken for.”

A look of blank surprise crossed Gunderson’s face. “Sorry, Sarge, don’t mean no harm in askin’—jest curious ’cause I knowed a nun from yer neck of the woods that… uh—” He cut himself short by clearing the phlegm in his throat.

Nettled, John returned the miniature to its place in the left breast pocket of his shirt and shoved himself away from the tree, ignoring the private's clownish expression. He glanced over at the group of soldiers falling in line along the road. Major General Sheridan was galloping up on his horse, Rienzi. Despite his small stature, Sheridan looked like an emperor atop the towering jet-black war horse. By the general's dignified, almost haughty carriage, John knew that his victory at Third Winchester two days before was not far from the man's mind. He appeared more ready than ever to seize the challenge Lieutenant General Ulysses S. Grant had put into his charge.

"Well, Private, looks like we're ready to march," John said, ensuring there was an edge to his voice that would let Gunderson know what he thought of blockheads.

"Sergeant! My horse—and get those men over here!" shouted the second lieutenant, pointing to a place behind John where ghastly successions of whoops and low chants issued. As he passed the reins over, John saw five or six soldiers crouched at the side of the road next to a muddy pothole, chanting something he could not understand.

"Whoop-whoop! Whoop-whoop!" Over and over again came the murmured mantra, disturbing in its minor key, as though it issued from the bowels of insanity.

They were scooping the miry clay into their palms, hideous expressions turning their humanness into animal passion as they slapped and plastered the mud on their necks and cheeks, uttering jeers that transformed them from fellow comrades into the bloodthirsty savages they imitated. Another soldier, standing alone on the edge of the road, quivered and panted as he practised a similar ritual, whooping and howling like a tormented beast as he painted his face with cartridge soot. But when John looked closer, he saw that the soldier was a boy, and he was crying.

"Seen it before, hey Sarge?"

It was Gunderson at his elbow.

"For three years."

"They ain't got no more compassion or remorse anymore, hey, Sarge?"

Compassion? John kicked the ground without answering. The virtue could not exist in a heart consumed with bloodlust.

Those boys were trying to dull their natural human feeling because they were sick of butchering men they could call neighbours and brothers and friends—sick of making widows and orphans with a rapidity that was as appalling as the French *la guillotine*. But somehow as he watched, reality faded out, swallowed for an instant by the grunts and grotesque, demonic sounds and movements of the men who suddenly began to fascinate him.

John Dallington did not need war paint. Remorse and regret could not weaken him. Fight sharpened his appetite, and a mob of walking Rebels waiting to be turned into bluish black corpses was enough of a spread to satiate that appetite in the same way that his body fed on its daily rations of dried beef and hardtack.

"They ain't human no more… seems," said Gunderson, wincing and crushing his kepi in his hands as he watched the men dehumanizing themselves. "Self-doubt is the dickens, Sarge. I know it. Beats the tar outta ya. Won't let ya sleep at night, neither—that's what them boys got now. Mud hides it, though."

John's eyes fixed on the mud pit. He never saw individual faces. With every man he felled he saw only one enemy. The one-man enemy whose face he saw in the face of every Confederate soldier, and whose shot he heard in every bullet that hissed past him through the din. That one-man enemy was the only enemy he knew, and his thirst for revenge the only master he obeyed.

"Boys! Fall in!" John bellowed suddenly. The men looked up at him, their eyes rolling back in their heads and the whites glistening in contrast to their fowled skin. "Fall in, you eejits! On the double!" He sensed a mounting rage taking over his senses. It was to be an eye for an eye and a tooth for a tooth this time. "We're going to outwit those Rebels and scorch the Confederate's breadbasket, aren't we?… Aren't we!"

"Yes, Sergeant!" shouted the men, each one straightening up as they abandoned their savage imitations.

"Then move it!"

The men seized their rifles and dashed up onto the sun-baked road, their full haversacks and canteens jangling as they ran.

"Company… Attention!" shouted the captain.

The men fell in line and stood like fenceposts, then gave a firm unison salute, listening attentively as General Sheridan gave his speech.

"We'll give Old Jube and his men no rest," the general said as he finished reiterating Grant's orders. "In less than two days we'll unravel Early's campaign down the Shenandoah Valley and Maryland and cut off his threat to Washington. Now! Forward… *March*!"

The company of men, in impeccable order, began their tramp along the dry dirt road, dust billowing a stifling cloud about them. John lifted his eyes. The towering heights of Fisher's Hill, the Confederate's seemingly impenetrable Gibraltar of the Shenandoah Valley, rose like a precipice before them, dwarfing Little North Mountain and Massanutten Mountain, which rolled on either side, gently melding into peaceful farms and fertile slopes that basked in the morning sunshine.

The peace of the Valley would soon be gone. Sheridan's surprise attack was only minutes away, and the general had plans to make Fisher's Hill and Third Winchester his twin victories.

John's nostrils burned with gun smoke. His own sweat was vinegar in his eyes. All around him blue and grey uniforms swarmed the clouded, blood-drenched slopes where horses and men lived like they were dead and the dead writhed like they were living.

Spirals of smoke ascended from torched houses and barns; animals dashed from flaming buildings; squirrels watched from tree branches as pigs squealed madly through the fields, pausing at length to chew on the lifeless faces of the men who had burned up their stys.

Over and over John discharged his Springfield musket, no less than three times a minute—sometimes four, if his eye and hand were quick. The rifle's wooden butt fit like a glove in the hollow of his shoulder. Squeezing the cold steel trigger and blasting the life out of Rebel after Rebel became second nature to him as his spirit grew drunk with the passion to kill. They outnumbered Early's Confederates three to one, and he would not be blamed for a lost battle.

But his ears roared and wept at once. Somehow neither the blast of musketry, nor the boom of cannons, nor the clash upon clash of countless swords and sabres could make them deaf to the screams of slaughtered men tortured in a manmade inferno where the hot sun beat down, baking and blackening the bloating, rubberized bodies of the unknown. Who could distinguish friend or foe, white man or Negro amid the human shells that littered the blood-soaked valley? And if he fell, too, then who would distinguish him?

It was time to reload. He lowered the Springfield and dove his hand into the tin-lined cartridge box at his belt. His gut twisted. Of the forty cartridges he had started out with that morning, there was only one left. Any extras he might have were out of reach in his knapsack. He tasted metal, then looked down at his hands; they were shaking, the cold sweat pulsing from his palms making the steel barrel grow slippery. Unrecognized voices shouted orders, men yelled and shrieked in terror; the buzz of hornets swarmed around his head and through his ears, stinging him. Was he losing his mind? He looked up. There! A short, grey-faced Rebel—a hundred yards away! Fifty yards—running toward him with death in his eyes! Screeching like a lunatic! His glittering bayonet slashing the air with the fury of a devil's pitchfork!

John seized the cartridge of gunpowder, bit the paper, tore it open. The bitter taste of black powder scalded his tongue. "Eejit," he gasped, pouring the powder and a mini ball down the muzzle of the barrel and shoving down the ramrod. Half-cock, and he reached for his belt, into the cap box—there! A musket cap! But his fingers were not his own as they trembled to position it in front of the hammer.

"Full cock, full cock—then fire! Eejit! Just *fire*!" he cried, pulling the hammer back. He could not breathe but somehow his vibrating arms raised the rifle, fitted it to his shoulder—

Whose voice was telling him he was already a dead man?

He stifled his breath, peered through the sight, took aim.

Steady… His right finger felt for the steel trigger. It was there, smooth and cold. He pulled the trigger back. Explosions went off around him—but where was his billow of smoke? His rifle crack?

There was the madman—still coming.

Panic gripped him. Over and over, harder and harder he yanked the trigger back, but the weapon refused to discharge. Then he remembered.

The bayonet.

He had never used it, but he would now. He reached for the black leather scabbard at his left hip and drew the weapon out. He grasped the socket in his sweaty palms, the pointed steel blade glistening in the sunlight as he affixed it to the muzzle of the rifle. It would impale his enemy. He looked up. Only ten yards separated him from the screeching red-eyed lunatic.

John rooted his feet and seized the spear. Suddenly the roar of artillery burst his ears. The ground shook and shattered beneath him with the violence of an earthquake and a smoky mass of dirt lashed his eyes and face like the barbs of a slavedriver's whip, blotting out the sun until it seemed midnight at noon. Instantly a force flung him backward, punching the breath from his lungs. He felt himself thrown through the air, then his body cast upon mangled corpses, then a shooting pang lacerate his left arm, leaving him writhing in agony.

Gunfire flew fiercely above him as he lay stunned, unable to draw breath. His chest throbbed; warm blood spurted; clotted salty liquid gathered in his mouth… Was he a drunken man now, that his head should reel like one? He groaned and drew a short breath, then rolled onto his side and pushed himself onto his knees. There was his useless bayonet attached to his useless rifle, two yards away, trampled by the feet of infantry.

"Get up!... I must, I must get… get up!" He went to stand, but his head lurched and spun, making him sick, and he staggered with no breath remaining as his body was cast back down to writhe shamefully upon the ground. He was going to die. Horror came then as his life and his sins crashed back, and he saw the great gulf fixed. Hell and the devil lusted over his guilty conscience, and they stretched forth their unclean skeletal hands from the depths of a fiery yawning chasm, saying that his unsanctified soul was rightfully theirs to lash and torment forever, and that he could not escape his punishment if he cried and begged for mercy like the rich man who entreated Lazarus to put a drop of water on his scorching tongue.

Then he remembered his children.

"O God!" he moaned and wept, looking above him into putrid clouds of dust and smoke. "If you will not have mercy on me, then have pity upon my children—give me one chance to make it right… once chance!" His head sank back onto the gory earth. Above him he saw the outlines of men with guns rushing and pounding past him, thinking nothing of him—not distinguishing him… Aye, leaving him for dead!

"Help me… Someone, help me! Please!" he gasped, straining toward the mob.

But no one heard him.

His eyelids rolled shut, and he allowed the terrorizing rumble of the battlefield to sink into the fibres of his crushed body and carry his mind away into the darkness that waited to consume him.

"Hey, Sarge!" A familiar voice sounded through the din. "Ya gotta get outta this hell hole, mister! Here!"

John forced his eyelids open and saw a lanky, broad-shouldered young man step out of the smoke and dash to his side. The left portion of the soldier's face was dripping with blood from a deep gash across his smudged, smoke-blackened forehead; but his eyes, blue and sharp as razors, were filled with life and energy. It was Private Gunderson.

Without wasting an instant, the young man bent down and lifted John from the ground. "Can ya put yer arm 'round my neck there, Sarge?" he shouted.

"I— I… yes," said John, wincing as pain shot through his system.

Gunderson pointed to a place shaded by a thick bunch of willow trees, then slung John's arm across his shoulders and retreated toward it. John glanced back just as a volley of cannons blasted through the air and blew up the very tract of ground they had deserted, creating a thunderous whirlwind of shattered debris behind them.

When they reached the shade, Gunderson lowered John onto a patch of wild grasses. He felt the private assessing his wounded arm; heard the quick lashing sound of a belt, the tearing of fabric—the private was tightly binding up his arm, making a tourniquet above his elbow. He heard the clink and slosh of a water canteen. It sounded like the promised land.

"Here, Sarge, have some."

John strained forward, desperate with thirst. He felt a hand support the back of his head and finally the open canteen reach his cracked lips. He drank greedily.

"You'll be okay here, hey, Sarge?" Gunderson said when the canteen was empty and John fell back, exhausted, to rest against a willow bush. The private straightened up and shifted the tattered haversack on his back, then lifted his blue Union kepi to scratch the unruly crop of hair that stuck out of his head like straw.

"Sure," said John, hardly suppressing a belch.

The young man grinned as he shouldered his musket, then turned around and began walking away.

John mustered his remaining strength to call out after him. "Private!"

Gunderson halted and looked back.

A lump in his throat made John gasp the words before his emotions got the better of him: "I owe you my life, son."

"Don't mention it." Gunderson's friendly eyes shamed John's former prejudice. "You'da done it fer me all the same, Sarge." He turned on his heel and faced the raging battlefield. A shift of his musket, a determined downward yank of his kepi brim, and then he broke into a run, disappearing into billows of blue smoke.

John sat propped against the willow, concealed by its screen of foliage. Was this his own body, weak and sunken with fatigue? His own mind, helpless with shock? Was that his arm that throbbed now, which only minutes ago had supported the useless bayonet and sought to impale a man? Was it really his own blood pumping from that arm gash, oozing out of the bandage and dripping onto the grass beside him?

No, it could not be possible.

— CHAPTER XIII —

A ROCK-BOUND COAST

Field hospital near Washington
Thursday, October 6, 1864

A cool breath of evening air wafted through the wall tent as the nurse opened the flap door and stepped out. That breath of air asked John to climb out of his cot and go outside despite the ache in his arm. He had been lying in the same hateful position for days, and if he was not sick from the pain, then he was sick of being cooped up like a dog in a stuffy white canvas hospital with seven other men, his nose constantly assaulted by the stench of blood, and sweat, and infection.

He flung aside the stained wool blanket covering him—pain lanced his left shoulder, and he grimaced.

Where was his opium gum?

He stood shakily. "No…no… Don't need the gum… shouldn't need the gum… I'm fine without the gum…" The blood rushed to his head. He reached out blindly, clutched the edge of his cot, and sat back down until the dizziness subsided.

After a moment he tried standing again. "Slow down," he reminded himself. "Slowly…" With his body still bent forward, he fumbled for his black goatskin-leather Bible lying next to his pillow, and from between the crinkled discoloured pages he retrieved Priscilla's latest letter, which had arrived that afternoon—just before his transfer to the General Hospital in Washington the next day. He had already delivered her bundle of linen shirts to the nurse. Her letter he would open once he had hobbled outside. But first: "Where's the gum?" he said again, and in blind desperation his throbbing arm forced his other hand to fumble in the haversack for the tin of opium. "Just a piece," he muttered, groping through the cluttered sack. "Field doc gave it for the pain, and that's all we take it for… The pain… Yes, yes, only… only for the pain…"

Ah, there it was! The little round tin. The pieces rattled inside as his shaking hand clawed the lid off. A piece or two fell out—no matter. He found another piece and rushed it to his mouth. There—no one saw it. But it was the taste of pleasure. Just put the tin back now, in the knapsack—there. He would get up and go outside now.

The tent was relatively quiet. Most of the other patients were asleep or dozing, and the doctor and nurses were performing an operation in one of the other two nearby wall tents that made up the regiment's field hospital. Picking his way through the narrow row between cots, John made for the flap door, threw it back, and stepped out from under the fly into the open air. Warm wind lapped against the back of his neck and rippled deliciously through his matted, unwashed hair, imitating the sense and motion of the water that hadn't cleansed it for weeks. He avoided the thought of his overgrown beard. It hadn't been touched by a razor since the day before Fisher's Hill, and he would doubtless look a stranger to his own children.

He breathed deeply of the cool air. The tinge of smoke still hung in it as a result of Sheridan's scorched earth fires all the way up the Shenandoah Valley—but it was nothing compared to the rancid smells of the tent. After Sheridan's army had taken the Valley's Gibraltar, John heard they had lost no time in executing the general's plan to destroy the Confederates' major food supply. All along the Valley, farms were sacked, their barns and mills and crops burned, animals slaughtered. Beyond where a log farmhouse and red barn stood out against a clump of trees, he could still see spires of black smoke rising from the devastated Valley as Sheridan's famous burning of Rebel provender continued. Yet, despite a decided Union victory and a hearty post-battle pursuit of the Confederates, it was obvious that the cunning Old Jube had once again slipped through their fingers.

John's bleared eyes swept the green meadow just outside the tent. White and black sheep grazed moderate pasture; distant bleating and the tinkling of brass bells comforted his strained ears and made him think of her… Cassandra, whose tender, innocent face leaned toward him through the weeping mists of years, yearning for him, not letting him go, reaching for him as though for mercy.

But why must his mind wander?

He shifted on his feet and stepped a pace or two farther from the tent, his eyes tracing the path of the aimless spires of smoke. Betrayal could not extinguish the longing, nor kill the passion he still felt for the woman whose heart had been a fetter to his own. He was only eighteen years old when it began; she, scarcely sixteen…

The time is half-past seven in the morning; the weather is clear and bright, the air fresh and moist with dew. It is the day of the shearing festival, and he and Geoffrey have just arrived at the Fletcher family's homestead.

Approaching them is Mr. Fletcher, the most prosperous sheep farmer in the area. He has been an informal acquaintance for several years and is known as the most amiable Roman Catholic man in the village area. Phlegmatic and kind, he prefers peaceful silence to religious debate, for Presbyterian neighbours are better friends than enemies, he believes.

"Shearing starts at nine, my lads, when the sun has dried the fleeces," says the smiling sheep farmer as he grasps their hands in welcome. He is a head shorter than John. "But ye can put the sheep into paddocks behind the barn and sharpen yer shears before the job commences."

At once John's eyes are distracted. A waif-like figure is emerging from the barn. It is a lass, clad in a bulky gingham shirt tucked into a sack-like pair of men's trousers cinched with a frayed piece of rope; her face is small, shaded by a wide-brimmed, blue-ribboned straw hat.

"John, Geoffrey," says Mr. Fletcher as the waif-lass comes

toward them, "this is my daughter Cass."

She nods cordially and smiles. It is a free smile, and the morning dew sparkles in her eyes.

At nine o' clock the men set to shearing with lusty vigour. And so does the lass—indeed, she can shear a sheep as fast as any man. Seven o' clock, and the job is complete, and the troop of shearers gather on the front lawn of the farmhouse to feast upon the spread prepared for them on the long hardwood table. They eat, and drink, and jest, and laugh together, and at last the sun goes down, leaving the air mild and dusky.

"Cass, will you sing for us?" says Mr. Fletcher, tasting his wine.

The waif-lass smiles sweetly; she rises from her seat next to her father. Evening shadows contrast her slender figure, now wrapped in a gauzy pink gown and encircled at the tiny waist by a soft cream sash, all poured upon by cascades of shining golden tresses.

John expects an Irish ballad, but instead she sings "Scarborough Fair."

A moment passes; he feels his soul rest in the soft sea of her violet eyes, and then all at once the guests are wildly applauding. Can it be the end? Can heaven itself have descended with her voice and left him enchanted, oblivious of time?

The lass receives the praise blushingly. She bids them all good night. She smiles at him—yes, she smiles at *him*—and then retires into the house.

Two years come and go… almost two years. Long years. John forgets about the waif-lass, for his parents die of disease, and Augusta deserts the homestead, and he prepares to assume the role of Presbyterian minister in the local parish in place of the late Peter Dallington. But then Geoffrey returns from England and taunts him, and somehow, a month before John's twentieth birthday, he receives permission from Mr. Fletcher to request his daughter's hand in marriage. Aye, she is shy—the pretty little waif-lass. But John knows she loves him implicitly, for she assures him that she was waiting for him.

The wedding is small but joyous, celebrated in the month of June. Cassandra's little sister, Feena, is the maid of honour;

Geoffrey is the best man. John's savings have purchased a simple ring for Cassandra, and his own tools have inscribed her initials on the inside of the gold band. It matters not that she is a Papist and he a Calvinist. The Presbytery may complain that they are unequally yoked, but Cassandra has vowed to love, honour, and obey him until death. And for John, that promise is sufficient.

There is no honeymoon, for they have no means. But there is a moss-encrusted thatched-roof cottage that has been carefully prepared for the waif-lass. A poor man's house, perhaps—but love may enchant it and turn it into a castle.

Love does enchant it, for a time. But then there is a day when John comes in late from the fields, and he is sweaty and hungry, and he is thirsty for her kisses that wait for him…

But she is not there.

The taste of opium on John's tongue drew him back to the present. He bit the inner corner of his cheek until a welt formed—he would think of it no longer. At any rate, there was Priscilla's letter to read, and daylight was fading fast.

Breaking the seal on the delicate envelope, he unfolded her customary rose-petal-scented paper and read the familiar Spencerian script:

Sunday, September 18, 1864

My dearest Papa,

I hope my letter finds you in good spirits. I pray to God every night that he will keep you safe, and that we will all come together soon.

Strange things have happened since I last wrote to you, and if it does not weary you to read about them, I will make this letter their chronicle.

It began two Fridays ago.

A dreadful rain and thunderstorm raged outside. All of us huddled around the glowing hearth in the front room. Peter perused his floor map, Auntie nested and chomped her vinegar pickles, Ellen knitted, and I sewed. A loud rapping at the door startled us. Ellen went to the door and opened it. A tall young woman in a wine-red cape stood there, and a child with golden curls was clinging to her.

I gawked stupidly for a moment. Without asking Aunt Augusta's permission, Ellen pulled the strangers in out of the downpour and slammed the door. There they stood, shivering and dripping on the front mat, hems and boots tarred with gumbo, them staring at us and us staring at them as though we had been from opposite worlds. The fire crackled, the old clock ticked, and the rain pelted against the glass windows—the only voices bold enough to speak.

What happened next is worth telling.

As the woman scanned the room, I felt her wild, fierce, black-painted eyes take hold on me. Suddenly she loosed herself from her child's grasp and threw back her wine-red hood to reveal a stunning cascade of damp strawberry-golden tresses swept back from a high, smooth, polished forehead. The loose hair shimmered and shone in the firelight, some of it tangled in her gem-encrusted earrings, some clinging to the sides of her ivory throat, where a pretty chain necklace and gold charm was fastened.

An instant later, propelled by one swift, unguarded impulse, she stretched forth her trembling arms and rushed upon me. Her face was at once beautiful and terrible. Her eyes, shadowed with green and sapphire powder and smoky paint, frightened me. Her cheeks were rouged, also. I felt her squeeze my hands in her icy fingers; I heard her gasp in short, impassioned accents as she stared into my face, her eyes like blue flames as she cried in a mild French accent, "Oh! C'est possible?" She waited for me to answer.

I stood stock-still, and stammered out my name, and attempted to extricate myself from her grasp.

She dropped her hands. "Oh, very sorry, mademoiselle," she said, then stepped back to her poor boy, who was shivering in the middle of a sad little puddle.

I asked the young woman if she would take a seat?

"No, merci, just the fire— I mean, may we dry off by the fire?" she returned.

Ellen fetched two quilts and made them comfortable by the warm hearth while Aunt Augusta began her squawking.

"Are ye sure ye won't sit down?" Auntie said, prickly as ever and looking down her nose. "We have chairs—in case ye didn't notice them!"

I thought the young woman would reconsider, but I think one look at Auntie resolved her decision to remain standing.

"Well then," Aunt Augusta whined, "I suppose you want something to eat? The child looks half starved! Do you even feed him anything? Will he drink warm milk and honey?"

The poor child shrank from the prickles and buried himself in his mother's skirts, then began to cry.

"Come, come—the child must eat!"

"Oh, yes— I mean," faltered the young woman, "very nice… The honey milk, merci."

"Ye could use some, too, lass, by the looks of ye. Ye're as skinny as a picket in the garden fence! What do ye live on—carrots?"

I nearly fainted with horror.

Auntie clucked and poked at Ellen, who was observing the little boy warming himself on the hearth.

"Ellen!" Auntie snapped. "The milk would get here faster if ye put it in a mug and carried it here, no?"

Ellen bustled away while Auntie scolded me and asked if, for the look on my face, I had just seen a murder.

Five minutes and Ellen returned with two steaming mugs that were gratefully received. The little boy looked all of a cherub with his milk moustache and his round face all rosy.

"Lass, where've ye come from?" Auntie asked flatly.

"Paris," returned the young woman.

Auntie's eyes plucked at her. "Paris? How's that?"

"I'm running away."

"Running away?"

"More or less, yes."

"And just who are ye running from?"

The young woman looked down. "From the father of my child."

"Yer husband?"

"No. My employer."

"Ye're not wedded to the fella, then, lass?" said Auntie, meaning that such a thing was the unpardonable sin.

"I am not."

A horrible silence came. Ellen and I exchanged glances, both embarrassed by Auntie's harshness. But before we could find something to say, Auntie did her cluck, and if her nose had been a little yellow beak, she would have peered down it. "What's wrong with the gentleman?"

"He is no gentleman. He intended to send my son to a French convent and then…" But she faltered.

"And then what?" Auntie pecked.

"And then finish using me," the woman blurted out.

Auntie's eyes popped. "And ye ran?"

The young woman nodded.

"And… where to?"

Only her silence answered.

Again, the hen-cluck. "Ye must have relations in these parts, no?"

"Family?" she said wearily. "I don't know."

"Don't know?" said Auntie. "And yet ye come searching for them nevertheless? Well ye must find out!"

"So I am here."

The young woman's voice was so calm that it made me shudder.

"Were ye born here, lass?"

"I was."

"Where?"

"In the asylum."

I heard a gasp and looked to see Ellen's palm come quickly up to cover her mouth while Auntie laid a golden egg.

"The Magdalene Asylum?" Auntie squawked.

"Yes. Then I entered a convent before I was twenty."

"A convent yet—even after that first workhouse?"

"Oddly enough, yes." She smiled a bitter smile. "I am coming back now because I'm—" She stopped short.

Auntie stroked Rufus until he squirmed. "Because ye're what?"

"Because I'm searching."

"For someone?"

She paused. "Among other things, yes."

"Looking in a convent, I assume?"

She nodded.

"Even if ye know which convent, lass, ye'll have to count on luck to find yer needle in that *haystack."*

"And if luck doesn't find me, I will still keep looking till I find it."

"Ye'll be grey by then, lass."

"Then I shall be grey, and happy."

This time Auntie laid two golden eggs, and the woman looked back at her calmly.

"I would like to find lodging while I am in Ireland," she said. "Perhaps you have room for me here? I have money and will gladly pay board for my son and I." Here she drew from within the wine-red cloak a rectangular leather wallet and opened it to reveal several bank notes, which she held out.

One look at the money stash was enough for Auntie. "To stay with us?" she clucked.

"If it is not too much trouble for you? It seems you are in a decent location from which I may easily branch out my search. It would be for only a fortnight, or perhaps two, depending on my luck," she added with a faint twinkle.

I'm sure to Auntie's eyes the bank notes looked like fat kernels of yellow corn. "We have a room upstairs," she cooed, and it was settled.

And so it has happened. Every day she goes outdoors, scouring the towns and villages and inquiring at Roman Catholic churches and convents. Occasionally she takes her little boy "Willie" but most often goes alone. She often comes home late at night, when all but Ellen are tucked away in bed. Ellen insists on sitting up to wait for her, never mind if it's midnight.

Sometimes I look out from my window at dusk and see her cloaked figure roaming the purple hills as the glowing sun dips into the sea behind them.

Tonight while we were sewing (she has joined Ellen and me in sewing shirts for the war relief effort), she told me that she has booked steamship passages to New York for her and Willie. Auntie flew off the handle when she heard.

"The United States of America?" she squawked, arms flapping. "It's an inferno hissing with gunfire and twelve-pound cannonballs!"

Collette—for that is her name—said she was not afraid. Not going, she said, would be worse than the risk. She had learned that a company of Nursing Sisters had departed there from Ireland, and she would follow them.

And so you see, dear Papa, what a strange time we've had. If any story is tragic, poor Collette's is. Ellen and I pray for her every night. Will you, too, Papa? I long to reach her, but she despises pity, and is bitter against God. She is like a broken water pitcher—empty and parched, with nothing to give and no heart to be filled.

But, as expected, I have written you a longer letter than usual, so I will bid you adieu. Please write back soon if you can.

I remain, as always, your most affectionate daughter,

Priscilla Dallington

P.S: I hear that Miss Barton was granted approval by President Lincoln to open the Office of Missing Soldiers, and that she is now travelling with the Union army as a battlefield nurse. They are calling her the "Angel of the Battlefield." Perhaps she has visited your regiment, and you have seen her? I hope this small contribution to her supply drives can be of help (the shirts, as usual, I trust will be delivered to her relief efforts wherever you are stationed.)

John lifted his eyes from the elegant calligraphy. His arm throbbed; the aftertaste of opium embittered his tongue; his chest tightened against the drilling thorn that said he was worse than an infidel.

Dusk had settled and a restless east wind ruffled the delicately scented pages, contradicting the stench of death and disease ushering from the hospital tent.

"Sergeant Dallington?" It was the orderly voice of the volunteer nurse calling behind him from the door of the wall tent. "Sir? Time to retire, sir. It is late."

He jammed the letter into the envelope, tearing a corner of the paper as he did so. He would trade all his limbs if it would get rid of the throb of that thorn. Slumping over, he turned and walked across the trampled grasses, already wet with evening dew. The oil lamp inside the tent was lit, and the white canvas glowed like a massive lantern against the gathering shadows.

He stepped under the canvas flap and waded through the cots toward his own. After depositing the envelope in his Bible, he tossed the battered volume on his haversack, realizing he had broken into a sweat. He grabbed the tin of gum, clawed it open again, stole a piece. Easing himself onto the cot, he stretched out and braced himself. He could close his eyes but he could not close his mind, and rest for his body was as far away as peace was to his soul…

Tired and hungry from a long day's work in the fields, he enters the thatched-roof farmhouse and walks up the narrow stairway to their bedroom. He reaches out and feels the icy heat of the doorknob. He is turning it, pulling it, wrenching it, shaking it for the millionth time.

But the door stands there, mocking him.

— CHAPTER XIV —

AT THE POTOMAC

Hall General Hospital
Thursday, October 6, 1864

It was just past nine o' clock in the evening. Rain drummed on the roof and water gushed down the swollen gutters like a bitter tide running away from itself. From her position at the second-floor window of the Third Ward, Kate pressed her aching forehead against the cool, foggy, dust-etched windowpanes and looked out into the narrow streets. They were deserted. Only one feeble glimmer of lamplight struggled out from behind a tightly closed shutter.

The recent summer in Washington had been worse than the first—almost unbearable. Enduring a third such summer was an insufferable thought. The reprieve brought on by rain would last but moments. Although sighs of relief went up following the abatement of the July and August suns and the spectres of infection and disease dissipated with the sweltering heat, close on the heels of the mosquito mobs and malaria came winter's bleak cold months, biting winds, and driving snows that left plagues of famine, scurvy, and monotony in their wake. Already, three of the seven Sisters of their company from St. Agnes had died of either typhoid fever or pneumonia, and malnutrition and death would once again visit the drafty halls, sniffing the heels of the wounded, the convalescent, and the medic.

Kate pushed away from the window, sweeping the side of her hand across the dust-laden windowsill. Dead flies and moths rustled as they piled up along one end of the ledge.

She looked at her palm, all covered in shrivelled insect wings and velvety grey matter. She rubbed them between her fingertips. Flies and dust were common in all the wards. There were too many men to nurse, too many letters to write, and too much laundry to wash to even think of keeping up with tasks as insignificant as swatting flies and cleaning windowsills.

She wiped her hand across the front skirt of her habit. What did it matter that she got it dirty? It hadn't been laundered in almost two weeks, and it stunk with her own odour and the smells of the gangrenous leg amputation they had performed that afternoon.

"Might as well wipe it all off," she said, "no one else will clean it." She swept her right arm across the sill and watched the billow of dust float to the floorboards. The rank odour of urine steamed from a nearby bedpan, reminding her that it still needed to be emptied.

"Sister Kate?"

It was Sister Bernice's voice, accompanied by the glimmer of a lantern as she approached to relieve her from duty.

She hid her dirty arm behind her back as she turned to acknowledge the Sister with a nod.

Sister Bernice smiled kindly. "You look weary, dear. I shall relieve you now."

Kate murmured a thank-you, making an effort to square her slumped shoulders, but she felt so tired. She motioned to the pile of dust and insects littering the floor beneath the window. "But the floor here needs sweeping before I leave—the bedpan is full also." She started to move toward the black cast-iron stove on the opposite side of the room, her eyes fixed on the broom resting against the back wall.

"I can take care of the sweeping, dear. Don't fret."

"No, no—I can do it," said Kate, eyeing the long broomstick wearily as her fingers closed over the familiar rough handle. Sister Bernice needn't clean up her mess.

"Dr. Hall is concerned about you. He told me to ensure you get more rest."

Kate's pulse quickened in her throat. Dr. Hall might have polite and studied manners when he wanted to, but with his sporadic drinking habits and a temper to match, he had no business worrying about how much sleep she was getting.

"I'm fine," she said, clenching her jaw at the memory of how he had watched her at breakfast that morning. His look had confused and frightened her. "Three hours a night is sufficient for me." But she still thought of how he had bragged about her to the other doctors who had come to work in the hospital during the rush of casualties from Gettysburg. He had declared that she was the most competent and attentive aide he had worked with. He had said that she would be fit to perform amputations without his supervision by the end of the war.

"Embarrassing flattery," she said under her breath, returning to the pile of dust. Though Dr. Hall was envied by his colleagues for his personal adeptness and skillful techniques as a physician, she would never flatter him back by alluding to such things.

"Really, dear, it is not much to sweep up, merely a little pile," Sister Bernice was saying in her soft tone. "Here, I will take the broom. You go to bed, please, dear? Take the lantern with you"—she placed it on the desk—"I need only the candle."

Kate decided not to argue, though she reluctantly handed over the broomstick before stooping for the bedpan. She emptied it and returned the bedpan to its place, carelessly wiping her hand dry on the skirt of her habit, which was wet from the lukewarm liquid that had dripped down the side of the tin. Then she took the lantern and moved down the long ward to the exit. Outside the ward, the corridor was dark and silent. Dragging herself to the base of the stairs, she climbed the winding ascent, pausing every three steps to catch her breath, wondering why her heart was palpitating in her throat. At the third story she paused in the vaulted gable before the door that led to the room she shared with Sister Anna-Maria. Her roommate was easily wakened by even the slightest noise—unlike Collette, who could sleep through a storm.

But she was not supposed to remember Collette.

Softly, Kate opened the door and peered within. The lantern light swayed eerily across the wooden walls of the small room.

One of the two low beds positioned against the back wall was rumbling and bulging with Sister Anna-Maria's frame. Kate tiptoed into the chamber and closed the door softly behind her, then glided to the washstand next to the east gable window and set the lantern on the wooden desk beside it. The least she needed to do before crawling into bed was wash the grainy windowsill and urine residues from her hands. Expecting to hear the slosh of water as she pulled the pitcher toward her, her grip tightened around the handle when she found it dry.

"She did not refill it," Kate muttered, her jaw tightening as she cast a glare at the occupied bed, from which a heavy snore issued in response.

Holding the jug and lantern, she retreated from the room and descended the staircase. The nearest freshwater was in the rainwater butt outside the back door of the kitchen. As she passed down the shadowy hall, she shuddered… was she back in the cold stone orphanage building, wandering the remote passageways and staircases?

Searching for something to eat?

The distant crowd of voices from the girls at the orphanage echoed through the crypts of memory: "Below the kitchen there is a frightfully dark cellar. Sister Emma-Margaret said that a hungry old rat lives down there, and he eats little girls who have sinful thoughts and say nasty things about the priests and nuns."

When Kate would lie awake at night, she used to imagine that she could hear the rat scuttling across the floor, searching for the bad little girls who were asleep in their beds. But how was it that the old rat had never discovered her bed? Surely her sinful thoughts ought to have rendered her flesh the rodent's dinner long before she had left the asylum.

Now she was at the kitchen threshold. Now she was smelling the buttery, spicy smell of baked apples and cinnamon. The sweetness was intoxicating. The cook must have baked pies with the bag of apples donated by one of the local farmers. Apple pie was her favourite, but she had not touched it since being at the convent… since the night that her aching belly had forced her to raid the larder at midnight.

She crossed the room and saw the storm-tossed moonlight illuminating three pies with flaky, delicately carved crusts and tops dusted with cinnamon and sugar. Her mouth watered as the old cravings returned. She took a step nearer and set the lantern on the counter, extending her hand that trembled—was it with fear or hunger? A knot tightened in her belly and she swallowed hard, yet she could not stop herself from breaking off a piece of buttery, marbled crust and bringing it to her mouth. But as she lifted her hand, nausea and a cold sweat made her shiver. She saw herself crouched in the shadows of the convent larder, devouring pie after pie, possessed with an insatiable, animal-like hunger. Had anyone discovered who stole those fresh apple pies? She had confessed her thievery to no one—not even the priest—and had never been able to shake the sense that hidden eyes had been watching her through the darkness. Despite not having eaten for days before that night, and not for a week after, the lump from those larder pies still felt like a rock in the pit of her stomach, indigestible even after years of feeling hungry.

Footsteps startled her. Did she hear breathing from the shadows? The scuttle of a rat in the cellar? She grabbed the lantern and wheeled around, searching the darkness. The only movement was the swaying lantern light glinting off the discoloured floral wallpaper; the only sound her own rapid, shallow, unnatural breathing.

Her eyes went to the piece of crust suspended between her fingers. Her palms were still filthy, smudged with fly wings and windowsill dust and carrying the touch of the rank bedpan—just as her mind carried the stench of an evil conscience. She had been taught never to eat with unwashed hands, and yet here she was, with not only unclean hands but a habit soiled and stinking, a mouth ready to bolt a piece of pie, and a heart ready to break one of the ten commandments.

Again she looked upon her hand, and a heavy wish to cut it off forced her fingers to loose their grip and let the crust fall to the floor at her feet. Deserting the lantern on the counter, she walked away, loathing her weakness to steal a second glance at the forbidden pie.

A numbness crept into her limbs. "When will I be satisfied?" she asked, then wrenched the back door open. It rebelled against her as it screeched loudly on its rusty hinges. Outside was dark and shadow, for the moon had become shrouded by heavy clouds. The downpour had abated to a misty rain, leaving the air damp and chill.

Her eyes sought the water butt on the left side of the porch beneath the eaves and she exclaimed. It was on its side next to a muddy hole dug into the clay, pushed over by the force of the rainwater that had gushed from the high, overflowing eaves. A sad dribble of freshwater trickled from the butt's spout and down the narrow trench into the filthy gutters. There it mingled with the green sludge that issued from the street corners, none of it fit to touch, let alone wash with.

The wastefulness made her feel like kicking the offending cask. "Water... clean water, it's all I need," she groaned, pressing her hand to her forehead and scraping it down her face. "I need to wash—I'll feel better if I can wash... wash in clean water... Yes, clean, clean water, somehow. Oh, somehow."

Then a vision of the Potomac flashed in her mind. Yes, of course—the rainwater ran down to the river. And the river was not far from the hospital... not far at all. She could walk there, within minutes, and bring her pitcher with her.

She stepped over a jagged rut and crossed the lonely street, the skirt of her habit trailing along in the murky waters, becoming heavy as she moved in the direction of the marketplace square. It was the square she could see from the window of her ward, where recruitment officers seemed daily to be rallying more troops to join the army—more troops to be slaughtered. More wounded to fill the hospitals. More bloody limbs to amputate, and letters to write, and deaths to watch.

On the outskirts of the square, she paused by the gutter beneath the shadow of a three-story boarding house. She stole a quick glance behind her. Silhouetted rows of wooden buildings hemmed the eastern skyline, dwarfed by the one great shadow that had—when she had first arrived in Washington—been the gaping, skeletal cast-iron form above the Capitol but was now the completed ellipsoidal dome that towered above rutted thoroughfares and trembling houses, embarrassing their homely, shanty-like designs by its imposing architectural brilliance.

Turning her eyes westward again as she moved on, she drew breath and smelled the reeking stench of death and human waste. Her eyes went to the ditch, and her stomach turned. There on her right, drifting half submerged in the thick ooze of the swelling gutter was a dead cat, and with it several long-haired forms that looked like the corpses of other domestic animals. She backed away, expecting to vomit.

The drizzle turned icier and heavier, angling itself southward with the bite of a cold north wind. A long line of living quarters stretched along the southern edge of the square, and from the lowest window of the final apartment, a feeble glimmer of yellow lamplight squeezed through a broken shutter, casting its shy reflection in one of the innumerable puddles littering the wide, rutted street outside.

It must have been the light she had seen from the hospital window.

Hasted by an urge to run, she darted across the square, then kept close to the shade offered by the buildings as she wandered a maze of streets and intersecting avenues. The back alleys, she had heard, were riddled with hoodlums, and despite the efforts of Union guards to patrol the main streets, criminal activity in the city was uncontrollable. If the patrol men saw her, they might shoot her like they would a common suspect. But worse even than patrol men and their guns were the demons that she could never hide from—that followed her now just like they always had. They thronged and pressed her and stalked her and said she was poor and frail, that her mind was polluted, that she was unfriendly and friendless. A mistake. That she was already a fallen woman.

The rain continued. The wind grew more bitter, sighing darkly through the hollow streets. She wished she had brought a cloak to wrap around her stiffening shoulders. But then rawness gnawed at her heart, and it said that even if she had the greatest cloak in all the world, it would not be great enough to hide the sins she carried.

Increasing her pace again, she turned a corner and glanced

back. A low, dark, lumbering shape caught her eye. It was creeping toward her along one side of the narrow thoroughfare, drawing nearer and nearer. Hair pricked the nape of her neck.

It was a shaggy old hound dog.

The great animal was dripping with condensation. It whined, then barked feebly. Kate hissed, attempting to drive it away. It kept coming. She waved her arms, she threw a stone, but it came on and on. After turning several corners, she looked back to see the dog pause in front of a puddle in a low corner of the street. The creature whined miserably, tilting his head to one side and fixing his sad large eyes on her as though to ask why he could not follow.

Finally she gained the outskirts of the city and vaguely saw the surging waters of the wide river as it passed beneath the Long Bridge, which joined the road into Virginia. She looked behind her and groaned, for there was the worthless tramp, still ambling along behind her.

She crouched down, picked up three stones, and threw them at the dog. It flinched back. She threw a fourth, then a fifth. But it kept coming, nearer and nearer until finally it was only a step away, and she could hear its breathing. She could have reached out and touched it.

"Get away from me, you stupid animal—get!" she said, stopping short.

The animal looked up at her with deep, sad eyes and tilted his head to the side.

"I said *get*!" Kate drew back her foot suddenly and kicked the animal in the soft area of its flank.

The dog moved back a step; it whined—almost sobbed, it seemed—as it looked at her with its sad eyes, asking why.

"I don't want you here, you ugly beast!" She clenched her fists as tears of anger and contrition burned her eyes at once. "Can't you see that?"

To Kate's surprise, the animal lay down on its belly in the middle of the muddy road, his massive head close to the ground between his great shaggy paws. And he groaned piteously.

Kate started—was that the tramp of horse hooves? The rumble of wheels? The shouts of a driver in the distance?

"Someone is coming!" she gasped, spinning around and looking. There, on the opposite side of the Long Bridge, the dim light of two swaying lanterns was rapidly approaching. Soon a hackney coach appeared, rattling as it raced through the slate-grey mists toward her.

Clenching the empty water pitcher, she fled down the slippery bank on the left side of the bridge. Suddenly her foot wedged inside a narrow gorge, and before she could keep herself from falling, the other foot slipped on a greasy section of ground. She sprawled face down into the mire, clay smearing her eyes and pain shooting through her lodged ankle as it twisted with the full weight of her body coming down upon it. The sound of shattering pottery mingled overhead with the thunder of horses, the rushing of wheels, the rattling of a carriage, all of it growing louder, pounding in her ears like a freight train coming straight toward her.

"Oh! They'll see me! They'll see me!" she cried frantically. "I can't let them see me!"

Floundering blindly, she tried to lift herself into a sitting position, but as she raised herself only inches from the ground, a leaden weight pulled her down like a magnet; her arms had no more strength left in them, and she fell back, wallowing. Tears cooled her hot cheeks but could not rinse away the grit scraping her eyelids as she looked down at her habit, drenched with rain and mud, and then at her sludge-blackened hands that were too weak to lift her body from the slime sucking her downward.

"Liars don't get into heaven!... Hypocrites are liars! Aren't I a liar? A liar and a thief? Oh!" she sobbed, her brain swarming as though infested with flies. "I cut off Collette's beautiful hair—stole it! And I stole those apple pies, too—filthy thief and gluttonous hypocrite that I am—I shall never make my heart as holy as my body looks!"

Her ears roared and screamed at her; it seemed lice crawled through her scalp and ate up her flesh as visions red with the fire of damnation surrounded her, scorching her brain, ravishing her senses with sickening lust. "Oh, someone help me!" she wept, clutching her head as she choked on a burst of tears.

"I have a name, but who am I? *Who am I?* Oh, it's no use! No use, trying to be clean when there is no water pure enough to wash away the stain!"

Her gaze wandered until it fixated upon the river. The brink of the fast-flowing dark current was only a yard away from where she had fallen in the shadow of the bridge. Had her foot not caught in the hole, she might easily have slid into it and drowned.

The black waters rolled and swelled like a living creature overturning in its sleep, the current flowing onward, always onward, as though pulled by an invisible force. She watched, holding her breath, gazing into the depths, mesmerized by what seemed to be a beast beckoning her to draw closer and look deeper. Then a strange sensation came over her: a terrible calmness, a realization both dreadful and possessive seemed to entwine itself about her like the smooth, scaly body of a python.

Escape… it was only two steps away.

She shivered, as she had shivered many times during the last hour. But this time it was not with the pain of her throbbing ankle, nor the icy dampness clinging to her bones, nor even the familiar stab of hunger.

Not caring about how the drenched fabric of her habit and veil dragged along in the mud, and just accepting that her already-ugly face was spattered with dirt and her arms and hands and legs and feet coated with the disgusting muck, she slid herself farther down the slope until her feet almost dangled over the edge, and she strained forward, willing herself ever closer to the threshold of the swirling, watery abyss…

She was a lying, thieving, covetous child of an adulteress woman—unworthy of happiness, unworthy of love, her heart crusted over with the excrement of sin that no water from a pitiful little pitcher could ever wash away. An eternity in heaven was only for people better than her. She wasn't good enough, or sinless enough, or loved enough to be noticed by God—she did not even know who God was. And, unlike rich people, she could not even buy her way into heaven because she had not a shilling in all the world. She envied the dead already.

They had escaped a miserable, seemingly endless existence. Were not their minds silenced now? If she were gone like them, no one would miss her; certainly no one would. She was one among the masses. One among countless women who could perform her task as competently as she could.

"Why didn't I listen to this feeling before?" she whispered, but tears were falling from her cheeks, and she was afraid.

Her head spun in circles; her heart beat wildly against her bosom; her eyes widened as macabre fascination slew reason with an overpowering blow; and her icy, trembling lips began to part in expectation as though she would invite the horrible rushing deep to swallow her up.

"Hallo!"

She started. Was someone calling her? She looked up. Was it a light?

"Hallo? Dat you dere, Sista?"

The man's voice seemed familiar, but the roar of the water and the vertigo in her head distorted recognition.

"You okay, Sista?"

The voice was louder this time, and the light was swaying, moving down the bank toward her.

Kate struggled to push herself to her feet. She staggered, for her feet were caught in the hem of her garment. She tried to release them but fell forward… forward… the mud would receive her in an instant…

But there was no mud in that spot. There were strong arms, for she felt them catch her under her shoulders, and as her body came into contact with a warm, muscular frame she heard a kind voice say above her head, "It was you, Sista! I knowed it when I seen dat lantern on da kitchen counta. Thank da good Lor' he send me out ta find ya. Lor' love ya, poor lamb! You's half-dead!"

"Sam?" she whispered, her body going limp as he swept her up into his arms and held her close like a child.

In a trance, she felt his gentle touch wiping away the mud and tears from her eyes, sensed him carrying her up the sodden edge of the riverbank, his chest ebbing and rising like a comforting tide beneath her head as it rested near his heart. When they reached the top and paused on the side of the road, Kate's eyes fluttered open, and she remembered the coach.

The vehicle was nowhere in sight. But as she peered deeper into the bleakness, she caught sight of a dark heap lying two yards away on the margin of the road. Again she looked, and as she looked, she gasped as she remembered.

Cast aside like a miserable pile of debris, the hound dog lay submerged in the thick mire with a pool of crimson gathering around its matted, mud-splattered skull. Only minutes before she had been stoning it away with heartless contempt, despising its persistence. She had even kicked it. Yet the peaceful animal had received the fate that might have been her own. Had she stayed on the highway, the coach might have smote and killed her. Had she yielded to the impulse to throw herself into the river, her wretched body, washing upon some unfriendly shore, might have been regarded as nothing more than this…

A sudden convulsive shaking seized her. She let out a frantic sob and turned her face away from the sight, burrowing it in Sam's rough jacket, clinging to him as though to life. "Oh, Sam!" she cried, her voice muffled against his thick shoulder. "It's dead—the poor, poor dog *is dead*!"

— CHAPTER XV —

THE NEW PATIENT

Hall General Hospital
Friday, October 7, 1864

The following day the autumn air was crisp with coming frost, the sky cloudless and motionless as a windless sea. Having asked Sam to keep to himself the knowledge of her "accident," Kate went on with her work, labouring to appear as though nothing unusual had occurred. Her ankle, which had endured a mild sprain, had swelled considerably, but she had slept three hours overnight with her leg elevated, then stolen away several times during the day to soak it alternately in hot and cold water. Thrice she had rubbed it with witch hazel, and thrice with Dr. Hall's turpentine ointment, rustled from his medical bag. After each application she had re-bound the ankle snugly in a doubled rag and then desperately endeavoured to use it normally.

Yet motivation was gone. Work and service were useless pastimes. Hollowness ate at her heart. Hour by hour her shoulders sank inward. Sam gave her an inquiring word, but she ignored him. He offered her a cup of licorice bark tea, but she refused it. Questions were a constant dread, and fear of them forced her to perform her duties as flawlessly as before.

At nine o'clock, in the grey dusk just after the bell rang for the shift change, five ambulances carrying new casualties rumbled through the streets and pulled up to the entrance of the hospital. The place was thrown into a whirlwind as bells rang and gaslights flared and all able bodies ran to assist the wounded.

"Sista!" called Sam as he and a contraband boy carried a stretcher through the door of Kate's ward. "Dat sergeant here—he don't look so good, Sista. Betta take a look."

Kate and the contraband boy helped him support the delirious man down the ward.

"Here, Sam," she said, "this one. I just changed out the straw in this mattress, and the linens are fresh."

They eased the man onto a vacant bed. Sam straightened up and tapped his long index finger on his own head as he added, "He's maybe a bit unhinged in da upstairs?"

Kate nodded in reply, and Sam withdrew with the contraband boy at his heels. Rinsing her hands in the washbowl, she grabbed a clean towel and dried her hands as she stepped to the side of the bed and surveyed the sergeant. He lay quiet and still, his eyes tightly closed, his brow contorted. His dark-brown hair and beard, streaked with white and grey, were uncombed and grungy, and his ears and neck were blacked with battlefield filth. The sleeve of his left arm was torn off at the shoulder to provide access to an arm wound that was bandaged with a thick, blood-spotted cloth that looked like it had not been changed for days. Around the bandage a telltale rim of brightly inflamed skin said that infection festered beneath.

"Sir?" she said in a low tone, leaning over him. "Sir, I am here to help you."

The man's eyelids flickered and opened, revealing hazy, bloodshot eyes. A murmured "Hmm?" was followed instantly by a sharp inward breath.

"Sir, I will wash and dress you, and re-bandage your arm."

He winced, then set his teeth together as his chest heaved and tightened. "No… it's not bad. I mean, it is… but I… can… do it…" His eyes drifted to her face. He started. "Prissy?... is that you?"

It was not the first time one of the soldiers had mistakenly addressed her as one of their loved ones. "No, sir, I am not Prissy. The light is poor, and you cannot see that I am a Nursing Sister." She placed her hand on his brow. It was hot to the touch. "It is all right, sir. The fever has upset you, that's all." Taking a damp cloth, she spent several minutes bathing his forehead. "It's time to clean you up," she said when she had removed the cloth. She glanced at his tattered, smoke-stained shirt. "We will get you a fresh shirt, sir, and I wish to check your wound and cleanse it."

"Forgive me, miss, it's just that… a young woman cleaning me up… I'm such a mess," he said, struggling against pain. "It just doesn't seem… proper…"

"Sir, your body cannot heal if there is uncleanliness or infection. We must get you clean."

He tried again to remonstrate, but Kate maintained insistence, and he reluctantly gave in.

She removed his shirt and smelly wool stockings, making a pile of the soiled articles at the end of the bed to be picked up by the volunteer nurse on laundry duty. Carefully, she unwrapped the stiff, crusted bandage that encased the arm wound, dabbing warm water on the final layer of cloth to soften the dried blood and thick, murky discharge adhering it to the partially scabbed flesh before she drew the bandage fully away. The gash was deep, and red, and swollen. "What was this from?" she asked.

"Explosion…"

Was his fixed gaze the result of the incoherence induced by fever?

"Ah," she returned, avoiding his eyes.

Was he probing her face?

Examining the wound, she noticed a tiny metallic glint wedged in the raw, oozing flesh, but the light was so dim.

She peered closer.

"Shrapnel," she murmured. She had seen it hundreds of times before, and she would need the doctor's help to remove it immediately after cleansing the area.

Grabbing a washbowl, she hastened to fill it from the large pot warming on the cast-iron stove. She pulled off one of the clean discoloured towels hanging stiffly from a line strung above the stove and seized a bar of brown lye soap from the wash basket that sat beneath it, then returned to the sergeant's bedside.

"Time to wash," she said briskly, then plunged into the task of sponge bathing him.

"You remind me of my daughter," he said as she finished cleansing his upper body "Have I never seen you before?"

Kate crouched down to scrub the dark earthy grime and pilled cotton particles from his reeking feet. She knew he had been studying her face despite the gaslight's dimness, and neither her evasive eyes nor the partial shade offered by her veil seemed to have discouraged his curiosity. Still, many patients suffered hallucinations. "I have never seen you before in my life, sir," she said, drying his feet with the towel as her cheeks grew warm under his scrutiny.

A crisp cotton shirt and a pair of clean woollen stockings were delivered by the contraband boy, and she pulled the stockings onto the sergeant's feet before moving to the head of the bed to begin redressing and wrapping his arm. Once the bandage was in place she secured it with a large pin, then helped him into the shirt.

"There, all clean now," she said when the task was complete.

As she turned to leave, he strained forward, reaching for the brass-buttoned Union jacket lying across the foot of his bed.

"Wait— I mean, please…" he began, grimacing.

"Sir," Kate said, reaching out to restrain his movement. "Lie still and tell me what it is."

"My uniform jacket… in the inner left pocket… Get the small miniature, will you?"

Kate fumbled with the jacket and withdrew a smooth dark-mahogany picture case from its pocket. The frame was decorated with gilt brass, clean and shiny. "This, sir?" she said, holding it up.

"Open it." His tone was rasping and urgent.

Upon unfastening the miniature, Kate saw the face of a young woman—a beautiful young woman, probably not much younger than herself. There was bloom and exquisiteness in the delicate, contoured features. The eyes were captivating. For a fleeting moment she wondered what it would be like to have her own portrait taken… But portraits—were they not like mirrors and window reflections? Snares for vanity of one's own image?

Kate felt her body go still and thickness gather in her throat. She looked up. The man was looking at her steadily. She looked down at the picture again and said quickly, "Your daughter is very beautiful, sir," then held out the open picture case.

"Aye—my pride and joy." A strange shadow crossed his face and his hand began to tremble as he grasped the picture case, pressed it against his chest, and closed his eyes.

Kate withdrew a few yards to the stove. She swept the dust and ashes from the area and arranged various items while watching the sergeant, who, despite closed eyes, was evidently not asleep, as told by his feverishly moving lips, his shaking head, and the restless flinching of his body.

The sweeping done, she returned to the patient's side and noted the beads of sweat glistening on his forehead, noted that his breathing was shallow, raspy, and unmeasured.

"I cannot escape it... God in heaven, why?" He was repeating the words again and again, tossing his head from side to side on the pillow, his hand crushing the picture case against his body. "Someone, give me something—something for the pain! Someone help me. Something modest for the pain... the pain!"

Kate lowered herself into a chair next to the bed and laid her hand softly on his burning forehead, hoping to draw him out of the delirium. "Sir?" she said.

His eyes flew open. They were glassy and fleeting and frantic. A blood vessel had ruptured in his right eye, making a crimson spot burn near its inner corner. His terrified look fastened unblinkingly upon her face.

"Please, miss—you have gum? Opium gum? I need it right now—need it for the pain, just the pain... okay? Look in my haversack... the one on the floor of the tent. There, under the flap... See?"

Kate looked, but there was no haversack. "You are in the general hospital now, sir, in Washington. Your haversack is not here. The doctor will come and check on you soon."

It seemed to quiet the man for a few moments, and he closed his eyes and tossed his head in silence. But it was not long before his mouth was again uttering a string of incoherent words.

"He spared me… he spared me… he spared me!" he panted. "This nightmarish vision of open fields drenched and sopping with blood—have you seen it, miss, have you seen it, too?" His eyes flew open. "There… there!" he wept. "It's strewn with black bodies boiling in an oven of death… Lifeless faces feasted on by maggots! Eyes plucked out by ravens! Bodiless limbs chewed up by hogs… My comrades! My friends!… My enemies! The men I killed!" He reached out his shaking hand and spread open his fingers, losing the picture case that fell to the floor, clattering loudly as he clutched her arm. "Say something… Say something, don't just stare at your hands! Give me something for the pain! I'm a religious man, miss, please! It's just something for the pain inside—inside my arm!"

Kate drew away from his touch, tensing with compassion and confusion. "Sir," she said almost desperately, "nothing happens to us but what is the will of divine Providence. At least…" she faltered. "At least, you can try to rest in that, sir."

"Rest!… Rest?"

He spat the word. Was he gaining coherence again as he continued?

"God's will—yes, yes, I know, I know!" he went on feverishly. "There is that—we must be thankful, I agree. But Providence? Explain. Explain it—you can explain it, can't you? I see you're a religious woman. Religious women know all about these things… Of course… of course they do! Aye, but will you tell me the truth, though? Or perhaps you're just here to convert me? Make me a Roman Catholic? Or better yet, a senseless Protestant? I know that game. You're here because your church forced you to come make more Catholics out of us half-witted hospital rats…" He grimaced and tossed his head back and forth, grinding his teeth. "I'm your enemy—you know that, right? What? Why do you look at me like that? You can hate me if you like. It'll make me feel better, actually—go ahead, hate me… Hate me good, really good!" he cried, then winced and swore as he clutched at his wounded arm.

Kate did not move.

He continued bitterly, "That's right, keep watching me. You know I'm in pain, but you won't give me anything for it—

that proves you *do* hate me… Yes, yes it does… You see, even if I did love a Catholic, or a Catholic loved me, love can turn coat—did you know love could do that? Ripping your bleeding heart out and, with bare hands like a savage, shredding it into a million red ribbons and eating it in front of you so that nothing no longer makes sense?... Swords and daggers and belching cannons can't do that—you agree, don't you?"

Kate repressed a shiver as the man laughed. "I have seen many men tormented by things they cannot forget, sir," she returned calmly.

"And what do you tell them? That Providence will close its eye to their past mistakes? That they're either animals or brainless machines that won't have to reap the consequences of their choices, and that free will is a complete lie? Or that thorns turn into roses like caterpillars turn into butterflies?"

Swallowing the lump that had formed in her throat, Kate shifted in her seat. "Is not inner peace the thing all people seek, no matter their station in life?"

The sergeant laughed at her, but did the laugh disguise a sob?

"You didn't answer my question," he said as his eyes began to water. He squeezed them shut, then reopened them, ignoring her concern. "What? Haven't you seen watery eyes before?" He blinked rapidly. "You swept up dust over there and it got in my eyes, okay? Now, stop staring." He rubbed his eyes, then kept blinking as he said, "Inner peace—sure, sure. Inner peace. Guilty men need that, too, don't they? Even ones that are half-dead, like me."

He forced another raw laugh, but this time Kate really did hear a sob in it.

"Tell me what to do," he continued. "Will you? Just tell me what to do because I hate myself."

She could scarce gather her thoughts, but the Sacrament of confession was first to come to mind, with the remission the priest could offer to penitent sinners humble enough to make a good confession. This man was tormented. Confession was the only true way for him to find peace. And it was her duty to tell him so.

"Sir," she said at last, meeting his eyes and forcing herself not to flinch. "You must send for the priest, and confess your sins to him, in order that he may grant you absolution and prescribe for you the true and just penance. We must confess ours sins one to another and pray for one another that we may be healed."

A touch first of distrust and then amusement changed the aspect of the sergeant's damp, fevered face. "Sure," he said with a shrug, "if your priest would like to confess his sins to me before I tell him mine, I will do it."

Kate's mouth parted as she tried to comprehend the remark, which sounded more like deliberate impudence than assent. No other man she encountered had ever displayed the audacity to challenge a church doctrine with such a ridiculous suggestion.

Rapid footsteps were approaching from behind. Having long since memorized the individual sound of each of the three doctor's footfalls, Kate knew that it was Dr. Hall. Not wishing to be found sitting befuddled in front of a patient when the surgeon arrived to make his rounds, she stood and said, "Would you care for a drink, sir?"

"Your priest might, but not I," returned the sergeant carelessly.

"Pardon me?"

The sergeant's eyes were still half closed and hazy, but his lips twitched at the corners. "I'm a man of temperance," he returned. "Just plain water for me."

Kate turned hastily away from him, trying to steady her hands as she poured out a glass of cool water and passed it to him. He received the drink gratefully, but not without a smug look that told her he was laughing at her confusion. When the glass was empty, she took it, and he laid his head back and closed his eyes obligingly.

The doctor stood next to Kate. "Well, I see you've got him cleaned up, just not shaved yet, eh?" He raised an eyebrow. "How is he?" His tone was harsh—his tone was always harsh when he was under strain. His cheeks were flushed, and the rank stench of whiskey hung on his breath.

Kate hated it and would not soften her bad opinion of him though she knew it was the excess physical and mental tension he was under and his need of a bracing sanity and function through turmoil that always drove him to the bottle. "He said he is in pain and wants opium."

The doctor scanned the patient with a critical eye. "Ah, another opium-eater? We'll have to wean him. If it gets too bad, I'll get him some morphine." He stepped forward. "Well, what'd you find?"

There was no running together of the doctor's words, but Kate still knew he was drunk.

"The sergeant has been badly neglected," she said, setting the water glass aside. "After cleansing the arm wound, I changed out the dressing and bandage, which appeared to have been unchanged for days. The wound was not properly cleaned out initially, and a fragment of shrapnel is caught inside."

"Spells infection, don't it?"

"It is badly inflamed."

He began his examination. Then he shook his head as his lip curled. "Those pesky field hospitals. Someone with any horse sense should get in there and make some order happen. Half of the volunteers they've got out there don't even know how to keep a scratch from turning into gangrene. Ah—there's the shrapnel. Hmm, you've a good eye. Blind brigands for surgeons out there. Fine—we'll dig it out, and if it doesn't heal after that, we'll amputate. How's his mind? He seemed a trifle patchy on his way in here."

"He's not well, I'm afraid."

"Hallucinations? He was flailing pretty good when I looked over."

"I believe so."

Dr. Hall crossed his arms over his chest and tapped his foot, as though remonstrating with himself. "Opium doesn't help. Better do up a letter to his family—you can do that, eh?"

Kate assented but wondered why he seemed so concerned, for it was rare for him to display anxiety over a patient.

He uncrossed his arms. "His name's John Dallington. I know him and his family. Lost his wife when I did my first

Caesarean on her to save his child—his son. How does a doc forgive himself for not saving two children their mother, and a husband his wife? I wouldn't know. It's enough that I didn't have a sober father to keep me home when I hit sixteen—world doesn't need more of what I was back then." He shook his head and put his hands on his hips. "Now those children are over in Ireland, staying at some relative's place, away from this war. If I don't fix him, I make orphans. But," the doctor added darkly, "I don't make orphans. And that letter—nothing long, eh? Just facts. Dispatch it tomorrow morning—Sam'll take it. Hopefully they get it before the snow flies." He shifted on his feet. "I need to do the rounds now, but that shrapnel's coming out first thing in the morning. Your shift changes at nine?"

Kate nodded.

"Then we'll operate at eight. Have my tools ready."

"Yes, Doctor." She went to the desk and prepared to begin the dispatch.

"Children's names are Priscilla and Peter Dallington. Family and military information, here." He handed her an open booklet containing the family and military information of each patient.

Finding the sergeant's page, Kate began the letter, expecting the doctor to leave, but he stood behind her as she wrote:

Dear Miss Priscilla Dallington and Master Peter Dallington:

This letter is to inform you that Sergeant John Dallington of Fairfax, serving in General Sheridan's army, was wounded in action during the Battle of Fisher's Hill, Virginia, on September 22, 1864. The patient is currently receiving medical care at the Hall General Hospital, Washington, DC, under the care of Dr. Robert Hall. The condition of the patient remains critical.

Yours, etc.,

Sister Kate; Third Ward Nurse, Hall General."

She folded and sealed the letter, then placed it in a stamped envelope and laid it on a pile of other dispatches that would go out in the mailbag with Sam first thing in the morning.

"Stay by him tonight," the doctor said over her shoulder. "He needs a good rest but a careful eye to watch him through it. Keep him quiet and comfortable, and in the same position so he doesn't disturb the wound dressing. Take care, though. He may be a good-natured fellow, but he's argumentative if you rub him the wrong way. Here's the morphine—you know how much. I'll check the boys in the next ward."

He stopped talking, but he stood there still, as though he would stay. Kate felt him watching her back and dared not look at him, her downcast eyes burning a hole in the sanded-over wood knot ingrained in the edge of the table. Fearing and impatient, she at last sealed her lips and glanced sideways. But he saw her.

"It's bad, but don't be gloomy. Makes it worse," he said with a twinkle. "Look here..." He tapped her on the shoulder, and a sudden thrill rushed through her. Then she stiffened. He was reaching into his vest pocket and withdrawing a long red-and-white spiralled candy stick. "Want a peppermint?" he said, holding it out to her.

Sudden confusion widened Kate's eyes as she stared at his offering. She stammered twice, quickly shook her head, and pursed her lips together when she realized they had parted.

A merry laugh rang through the hall. The doctor had thrown his head back—he was laughing at her. It was a long, rippling laugh, accompanied by a pleasant smile that she didn't know he had.

"Can't figure you out!" he said, shaking his head. "First you steal my turpentine, then you're rude to poor old Sam, and then you act like you don't have a sprained ankle when you really do! What's the point?" He laughed again.

A fluttering sensation took hold of Kate's stomach as she saw a look of longing soften his eyes. He flourished the peppermint stick and looked away from her.

"Oh, well," he said, "that's just one more candy for me—better than whiskey, ain't it? And I like peppermints, even if you don't." He strode toward the exit, then turned and took another look at her over his shoulder, depositing the notorious peppermint between his lips and holding it there like a colourful cigar. He grinned playfully. "My dear Sister Kate, several centuries ago a wise poet under the *nom de plume* of William Shakespeare once said,

'This above all: to thine own self be true,
And it must follow, as the night the day,
Thou canst not then be false to any man.'

"I don't know about you," he added, plucking the peppermint from his lips and twirling it between his thumb and forefinger, "but I intend to do just that—even as regards this poor little peppermint." He then retreated from the doorway, whistling the familiar chorus of "Battle Hymn of the Republic" and letting it ring like the tune of a mad piper through the long corridors of the hospital.

For a long time Kate sat motionless in her chair. What conflict was this? What tearing within? What sweet sensation that came with his look? Her eyes fixed on the ring that girded her finger; her ears rang with the sound of his pleasant laugh. Who was this man?

A puddle of water… a pile of knots… gathering by turns in her stomach—and she realized that a new feeling was there, even if she denied it.

"But a silly man with whiskey hanging on his breath," she suddenly said, steeling herself, chiding the weak mind that took pleasure in entertaining itself with foolishness.

Ah, yes, Sister Kate! Sweep that puddle and those knots aside! Sweep them aside like the dirt and fly refuse and bloody rags littering the floor! Renew the old repugnance! Will your heart to harden! If he will look at Sister Kate that way again, let her withdraw the more, for emotions will not rule a woman whose capacity to love is not greater than her resolution to guard it!

"I am a married woman," she said to herself… to Sister Kate.

She was content. Human love was of no consequence; family attachments?—of no consequence either. Would not her ring remind her of that? And her final vows… Yes, when she returned home, stepped behind those iron gates—then she would forget him. That day would come soon, and it would certainly seal her soul to God. She would be decked in red velvet! She would walk down that aisle! And she would lay herself down in that casket, and suffer, and die, and serve the needy, and pray for lost humanity, and experience the bliss of divine love that was not to be experienced except within the confines of a life devoted to Consecrated Virginity.

Ah yes—that was Sister Kate.

— CHAPTER XVI —

A SPARROW FALLS

"Sister Kate?"

It was a damp, chilly autumn night and Kate was prodding a piece of dry spruce into the struggling fire of the cast-iron stove when she heard the voice of one of the Sisters behind her.

"Yes, I'm coming!" she said, giving the stick a shove and snatching her hand away as hot flames began licking at the edges of the crisp wood.

Sam had spent the whole of the previous day perspiring in the sweltering afternoon sun, chopping wood in the backyard behind the kitchen because he "smelled rain in da air." None had believed him. But as a steady downpour settled in for the night, no one could pick up a stick of firewood without feeling grateful for the old Negro's auspicious foresight and initiative or doubt that his weather predictions were as good as his word.

Finished with the stoking, Kate latched the stove door with a clang, coughed away a whiff of smoke, then wiped her sooty hands on a rag hanging from the wash line strung behind the warm chimney.

"Sister Kate?"

Kate turned to see the sober face of Sister Anna-Maria. It was drawn and pallid, signs of the stress they had all been under since the influx of soldiers had arrived at the hospital the week before. Workloads for all volunteers and doctors continued steady and overwhelming; sleep those days was a rare commodity, and death was a daily occurrence.

"Yes, Sister Anna-Maria, how can I help you?"

"There's a poor boy in my ward who's lost his left arm," she said. "He was shot in the back, too, and the ball broke two ribs and punctured his right lung. He's been dying, slowly and painfully, ever since getting here. I've done all I can, but I do fear he won't live out the night. He has asked for you. He's wanting to write a letter home to his mother now, before he passes, and would like to know if you'll do it for him?"

Kate narrowed her eyes. During her two years of service in the hospital, she had seen countless men, young and old, pass through its doors, but she had never seen the same face twice. She tried to remember faces, names, even conversations, but everything seemed to crowd and blur together—a ghastly cargo of unorganized memories surrounded by the horrors of war. The crackling of the fire in the stove grew louder, and she bent over to close the damper halfway.

"He did ask for you, Sister Kate—rather emphatically. He was sure he knew you. Even when I offered to write the letter, he still insisted he wanted to see you. If you'll consent to going, I will stay here to watch the Third Ward until you return."

Kate straightened up slowly. "Well," she said, "I suppose I can go since there is not much to be done here tonight. Which bed is he?"

"Number seven, on the left side going in."

Kate left the ward and glided downstairs. She didn't often visit the Second Ward, but because the room was directly below hers, she had often heard the music from the upright piano in its centre either pounding, jumping, or floating through the rafters and floorboards, sometimes mingling with more than one voice singing cheery folk tunes, dance songs, and hymns she didn't know. The organ was the only musical instrument she was accustomed to, for any other instrument besides it and the human voice were considered worldly and even sensual forms of entertainment, unfit for more spiritually minded individuals, especially those sanctified for the religious orders.

When she entered the ward, she paused in the dim light and located the patient. He lay on his back with his eyes closed and his thickly calloused enormous right hand resting across his broad torso. She approached quietly, curious if she would recognize him, and as she stepped closer the sight of a homespun blue woollen coat with patched elbows hanging on the corner of a nearby chair made her smell the honied, musty odour of horse sweat and dust. The soldier's face, tense and bruised, was damp with fever, and the effects of malnourishment traced themselves in the sunken tissue beneath his jaw and cheekbones. A ghastly white scar distorted the left side of a broad forehead spanned by dark, expressive eyebrows. Obviously, the nurse who had bathed him hadn't succeeded in scrubbing his remaining hand entirely clean, for grime still shadowed the tips of the yellowed, uneven fingernails—grubby fingernails that reminded her of bony knees and driving lines.

Just then the soldier's eyes fluttered open gradually, sleepily. For a long, uncertain moment his bleared vision seemed to labour to regain focus. Then a dreamy smile crept over his face and his blue eyes brightened.

"Howdy, marm," he said with effort. "If I'm glad to see a face after that filthy bloodbath, it's gotta be yer's. I'm jest 'shamed it's only half a man—and an ugly one at that—who's greetin' ya this time."

Kate's mouth lifted with a warm expression. "Brother Gunderson, it is good to see you again."

The stagecoach driver's countenance had lost its ruddy glow, but his eyes still twinkled. "I reckon we've done that conversation once before now, marm?"

"I beg your pardon?"

"Ya know"—he nearly laughed—"'bout my bein' fancy 'Brother Gunderson'?"

Kate was not sure if she should smile or maintain a waveless expression, but as she recalled Jack's memorable reproof during the long wagon ride, and how he had scorned the whore's dripping gaze during their drive through Washington, she knew it was safe. "Yes, I remember," she said, smiling fully.

"Did that… uh… Sister Mary-Maria tell ya?" he asked, struggling to recall the name. "I wanna write a letter if"—he cleared his throat of a hoarse rasp—"if ya give me a hand?" His clear, kind eyes were searching, his voice almost pleading. "Never did learn to read and write, marm. And I lost a point bein' born left-handed," he added with a weak grin, "but if I had learned, and the left arm had a' followed me here, I'd've least tried."

"Of course I will help you," Kate said, about to reach for the small writing desk, but he began speaking, so she paused and listened.

"Ya know, marm, I never was the kinder feller to go a sparkin' like all the other boys did. Couldn't find a gal what liked me and I liked her well enough to make it happen. The best kind are lilies among thorns, like my ma'd say." Jack coughed a few times, then laid his head back on the pillow. "But ya know, marm, I like ya, and ifin ya wasn't a nun and all—and ifin I wasn't in such bad shape, 'course, well, I reckon I jest might try it." His eyes grew soft as he offered her a sad, tender look.

A strange heat crept across her cheeks, and she looked away.

"Lookee," he said, "I'm the kinder feller to say what's on his mind plain and simple-like, so you'll have to pardon my bein' frank. But seein' as I'm gonna be crossin' over Jordon soon, I want ya to know somethin'." A fit of coughing overcame him for a moment, then he persisted. "I know nuns ain't the marryin' type, but that's 'cause they forget that a man needs a honest woman to love him. And, marm, besides bein' downright good-lookin', you've got smarts and sweetness buried deep down what makes ya real 'tractive. 'Member," he added, "the Good Book says it ain't fittin' fer a man to be alone—that's why God took Adam's rib and made it into Eve. And, marm"—his voice grew raspy, his accents lurching and broken, and a shadow passed over his face as he added slowly, with a short, bashful laugh—"I'm of the same mind 'bout you findin' yer man, and fixin' the cleft in his side."

An ache rubbed Kate's heart. Childhood dreams visited her, and she was a happy little wife in a home of her own, with a man who would make her his favourite…

And then she remembered Thaddy Murray.

Only days before she and Collette were to enter the Postulancy, Collette had told her he was marrying Brigid O'Sullivan.

The memory still had a scar on it; years and religious vows could not heal it. They might bar her from the opportunity to legally marry, but they could never dull the sting beneath. Yes, she had gotten her own wedding day, her own white wedding garment, her own little golden wedding ring. But still she was not happy. Kate did not want clothes and flowers and rings. No, she longed for closeness—for her spirit to be understood, her soul to be united with a companion, herself to be seen in the light of the very best that she could be.

"And, marm, listen," Jack added, drawing her from reverie. "Real men ain't fully built till they snip themselves free of their ma's apron strings and strike out on their own. Make sure yer feller has waved goodbye to babyhood, okay? Or else his ma'll upset the marital apple cart. But heck—" He winced suddenly. "Would ya bolster me up a bit there? This here way of layin' is the pits." Jack began straining in his bed, trying to hide a pained expression with a lopsided smile.

Kate moved quietly about, carefully arranging the bed-sheets and pillows around him until he was comfortable.

Jack was everything but Thaddy. Thaddy had been cold, distant, regal, strikingly handsome. He had a smile that could charm any girl and a mother who made all his opinions for him. Jack was no comparison. He was just plain Jack. Jack with the homely face. Jack with the windmill limbs. Jack with the tobacco habit.

But Jack had a heart, and it was that which made the ache go deeper.

Assured of his general comfort, Kate pulled up a chair and sat next to his bed and opened the writing desk. Retrieving her favourite nib, she inserted it into the pen and selected several blank sheets of paper. She dated the first, then waited for his direction.

"Start 'er like this," Jack said, seeming to muster his strength as he began. "Dear Ma, forgive me fer not writin' sooner—" He coughed and wheezed a few times before he was able to continue.

When he began again, it was to repeat the same interruption nearly a dozen times before the letter was finished. "I've been through the mill fer the last time. But Ma, I ain't afeard of dyin'. More than anythin' I want to die the Good Death, and meet my Maker with a clean slate. Seems now I'm near it, I recall words ya said when I was jest a young 'un. Words of love and peace. Words that make me right sorry fer my sins—and wish fer a chance to make 'em right. Ya see, I ain't thought much 'bout God before now—except I knew he dis-proved my tobacco chewin', like you did. But God seemed so far away, 'specially after Pa died. But I figure it's a mercy I've been given a slow crossin', since I've had time to think o' the world beyon' and give God a fair and honest trial—see him as the Father he is to me. And, Ma, I reckon that all ya said 'bout God, and heaven, and Jesus on the cross and risin' from the dead to save us from our sins ain't a fairy tale after all. Give my love to Louisa and little Freddie. Tell 'em I couldn't've had a better brother and sister. I'll see ya in the great beyon'. Yer lovin' son, Jack."

Kate's nib scratched rapidly along the page as he dictated, but her eyes watered, and by the end she was hardly able to see to steady her hand as she signed the letter for him. When a tear spilled onto the page and turned his name into a blotched puddle of water and ink, she knew she was weak.

"Thanks… fer… fer doin' that fer me, marm," he said, wheezing and tensing.

She had never thought of Jack as a gentleman, but now she suddenly did. Gentlemen did not wear stiff cravats and ironed trousers and fancy coattails or flourish smooth speeches to be charming, like she had imagined; gentlemen were gentle. Gentle like Jack.

Dashing away the wet on her cheeks, she laid aside the letter and writing desk, sat on the side of the bed, and supported his quivering frame.

"Could ya hold my hand, too, marm?" he said, wincing. She gave him her hand, and he squeezed it, and she remembered the time he had offered her his hand when she had jumped down from the stagecoach.

He had been kind first.

Time passed. He coughed, and a fine mist of blood sprayed onto the white sheet. With her free hand, Kate reached for a cloth and wiped away the crimson spittle around his dry mouth and chin. The coughing began again, lasting several minutes. The attack abated, and she laid him back on the pillows. Then he closed his eyes and fell into an exhausted slumber.

An hour went by. Kate kept a watchful vigil by Jack's side.

He did not move. Restless, she stood up, walked to the window, and looked out. The cold night was still and silent; the rain had ceased and the stars glittered brilliantly like innumerable diamonds cast across a carpet of indigo velvet. Walking back to the bed, she regained her seat and allowed her gaze to drift toward Jack's sleeping face. She studied its lines, its homely features, its most recent scars.

What was the state of his soul? Was he ready to die that night? If he should die suddenly, how long would his unsaved soul burn in the fires of purgatory? What gates would open to receive him when his soul should leave its broken frame and pass into 'the great beon'?

And where was Father Andrew? Perhaps she ought to send for him so that he might hear Jack's last confession and administer Holy Viaticum? Yes... yes, of course. Of course she must send for Father Andrew—send for him directly; for poor Jack must receive food for his journey, and be preserved from the wicked enemy, and be led into everlasting life.

Kate was about to stand up, but suddenly her train of thought was interrupted by the sound of a voice—tender, steady, sweet, and pure—borne from the centre of the ward. It was Sam's voice, and he was singing:

"Rock of Ages, cleft for me,
Let me hide myself in thee!
Let the water and the blood,
From thy riven side which flow'd,
Be of sin the double cure,
Cleanse me from its guilt and pow'r."

The gentle notes of a piano touched the melodic vocal strains with soothing harmony. Together they penetrated the heavy stillness, floating on the midnight air, falling on her ears like raindrops. She glanced over and made out the large dark shape of Sam sitting hunched on the low bench before the instrument.

"Not the labour of my hands
Can fulfill thy law's demands;
Could my zeal no respite know,

Could my tears forever flow,
All for sin could not atone;
Thou must save, and thou alone!"

Kate did not recognize the hymn, but the words, the voice, and the music carried with them was a mysterious balm that made the tension flow from her body, leaving her quiet and still.

Jack's coughing startled her. She looked to find him awake, his face sharply contorted, his skin clammy with sweat. If she had ever felt for someone else's pain, she felt it in that moment, and realized, too, that the years of nursing school, textbook study, and practical medical training could never have taught her how to feel what she was feeling now.

Now his eyes were welling with tears, yet he made no cry. He did not curse. Jack had never cursed. Plenty of men cursed and swore when they were in pain. It was common among soldiers, something she had come to expect in the circumstances. But Jack was not like other men; he was quiet, patient. It seemed that the suffering did not matter to him—that he saw, as in a vision, an unspeakable victory at the end of it.

She rose from her chair to sit on the edge of his bed, then reached out to smooth back the coarse tawny hair clustered over his moist brow. He struggled to lift his face, then looked at her with his tired eyes and whispered, "Do ya hear it?"

Kate smiled. "I do."

"Guess it's my turn to be homesick now," he said. "Homesick fer heaven—you, too?"

Kate couldn't answer. She was looking away, weeping.

"I can't carry a tune in a bucket, marm"—he struggled to say, laughing slightly, his tears answering her own—"but if I could sing with him now, I would."

"Nothing in my hand I bring,
Simply to thy cross I cling;
Naked, come to thee for dress;
Helpless, look to thee for grace;
Foul, I to the fountain fly;
Wash me, Saviour, or I die.

Whilst I draw this fleeting breath,
When my eyestrings break in death;
When I soar through tracts unknown,
See thee on thy judgment throne,
Rock of Ages, cleft for me,
Let me hide myself in thee!"

Kate blinked back the tide as she watched Jack. A deep serenity descended upon him as though the words of the hymn had been to his soul rivers of water quenching a thirsty desert.

A comforting smile shone in his face. The struggle seemed to fade, and he murmured, "I'm so glad… I asked Jesus… and now he forgives me… fer all the wrong I've done… I know… Jesus… for-forgives me." His eyes radiated as though they saw a precious treasure. His voice dwindled but still his lips moved, and she wondered if he was singing.

She had sat by the side of many dying soldiers; she had heard the last words of many men; she had watched them fight, seen them breathe their last breath. But she had never had to struggle so hard to maintain her composure with any of them as she did now. Jack had just grasped something she wanted. Even in his poverty, he was richer than she was because his mind was free. Jack's was a knowledge, a comfort, a hidden strength, a filling up of the spirit and rescue of the soul that she had never learned in the convent. Her concern about summoning Father Andrew grew dim. The last confession, the usual and necessary administration of Holy Viaticum—all of it felt meaningless now when mingled grief and peace looked up to heaven, and heaven smiled down with simple majesty to crown the most childlike faith she had ever seen.

Jack was coughing again, each spasm frailer than the last. Reaching between the pillow and his back, she gave support by cradling his head and shoulders in one arm while with the other she held the white cloth near his lips. The fine scarlet mist issuing from his parched mouth became large clots that soaked through the linen. His head swayed as though he were growing dizzy and had lost the strength to support it. His breathing grew quick and shallow as his eyes closed in weariness. The coughing ceased. A moment passed. His jaw loosed, his lips parted and uttered a feeble cry. A heartbeat pulsed through his body—Kate felt it, for the stillness that followed told that it was his last. Gradually, his body became limp, and Kate knew that he had drowned in his own blood. His eyes opened then; dilated pupils stared into nothingness; they rolled back in his head, as though chasing the path of his mind. A grey shadow crept across his face. She had often seen that shadow.

A tremor passed through her frame. Tears would come, and she let them. Slowly, she laid Jack's head back to rest on the pillow. She dampened a clean square of linen and dabbed away the red spittle draining from the corner of his bloodless lips. Though her fingers feared to touch him, she reached out and drew them over his face, closing the lifeless eyes. The skin was already paling; the flesh, already chilled.

For a long moment she gazed upon the corpse, feeling an overwhelming sense of loss. The heartache that throbbed so deep seemed vaguely familiar, almost confusing, until she saw Collette's face, and knew why…

Ah yes, Collette's face—staring back at her through the rapid recollections of years gone by, fearfully and beautifully cold; staring back at her now from the day she left the convent… from the day when sweet autumn blended with warm winds and a harvest sun, and the song of the haymakers floated on the air.

And now it is night: Kate creeps into Collette's cell. Ah, into Collette's cell she creeps—the stolen key of Collette's door gripped in one sweaty hand, the garden shears in the other. Collette is a deep sleeper—she will not wake.

Forward—into the darkness; forward into a murky atmosphere drenched with fire and ice. She is still there, in her mind, and she shivers as she finds Collette's narrow bed, reaches out her skinny hands, feels the lengths of hair shimmering like water escaping her grasp, almost weeping, begging her not to do it—not to cut them off. But the shears do not listen—they have a mind of their own, don't they? They open wide their mouth, and close upon the helpless locks, and hiss with glee over and over and over again as they send them plunging to the ground in waves—surely the shame of a shaven head will force Collette to stay.

"Thou shalt not steal," says a voice.

And Kate replies, "Mary Mother of God, pray for me, a sinner."

And now it is the next day: Will Collette leave St. Agnes?

Kate crouches in a covert under the winding stone staircase that leads to the attic. She watches as Collette emerges from her cell.

What an ugly grey dress she wears! What a plain, silly homespun linen chemise beneath it! What horrible, itchy-looking wool stockings stuffed into such old brogues that will certainly hamper her feet when she walks! And what a disgusting red linen scarf tied about her head—why would Collette wear something so hideous?

But Kate gnaws her lip suddenly, for she feels again the cold, heavy weight of the shears in her palm, and the golden locks rippling through her fingers. That disgusting linen scarf: surely it is meant to conceal the ghastly haircut that her own two hands have inflicted upon Collette.

Now Collette is bidding farewell to the two Sisters standing at the door; one of them is escorting her outside, into the sunshine.

Kate slips out of her hiding place; she glides up the turreted staircase and into the dingy attic where a long, narrow window commands a view of the garden and the green valley that slopes away to the southeast, blending with the thickly wooded forest below. She sees the dark shadow of the Sister moving down the long open avenue a few steps ahead of Collette's willowy, jaunting figure as they approach the black iron gates.

The Sister draws a heavy ring of keys from her pocket. She selects one; she applies it to the iron lock. The three pots of daffodils at the entrance seem to disapprove of the action, for their once-yellow flowers are now reduced to a cluster of lonely green stems. At one time, daffodils had been Collette's and Kate's favourite flowers.

But not any longer.

Even from a distance Kate can hear the gates—they are opening now, with a low groan. Collette is slipping through them now, almost dashing into the old dirt road, and she is turning around now, motioning to the Sister, flashing the Sister her most disarming smile—the smile she uses on boys.

But the Sister won't be fooled, for she already knows Collette's tricks.

The iron portal clangs shut. The key and lock grate and clank together against the iron bars. Is it now the sound of the soft, measured tread of the Sister's footsteps as she retreats through the grave-like hush of the enclosure that Kate hears? Is it now the sound of silence—swallowing up in shadows the souls and voices that crowd and press within the stone walls and stone turrets and yawning stone archways—that forgets that Collette is left standing a lonely orphan on the other side of them?

Collette stands in the road, her face toward the east. Is she shaking out one leg? Yes—yes, she is shaking out one leg. How outlandish! What? Shaking off the ugly brogue? Yes—there! It is flying off her foot now! And crashing against the side of the gate now! And the other one is flying, too, now, followed close by a tugging and tearing and ripping of stockings and a sudden flinging of them up into the air, where they soar for a moment before decking the sea buckthorn hedge on the side of the road. And what will come next? Is it to be the poor, disgusting red head scarf? Yes. She is untying the knot, yanking it from her head, holding it on both corners and tugging—what? Tearing it down the middle? Yes, tearing it down the middle and discarding it like a piece of trash to blow down the ditch in the wind.

She is a bare-headed, barefooted savage now. She stands there, breathless, relishing the kiss of the sun, and the touch of the breeze, and the delight of her sin.

But then suddenly the face of the savage turns around and looks—looks up at the window and stares into the turret at the place where Kate is standing…

❧

And even now, the face still stared at her.

— CHAPTER XVII —

CONSPIRACIES

A quick, halting step sounded behind Kate, and Dr. Hall's rough tones jolted her back to the present.

"Boy's gone, is he?"

She avoided looking at the surgeon. She took Jack's letter, folded it hurriedly, and placed it inside an envelope.

Dr. Hall ambled up to the bed and stood looking over the dead body. He shook his head once. "Death, that old spook," he said. "Those who deserve a good long life and a family to enjoy it with—the strapping youths, the innocents, like this kid—are the ones he claims, while those sick drunks and brigands and prostitutes—wretches who don't give a continental—he lets go, permitting them to go on wasting their lives and wrecking the lives of others." He combed his fingers through his dark hair. "It'll be a cold day in hell when I finally understand why."

"It does seem partial, perhaps," said Kate hesitatingly. Emotion crawled around her, stealing her courage. "Let us find comfort knowing that God sees what we do not, and knows best despite our questions of why." She had hoped to sound philosophical—at least spiritual—but the words came out flat.

The doctor tapped his foot. "That," he said coolly, "is precisely the reason I don't believe in God." He crossed his arms over his chest, and a strange look crossed his face. "I'm a scientific man—not an emotional one—and my observations report to me that 'God' allows a good boy to die but splits no hairs about them bad eggs, bloody blowhards, and fancy girls walking the streets outside these doors. I see war—but does God see war? It flays men with bullets as fishermen flay their cod. I see men with white skin who kidnap men with *black* skin merely because it is black—does God see that, too? It drives the lot of them to pick out their bullets, and pull back their triggers, and make orphans—and you know what that's like. But who can tell if your merciful 'God' is not actually blind, since he appears to do nothing to stop it?"

"Man cannot blame God for the unfortunate consequences that may befall him if man's personal choice has been to shackle a Negro and then kill his brother, sir."

He looked at her straightly. "Agreed!" he cried. "But what," he added with a grin, "is your remedy for man's free choice when man *blunders*?"

"Providence."

He laughed disparagingly. "I despise vague answers, Sister Kate. There's more you're not alluding to—like priests that can forgive your blunders and penance that can save you. Men are not brainless machines, no matter how much 'providence' there is splashed across Copernicus's heliocentric universe. The Eye of the Freemasons, the karma of Buddhism, and the leaven of the Pharisees all say it in different words, but their agenda points to the same thing as yours does, their religions concoct the same do-good-works formula as yours does, and their gods—like yours—are as impersonal as a planet. But," he added, "what does the boy say?"

He planted his hands on his hips and fastened his stormy hazel eyes upon the corpse, as though awaiting a response. "See what I mean?" he huffed and flung his arms into the air with an exasperated motion. "He has the answer—but who's got the power to bring him back to tell us? These religions? Not a chance. They breed false hopes and are a sorry waste of time and money."

Kate frowned. "A waste of time and money?"

"Precisely. Muslims waste time and money on their pilgrimages to Mecca; your people waste time and money on your pilgrimages to Rome. Both of you fought over Jerusalem—and that was a waste of blood."

"We are different in many ways."

"How? You both pray rosaries, kiss and worship stones—face or no face—and bless the new world order when you claim that there is no salvation outside of either religion—and even *that* salvation is morbidly uncertain and hopelessly reliant upon your dead works."

"We believe in the Trinity, Doctor. Islam does not."

"Ha! You think that's enough to convince me? Your priest is his own masquerade of a trinity. And in case you didn't know, his triangular *Trinity* word is a pagan invention in the first place, not even mentioned in unadulterated scripture manuscripts. Add sin to sin when Muhammad married a Catholic nun. Will you still say the two cults aren't joined at the hip?"

"Yet we cannot argue that Islam denies the divinity of Christ, Doctor."

"So does Catholicism. But Turks come by it honestly—Romans makes their priests do it."

His eyebrows arched at her silence. "If anything makes me gag, it's hypocrisy. If there is a merciful God higher and more omniscient than the Eye of the Freemasons, my eyes will see his hand move. But until that day comes, I will doubt."

Kate lowered her gaze involuntarily. "Doubt is unnecessary, sir, for the souls who have confessed and put their faith in the Lord Jesus will certainly receive the blessing of eternal life."

"Ah, but the question is, Sister Kate, do you really believe that? Do you know where *your* soul will spend eternity?" He scrutinized her, his words splitting the air like a pistol crack.

"Dr. Hall, we are all sinful creatures. But our penance, and the merciful aid of the Blessed Virgin Mary, our Queen of Heaven, who intercedes for us and subdues the wrath of our Father Jesus, grants us forgiveness and the hope of eternal security."

He laughed disparagingly again. "You're sounding worse than a parrot—you know that, right?" He paused and his eyes turned to slits. "Security where—heaven or hell? I want *your* own opinion on the subject. Not your priest's."

"It seems by your question, Doctor," she said, lifting her chin in defiance, "that you would like to see me contradict myself?"

"You've been given a keen mind. I would beg you not to slaughter it on the altar of your Pope."

"I am a Mercy Sister, Doctor. I have devoted years to the study of my profession. The opinions you hear from me are my own."

He looked at her as though doubting her honesty, but then he said, "Fair enough" with a decided inclination of his head and a purse of his lips. "But you must also explain things if you're going to believe them—explain things like, for example, what you will do if there's nobody around kind enough to pray for your soul to get into heaven once you die? I'm sure you're not fond of the idea of sweltering in purgatory?"

"Faith is not science, Doctor. It is a belief."

"Not a science?"

"Science relies upon observation, repetition, and such things. Indeed, if science could prove even God's existence, we would have no need of faith."

"Granted," he said, as he commenced rocking back and forth on his heels. "But then tell me, if your faith is not a science, as you contend, why does it rely upon relics, robes, and repetitions—not to mention a slew of dead saints mouldering in their graves?"

Kate looked at him steadily. "I do not question Papal teaching, Doctor, nor do I doubt its authority or its infallibility."

"Sister Kate," he said with special emphasis, "it is a practical observation that only dead fish swim downstream. In view of such a conclusion, will you tell me what role your personal intelligence, free will, and free choice play in the matters you reference now?"

"The Virgin Mary was given the gift of bearing the child Jesus. Except in the voluntary submission of herself to the authority of God, she had no choice in the matter concerning the conception of her privileged son. For myself, as a Sister ordained to the service of the Mother Church, I, too, consider myself a privileged child—as Christ himself was—in the arms of the Mother of God."

"And your free will bows to her authority?"

"Indisputably."

"A most curious phenomenon—this Mother Church," he remarked, crossing his arms over his breast. "A face-painted

Jezebel. Her manipulation is brilliant—positively brilliant! Ahabs and eunuchs—slaves to her whorish tactics. Four hundred and fifty prophets of Baal leaping on their altars, cutting themselves with lancets to pay her homage, gawking stupidly as she takes the ten commandments in her bloody hands and 'dispenses' with the fourth." A sudden spark lit his eye. "But does the Mother Church still bet her crimes will escape Elijah? Dogs will eat that harlot's flesh again, whether she likes it or not."

"'Dispenses with' the fourth commandment?" Kate repeated, looking at him sideways. "Dr. Hall, I fear that your prejudices have caused you to become sorely misinformed."

"You think? Don't your bishops and priests teach you the history behind 'the venerable day of the sun'? There's a reason why they face east during their Sunday morning massacres—and it's a whole lot more about leading their silly women to weep for Tammuz than showing off that pretty stained glass."

"Emperor Constantine was a convert to Christianity, Doctor."

"Ah—merely to get his way. Undercover he was always a sun-worshipping pagan."

"You err, Doctor. Constantine's many good works, including his civil law regarding Sunday rest, brought many pagans into the knowledge of Christ."

"And made those same pagans laugh at the spinelessness of professed apostolic Christians, who halted between two opinions and then changed their seventh-day Sabbath to Sunday just to save their bacon." The doctor harrowed his fingers through his hair. "The intention is in plain view—but, according to your catechism, the Councils of Laodicea and Trent no longer transgress the fourth commandment since Sinai is dwarfed by the infallible meddling of your Church Fathers."

"Sunday is the Lord's Day, Doctor, and the day upon which St. John received his Revelation on the island of Patmos. There may have been some heretics, such as the Waldenses and the false churches in Piedmont who undermined the supremacy of Papal power and Rome's enforcement of Sunday law, but such heretics, it may be understood, were dealt with by the Holy Inquisition in ways which I trust were equitable to their crimes." Kate turned away to organize the table near Jack's bed.

"As for myself, Doctor, I will maintain that the first day of the week is wholly sanctified, as our Popes and prelates assert, and upon that day we will continue to celebrate the resurrection of our Lord, according to the tradition of that blessed first Easter."

"Ah yes, certainly. Jezebel and her priests adore reminiscing Nimrod's Babylon by feasting on the roasted pig that killed his son Tammuz. Who cares if they ogle at Easter bunnies that lay chicken eggs dyed in the blood of human child sacrifices? If my last decade's obsessive exploration amidst the dusty columns of ancient history serves me now, I'd say that there's a wall of honest history dividing Egypt's Ishtar and the Hebrew's Passover—in case your priest forgot to tell you—and celebrating the festival orgy of a goddess's incredible fertility is not the side you want to be on."

He flicked out a cigar and lit it, then began to pace while his voice pitched into a fever as he began lecturing the air, his darting figure pursued by a woody-smelling storm cloud of cigar smoke.

"If Nimrod thinks he can look down from Olympus," he expostulated, "and use his sun rays to impregnate his mother-wife Semiramis and produce their divine child, Tammuz, where else shall we discover the incestuous Madonna and Child? Where else the 'Queen of Heaven'? Where else those stolen Sunday morning cakes and the first *Cahna-Bal* who sports the robes of a Romish priest while he dines on human flesh and gulps down human blood? Is this all just Baal-worship cloaked in rustled names? Oh—no! Surely, it couldn't be!" He stopped in front of her and held his smoking cigar between his fingers. "Do you know," he said, pointing his finger at her, "how many men and women have preferred to burn at the stake or lay their necks on the block and receive the executioner's axe rather than drink the cup of devils through Rome's transubstantiation?"

"Pardon me, Doctor, but I am quite ignorant to the history you reference, and therefore have no commentary to offer on the subject."

"Sister Kate," he said, stepping closer so that she could nearly feel the breath in his presence, "all I ask is that you trust your senses. Become a skeptic for once, and observe that the *hocus-pocus* chant of your priest that magically turns a piece of bread into the literal flesh of a dead god suitable for cannibals to eat is in total opposition to the dictates of plain reason."

"Doctor, I am sorry, but I fear there is a misunderstanding," she said, looking at him squarely and drawing breath. "Thank you for elaborating your views so clearly, but I trust you will now be kind enough to see that I do not wish to continue an argument that is leading nowhere."

"Nowhere? Ha!" He resumed his pacing. "You're red enough in the face to suggest otherwise."

Kate swallowed hard; her hands fidgeted against her will—she must find a task to busy them. There—a stray linen bedsheet! Freshly washed, draped across the back of a chair, ready to spread on the next vacated bed—Jack's bed. Seizing the long sheet, she began folding it. The piece was unusually awkward in her confused hands. She felt the doctor's eyes tracing her movements, examining every tremble of her hand—was he laughing? Then she dropped one corner, and it swished down and swept over the dusty floorboards.

Just then Dr. Hall stepped up and reached for the drooping corner. "What is the misunderstanding, Sister Kate?" he said in a low voice, taking the sheet, drawing it up, and casually meeting his end with hers.

"Doctor," she said, grabbing both sides of the sheet and looking fearlessly into his eyes, "you talk of cannibalism. I know nothing of such things. I am a nurse. I am here to serve. Anything associated with heathenism or this Baal you accuse the Mother Church of celebrating is a complete mystery to me." She finished folding the linen, then held it under one arm while her opposite hand clutched the folded edge. "But there is one thing I can tell you honestly, and it is that the Mass reflects upon nothing other than Christ."

"What Christ?"

"Christ Jesus, the one and only."

"The living one, or the dead one?"

First the unfeeling corpse fastened to the crucifix flashed in her mind, then the breathless image of the Virgin Mary, and her ears pricked to the quickness of the doctor's breathing, as though it raced to keep pace with the beating of his heart.

"I know—we're thinking the same thing," he said. "But I suppose you wouldn't deem idolatry a sin, would you—since your Pope justifies it?"

"I do not know what you mean, sir. Sin is never justifiable, and the Pope would be the first to concur."

"Of course he would—after he's annihilated the very commandment that forbids the sin."

"I beg your pardon?"

"Idolatry. Compare your adjusted catechism to the Papists' hated translation of the Bible under King James, and you'll notice the discrepancy. The second commandment of the ten forbids bowing down to graven images—but does such a commandment remain in your catechism today?"

"There are ten commandments there, sir, I can assure you."

"Ah yes, because, to Rome, to covet another man's house is a separate violation aside from coveting his wife."

"That is correct."

"But my point, Sister Kate," he said as he locked his gaze with hers, "is that, in order to make the *annihilation* against graven images as seamless as possible, Rome plucked out the second commandment and then conveniently knocked the other nine back a step, then split the last down the middle to make two."

Kate's mouth went suddenly parched.

Just then she heard shuffling footsteps sounding along the corridor, ushering from the direction of the piano. Someone was coming.

The doctor leaned in closer to Kate, looked at her; his facial muscles tensed and quivered as his voice, calm and low, spoke with forced restraint: "You know, Sister Kate, there's a conspiracy in everything. Even in religion. A person just needs the wits to see things for what they really are in order to believe it."

The hunched, ponderous figure of Sam approached from the shadows. He held a flickering candle in one hand.

Dr. Hall stepped away from Kate and summoned the Negro with a wave of his arm. "Sam," he said, "get one of your contrabands and bring this boy's body out to the dead house."

"Yes, suh."

The doctor muttered something about needing to refresh himself with another swig of "bark juice," then bade Sam and Kate a stiff good night and abruptly left the ward.

Sam stood by quietly. Even in the dim candlelight Kate could see the whites of his eyes as he glanced in her direction, tilting his head as his eyebrows drew together, asking her: Was it Jack?

She swallowed and nodded silently. He understood, for his eyes answered as they welled with tears and his head bent with grief, and he went to work slowly, reverently, preparing the body for its shroud.

It was now well past midnight. Streams of moonlight filtered in through the long side windows, bathing the centre of the room in a pool of silvery light. Sam had finished his task. Another contraband had entered and was standing by the bedside to assist the removal.

"Good night, Sam," she said as the two men left.

With deft motions she stripped the bedclothes and discarded them in a pile at the foot of the bed. She would make the bed. But where was the folded sheet? There, on the desk where she had mindlessly placed it during the discussion with the doctor. She drew breath. Still, she could sense the unsteadiness in her limbs, the confusion of feeling in her mind, the fluttering sensation in her heart as she remembered how the doctor had looked at her that last time.

Impatiently, Kate seized the bedsheet and flung out the folds till it billowed like a cloud on a wind. It descended on the bed, and she straightened the corners, tucked in the edges, and pressed out the wrinkles, then replaced the soiled pillow and wool blankets with fresh ones.

"Does he not see that I am a Sister?" she said, shaking her head to ward off the thoughts that plagued her.

Gathering up the pile of old blankets and sheets, Kate prepared to return to her ward and relieve Sister Anna-Maria. She passed by several sentinels standing erect near the entrance as she glided out the door, their gleaming muskets thrown over their shoulders. Others she passed as they made their rounds along the corridors, their low, steady tramp sounding through the building like the echo within a desolate tomb. She deposited the armload of soiled linens in the laundry room and then stepped into the Third Ward. Moonlight was flooding the room like a lamp. She walked into the midst of the natural spotlight, surveying the room to find Sister Anna-Maria.

When she saw Kate, the Sister came forward with a candle and the two exchanged a few words on the condition of Sergeant Dallington, and then the Sister withdrew.

Left alone, Kate trod softly along the aisle. By now most of the soldiers were sleeping. She saw only three awake in their beds.

"God bless ya, lady," whispered one of the men in cracked tones as he smiled and raised his arm to salute her when she passed by.

The second man said nothing but observed her movements with an inquisitive stare. The third gave her a bashful glance before he buried his face in his pillow.

Somewhere out in the world the families of these men waited and worried for them. Somewhere out in the world Jack's family waited and worried for him. Everywhere the blood of sons, and brothers, and fathers, and lovers had been sacrificed. Was there a home in this nation that did not house the voice of one who cried out to God in agony for their irreplaceable loss? Though it had been issued by President Lincoln nearly two years earlier, was the emancipation of persons held as slaves a reality today, or was it to remain nothing more than a glorified idea embellished by eloquent speeches and eternal rivers of blood?

Her eyes wandered to the bed where Sergeant Dallington lay, asleep. The man's words, his false accusations against her, his unkind assumptions and the prejudice that made her his enemy—why was he so bitter? The sergeant stirred. His face contorted in sleep. She watched him.

Her duty remained unchanged. She would nurse the man still, though he had cut into the quick. Yet whilst she pitied his tormented state, she wished she would never have to look at his face again.

— CHAPTER XVIII —

THE VISITORS

"Get the amputation instruments ready—we start in an hour."

Dr. Hall strode toward Kate while she swept a pile of soot out from under the stove door of the Third Ward. He came from the direction of Sergeant Dallington's bed. The dark cloud hovering over the doctor's contracted brow mirrored the gloomy aspect of the chilling, wandering wind that moaned a solitary spirit across the snow-encrusted fields and hills, the leafless forests, the disgusting, mud-plastered streets outside the hospital. It told of an emergency.

"A sliver of uniform or dirt has bred that gangrene in the old boy," he went on. "We're not waiting any longer. We amputate that arm tonight, or it'll kill him."

Several weeks had glided by since Jack's death and the interview with the doctor. Since then, the condition of Sergeant Dallington was not improved. As scheduled, the remaining shrapnel had been removed from his arm the day after he had arrived from the field hospital, and for a time he was moved to convalesce with other patients in a nearby home, but he was later brought back to the Hall General when gangrene was detected in the wound.

On the day he returned to the Third Ward, the sergeant's body and brain were already racked with the agitation brought on by a mounting fever. For hours a day Kate watched him in a miserable, sleepless slumber as he tossed his head madly back and forth on his pillow, muttering incoherent, terrorized utterances and crying out in anguish as though overtaken by a ghost.

"Yes, Doctor," said Kate, and the dustpan clanged loudly against the metal waste bucket as she emptied it and set it aside along with the broom.

"After you get the instruments, stay by him, will you?" he said as he almost ran to the door. "There are two boys downstairs I'll check on before we get started."

Kate went directly to the operating room and took out the amputation kit. She ran her eyes over it. There were the two trephines; there, the bone nippers; there, the old bone saw that Sam had just sharpened; there, the tourniquet; there, the tenaculum; there, the forceps; there the scalpel. All of it in perfect order, as she had left it. Washed and ready for use. She gathered several cloths and sponges and arranged them on the washstand, then filled a large basin from the rainwater butt outside the kitchen door and set it in place beside them. Standing on tiptoe, she strained to reach the top shelf of the cupboard and retrieved the tinted bottle of chloroform, then set it out on the old wooden table next to the cone-shaped inhaler.

Straightway, she returned to her ward and went to the sergeant's bedside. His eyes were closed and he was unusually still, but she doubted that he slept. She sat down on the nearby chair. She took her rosary beads between her fingers, bowed her head, and closed her eyes while her lips commenced the first decade.

But behind her eyes she saw neither what she prayed about, nor heard what words her lips were speaking…

She saw great army encampments, like small villages, lay spread out over the frozen ground of the hillsides outside the capital. She saw dark masses of men moving about as they performed their drills. She saw a sea of soldiers in rows and rows of hospital beds. She heard their broken voices pouring out memories of family and children and lovers they would never see again. She saw Father Andrew bent over their bedsides administering Holy Viaticum… listening to the secret sins of the dying, feeding them *le Bon Dieu,* making the sign of the holy cross upon their foreheads, forgiving them, and sending their souls on the next stage of their journey. And she saw the sergeant refusing *le Bon Dieu*, as he had done the day before, and the day before that, and the day before that; heard his voice swearing that ill health—even death—could not force him to submit himself to the abominable practice of auricular confession.

The decade was done. Kate opened her eyes. He still slept. She rose from her seat and made the usual rounds, examining wounds and administering dosages to the fifty men in her ward. She stoked the fire in the cast-iron stove. It crackled merrily, but the heat could not entirely dispel the cold draft that stole into the building.

Still hunched before the stove, she noticed a figure enter and looked up to see Sister Bernice standing in the aisle at the foot of the sergeant's bed, beckoning Kate.

She straightened and went forward. "Yes, what is it?"

"There is a young lady here to see Sergeant Dallington," Sister Bernice replied in hushed tones.

"Who is she?"

"She says she is his daughter come all the way from Ireland. I wonder, is he well enough to see her?"

"What—his *daughter*?"

"Indeed. Her name is Priscilla Dallington, she says. She received the letter you sent over a month ago and is most anxious to see the sergeant. Another woman and a child have come with her. They are special friends, apparently. Shall I show them in now?"

Vacillating between the opinion that her patient should not be disturbed and feeling an obligation to allow his daughter to visit him before his surgery, Kate reluctantly consented to allow the visitors to enter, with the admonition that they must not stay long.

Sister Bernice soon returned to the room, trailed by a beautiful young woman in a sweeping dark-green wool travel suit. A beaver fur hat and a cloak trimmed in matching sheared beaver fur kept off the chill of the autumn night, and to ward off the offending hospital stench a delicate white satin handkerchief was held to her nose with a hand gloved in Swedish leather. Despite the concealing garments, however, Kate instantly recognized the woman as the one in the sergeant's miniature.

The young woman followed Sister Bernice to the sergeant's bedside, and without ceremony she rushed forward and fell to her knees beside it.

"Oh, my dear Papa!" she cried in a feminine whisper, clutching his hand and pressing it to her full lips. And then she laid her cheek against the back of his hand, rocking back and forth in silent grief.

"Miss Dallington, this is the sergeant's nurse, Sister Kate," said Sister Bernice with an introductory motion.

The woman gave hardly a lift of her head in notice. And then the sergeant stirred.

"Prissy, my darling daughter…" A moan escaped him before he opened his eyes. "God in heaven, can it be her?"

The feminine chin quivered as she stroked his matted hair. "Yes, Papa, I am here."

"They sent for you, did they?"

"Yes, Papa. A letter arrived at Aunt Augusta's saying you were wounded. We took the new tramway from Dublin to Queenstown and booked passage onboard a steamship, sailing almost immediately after."

He reached out and stroked her wet cheek. "I've missed you, sweetheart."

His voice was softer, kinder, more tender—was this the same man she had been nursing? She felt a tightening under her eyes as she wondered what it would feel like to have a father who spoke that way to her, who called her sweetheart and told her that he missed her, who stroked her cheek that way.

Miss Dallington turned his palm up and kissed it. "Papa, I've missed you, too… more than I can say."

"Where is Peter?"

"With Auntie. He and Ellen are to travel home in the spring, after we send word."

"Aye, yes"—he dotingly traced the dimple in her cheek—"it will be good to see my brave little soldier again. And Paul, darling… have you heard from him?"

"He writes nearly once a week and tells me he is in good health and spirits. When he was with the XII Corps at Antietam, Papa, he even saw Miss Barton from a distance when she was giving aid to the wounded soldiers on that terrible day in the cornfield. Paul has been lately promoted to the position of corporal, also, Papa. He said he saw you before your unit left for Fisher's Hill?"

"Briefly—just briefly. Now… Samuel Richardson—does

he know you're back? You must stay with his family in town. The army took over the farm—a field hospital now… one of our boys here told me."

"Of course, Papa, I will do that. Tonight we will go there. Since I am back home, though, Papa, I hope you wouldn't be opposed to me offering myself as a nurse with Miss Barton's relief efforts?"

"No, no—too dangerous, sweetheart… You are not old enough—too beautiful. The Union needs supplies as much as they need nurses… continue sewing, Prissy. Stay with Mrs. Richardson and her little ones… you can sew there, sweetheart—yes, sewing… Sewing linen is good; it is safe, Prissy… very safe for you." He groaned, then closed his eyes as his voice drifted off.

Kate dipped a cloth in cool water and bathed his forehead, hoping his daughter would discern the action as an indication that she should leave, for his exhaustion was evident. The young lady seemed blind.

"Excuse me, Sister," the young woman said, struggling to her feet as she unwound herself with delicate effort from the copious folds of wools and silk petticoats that appeared to have left her legs in a tangle among them. "How long has my father been here?"

"Over five weeks in Washington, miss," said Kate. "He convalesced elsewhere for a time before his wound became gangrenous. The notification letter was sent the day after he arrived on the ambulance."

"Do you know how it happened—his wound, I mean?"

"A shrapnel explosion. Unfortunately, even after the removal of the shrapnel it seems a piece of his uniform or some debris was missed, causing the infection."

"They won't need to amputate it, will they?"

"I am afraid, miss, that Dr. Hall has prescribed it as our last option."

The woman's face went still.

"That is," Kate added, "if the sergeant is to be saved from gangrene poisoning."

A fragile "Oh!" Then, "Do you know when the doctor will operate?"

"Tonight."

The young woman began to weep. Her shoulders shook and muffled sounds issued from within the gloved hands that hid the feminine face.

"No fretting, Prissy… remember?" Hoarse and laborious was the sergeant's voice. "You've met Sister Kate, my nurse, I assume? Ah, Sister Kate—see? My daughter, Priscilla."

Kate inclined her head. "Yes, I am pleased to meet you, Miss Dallington."

Miss Dallington mumbled and nodded and knelt beside the bed, and then Kate glanced up and was arrested by a tall shadow gliding two or three paces away from them, emerging into the glaring shaft of gaslight.

"You have another… visitor… sergeant?" she said almost inaudibly, for at the same instant her voice seemed to lose its power and trail off as she watched the elusive shadow become the stunning figure of a tall woman. The woman was clad in a perfectly fitted corduroy maroon travel suit; her face was partially concealed beneath the brim of a riding hat, her eyes shaded by the trim of a short veil constructed of black netting. Golden hair tastefully turned up and braided hemmed the lower part of the hat; glossy tendrils escaped the ear and temple area to frame a chin and jaw that were as impenetrable as they were exquisite. As exquisite as they were recognizable.

"Mama? Who's that?"

A child's voice. Kate started. A rustle of fabric near the woman's skirts and a little boy hiding behind them.

"Never mind, Willie. Hush now."

The woman's voice. She knew it. Her stomach wrenched.

With a smooth, strong, graceful stride, the woman came forward. Was that sudden flare of gaslight glinting off a piece of gold at the woman's bosom?

Yes. There was no doubt.

Shock, and stark realization, and electrifying tension made them gasp together.

"Collette?"

"Katie!"

The thin lips, like two scarlet threads, lifted at the corners, and delight beamed from the face as Collette's eyes animated.

Kate shuddered, and her hands flew to her ears, and she tore her gaze away. Oh, the exit! The exit! She must run and reach the exit!

Hot tears stung her eyes; emotion thundered in her chest as, chased by fear, Kate fled from the room, down the steps, through the halls, and toward the office. Eyes scorched and lungs burning, she reached it and slipped into the dark empty room and locked the door behind her, where she stood for a moment, her back against the cold oakwood, trembling.

"I will not speak to her! I will not forgive her! I will not! I will not!" she cried, sobbing and gasping by turns, clutching her sides.

Then she moved into the darkness and groped for the oak desk she knew was there. The tips of her fingers brushed its rough corner; she grasped it and slowly lowered herself onto the cold wooden floor. The draft crept up. It stole into her limbs. It made her shiver. The silence seemed to close in upon her. To suffocate her. At that instant she became conscious that something had followed her. Something dark, unseen, spiritual. Was she delivered to the tormentors now? Was hell closing in upon her? Was that the devil's laugh, laughing at her as he laughed at all his slaves?

A cold, involuntary spasm passed over her body; her mouth became dry; her eyes began to water—but not with tears. The blood seemed to drain from her limbs, rendering them stiff and lifeless. Did she hear the old cellar rat returning? Was he coming to eat the naughty little girl who had bad thoughts and said mean things about others?

She became nauseated, her mind overcome by sudden terror.

"Help me!… Why— Why… am I… like this? What is… what is wrong with… with me?" Her icy, clammy arms fumbled to hug her body. Rocking back and forth rapidly, feverishly, she uttered, "*Pater noster, qui es in caelis, sanctificetur nomen tuum. Adveniat regnum tuum. Fiat voluntas tua, sicut in caelo et in terra. Panem nostrum quotidianum da nobis hodie, et dimitte nobis debita nostra sicut et nos dimittimus debitoribus nostris. Et ne nos inducas in tentationem, sed libera nos a malo.* Amen."

Her posture unchanged, she continued The Lord's Prayer without pause or cessation. But alarm was gripping her, anxiety was engulfing her, fears were sucking and pushing and bullying her down into a swamp where the devil and his rat mocked her frail, floundering heart.

"Oh, Collette! Why? Why did you have to come back?" Tears coursed down her face as she broke the hypnotic rhythm of the Latin repetitions. Her words, low and aggressive, suddenly leapt with fright. "After all these years—banishing your memory—and now you come back! Why? To destroy me? Oh yes, I know—I know all too well that you'd drag me down to hell with you if you could, Collette Clayton!" She stopped short, gasping for air. "God preserve me from such witchery as yours! I shall never forgive you for what you have done to shame the name of God! If you think to change my opinion, you're wrong! You're wrong, wrong, wrong, I tell you!"

Kate rose to her feet, seething with an anger that would rival her fear of Collette's influence over her. Her jaw set in iron determination, her soul burned with a fierce, unconquerable passion that cried against all sympathy and humanity and declared them weak and foolish. "I am not afraid of you, Collette!" she cried. "Nor do I care what you, or anyone else, does, or thinks, or says about me! My duty is to God—and God forbid that I should ever fail him!"

An unclean presence invested the room. It was heavy, tangible. It reeked and burned and howled.

But her accusations against Collette were warranted—were they not? The woman was a heretic. An apostate. She had rebelled against the Romish Church, and every charge laid against her could be in every way justified and unforgiven.

But this inner conflict—this suffering that left Kate unconvinced that Collette's presence alone could exercise such an influence over her body and mind—what was it? This shadow on her life, this power of something she could neither see nor understand, much less identify—was it a man? Was it a woman? Was it a spirit? What unknown iniquity of an unknown family member had left her alone to bear the punishment of their unknown sin?

Sweating with trepidation, Kate peered through the darkness, thinking she had seen movement. But there was nothing there. She sensed something behind her and whirled around. The door was the only thing she saw.

The door…

If she left the room, she could escape the torture, the suffocating pressure that seemed to entrap her, to crush her like the coils of a python. But she might meet Collette, and that would be a fate worse than the darkness. Deception waited where Collette did; humiliation, the blackness—it would not be just this momentary fear of the dark.

Light footsteps sounded outside the door. Faintness made her sway, made her unable to catch her breath. The locked door was a fleeting sense of security. There—a slow grating in the lock, like a key being turned in it… turning, turning… turning…

Snatching wildly at the rosary on her left side, quivering and murmuring by turns, she gathered the beads and Mercy Cross in her wet palms and crushed them against her palpitating bosom. The door handle clicked. She made a wild dash for the corner of the room, where the bookshelf stood next to the long curtained window. The shadows provided by the thick drapery formed a covert in which she might conceal herself. There she crouched, hardly daring to breathe and shaking like a child just awakened from a nightmare.

The door began to open. It seemed to yawn by degrees, like the mouth of a great beast, and the wavering light of an oil lamp, like a serpent's tongue, seemed to lick up the cold shadows gathered around her quivering frame.

Kate lifted her eyes, and there, in the centre of the open doorway, stood a dark-robed figure.

— CHAPTER XIX —

THE AMPUTATION

"Hello? Is someone in here?"

The kind voice of Sister Bernice fell on Kate's strained ears. She scrambled to her feet, too stunned to speak and too mortified to step forward into the full light of the lamp. Sister Bernice entered the office and placed the lamp on the desk.

"Why, Sister Kate!" she exclaimed upon recognizing her. "Are you all right, my child? You look frightened."

"Oh my! Please, Sister Bernice… I, I, well…" Tears of relief sprang to Kate's eyes. "I'm afraid that… well, I should not have allowed Sergeant Dallington's visitors to see him. Could you please kindly tell them they must leave immediately?"

Sister Bernice came near and touched Kate's hands—oh, how her hands trembled so! She could not steady them!

"Of course," said Sister Bernice—how kind her voice was! "But do go warm yourself by the fire, child. It is cold as an icehouse in here, and your hands are freezing." A moment's hesitation; a looking upon Kate with what seemed like mingled confusion and concern; and then, keeping the door ajar, she withdrew, leaving the lamp still burning on the desk and Kate standing alone in the centre of the room.

Kate knew not how long she stood there, unable to move, waiting for she knew not what. But presently she heard a rush of footsteps coming down the stairwell, flowing along the hall, coming toward the office, and along with them the sound of female voices speaking in hushed tones.

"Is there a position that needs filling in this establishment, Sister Bernice? I know there are restrictions as regards the, uh"—there was a mild clearing of the throat—"the type of women who are permitted to work in these places, but I feel it my duty to at least offer myself as a volunteer. I am strong and can work long hours if you require it."

"We are always in need of fresh volunteers, my dear, and I can assure you that Dr. Hall is not particular in his selection as I know some are. He welcomes anyone who is plain, hardworking, and willing to learn. And I can tell you now that we are in particular need of a second laundress."

"Ah! Well, you need not look any farther. I may not appear plain in these travelling clothes, but that can be remedied, and I am quite used to tackling piles of filthy linens. When shall I start?"

"I'm sure if you come by tomorrow, we will be able to arrange a suitable shift for you. Have you ladies secured a place to board while you are in town?"

"Yes, Sister Bernice, Miss Clayton and I have already secured lodging. Samuel and Elizabeth Richardson—the family live not far from here."

There was a cordial thanks, a general farewell and goodnight, and then fading footsteps told that the visitors must now be gone.

Kate clenched her teeth as her hands turned to fists at her side. It was unthinkable, scandalous. Collette, a fallen woman—a woman with no husband and a child most certainly born out of wedlock. A woman younger than herself, an obvious scourge upon society—a woman with a beautiful face and a heart like a snare. And yet she was being hired as a laundress in an establishment devoted to the care of wounded soldiers—of *men*?

Dr. Hall knew nothing. And Sister Bernice was most imprudent to approve Collette on his behalf.

She crept to the door and stood in the shadow of the door frame, waiting in the empty stillness. Was it breathing she heard in the hall? Was there movement, like a faint rustling of skirts or a delicate twitch of a handkerchief?

"Miss Dallington?"

Kate's ears pricked; she stopped her breath short and listened.

"Yes?"

"There is something I must ask you."

"Of course, Miss Clayton, what is it?"

"Would you be willing to help care for my son while I offer my services at this hospital? William must not be neglected, and I know I can trust you with him. I have money. I will pay you well."

"Oh, of course, Miss Clayton, yes. It is very kind of you to volunteer, and I am sure they would appreciate your service a great deal. To care for your son while you are here would be a joy for me. But I would not do it for money."

"Well, thank you." There was a short laugh. "But I must give you something."

A moment passed. Kate found herself straining to listen. What kind of woman had Collette become? Wealth and privilege exuded from her presence. Where could she have acquired the means—except by prostitution?

"Oh, Miss Clayton! Why, you are shaking. Is something troubling you?"

"No, no, it's nothing." A pause; a sniff; a violent blow into a handkerchief before: "Except that… well, visiting this place brings back many memories from… from my past life. But I thank you, Miss Dallington. I thank you very much for your kindness, and for everything you and your family have done for my son and me."

"Well, I am just grateful we are able to be of help to you. Shall we be going now? Our carriage driver will be waiting. We will go to the Richardsons' place—they are only a few minutes' drive away from here. Come."

The sound of footsteps began. They went in the direction of the main exit. They died away. A creaking of doors, a dull thud announcing the front doors opening and closing, and then silence in the hall.

Kate stood motionless.

Outwardly, Collette had changed. Five years could do that. She was a woman of the world now, with its mark branded upon her forehead and displayed in the thick tresses that crowned her head with the same vanity she displayed as a child. But inwardly she had not changed. She was still apostate. The same evil spirit that had driven her away from the convent was driving her here now.

"Her motive in taking up employment here is not because of the patients or the cause," said Kate, filled with loathing as she paced the floor. "It is because she intends to cross paths with me! Surely, surely that is why! She intends to ask questions, and make peace, and trap me!"

Just then the clock in the hall struck the eighth hour.

"The amputation!" Kate's hand flew to her mouth. "I'll be late!"

Breaking almost into a run, she rushed to the operating room, which adjoined the hospital's largest ward on the main floor and was situated several yards up along the same hallway shared by the office. A light shone underneath the door. Passing footsteps and hurried voices sounded from within. Kate paused to catch her breath and steady her nerves, then pushed the door open.

The room's aspect was ghastly and severe. The shutters were tightly closed and the gas lamps glared, casting unnaturally sharp and elongated shadows along the bare walls. Two or three candles flickered atop the old wooden table, illuminating the harsh, glinting steel of the amputation instruments. There was the high operating table, and Dr. Hall in position. He was examining Sergeant Dallington, who lay stretched out on top of the table. The two male assistants were nearby, and Sam stood in the background, ready, as usual, to carry amputated limbs out back.

Without glancing up to ascertain that it was her, the doctor gruffly demanded that Sister Kate record the date for the left-arm amputation of Sergeant John Dallington.

Kate moved to the table, took up the little brown book and its corresponding pencil, and began to write.

"Ready, old boy?" said the doctor as he rolled up his sleeves.

"Ready," the sergeant returned, his face damp and rigid, his eyes glazed and brilliant with fever. "Did you sharpen your saw?" he added, as though trying for lightness.

Dr. Hall did not look at the sergeant. "It's sharp," he said calmly, but the tightened muscles of his face and the forgoing of his wont sarcasm told Kate that he was unsettled.

After entering the necessary information in the book, she took her place at the doctor's side, and the familiar rank stench of perspiration wafted under her nose. As custom had it, Dr. Hall had likely not bathed or changed his clothes in weeks.

"Hand me that bottle of chloroform," he said to her.

She held out the bottle as well as the inhaler. He snatched the bottle but ignored the inhaler. "Don't need it," he said, grabbing a cloth from the table. He applied several drops of the sweet-smelling transparent liquid onto the cloth and administered the anesthesia by holding the cloth over the sergeant's nose. Suddenly, Kate realized that the doctor's surgical apron was yet soiled with blood and pus. It was the one item she had failed to wash and ready for him. Doubtless, he would scold her for it.

In several minutes the anesthesia rendered the patient senseless. "Boys," said Dr. Hall to the assistants, "get ready to hold him. Sister Kate, stand over here"—he jerked his head toward the side of the table across from him—"and hold up the limb for me. Wait, give me the scalpel knife first."

Kate handed him the scalpel.

Grasping it, he looked at her. His eyes pierced her. A muscle twitched in his face. "Remember?" he said. "I don't make orphans."

He proceeded to make a circular incision through the flesh and sinew of the arm just above the elbow, leaving two flaps of skin on each side that would later be sewn over the stump. Warm deep-crimson blood touched Kate's fingertips as she found the main artery and held it closed.

"I'm your enemy—you know that, right?"

The sergeant's words throbbed against her brain; she closed her eyes but could not shut out his voice; it was as strong as the pulse she felt in her own body.

"You can hate me if you like. It will make me feel better, actually."

Strong feelings of pity and confusion surged through her. She didn't see him as her enemy—why did he hate her? Was it her clothes? She had done her best to serve him in his hour of need. But he had wished her to hate him instead.

Her stomach reeled and knotted with a sensation of nausea as a sudden, unusual desire to flee the room seized her faculties.

"Stop trembling!" the doctor snapped.

"I'm sorry, Doctor," she almost cried, struggling to ignore the dizziness fogging her vision. She bit her lip until it stung. Her eyes watered with an unknown pain that touched her heart and made it weep.

"What's wrong with you tonight?" he said. "You've done this hundreds of times before without flinching—why can't you do it now?" But he did not wait for a reply. Once he had cut down to the bone, he exchanged the scalpel for the bone saw and began to speedily sever the limb.

The rasping, grating noise seemed to rouse the patient; he began to moan, his legs writhed, his head began to toss.

"Keep him down, boys! Keep him down!"

The assistants braced themselves as they fastened their hold, but Kate saw their eyes—were they doubtful?

"He's in the fog—can't feel a thing." Dr. Hall shot them a look of warning. "But don't dare let him move."

The bone saw began rasping and scraping again, pulsing back and forth as though it were a living thing. Soon the limb was detached. Kate caught it—it almost slipped from her quivering hands—then she quickly wrapped it in a cloth, placed it in a basket, and handed it to Sam, who took it away. Dr. Hall seized the forceps and pulled out the nerves of the stump before cutting them. Kate caught up a piece of silk thread and quickly tied off the arteries then took a needle and thread and assisted in suturing the stump. Within ten minutes the operation was completed.

"There—that's right," said the doctor as he watched Kate's finishing motions with the needle. "Be careful to leave a clean drainage hole there." Three firm strokes across the front of his filthy apron and Dr. Hall declared himself clean. "Boys, transfer him back to his ward upstairs. You"—he looked at Kate—"give him a dose of morphine and stay by him for the remainder of the night."

"Yes, Doctor," she said as the assistants laid the sergeant on a stretcher and transported him out of the room.

Dr. Hall untied and pulled off his apron. "Make sure this thing gets washed, will you?" He tossed it on the table with the pile of bloodstained rags and instruments. “And keep your wits about you next time, for pity’s sake.” He wheeled and went to the door without looking at her, muttering, “I need to steal a jug of bark juice before my legs buckle.”

— CHAPTER XX —

THE DOCTOR SPEAKS

The advent of spring found Kate feeling the effects of the winter's long months of strenuous work and cold. Neither frequent walks in the fresh winds nor the sights of bright flowers blooming wild in the ditches could defeat a rasping, straggling cough that had affected her for weeks, nor could it subdue the general fatigue that by noon each day made her limbs feel heavy and often immobile.

On a pleasant evening in early April, the sun began its downward course behind the purple hills while a wild spring breeze frolicked through the open windows of the hospital as Kate administered dinner to the patients in the Third Ward.

Sam walked up to her and said in a low voice, "Sista Kate, da Doc, he want to see ya in da office straightway, when you's finished up, Sista."

Kate hesitated. Dr. Hall proved a constant distraction, and his attentiveness to the state of her health was an additional source of increased emotional strain.

"What does he want, Sam?" she asked, gathering up the remaining dishes and utensils.

Sam shrugged. "Don't know, Sista," he returned, scratching his head. "Just says he wants Sista *Kate.*" The added stress on her name made Kate cringe. For months she had been assiduous in performing all hospital duties with the most disciplined manner and perfect formality. But what unspoken current of thought lapped the sandy edges of even the most regular tasks, eroding the safe confines of their common regularity? What living tension strained like an unruly tide of emotion between her and Dr. Hall, defying all her practical explanations to push it back?

Sam still stood there, mute, waiting for her answer.

"Thank you, Sam, I'll go see him," she finally said.

She made her way downstairs, depositing some dirty dishes next to the two Nursing Sisters already engaged in washing and drying the mountainous pile of plates and bowls and cutlery collected from the evening meal.

Indeed, day by day the doctor's attentions had increased. He made unusual visits to her ward on pretense that he required some trifling article or tool, or he came on errands to which Sam and the other attendants were designated. Even at meals she would feel her empty stomach rumble while her mind resisted, and then she would look up from her full portion of meat and potatoes with butter and gravy still steaming on her plate to find him looking at her across the mess hall table, and she could almost hear his voice speaking through his eyes, saying quietly, "If you're hungry, Kate, then eat." He may have endeavoured to keep her unaware of his loyalty; but Kate could not deny the tender concern she felt from him. It was a loyalty which she was unable to rebuff without making his advances appear even more obvious.

Untying her white apron, Kate made her way down the corridor toward the office. On her way she passed the open doorway of the main lower ward. The sounds of weeping met her ears. She paused and looked into the room. Kneeling at the bedside of one of the patients was a pretty young lady dressed in lilac-and-green calico. But the woman's face was contorted with suffering and terror, her long hair dishevelled as she tore at it with hands frantic, shaking with the intensity of her grief.

Beside the woman was a little girl dressed in matching calico print, whose face was white and drawn, nearly emotionless as she watched the painful demonstrations of her distraught mother.

Footsteps approached them. Kate looked over and saw Collette. Sympathy glowed on Collette's face; tears stood in her eyes.

"Ma'am, I'm so sorry," said Collette as she knelt on the dirty floor beside the woman and put her arm around her quivering shoulders. "I'm so sorry you've lost him."

"Oh! He was good! So good to us! My husband! My husband!" Rocking back and forth, pressing her hand against her mouth as her face contorted with grief, the woman cried and murmured and wept. “He was such a good, good man!... Wasn't he? Wasn't he?”

“Yes, he was—a very, very good man.” Collette rubbed the woman's back, her face expressing pity and grief. And the little girl looked at them both, a lost expression in her tearless eyes; and then she looked upon the corpse of her dead father as though she struggled to understand the difference between slumber and death.

“Oh! Oh! Oh! How shall Polly and I go on without him? How shall we? How shall we? Oh!”

Collette offered the woman a handkerchief; the woman dabbed it on her swollen red eyes, then collapsed into Collette's arms, breaking into repeated spasms of tears. Sympathy, warmth, compassion—all showed in Collette's honest look as she cradled the woman's head against her bosom and swayed gently from side to side, weeping with her.

“There's no known substitute for the milk of human kindness,” Dr. Hall had told Kate when she had gone to him months before, explaining the obvious facts of Collette's fallen state that would justify her hidden scruples against the woman and—she had hoped—send her away from the Hall General. “If that woman can provide such a rare substance to this hospital,” he had concluded, “then I'm happy.”

Kate shook her head against the recollection and hurried away down the hall. Forcing back the tears that pricked her own eyes was nothing but a vain effort. All through the winter, Collette's presence in the hospital wards had been a constant source of strain, though the two had never exchanged a word. For months Kate had striven to maintain a perfectly composed exterior that would give the impression of a spirit that was both settled and resigned, but the haunting ghost of bitterness and the shadow of resentment were both as raw as the wound still bleeding from Collette's divorce of the Romish Church. But now there was a new knowledge: the deep sympathy and comfort that Collette was capable of showing—and it proved right Dr. Hall's initial conclusion about her. Whatever secrets were held in Collette's past, they had not hardened her heart.

Whatever wrongdoings and pain she had experienced in the world, whatever guilt had sullied her conscience, seemed to have wrought the very opposite effect, producing a kindness, a meekness, an ability to mourn that Kate knew nothing of.

She dashed away tears and approached the office. She peered into the room through the half-open doorway and saw the backside of the doctor. He stood before the long open window, his posture slumped and a full whiskey bottle made of green glass on the desk behind him.

Stepping away from the opening, she took in a steadying breath, pushed aside the thoughts of Collette, then raised her hand and made three light taps against the solid wood.

A solemn "Yes?" issued from within.

Keeping her eyes bent on the floor and her lips sealed, Kate pushed the door open and slipped in, consciously leaving it standing fully open behind her.

"Ah, Sister Kate, thank you for coming." The surgeon shifted on his feet and turned around as an unsettled expression deepened the lines in his forehead. He cleared his throat uncomfortably once or twice, then lifted his dark eyebrows, looked at her, and said, as though trying to sound casual, "Please, step in—you can shut the door."

Kate did not move. Closing the door of the office with them alone together in it was like asking her to take up a viper in her bare hands and not expect it to bite her. She would do no such thing. Her eyes lifted for an instant and she cast the doctor a reproving glance.

"Ah yes, I suppose I don't much resemble your priest, do I?" Sarcasm flashed in his bloodshot hazel eyes.

"I beg your pardon, Doctor?"

"Well, you split no hairs about being in a confined area with the physician of your soul, I merely thought you would not be partial when a similar situation concerned me."

Kate drew in an unsteady breath. The peculiar suggestion in the doctor's manner as he presented the picture made her wonder if he was calling her a hypocrite. "I have not asked you to be the physician of my body, sir, if that makes any difference."

He ignored her. "Close the door only partially, will you?"

But she stood resolutely on the threshold—unmoving, resolved to wait for his instructions with silent, businesslike patience—and hoped that he would be as quick and unassuming in his matter as she had been in responding to his summons.

"Very well," he finally said. He hemmed and reached for a cigar. He struck a match on the heel of his boot, lit the tip of the cigar, and placed it between his lips. The cigar rocked up and down several times while he performed the preliminary puffs that would cause the smoke to boil out of him like lava from the centre of a volcano. "It's been a long day," he commented, harrowing his other hand through his hair—greasy hair, as usual, which firmly held the deep furrows made by his fingers.

He seemed wholly unconscious of any urgency to bring the interview to a close, and Kate wondered if she ought to press him. But just before she was about to say something, he turned to face her fully. The boldness in his manner made her stiffen; her gaze darted away for one instant before she gathered herself together—no, she was not afraid of him—and she then lifted her chin in an effort to draw out the boundary line between them with more accuracy than a single word could do.

He appeared to understand the action, and to suddenly regret his cigar with uncommon contrition, for he plucked the smoking piece from his mouth and discarded it in on the desk. Then, with a loud exhalation from his nose that brought smoke pouring out of his nostrils, he began to pace the room, both hands clasped tightly behind his back. "You are not well, Sister Kate," he said bluntly.

"I am as well as may be expected, under the circumstances."

"Precisely," he said. "You're working too hard."

"I appreciate your concern, Doctor," she returned without flinching. "But I assure you, I am not working too hard."

He pursed his lips and wagged his head. "Denial is a more difficult dilemma to cure than physical disease, isn't it? I'll be frank: if you don't slow down, you'll kill yourself with exhaustion."

"It is doubtful whether any of us can expect to maintain our positions here at the hospital without any small degree of physical strain."

"I am not merely speaking of 'physical strain.' I refer to the deterioration of your general health, which will be the direct result of mental and emotional exhaustion."

"I feel in perfect health, sir. I am merely behind in sleep."

"And decent food," he added quickly. "Sister Kate, I'm a doctor. I know illness when I see it."

A growling in her stomach confirmed the doctor's accusation, and Kate felt herself colour with embarrassment. Despite her workload she had studiously maintained her regular fasting routine, and she knew the practice enflamed the doctor.

He inhaled, and a strange look stole across his face. "We all have our vices, don't we?" he said quietly.

"I beg your pardon?"

"I mean, we're all servants to a master." He glanced at the whiskey bottle on the table, then reached for the smoking cigar and examined it. "You have a habit and veil. I have a bottle and cigar. Makes us even, right?"

"Forgive me, sir, but I am afraid I do not understand the metaphor."

"I said we're all servants to a master," he repeated with emphasis, "and we each decide who that master will be—understand now?" He carelessly looked her up and down, jutted his chin at the whiskey bottle, and deposited the cigar between his lips. "These things come to us as consolations, but in the end they become the vices that control the way we live our lives. Like a mask, they hide who we truly are."

Kate lifted her chin again. "Doctor," she said impatiently, "I believe you called me here because you required my assistance?"

"Not your assistance. Your attention. Forgive me, I understand you are a busy woman." He hemmed loudly and assumed an official air. "Sister Kate, upon closer inspection of your generously robed figure I've concluded that you've grown dangerously thin underneath it." Deftly, he plucked the cigar from his lips, twitched it in her direction, and glanced over her figure, transferring his weight from one foot to the other as he performed the examination. "You eat next to nothing," he reported gruffly. "It's a known fact. The fresh buttermilk that Cook tries to feed you in the morning would be the best tonic, but you refuse it and eat herbs instead. And all for what? Vanity? Pride? Is it because you want to become a saint or something? Or just a vestal virgin? You baffle me. You're a rack of bones and still you insist on fasting compulsively."

His lips formed a thin tight line that grew almost white, and he flexed his sinewy fingers. "Do you consider these things, Sister Kate?"

"Doctor, I assure you that my fasting has no frivolous motive attached to it, as your questions uncharitably assume. It is exclusively a spiritual exercise."

"Indeed," said the doctor, sarcasm edging his tone. "Just like celibacy—a *spiritual exercise*, as you modestly point out, designed to starve the passion out of you while teaching you to embrace the corpse of paganism in an attempt to satiate the insatiable need. You think it will do it?"

"I fail to see your point, Doctor."

"This unique marriage of paganism and religiosity—do you think it will kill the need you have?"

"I have no need but the need for God, Doctor."

"That is precisely what I mean: will this marriage satiate you?"

"Man's sole need is his need of God. To know him, and to hear him speak. And yes, I believe that God will satiate that need for me."

"And permitting such a conviction, what becomes of human love? Is it a sin?"

Her lips came tightly together and she lifted her chin. The fear she had of herself in that moment could hardly outweigh the pained expression in the doctor's eyes. She cleared her throat then, and said, "Doctor, it is fair to say that each man and woman walks alone with God. It is before God that they each must settle their minds and wills, and reconcile their desires. I have chosen my path, and you have chosen yours. Let us be content."

"That is the fascinating thing about us single folk, isn't it? We have something to reconcile." He smiled bitterly as he put the cigar between his lips again and puffed. "Married people can't understand it, though—this constant search to fill the human need. They forget how it feels to ache. Therefore, in the midst of their marital boredom, they resort to playing the critic toward those poor, conflicted spinster and bachelor nomads whom *they* think will *only* be happy if they, too, resort to the partial satiation advertised about in the news of holy matrimony. Walking nuns, of course, know nothing of such discrimination"—he shrugged and put his hands on his hips, pushing out his lower lip where the cigar wiggled loosely—"for their religious costume mysteriously deters the inevitable judgment that the unmarried celibates have been doomed to suffer for millennia."

"I think our business in these matters does not concern each other further, Dr. Hall."

"Well!" said the doctor, half laughing. "It concerns me in part, I must argue, because I work with you." He extracted the cigar from his mouth, holding it between two fingers as he resorted to pacing the floor again. At length he halted before the window and looked out across the street. The cigar twitched. "You know," he exclaimed with sudden impatience as he turned around to face her, "since working with the nuns I've never been acquainted with one who's as dedicated and skilled as yourself. But of course I won't waste time flattering you by making an exhaustive list of your attributes as a nurse—you're clever enough to know that when I say you are valuable here—and we can't afford to lose you—I mean it."

"Dr. Hall, again, I thank you for your concern," said Kate, battling against a feeling of weakness, "but permit me to plead my case over my fellow nurses who have sacrificed their lives serving as I do now. I hope you can understand that I do not expect a fate less honourable than theirs."

"But, to prevent an untimely death, will you listen to advice? You know, negligence of one's own health is as bad as neglecting that of others."

Her neck and ears grew hot beneath her wimple, and her gaze fell. "If God has sent me here, then I am fully convinced that, should I live or die, he will accomplish his desire."

The doctor eyed her narrowly. "Philosophy isn't logical here, Sister Kate. Don't kill yourself."

She offered no response, determined to inform him of her opposite opinion by maintaining her silence.

He picked up his pacing across the room again, seeming to weigh out the different options his circumstance allowed, yet not without a keen frustration that manifested itself in the tight clamp of his chiselled jaw. "Sister Kate, what is it that motivates you?"

She looked at him squarely, ignoring her instinct to evade. "My purpose is to become an acceptable sacrifice in the eyes of God."

"But this god of yours—does he have no compassion?"

"We do not always understand his ways, Doctor."

"But he still wants to keep you crawling back to him so he can keep his foot on the back of your neck?"

"He requires the continual chastisement of the indomitable enemy."

"Ah!" Dr. Hall gave a sardonic huff, walked to the table, and tapped his cigar against the ashtray to dispose of its inch-long ember. "And, uh… just *who* is this… this 'indomitable enemy,' and just how do you chastise it?"

"The enemy is our flesh, sir. And we chastise it by suffering bodily on behalf of the Mother Church. In turn we shall certainly receive the forgiveness of God and the favour of the Heavenly Bridegroom."

Blood rushed to his face; suddenly, he flung the cigar on the table, slapped his palms onto the tabletop, then clenched is hands into fists as his knuckles turned white. "What drunken bastard told you that?" he burst out, turning to look at her as though upon some intangible, evasive obstacle that he would stop at nothing to strangle and crush the life out of if only his hands could reach it. "That's a bunch of hogwash—hogwash! You know better—I know you do! But you don't fear God, you don't serve God—you fear and serve this institution, this *man* that you only *think* is God—right?" he almost screamed as he pushed himself away from the table and approached her. "Right?"

Kate stepped backward toward the door, reaching her hands behind her, feeling for the wall, afraid he might reach out and grapple her.

"You're so insufferable!" he went on angrily, stopping short and pressing his forehead with his palm. "So stubborn and headstrong and proud that you will insist black is white and bitter is sweet and believe that evil is good and truth is a lie! You know this hospital needs you—right? You look around and see it every day, right? You know the sick and wounded boys need you—you know *I* need you!"

His voice shook as he looked into her eyes, and her heart thrilled for an instant as she read in his glance the truth of his feelings for her.

"You know what?" he said. "I look at you and wonder, 'Why? Why! Why in tarnation does Sister Kate do this? This inhuman *torturing* of herself?' You can't even enjoy the simple pleasures of life! You can't smile or eat without confessing later—next thing you know you won't be allowed to *breathe!* It's foolishness. No, it's worse than foolishness. It's insanity—pure insanity! It's as though you like being in prison—this prison you call religion!"

"Dr. Hall, please—"

"And do you know what I see?" he said through clenched teeth. "I'll tell you what I see. You—the pure, pious, untouched little nun—searching for someone who will care for you, someone who will love you, accept you, help you like the poor, lonely little girl that you are inside… But you would walk to the scaffold tied up and gagged sooner than admit the fact!" His face turned white. His chest heaved. "It maddens me to no end to see you willingly— No, stupidly… stupidly suffering disease and depravation by your own hand."

"Dr. Hall, my moral obligations and the nature of my position here demand the highest level of service. You cannot ask me to limit myself in this."

"Moral obligations? Moral obligations?" He uttered an oath. "Whoever said I was asking you not to fulfill your 'moral obligations'? When did I ever tell you to 'limit your abilities'? Who the hell gave you the boneheaded idea that I don't expect the 'highest level of service' from you—or from anyone else working under me? But do you seriously think that a man worth his salt is going to stand aside and watch a woman kill herself as you do?" He stopped directly in front of Kate and glowered at her, then looked at her imploringly, as though tottering between the two vulnerable extremes of rage and weeping. "You know, I've had it up to my eyeballs with all your neat sidestepping—your conceited modesty, your twisted spiritualizing and philosophical drama. For once why won't you be honest with me—honest with *yourself*?"

Kate, shocked by his passion and sensing in herself an overwhelming fear that threatened to topple the usual appearance of self-possession she could exude even under tension, stared back at him. "Dr. Hall, please... Compose yourself, please. This outrage is unnecessary—I assure you."

He dealt her a stormy glance, grinding his teeth together. "You'll tell me what to do now, eh? Tell me bloody well that I'm blind?" he said bitterly. "Oh no. My eyes and ears tell me when I see pearls cast before swine, and now I see that those swine are turning on you and rending you to pieces in front of me!" He drew his sleeve across the sweat beading his forehead and took breath. "But I won't mince words with you. If you insist on ruining your health on account of your own stupid obstinacy, then my hands are tied." He looked down at the half-finished cigar still lying neglected on the tabletop, a thread of smoke twisting above it. He seized it, flung it on the floor, and ground it with the heel of his boot. Then he stormed passed her, grabbing his hat and coat from the wooden bench. He was about to leave the room, but when he reached the door he halted abruptly, as if arrested by a sudden thought. Spinning around and brushing past her, he made for the desk and seized the whiskey bottle by the neck. "Only a dog returns to his vomit," he said, glaring at it. Then he hoisted the bottle above his head, drew back his arm, and hurled the bottle across the room, where it crashed against the corner of the back wall, showering glass splinters and whiskey in all directions.

Kate shrank back and gasped, her hands flying up to cover her ears from the shock of sound shivering the air. And then it was suddenly quiet. And moments passed. And there was no movement. Only a heavy, horrible silence. Finally, she looked up at the doctor, terrified, and her legs went weak when she found his penetrating eyes fixed upon her. They were wet with tears.

"Kate," he said huskily.

Her heart skipped a beat, knowing he had intentionally addressed her without the customary prefix. By the slack look on his face, he appeared to have received a sense of relief in doing so.

"I once told you I didn't believe in God, but now," he said, dashing the heavy stream of tears from his cheeks with the heel of his hand, "now I believe differently. Now I know there is a God, and I know he loves you, and I know he sent you here to find that out." His lip quivered. He bit it, then turned on his heel and rushed from the room.

Only Kate's determination to preserve her dignity, even in private, saved her from a complete breakdown. She shut the door and bolted it, then flung her body against the wooden frame as she fought through the tempest of emotions whirling inside her. Provoked by his words, enflamed by his very presence, a violent sob escaped her as she crushed the innate desire to respond.

He had unearthed a secret she had kept concealed even from herself; and now, drug out as it was into the naked light, she felt frightened, insecure, and betrayed. Betrayed not by him or by anyone else, but by her own self, by her own inability to conceal the dream of human love to which her stubborn heart still clung with desperate tenacity. Now neither determination, nor mental powers, nor endless resolutions were enough to calm this stormy sea that flung about the wreckage of hidden desire and beat it against the cruel rocks as though it had been nothing but a drifting mast tossed about on the salty billows.

"He thinks I, I'm crazy—mad…" she whispered rapidly. "Am I? Am I mad?"

Her body shook and vibrated. She could not control it. She paced the room and saw the shattered glass and the puddle of liquor cowering in the corner. What made him give it up? What made him suddenly hate it even more than she had hated it?

She walked to the window and looked out. A single strip of crimson stained the western sky. Two birds flew just above the horizon, imprinting their inky silhouettes against the blue and orange and purple dusk of the zenith. She watched the birds until they disappeared in the distance. "Little birds... why can't I follow you?" she said, beginning to cry.

The evening was not cold, but she shivered. She wrapped her thin arms about her sides and bowed her head; tears wet her cheeks; she whimpered. Lowering herself into a kneeling position on the floorboards, she felt for the rosary hanging at her left side. Her fingers caressed the smooth, familiar burnished wooden beads. She prayed, beginning with the Hail Mary, but even as she continued through the decades of the rosary, a familiar voice wandered into her mind, interrupting her, reproving her. It was the priest speaking, on the day of her First Communion.

"It is always God's will that a young girl offer herself willingly upon the altar of service to the Church of Rome."

The words scalded Kate's brain. "It is God's will—God's will! God's will that I do what I do! It's for God, and for my family! I must do it, and do it well!"

She tried to ignore the suffocating sense of confusion that enveloped her by beginning another decade, but her schooled repetitions could not drown out the flood of longings and questions that began slowly, gradually at first and then more forcefully, to inundate her mind. She found herself beginning to wonder why she was doing what she did, to wonder how the words she uttered in prayer—and had uttered a hundred times before—suddenly seemed so strangely empty, so unavailing, as though they laughed at her.

"Poverty... Chastity... Obedience... Service! My vows! My vows! My vows!" she whispered, dragging her mind through the mire of the past and back to the present.

Time passed. The decades dried up on her lips. Her cold, trembling, raw-boned fingers halted their measured course along the beads. It was impossible. Stillness would not come.

"Our Father, which art in heaven"—at least that prayer she had learned in English from hearing many of the soldiers recite it over and over on their deathbeds—"Hallowed be thy name. Thy kingdom come. Thy will be done in earth, as it is in heaven. Give us this day our daily bread. And forgive us our debts, as we forgive our debtors. And lead us not into temptation, but deliver us from evil: For thine is the kingdom, and the power, and the glory, for ever. Amen."

She shuddered. "Oh, I am wretched! Wretched! Wretched, aren't I?" she cried, then she bowed her head and buried her face in her wet, trembling hands. "Is he right? Is the doctor right about me? Am I just afraid of man and not of God—or am I just afraid of myself? How shall I know? How shall I *know*?" She suddenly turned her face upward; tears coursed down her face, and though her words were broken, convulsive, as she struggled to draw enough air to breathe, she cried, "Father in Heaven… I know not what to pray, except that thy will be done! *Thy will be done!*"

With a moan of bitter agony, she cast herself face down on the floor, stretching her quivering body out upon the cold boards with her arms extended away from her sides, allowing herself to be swallowed up in the dark yawning valley of a painful helplessness—a valley in which the remotest star that twinkled in the gathering gloom seemed nearer than a God in heaven whose heart might or might not beat with a low, steady, warming thunder…

He seemed ten thousand miles away.

— CHAPTER XXI —

TWO OPINIONS

It was finally Sunday, and John sat upright in his bed feeling unusually amiable and sharp. His worn copy of Calvin's *Institutes of the Christian Faith*, which he had studied all morning, was drooping now, by degrees, toward his lap. The morning sunshine filtered through the east casement opposite his bed, and he plucked his spectacles from his nose, more inclined to watch and listen as the sun rose above the awakening city and to hear the church bells chime eight o' clock than to read the passages he had perused and practised and preached to the boys ever since his returning health had permitted him to do so.

His interest flagging with the decline of Calvin onto the blankets, he was reminded of the innocent diversion he often enjoyed in secret. Though plenty of the men in the ward did not care that *their* dependence on it was generally known, he preferred to practise discretion in his personal habits—and this particular habit was justified, certainly, by the reality that the boys' habits were considerably more advanced than his.

As John considered the idea, it burned his brain—for certainly he needed it—and its goading flame induced his hand to creep into his pillowcase and withdraw the battered tin of opium pills. Aye, but there was a decent twinge of pain in his arm yet, too—enough, at least, to justify him an opiate for today.

John opened the tin, hastily inserted a pill into his mouth, closed the lid tight. At that moment, bustling sounded in the hall outside the recovery ward, followed by the entrance of half a dozen nuns, maids, and convalescent men; among them was his nurse.

"Why, top of the morning to you, Sister Kate!" he cried, smuggling the tin back into the pillowcase with a broad grin.

"I'm feeling quite well this morning. How are you?"

She was now approaching his area carrying a tray loaded with the morning's rations, preparing to distribute them along the row of men. But she did not answer him; in fact, she hardly looked.

The air quickly filled with the stimulating aroma of fresh-brewed coffee, the prattle of voices, the swish of bustling movements, and the clatter of utensils. The men who could eat smiled gratefully as they received their breakfast, uttering choruses of "Thankee! Thankee! Thankee, ma'am! God bless you, ma'am! Best coffee I've tasted, ma'am!" as they prepared to relish the steaming fare.

"Here's your breakfast, sir," said Sister Kate to him, neglecting to acknowledge his former address. A studied reaction, no doubt.

John glanced doubtfully at the steaming tray of food. "You got any coffee left? The brew the attendant perked early this morning was about as thick as mud soup and tasted as bad. I dare say the boy was slightly overenthusiastic about the long sweetening, too."

"You do not prefer molasses?" she returned tartly as she dished out a steaming bowl of porridge. "This coffee pot is empty, sir. But if you did not care for the first brew, I am sure Fritz will be happy to make you a new cup."

"Ah, Fritz, was it? The dear fellow… he likes his mud water." He let his eyes sparkle with humour as he glanced at the full mug. "Well, in that case, a drink of *water* will do fine." He feigned a cough in order to conceal an outright laugh as she poured him a glass and handed it to him. "Well, I've been knackered long enough—I'm a happy man today to have my strength returning and my children visiting me after church on my last Sunday in the ward. What else could a man ask for?"

Her gaze flicked up. "Shall I get you anything, sir?"

John finished the water. She was always so cold, so reserved and impenetrable, and he wondered for a fleeting instant how he could pry a smile out of her before he left the next day. Even though she had always been kind to him, the young nun was all—and only—business, and to think up a scheme to outwit her with humour at that time or any other would be futile, since her duties always claimed her first and best moments of attention. "No, I'm quite all right, thanks," he finally said, plunking down the empty glass on the bedside table. He glanced at the bowl of cornmeal porridge and promised himself that, after only twenty-four hours were expired, he would never eat the tasteless mash again.

"Then if you require further assistance, please send for Sister Bernice. When I am finished here I will be assisting the doctor down the corridor." She turned briskly and dished out tasteless mash to the next patient.

Avoiding his own bowl of porridge and the first brew of cold mud water, John's eyes fell easily upon his Bible, which lay on the stool next to his bed, opened to the seventh and eighth chapters of Hebrews. He had been reading the passages the previous evening, and if there was one point that would solicit attention from the taciturn little nun, it would certainly be a conversation on doctrine; and since it was Sunday, such a topic could not but be eagerly entered in upon by her—most especially if it involved the subject she always seemed so adamant to suggest to him as one of the most important of all her seven Sacraments.

When she was passing in front of his bed about to leave, he raised his arm and cleared his throat loudly.

"Ah… yes… Well, actually, Sister Kate," he began as she looked around to ascertain the speaker, "would you have time for a few questions? Before I leave, I would like to resume our conversation regarding confession." Her head turned slightly to the side, and he added, "That is, if you have the time?"

Her shapely dark eyebrows curved upward in a delicate expression of surprise. "Questions, sir?" she said. "About confession?"

The bait worked. "Ah, yes, Sister, that's right."

"I will do my best to answer your questions, sir." She stepped up to the side of his bed.

Aye, very cordial, she was. Very cordial indeed.

"Much obliged," he returned, nodding sagaciously. Then in an easy, forthright manner, he began. "How can one be certain that the priest is he who has the power to grant the absolution of sins?"

The young nun hesitated only slightly, and he imagined she was collecting an often-rehearsed answer.

"The Church Fathers have clearly stated that confession must be made to an ordained priest. Take Cyprian, for instance, who says that 'only through the priests' may forgiveness of sins be obtained. Ambrose says that 'this right is given to priests only.' Because Christ cannot be with us in the flesh, it is more than obvious that we require a representative of him in order to not only make a proper confession but to be assured that our sins have been properly confessed and forgiven."

"Then, for you," the sergeant said with a shrug, "any kind of faith in a risen Christ would seem entirely meaningless—especially if one takes into account the first verse of the eleventh chapter of Hebrews where the apostle states that faith is, in itself, 'the substance of things hoped for' and the very 'evidence of things not seen.'"

"I am not familiar with the passage, sir, although I trust that the Church Fathers have made theologically sound conclusions in their teachings regarding the Sacrament of confession. You see, the common man is a finite and fallible creature with a finite and fallible mind that cannot comprehend the vastness of the infinite or the infallible. What he cannot see, he often will not believe. This understanding, therefore, spurs the physical requirement that, in order for his faith to be strengthened, man's physical eyes and ears must see and hear the voice of Christ. This need is satisfied through the ordination of the priest, *in persona Christi*."

"Which is your Father Confessor?"

"Yes, sir."

"However, to me, the practice of confessing to a mere man who masquerades as the intended representative of the Lord Jesus—as you describe—seems nothing short of an outright attempt to not only discard the need for a simple faith in the Son of God—who, Scripture says, has done away with the Levitical priesthood and become our one and only High Priest—but, in the entire scheme of things, to actually justify the nullification of the sovereignty of God's grace. Besides," he added, "will not this 'physical requirement' facilitate the whims of a doubting Thomas?"

"I am afraid you misunderstand me, sir," the young nun said, still businesslike as she cleared her throat. "The power of Christ to forgive sins was transferred to men when our Blessed Lord breathed on his disciples and said, 'Receive ye the Holy Ghost: Whosoever's sins ye remit they are remitted, and whosoever's sins ye retain, they are retained.' The Church Fathers have interpreted these passages to mean that God gave to other men of the Church the same power to forgive sins that Christ himself exercised while he walked with them."

"Jesus also said that the servant is not greater than his lord; neither he that is sent greater than he that sent him. And pray," he added quizzically, "after your priest has so generously absolved the sins of his penitents, who will be there to absolve *his*?"

"I do not concern myself with the affairs of my superiors, sir. And to clarify my position on your statement, I believe that it is utterly impossible for a human being to usurp the sovereignty of Almighty God."

"Yet is such an attempt beyond human ambition—particularly when it concerns the attainment of infallibility? Lucifer's pride knew no bounds where his jealousy was concerned."

A brilliant flush painted her usually pale cheeks, and John knew he had touched a nerve.

"If you refer to the infallibility of the Pope, sir, and the doctrines within the Mother Church, I do not believe a compromise may, or ever will, be found within her."

"Ah—and with your linguists?"

"Linguists?"

"Jesus said, in verse nine of the twenty-third chapter of Matthew, 'And call no man your father upon the earth: for one is your Father, which is in heaven.' How do they justify their obvious transgression?"

"As I said before, the Father Confessor represents Christ for us. His title is merely that—a title."

"You know, Sister Kate," said John, flexing the fingers of his right hand, "it behooves me to tell you that the devil himself is represented under a similar father-title."

She did not flinch. "Oh?"

"He is called the father of lies."

He noticed her nostrils flare and her jaw tighten.

"Then if that is so," she said, her gaze fixed steadily upon him, "then I pity that you, sir, should be bound by him."

"But Sister Kate," he said, almost unable to keep a burst of laughter from spoiling his gravity, "let me finish. Before Christ ascended into heaven bodily, do not the scriptures give plain witness that he had already remedied the situation of his absence by promising, in John fourteen—I'm sure you know the passage?—to send us in his name the Comforter, which is the Spirit of truth, to indwell in us and by himself teach us all things? Tell me one thing: can a priest's mortality sustain this very unique and most supernatural requirement of *indwelling* in us?"

"The priest has qualified and separated himself exclusively to the service of God and the Church through a celibate life. Just as Jesus indwelt Mary, even so the priest may enter into the secret places with his penitents and both hear their auricular confessions and offer them solace." Her voice remained steady and measured as she looked at him squarely, but small creases formed at her lip's nethermost corners.

"Is it not precarious?"

"I do not know what you mean."

"An unmarried man, a woman—together in the dark?"

"You obviously have not entered a confessional, sir. A metal grille separates the priest from his penitent."

"Ah, that is reassuring. Well then, back to my question." John fixed his eyes exactingly upon her face, not willing that she should overcome him with her own deliberate stare and not softening the pique intended by his impending question. He glanced down at her long black habit. "Do you believe God to be a *personal* being—or even Christ to be a *personal* saviour?"

A curt exclamation almost like a laugh escaped her, and her gaze darted once. "Well," she said, a note of offence edging her tone, "I should think it quite obvious—simply by my choice of apparel—to realize that I consider Christ to not only be a personal saviour but my Heavenly Bridegroom as well."

The opposition he encountered in her spirit did not surprise him. Of course she would consider her profession supreme, for her entire life was clearly pledged and bound up in it. He already knew the arguments. He had debated with enough Catholic neighbours and acquaintances in his earlier days to understand their dogmatic views on the subject. But even so, the nature of her reply was exactly what his argumentative tendencies relished; and he would not allow the debate to be squelched until he had securely won it. "Then why do you maintain the necessity of a *physical representative* of Christ?" he said, squinting. "Is that not a contradiction?"

"Man is finite, sir, as we have previously discussed, and his human faculties are bound by many earthly hinderances which, unless facilitated, may cause him to fall into the snare of the devil. This knowledge initiates our need for the priest.

"Have you ever *seen* your Heavenly Bridegroom?"

She looked at him askance. "No," she said quietly.

"How do you know he is your Bridegroom, then?"

"The priest represents him, sir." But instantly her face reddened.

"Your Bridegroom—he represents your *husband*?"

She faltered; he saw her swallow hard, then lift her chin carefully. "To a certain degree, yes. But the relationship is purely spiritual, sir."

"Ah, but if it is *purely* spiritual, then how can your finite mind believe that the relationship even exists?"

"I wear a ring, sir, and a veil, which you can see."

"Oh! How stupid of me!" John burst out with mock realization as he slapped the side of his leg. "I forgot—if I did not *see* it, I would not *believe* it, right? But of course this makes it much, *much* clearer for me, Sister Kate. You are a married woman—you wear a ring. This, certainly, I can understand—except," he added, furrowing his brow concernedly, "for the fact that I cannot *see* your husband in front of me."

Her brow twitched; there was a slight darting of her eye, a slight gnawing of her lip. She was distrusting him. "I understood, sir, that you were concerned about the Sacrament of confession—*not* marriage."

"Yes, that is correct. I see our conversation has deviated slightly—my apologies. Now, the next question concerns imposters, for the word says"—he took his Bible and opened it—"here, in the twenty-fourth chapter of Matthew: 'many shall come in my name, saying, I am Christ; and shall deceive many.' I fear exposure to deception, Sister Kate. Will you tell me if you know of any?"

"Any what, sir?"

"Imposters."

"Of who?"

"Christ."

"I know none."

"I thought you employ the priest's incantations to embody Christ inside a flour wafer?"

Her knuckles whitened as her grip on the food tray tightened. "The doctrine of transubstantiation is one of the great miracles."

"Of the priest?"

"Of our Father."

"Ah—the Father Confessor?"

"Of God the Father— I mean, sir, through the Holy Spirit in the priest."

"Of the Father Confessor who impersonates the Holy Spirit?"

"Of the Father—the priest, I mean—who represents—"

"An antichrist?" John rubbed his thumb and fingers together as he pursed his lips. "The name of blasphemy is smeared across that man's forehead, Sister Kate. You'd be blind not to notice."

Her chin elevated. "Blasphemy is a very strong accusation, sir."

"I know it is. But you yourself have admitted the crime of your priest just now."

"I beg your pardon?"

"Father, Son, Holy Spirit—he denies the divinity of Christ by replacing all three with himself, does he not?"

The young nun shifted on her feet. John glanced around the room when he saw her gaze darting again, and he noticed that they had unconsciously gained an audience of several men who were silently chowing their breakfast, their eyes animated and faces bright as though, along with their coffee and corn-meal, they enjoyed the added stimulus of theatre.

"Excuse me, sir," Sister Kate said brusquely, raising her voice as she focused her attention on him, "but I am afraid I am left to wonder one of two things. Either you are a truly penitent sinner who wishes me to send for the Father Confessor, or you merely wish to boast the superiority of your religious dogma by taking sport in interrogating me with your questions. If the first, I will gladly send for the priest, for I do believe your soul is precious but is currently on the brink of destruction. If the second, you should know already that I am a woman whose course has been chosen by God, and no attempt to weaken, persuade, or mock me will convince me to accept yours."

"Well, if it's a case of dogma against dogma, as you suggest—"

"You suggested it yourself, when you argued the authority of the priest, sir." Her green eyes turned grey. They flashed like a bayonet.

John raised his right arm and inclined his head, forcing himself to speak calmly but deliberately. "Please forgive my bluntness, Sister, but whose blood was shed on the cross—Christ's or the priest's? I simply cannot reconcile your dogma with plain scripture."

A modest round of applause from several of the men nearby brought a rush of warmth to John's face.

"Say on, Preacher!" came a murmur from the back of the room.

"Hurrah for the man of the cloth!" another cried.

Sister Kate drew in a sharp breath. "I take it, sir, that you are a staunch Protestant, with a particular prejudice against the Mother Church."

"Strictly speaking, yes. I am fortunate that my father himself was a well-to-do Presbyterian minister from England."

"Well then, if you will look more closely at your apostate doctrines, perhaps you will see that it is your very arguments which prove the reason for the Pope's institution of interpreters for the scriptures. Interpreters are instituted to maintain order and consistency in our traditions and our profession of faith—which you seem to take so much pleasure in mocking. But when men take the Holy Scriptures into their own hands and attempt to interpret them privately in order to fit their own schemes, it is easy to see that even God's word can soon become convoluted, deceitful, and even dangerous for the common man. You quote doctrine and scripture well, sir. I do not believe I have ever heard anyone quote anything from the scriptures as quickly and as readily as you do. But when such knowledge is used to humble and even debase an opponent, I cannot help but think that it is less than desirable, for it will lift up that man in his own eyes by putting others down, denoting nothing short of a pride that makes the spiritual topics of our Blessed Lord into a stumbling block for those he wishes to shame. Now, will you eat your breakfast before it gets cold?"

Maintaining her poise and relative calm, she looked at him curtly and shoved the neglected bowl of mash at him.

John was not ready to give up his position so easily, so he took the bowl just to oblige her and put a spoonful of the grainy mush into his mouth before saying, "Sister Kate, I beg you to consider one last item." He swallowed hard as the lump of sludge-like, tasteless corn sank gradually down his throat. "Is man fallible?"

"He is both finite and fallible, sir, as I assured you before."

"Is God *in*fallible, then?"

"He is, and the Pope represents such."

"But God is still personal, as you pointed out earlier—though he be represented in the body of a Pope thousands of miles away?"

"Correct—we require physical representation of God to stabilize our faith in him."

"And what of Jesus Christ? Is he the Way, the Truth, and the Life—or can man climb up to the Father some other way?"

"There is no salvation outside the Roman Catholic Church, sir, I assure you. Any opposing teachings are false."

"But men are fallible, as you said, correct?"

"Correct."

"Then why would an infallible, personal God intend fallible men to institute fallible interpreters of his word? Where in the Bible has God asked for innumerable *and* fallible representatives of his Son to be the finite man's substitute for the Holy Spirit? Sister Kate, would such a practice not void one's faith entirely? Would it not kill any hope of man's *ever* attaining the unadulterated truth—especially when one considers the many *changes* made to Rome's teachings and practices, including Papal documents, particularly where this novel dogma of the Immaculate Conception is concerned?"

Her eyes squinted suddenly. "Flatter yourself you may, sir, into thinking you will win this argument." It was the first time her tone became sharp and flinty. "You say our Church Fathers are fallible? Well, can you prove to me that your *own* doctrine is flawless and your dogma consistent? That your own *personal* interpretation of the scriptures is not itself fallible in some way—for you yourself are a fallible human being, sir, are you not? Can you answer for the many different denominations spawned by the apostasy of your own Protestant faith? And tell me that, if there can be no private interpretation of the scriptures, as you seem to suggest, then *who*, in the end, shall lead our souls into all truth?"

"Ah! Hear! Hear!" a man shouted from the back.

"Excellent rebuttal, ma'am! Excellent rebuttal!"

"Aye—let him answer it! Answer it, Johnny, boy!"

A general chorus of voices rose in agreement, stirring around them, exuding admiration for her rejoinder; and John saw a flush of momentary satisfaction flash its sweetness across her face.

He nodded to her in acknowledgement, but he did not relinquish his argument. "I am not saying that my doctrine or my denomination is entirely faultless. I am not saying that *I* am entirely faultless. It is the Holy Spirit, Sister Kate—something we cannot see with our eyes, mind you—who convicts men's hearts and will direct their steps in truth when they trust themselves to Christ. But I will maintain that if I should elevate my religious practices *above* my love for God himself and the truth in his word, then, whatever religious practices I may cling to, the essence of them becomes nothing more than the sound of clanging brass or the tinkling of cymbals."

Her eyes seemed to surge as she stared at him blankly, her trembling fingers revealing their sudden clumsiness as the tray of dishes tilted and an empty tin cup crashed to the floor. "Do you mean to tell me, sir, that to you I sound like nothing more than clanging brass?"

A ripple of suppressed laughter sounded around the room.

John shrugged. "I merely pointed out that the justification of your religious dogmas might."

She stood there, blinking once, then twice, while her clenched fingers on the serving tray seemed to absorb the retort her tongue was forbidden to unleash. Scarcely, it seemed, was a breath drawn in the entire room. John looked around: even the men in the farther corners of the ward, who had earlier found nothing to interest them in a debate centred around religion, had laid aside their cards, books, checkerboards, and other sources of amusement and joined the audience of men who observed the scene with rapt attention.

Just then a jolly whistle came from the hall outside, and soon the sanguine face of Dr. Hall made its blithe entrance into the room. All eyes turned toward him, and he stopped in the centre of the doorway and scanned the room, looking amused by the uncommonly attentive countenances of his patients. He raised his right hand in a partial salute. "Good morning to you, boys!"

"Lookin' like a dandy this mornin', Doc!" shouted a man from the back of the ward.

"Great Scott, mate! The old doc's goin' sparkin'!"

"Yeah, lookee!" rejoined another. "Hair pomaded, whiskers shaved like a reg'lar gent—how's that, Doc? Ya got yerself a lady friend?"

A general laugh rippled through the room, followed by several more jests as the doctor strode into the ward, thumbs hooked in the armholes of his dark-green vest as he surveyed the room with a humoured expression. Then his eyes fell on the figure of the young nun, and he stopped short in the middle of the room.

She had turned away from John, but not before he noticed her face blush painfully. No sooner were the jests being tossed through the room than she was rushing down the aisle in the direction of the exit. But the path was obstructed by the doctor, who had—almost strategically, it appeared—planted himself in her way. His face took on a sudden look of fun and mischief as he reached into his vest pocket and extracted a red-and-white peppermint stick and wagged it in front of her, forcing her to halt abruptly while her hand shot to her mouth to smother a gasp as she looked up at him.

"Peppermint, Sister Kate?" he said, and winked at her.

Instead of another general ripple of laughter, an uproar of hoots and whistles and vigorous applause ensued, which accompanied the hopelessly confused nun as she fled past the doctor and out the door.

With an innocent expression on his face, the surgeon glanced behind him as she disappeared. "Ah, a trifle feisty today, is she?" He chuckled, then examined the candy stick. Casually returning it to its place in the vest pocket, he picked up his stride again and scanned his devoted audience with a generous smile. "Oh well! Reckon she just needs to learn how to take a dash of humour now and then, eh? Someone's got to teach her."

The doctor made his rounds and presently came to John's side.

"Good morning to you, Mr. Dallington." A wide grin lit up his face and he gave John a knowing look. "Glad to see that your eloquent, animated self is getting back to the old boy."

John laughed as he glanced in the direction of his missing limb. "Well," he said, "at least it's getting back to *most* of me."

"How are the vittles?" He swung a chair in front of him and planted it backward next to the bed, sitting with his legs straddling it while his hands dangled from the backrest.

"Highly suspect, I dare say."

The doctor eyed the bowl of porridge. "Huh, looks a trifle cold, at any rate. She must be used to eating gruel herself or she wouldn't serve it to her patients." He cleared his throat and produced the formerly neglected candy stick. "Peppermint for you, perhaps? I guarantee it'll taste quite a bit better than what's in *there*." He motioned toward the infamous bowl of porridge.

"Aye, will you give a poor man one more for his dinner?" John said with a look of mock petulance as he received the candy stick. "And don't tell her, either?"

"Just between you and me and the fencepost, then, eh?" Dr. Hall chuckled again as he retrieved a second candy stick from his pocket. "And don't worry," he added with a wink, "they're sweet. The sourness just left." He tossed a witty glance at the exit.

"She's got some neck," said John, shaking his head as he wiped tears of laughter from his eyes. "I thought she was impossible to humour, but at least you got a reaction, Doc. All I got was a tongue-lashing."

"A tongue-lashing? Son of a gun—never thought she would have the nerve to tongue-lash her own patient." His eyes narrowed. "You pulling my leg?"

"Hoots, man, no. Talk religious controversy and she's stubborn as a mule."

"Ah, that's what you mean. An argument?"

"You've had your fair share of them, too, I take it?"

The doctor nodded slowly as an inward look pooled in his eyes. He looked down. "She's a tough shrew to tame, that one."

"People won't see unless they want to. Some even go blind to their death just to save their pride."

"Still," returned the doctor with a careless shrug as he rubbed his hands over his knees, "a decent man can hardly criticize the fierce loyalty she exemplifies—even if that loyalty is grossly displaced. Turned in the right direction, it could transform that woman into a thing that even demons would tremble at." He cracked his knuckles as though to indicate that the topic had lost its interest with him. "Well, Sergeant," he said gruffly, "shall we get down to business?"

"If you please, sir."

"All ready, how's the old stump healing?" He stood up, drew the chair out from under him, set it aside with a harsh thud, and, striking up his whistle again, he examined the amputated limb. "Any phantom pain? Hmm…" He prodded the stump until it pinched. "A bit of swelling happening here—"

"Gently, Robert!"

The surgeon's eyebrows flickered up. "Touchy, are we, now?"

"Just a little."

The doctor chuckled and took another minute to examine the area.

"No booze on your breath this morning, aye, Doc?" John commented with a grin, noticing the unusual normalcy of the doctor's breath. "You studying seminary now?"

The doctor, still intent on his examination, pursed his lips forward with satisfaction. "Just abstinence, sir—health reasons," he commented with a frown that suggested humour as he straightened his back and planted his hands easily on his hips. "Alcohol irritates my bowels. And now, Mr. Dallington," he went on casually, "lookee you—an old boy fit as a fiddle, and still expecting to be sitting content as a baby before his own hearth with his children around him by tomorrow night. How does a grand old Irishman like that for his morning report?"

John grinned as the doctor moved on. "I'm indebted to you, Hall," he said, shaking his head. "You're a good man—there aren't many of us left."

"Still a handful, though," the doctor remarked as he walked away. "Just beat the opium, Sergeant, and we're both walking with King Solomon."

— CHAPTER XXII —

THE CHURCH BELLS RING

Kate fled out of the Third Ward, nearly colliding with Sam, who was just then coming along the hallway with a steaming pot of fresh coffee.

"Everythin' all right in dere, Sista?" he said, stopping short.

"Fine—fine, yes," Kate said, hurrying past him lest he should notice the red spots scorching her cheeks.

"I gots more coffee here 'case da men wants more," he called after her. "Do dey, Sista Kate? Do de boys wants more coffee?"

"That's good, Sam," she called back without bothering to answer as she hastened toward the kitchen. Her efforts could not keep the tin cups and dishes on her serving tray from rattling loudly all the way down the hall.

The kitchen atmosphere was stuffy with a myriad of disunited putrid and savoury smells. Three or four people bustled and clamoured about while three or four others rushed and scurried and ducked to avoid colliding with the former. Dishes clanged, utensils clashed, and cries for potatoes to be peeled, roast to be salted, dishes to be washed, and a stray cat to be shooed out the door arose like an unholy din that made Kate feel that, unless she got away, she would be smothered any moment and her already hot, frenzied brain would be driven to madness.

"Five minutes—just five minutes in the open air!"

Holding her breath, she dove into the swarm of bodies and pressed through to stack her serving tray with its dirty dishes onto a rickety pile of several other trays awaiting the soapy washtub. The tower of trays swayed unsteadily, but she did not attempt to secure it.

Stooping down to avoid becoming the target of the soup ladle that was being flourished like a weapon by the head cook shouting out directions, Kate pressed back through the bodies and made a dash for the doorway. She gained the empty hall and broke into a half run, chased to the front entrance by the fear of being detained by someone. She pushed the doors open and emerged onto the top of the staircase landing and into the clear morning sunshine.

"Finally!" She exhaled, then took a steadying breath as she wiped the perspiration trickling from beneath the wimple line embedded into her forehead.

The streets below the hospital resounded with the rattling and clatter of a throng of carriages, streetcars, omnibuses, and pedestrians rushing to and fro.

"Perhaps no quiet serenity," she said to herself. "But at least there is fresh air to breathe and only strangers."

She padded down the steps, turned right, and, keeping her head turned down, blended into the flow of people surging along the muddy boardwalk. On and on she went, quickly at first, dodging puddles and people, but as the Hall General got farther and farther away and the crowds grew smaller and smaller, she slackened her pace to an easy amble and lifted her face slightly. The sun was warm on her skin; and yes, the air was refreshing.

Across the street, slumped sheds and dingy houses were eclipsed by two three-story hotels and a boarding house whose neglected shutter dangled wearily from a lofty front gable window. Below the scuff-marked front steps, a group of ragged, barefooted children were playing marbles. Harvey's General Store was on the left. It was a squatty, mud-spattered building with ugly yellow-green siding, a false square front, and a sorry representative of carpentry substituting for a veranda.

"The kernel of controversy," Dr. Hall had fondly called it. The staff at the hospital knew that if the doctor accidentally had a scrap of personal time on his hands, he liked to "slip down to Harvey's," where a colourful array of farmers, contrabands, businessmen, and soldiers gathered to catch and debate the latest news and phenomena surrounding American politics, conspiracies, and the war.

The street ended where a mature red maple tree stood in an inviting sward of grass. A few small buildings and homes occupied the area. It was quiet, for the uproar and general commotion of the busy street corners and squares were faded out several blocks behind her. The maple's spreading boughs made a pool of shade that offered a comfortable seat.

"Only for a moment," Kate promised herself as she reclined against the sturdy trunk. She tilted her head back. Little patches of blue sky played peek-a-boo between the green canopy of leaves; folds of shade enveloped her like water.

Several moments passed. How heavy her eyelids felt now! How she would like to close them and rest awhile!

"One minute," she said. "*Just one…*"

She was gently wakened by sweet music. The ebb and swell of a melody ascended, and she listened, stilled by the sound. A pump organ made a full, resonant wave that supported stringed instruments and harmonies of male and female voices blending like brooks and rivulets flowing into one broad, smooth river.

"Amazing grace! how sweet the sound
That saved a wretch like me!
I once was lost but now am found;
Was blind but now I see."

Somewhere, a horse nickered. Kate opened her eyes. A company of horses and mules harnessed to buggies and wagons was tied and hitched to the trees or hitching rails outside a small whitewashed building directly opposite the road. A flight of five steps led up to a modest square porch and a set of red arched double-leaf doors. How had she not noticed the church before?

Presently a general commotion of voices and footsteps preceded a sudden surge of people as they poured out of the building. Women, children, and old men—all of them smiling, talking, even laughing—were ushered out into the noontide glare of sunshine. Where was the example of sober piety?

The church bells were ringing now—grandly, cheerily, as though rejoicing from their heights in the belltower.

Her eyes scanned the crowd. Was that woman's face familiar? Yes—that woman, there—walking down the steps with cheer wreathing her countenance? Ah yes, of course. It was Sergeant Dallington's daughter. And who was the woman with her, whose head was bent as she removed the white lace shawl draped over it… it was falling to the woman's shoulders. A glorious crown of shining golden locks was revealed. Graceful arms were drifting to her sides.

Yes, it was Collette.

"Apostate!" Kate muttered through clenched teeth. "How dare she!"

The bells were still ringing out—more loudly now, it seemed. She scrambled to her feet—at all costs, she must not be noticed. Retreating behind the maple, she paused for a moment, took breath, and then, without risking a backward glance, mounted the boardwalk and hurried toward the hospital. Progress, however, was hindered by an increased flow of traffic that was travelling, it seemed, in all directions but the one in which she wished to go. Dodging sluggish pedestrians, ducking from the notice of stony-faced patrolling Union soldiers, dashing in front of riders on horseback to gain the other side of the street before she had to wait another moment all left Kate's neck and palms sticky with sweat and her habit and wimple clinging to her skin as if adhered by glue, for every crunching of hooves, every rattling of every carriage and omnibus behind her seemed to be the dreaded one in which Miss Dallington and Collette might be riding.

In five minutes she was on the boardwalk opposite the Hall General. Only one final road crossing, only five stairs to climb, only two doors to open…

"Sister Kate! Sister Kate, is that you?"

To her horror, she saw the face of Miss Dallington leaning out from the window of a carriage that had just drawn up beside her.

"Yes—good day, Miss Dallington!" Kate called back desperately before tearing across the street and clattering over the boardwalk. She gained the stone staircase, ran up the steps, and fled into the hospital, panting for breath as she slammed the doors behind her. "To my ward—quickly! Quickly!"

Blindly, she found the Third Ward. Inside, she paused for an instant and scanned the room. What patient needed her? There, that one at the back of the ward! The Pennsylvanian farmer with the bandaged head and broken wrist was struggling to eat his bowl of lentil soup. She would help him.

She walked briskly down the aisle and gained the side of his bed. "May I help you, sir?" she said, raising her eyebrows and speaking as pleasantly as she could.

"Sure, ma'am, that'd be mighty kind of ya—thankee," returned the farmer with a toothless grin. "Lady, you's my favourite nurse anyhow—ain't I a lucky bloke today?"

She did not answer as she sat down, plagued by quivering nerves. She seized the bowl of soup and commenced the task of spoon-feeding him. He slobbered and dribbled and belched, but she hardly noticed as she wiped the spittle from his wiry red beard and offered another spoon. Surely within minutes she would hear the voices of Sergeant Dallington's visitors coming to pay him his usual Sunday afternoon visit—would they notice her? Would they question her? What mortification would she be doomed to endure if the sergeant discovered that she had been noticed in front of a Protestant church only a few minutes earlier?

Within minutes the visitors entered the ward. Though her back was turned to them, their voices filled her ears. Tones of introduction were a prelude to a string of lively chatter and laughs that she could scarcely tolerate.

"To be home—all of us together once again! Oh Papa! And by tomorrow evening!"

"Wonderful, yes, darling; it will be wonderful. And how are Samuel and Elizabeth?"

"Oh, the Richardsons are such lovely people. So kind and generous. Mrs. Richardson has promised me some ducklings when we are settled back home."

"Ah! That's grand. Ellen, you will consent to being commissioned to make your Scotch duck eggs for our breakfasts again, I daresay?"

"Aye, Mr. Dallington, that I will."

"Collette loves Scotch eggs, too, Papa. As soon as her work abates somewhat here at the hospital, I have insisted that she and her son visit us for at least a month."

"A charming idea, darling—charming. Perhaps your friend

is fond of horses and would care to ride while she stays with us?"

"I am sure of it, right, Collette?... Oh dear, Collette, what is it? You are pale—are you ill?"

"No. No, I'm quite all right, Miss Dallington... Indeed I am."

Kate blinked away the mist covering her vision. The toothless farmer was waving his hand in front of her, saying something.

"I'm sorry, sir," she said, struggling to regain focus.

"It's kindly of ya, lady, but the gut's full now!" He was chuckling and patting his belly.

Kate set the empty bowl and spoon aside and stood up, hardly seeing his grin. "You're most welcome, sir." But what should she do now? She dare not walk or even look in their direction. They would notice her—or had they noticed her already?

"Just some water now, lady, afore ya go, if ya please?"

"Water...? Oh yes, water. Of course."

She desperately filled the water dipper in the wooden water bucket a few feet away. With haste she carried the full dipper to her patient and held it to his lips as he drank.

Instantly, she was aware of pressure. Was it the pressure of someone's gaze following her with an invasive curiosity that hurt worse than words? Yes—yes, of course it was. They were watching her now, their critical eyes following her every movement, boring into her, inspecting her just as they would inspect an unearthly creature. Perhaps they imagined that she was unfeeling, too. Perhaps they would not care that she did not have a father as they did. Perhaps they did not care that Kate would like to have gathered around a father, and smiled, and laughed, and talked with him, the way those children did with their own pa. Perhaps they did not know that what they had was precisely what she wanted.

They were chattering again. They were laughing. And she was depositing the water dipper back into the wooden bucket, her gaze fixed stubbornly on objects she could hardly see for the cloud of self-consciousness and pain shutting out perception.

Kate would not cry. No, she would certainly not cry. Life was not fair, and Sister Kate must accept that.

~

Kate spent the latter half of the day administering dosages, bathing patients, and writing letters. As was her usual habit, a particularly calculated effort ensured that the timing of her duties did not take her, even inadvertently, into Collette's path; and by nightfall she had acquired not only an exhausted frame but a severe headache.

At the ten o' clock chime, Kate dragged herself up the narrow staircase into her musty old garret, thankful that because Sister Anna-Maria was on night duty, she had the room entirely to herself.

Inside, the garret was thick with shadows. She would need a candle. Going forward into the inky darkness with her arms outstretched, her hands fanning the air, she finally grasped the rough edge of the old crates that Sam's innovation had transformed into a makeshift desk. The mice were troubled by her presence—they were scurrying about her feet. Blindly, she reached for the candle but felt her catechism. She drew her hand back and it knocked against the candleholder; the candleholder wobbled. The smooth stick of the wax candle was under her fingertips now; next she groped for the tinderbox—she had groped for a tinderbox like this one once before, in the dark of a convent cell, the night when Collette had tried to hang herself…

"Quiet!" she said, and struck the match, lit the candle, and watched for a moment as the tiny explosion of light ate up the blackness. The dust and cobwebs tangled about the corners and rafters were not as visible as in the daytime. The scanty afghan, flat pillow, and short straw mattress on the low bed in the corner invited her to rest. Certainly tonight she would be fast asleep long before the mice returned to disturb her with their sounds.

Having unfastened her leather cincture at her waist and lain it over the back of the chair, Kate was unpinning her veil when she heard a knock at the door. She paused an instant before securing the pin again, then went to the door. "Yes?" she said as she opened it. Her eyes, not yet adjusted to the dim shadows of the stairwell, did not discern the visitor.

"Katie?" said a familiar voice in low, urgent tones.

A cold hand touched her arm, and she shivered. "Collette!

What are you doing here?" She wrenched her arm away and drew back, about to close the door. But a strong weight held it fast.

"No! No, please, Katie—wait!" Collette whispered.

"I don't wish to speak to you—leave me alone." Kate gave the door a shove, but Collette's hand held it fast.

"Alone! Alone? Katie!" exclaimed Collette in an impassioned whisper. "I saw you today—just outside the little church in town, when the bells were ringing—and all day I have been burning to speak to you and know why! But each time I pass you in the hall, or find you in a ward, or look at you, you as quickly find a way to escape me! Oh, Kate, can't you see how I am trying? For nearly five months you have treated me as though we were perfect strangers—why are you this way?"

"I was merely outside taking a breath of fresh air and happened to wander in front of the building at the same time as you exited it." Kate pushed against the door.

"Katie, wait!" cried Collette, applying her own weight against it with more determined force. "Let me tell you— Let me speak to you, just this once, I beg you! I know you are not so cruel as you are trying to make me believe. I know you're not! I know it! All these months you've acted as though we are perfect strangers even though you know in your heart that I seek only peace between us!"

"Peace?" Kate shivered with dread. "How can there be peace between us when we each walk two different roads—so dissimilar from one another as to render us even more than perfect strangers?"

"But Katie, you know I'm not that," said Collette, her tone halting and lowering as though she were about to cry. "You know I'm trying to do what is right, even though my way is not what you think it ought to be—don't you?"

Kate's heart stirred, her reserve slackening at the sound of tears in Collette's voice. Her arm seemed to lift of its own accord, wanting to take Collette's hand, wanting to soothe and comfort her—she forced it back. Biting her lip, she stiffened her posture and braced her voice. "You have given me no reason to change my opinion. You are an apostate, which gives me no other choice but to consider you a kissing enemy."

"Is that how you see me, then, Katie... as Judas?"

"You rebelled against the very people who raised and nurtured you from an infant. You have wrecked your life! You have abandoned your duty to your poor mother just to become exactly what she was—and *still* you have no guilt! And furthermore, if I were to make friends with a heretic, Collette, I would be excommunicated."

"Kate, yes, I was ungrateful! Yes, I left the church! But I have not abandoned a person who is already dead—I have not, for I *cannot*! Our mothers sinned—but Kate, we have *all* sinned! And if there is a merciful God in heaven, and if our mothers begged his forgiveness, I believe he gave it! Kate, their iniquity is not upon us! It does not hound our steps! We do not bear the punishment for the sins of others—it is a lie you have believed! It is a lie, I tell you! A lie hatched in the pit of hell! Be free from it, Kate! Be free from the bondage you have submitted yourself to! You have a mind that can think! A heart that can feel! A body that breathes and possesses free will—these are not things you can sign away with a vow! Katie," she said passionately, her voice lowering distinctly, "there is more to life than suffering! Somewhere there is truth! Absolute truth! Waiting for us! Waiting to give us freedom! Oh, Kate! If I should stop seeking without finding *that*! Oh! Then yes! Yes, *then* I would be both guilty and apostate!"

Suddenly, Collette clutched at her throat until her fingers grasped something and drew it out of her bodice. "Look, I still have it. See?"

Gold glinted through the darkness, touched by feeble candlelight, and Kate saw it—the viper—and recoiled at its sight.

"I will find him, Kate."

Kate stood still. Tension burned in her muscles as she kept her eyes fixed upon Collette's face.

"Katie? Won't you say something?"

"There is nothing to be said," she returned sullenly. But tears stung the backs of her eyes.

"Katie, I— I want to be your friend again. Can you not see that?"

Indeed, Kate could see it. But to be civil to a heretic was hardly acceptable; therefore, friendship was out of the question. The woman must first recant.

"You have slandered, mocked, and scandalized the Church to which I owe my life," said Kate, struggling to keep her voice steady. "You lied to me when you broke your promise. Why do you expect me to change my opinion of you?"

"Because *I* am changing, Kate!"

"You? Changing? I still see the same rebellion in you I saw five years ago. It stains you, Collette—like the blood of the grape stains white linen, you cannot hide it!"

The dark outline of Collette's form tottered and shook. All was silent, and even Kate shivered in the gloom.

"You want to keep me buried in my past just like the Romans want to keep Jesus buried in that tomb," Collette said, sobbing. "Why?" She reached forth her trembling hand. "I don't understand!"

Kate stared back, drawing herself away from the touch as tears blurred her own eyes. She did not understand either—but who did?

"Please, Kate." The tone was weaker, wearier—was she weakening, too? "Don't act this way—it is an act, I know it! A stupid, unfeeling *act*! You are not so cruel and heartless as this—I know you are not! I know it! I know it! You saved my life once when I nearly killed myself! Please, Katie—forgiveness! Forgiveness, between us—love like we once had as the sisters we once were! It's all I ask—I beg you!"

Kate waited, suspending the silence for a terrible moment. She must drive the shaft deeper. "I once begged you, too, Collette. Do not expect to reap treatment less painful than that which you sowed to me."

Collette's pressure upon the door weakened. Kate pushed it again. It gave way without effort, and she guided it closed. Her cheeks were wet, but Collette would never know.

After bolting the door she stood still for a moment, shivering. All was silent in the hall—deadly silent. Kate listened but heard no movement, only a feeble whimper that told her Collette was still there. Suddenly the day of her First Communion was before her: Collette had secretly saved Kate one of her own oatcakes… and that same night, when Kate had done penance by sleeping on the floor, Collette had slept next to her, and covered her with her own blanket to keep warm.

Bracing herself against a temptation to soften and open the door again, Kate swiftly returned to her preparations for bed, drying her cheeks and pursing her lips to keep them from quivering. When done, she cupped her palm behind the candle and leaned forward, about to extinguish it. Suddenly, a terrific shriek rent the stillness, followed closely by the loud crash of something striking violently against the stairwell platform outside her door; then a rapid, weighty, washboard-like sound scudding down the staircase, then a leaden thud that shook the room's unsteady table and made the candle flame shiver with dread.

Kate jolted with alarm and halted, her hand falling to her side as she listened to the breathless silence that followed the noise. A moment passed, two moments, three. She could almost feel again the tight death knot that had choked the breath from Collette's throat that night in the convent cell. It was happening again.

Kate bolted to the door. Wild with fright, fearing she had waited too long, she tore at the latch just as the bell pealed madly through the halls. She flung the door open, about to dash into the hall and down the staircase, but just then the rush and patter of footsteps along the corridors below made her halt upon the threshold.

The shrill voice of one of the contraband maids echoed through the building. "Oh, Docta! Docta! Come quick! Come quick! Miss Clayton's just had a terrible fall, Docta! She's fainted clean away! Come quick! Come quick!"

Fresh tears sprang to Kate eyes—tears of remorse that scourged her conscience worse than a whip. She tried to force them back, but they would not obey. If only she had not been so cruel to Collette only moments before—if only she had acted more quickly to help her. But now it was too late. Someone else was there to help. Her hands would not be needed.

Stiff with shock, she retreated into her room and closed the door, strangled by inner emotions that could not break free of her body. The door muffled the scuffling sounds from downstairs, but it did not silence them. Those sounds just asked her why she was so cold and unfeeling—why so scared?

They condemned her cruelty.

Limbs shaking, pulse racing, she slumped into the desk chair. Her hands pressed against her pounding temples. "What has become of me? My heart… where is it?" She bent forward and covered her head with her hands as the familiar sting of emptiness and guilt made her weep with renewed shame.

PART THREE

— CHAPTER XXIII —

THE BREAKERS ROAR

On a chill, windy night two weeks following his family's re-establishment in their country home, John sat, pen in hand, before the scuff-marked mahogany desk in the parlour. The effects of the war had left themselves in the vacant spots from which the family's furniture had been looted or spoiled. The desk, though damaged, had remained, evidently a piece too cumbersome for the looters. The curtains were gone, perhaps having served to bandage a soldier's wound or mop a surgeon's bloody arm. Ellen would have to sew new ones to replace them. The glass globes of the two kerosene lamps were shattered. Several sheets of smoke-stained wallpaper drooped sadly from the chipped mouldings along the back wall. The room smelled musty. Second-hand smoke fumes burned his nostrils—or was that only the stench of memory?

Having refused his children's company following the family meal, John had bade them good night and retreated to the parlour—but Priscilla's miniature portrait, brought back with him from the hospital, was there on the desk, and her eyes were watching him, waiting, almost listening to his thoughts.

The volumes of Calvin's *Institutes* and Dabney's *The Five Points of Calvinism* lay open before him; beside these lay a heavy leather-bound journal, a small notebook, and the Bible opened to the fifteenth chapter of Luke. Sunday was approaching, and he had agreed to fill the place of interim that week for the absent parson at Falls Church. Yet, as he strove to construct a sermon that paired the doctrine of Irresistible Grace with his personal commentary on the parable of the prodigal son, words, paragraphs, and ideas swam before him, their meaning lost in boundless labyrinths of restless imaginations.

Still, his pen laboured. Inspiration or not, sound Christian theology must be made clear for the sake of the sheep that he had committed to shepherd that Sunday. Certainly, there would be prodigals in the congregation. Prodigals who were devouring their father's living with harlots, even now—their own lives an ignorant imitation of the lost son in the parable. Prodigals who must come home to their father. Prodigals who had a Father that would run toward them, forgive them, and kill the fatted calf in their honour, if only they would repent.

For their sakes, he must deliver a first-rate sermon.

Outside the window lay the dark valleys and black woodlands, where the wind was wailing and roaming, seeking prey like the devil tempted boys to waste and riot and seduced women to be unfaithful to their husbands.

John gripped the pen and set his teeth together; he glared at Priscilla's portrait—even the wind recalled his past to him.

Just then a fitful shriek swept down the western hill and hit the side of the house, shuddering the windowpane with the force of the blast. John's gaze bolted to the window. Branches of a rusty black haw scraped along the glass like the claws of a cat trying to find the latch hook.

John's hand dropped the pen and went to his pocket—the tin was right there; it would solace him.

But no—not now. He was writing a sermon. Prissy was watching him. When was the last time he had sat at that same old desk? Let him think… Ah yes—it had been when he composed his letter to Augusta...

"Eejit!" he exclaimed, for even a stupid old desk could recall the thatched-roof stone house and remind him of Priscilla's letters: the ones she had written to him while she stayed there; the ones that maddened him with their clarity.

Why had he obliged Priscilla by allowing her friend and young son to stay at their home? He regretted it now. The young woman was still recovering from her illness—her health seemed nothing improved from the day she arrived. Now Priscilla was growing fond of them both; indeed, she had become the nurse for the invalid. And Peter had even taken a fancy to the boy; the two of them romped and ransacked like holy terrors, imagining themselves the only two Billy Yanks who had sniped the Johnny Rebs.

Granted, the child was the brother Peter never had, and Peter could not have been happier; but the constant activity of boisterous youngsters was growing irritating, and the woman and her son would need to be sent away at the first available opportunity.

John flung the pen aside and leaned back in his chair, then glanced toward the mantlepiece. The wall panelling near the fireplace looked rich in the lustre cast by the crackling hearth fire. He looked up at the oil painting above the mantlepiece.

Upon returning to Dallington House, John had not been surprised to find Caspar David's masterpiece missing from its place. But in walking through the deserted room strewn with stinking leftover dressings, he had disturbed a pile of soiled blankets and mouldering bandages to discover the prized painting lying face down on the floor. It was dusty and had endured scuff marks and chipped edges, but it was still worthy of being returned to its original place above the mantlepiece.

He watched the Wanderer. The painted man still stood there, his back toward John, observing his painted wilderness. Masses of fog clouds curled and crested like ocean whitecaps below the peak of the dark jagged precipice upon which he stood. That Wanderer was him. The indefinite mists, the unseen landscape, the rocks—all of it: they were the years of silence and the marks of pain.

His thoughts were interrupted by a light knock at the door. But perhaps the sound was a figment of a hackneyed imagination?

But there—the knock again, repeated with more insistence. He leaned forward, placing his right elbow firmly on the desk. "Come in," he said.

The door creaked open. A rustle of petticoats accompanied the appearance of the short, matronly form of Ellen. Her rusty-coloured hair seemed almost red tonight.

He smiled tightly. "Good evening, Ellen."

"Good evenin', Mr. Dallington." She entered and closed the door behind her.

Was her calm, decided manner deliberate? With any luck he might discourage her from accepting a chair. He would allow an unwelcome tone to chill his voice.

"Will you take a seat?" He motioned to the chair on the opposite side of the desk.

"Thank ye." She took the seat and folded her hands in her lap with a measured sigh.

Ah, look—the unusual elevation of her chin, the compressed lips, the rigidity of her expression, the spark in her eye that would not let him forget her determined, sometimes insubordinate nature. Indeed: he had not contended with that side of her for many, many years.

He pursed his lips and picked up the pen, glancing at his books and papers as he adjusted his spectacles on his nose. She enjoyed making him feel berated, didn't she?

"Well, Ellen, what can I do for you?"

"Sir," she began, "I knocked on yer door tonight because I'm needin' tae speak tae ye on a hard subject. It concerns yer bairn Priscilla, an' two other lasses ye'll know, sir."

"Hmm?" he said. "And who might they be?"

"Two young nurses. One a lass from Europe—"

"Ah, you mean the hospital volunteer living upstairs, possibly? Is her health improving yet?"

"Poor lass. She dinnae make a fuss, but she's still weakly. I've asked Doc Hall tae come check her."

"Well, I am sure he will manage to get her back on her feet lickity-split."

"The second lass is a Nursing Sister who works at the Hall General."

"There are several Sisters working at the Hall General, Ellen." Let his tone be scathing: if Ellen had the neck to come to him this way, then she could handle a touch of sarcasm.

"Aye. I mean Sister Kate, sir."

He arched his eyebrow. "You know her?"

"I know of Sister Kate."

"Ah, you know *of* her? How nice."

The old clock on the mantlepiece ticked away the minutes, and the fire crackled and hissed like a temperamental spirit;

John plucked the spectacles from his nose and twirled them in time with them both. "Well? What about her?"

"Sir," she said, "I wish tae speak my mind tae ye, but I cannae do it good save tae bring up yer past. An' that, sir, I know might fash ye." Ellen's Scottish dialect was taking over, the telltale of nerves.

"Hmm? And what interests you about my past, Ellen?" He was winning: a careless manner would be perfect.

"I dinnae wish tae disrespect ye, sir, but the old pains ye is still holdin' inside, ye willnae 'scape till ye face them. An' savin' I speak what's been fashin' me so long, I cannae bide myself, neither. Lord God Almighty knows it, an' I want more than anythin' tae have my heart right in his sight."

"Well, in that case"—he sat back in his chair and drummed his fingers on top of the desk, suggesting her opinion would automatically become the target in the crosshairs of his judgment—"you may speak your mind."

"'Tis about Cassandra, an' the poor lass's bairns, sir."

That name—his heart stopped for an instant, though his fingers kept drumming.

"Mr. Dallington, I see yer Bible open tae the gospel of Luke, tae the parable of the lost sheep."

"Actually the parable of the prodigal son," he corrected. "But continue."

"Very well—they are the same, and there are many lost ones, Mr. Dallington."

"I know that, Ellen. Which is why I write a sermon on the subject. Have you come to assist me with that?"

"I am a midwife, an' I ask if any decent one can mind the awe of catchin' twin lassies an' later forget who their father was?"

"I have *one* daughter, Ellen."

"Aye. An' the other is the lost sheep."

"Ellen. I am a shepherd with one daughter and one son."

"But sir, yer eyes saw two cradles, with *two* wee bairns in them—yer own flesh an' blood. Ye knew that Cassandra's last child had nae shepherd at all, an' yet ye went not after it."

"Oh, so it is *two* orphans now, is it? I suppose you now expect me to run a charity by adopting the illegitimate one, too?"

"Sir, ye can do more than I—but what I *can* do, I do now."

"They are not my concern, Ellen. Both of those children are adults by now, fending for themselves. It is as simple as that."

"Ye lie, Mr. Dallington."

"Oh really?" He laughed.

"Think of Prissy an' Peter—will ye look tae the Lord God on the Judgment Day an' tell him that yer sweet bairns couldnae know the truth on account of yer own pride?"

"Miss Kelly," he said, straining against emotion, "I forbid you to speak to me about my children. It sickens me to recall the past. How can you impose upon my unwillingness the unnecessary obligation to unveil to my two children those things that should only corrupt their innocence and upset their current happiness?"

But his flesh trembled, for suddenly it looked for the first time upon the seething brimstone and the smoking black billows that rose from the lake of fire where all liars would have their part. He shook himself, and his jaw contracted rapidly as he stood and strode to the fireplace, halting before the hearth with his back toward Ellen. He plunged his hand into his pocket, felt the tin. She had no idea it was there—she never would.

"Mr. Dallington, forgive me, but how can ye look upon the hungred, an' give them nae meat? How can ye see the thirsty, an' give them nae drink? The bairns are strangers, sir, yet ye willnae take them in; naked, an' ye willnae clothe them; sick, an' in prison, an' ye willnae visit them?"

"Ellen, your speech is eloquent indeed, but it is quite irrational in my case."

"Do ye mock me, sir?

"No—I conclude that their mother took them in, and I merely washed my hands."

"But of duty, sir?"

"Duty? What right do you have to question the execution of my duty?"

"The right of one who knows tae do good—an' knows that to *nae* do it would be sin."

"Sin?" John laughed, but the sword pierced deep as his gaze darted here and there in time with the restless flames. "There was a door that was shut and locked on me many years ago. The two behind that door were sinning, Ellen, and I do not intend to try the latch again."

He heard the rustle of skirts and the grating of a chair across the floor as Ellen said, "The kingdom of heaven is like a king, sir, which would take account of his servants. One servant owed ten thousand talents. But that servant begged patience from the king, an' the king was moved with compassion, an' loosed him, an' forgave him the debt."

"Don't use scripture on me, Ellen."

"But sir, the same servant went out an' found his fellow servant who owed him a hundred pence, an' the man demanded payment. That fellow servant pleaded mercy, but instead was cast intae prison till he should pay the debt. Mr. Dallington, what will the king say tae the unmerciful servant—what will he *do*?"

"I know what is best for my daughter and son, Miss Kelly," he said, but every muscle in his frame vibrated, for he knew the parable, and knew that the king had already delivered John Dallington to the tormentors. He turned his head to look at her through bleared vision and, anchoring his voice, said, "Neither of them must know anything of the shame that Priscilla's mother brought upon me. You understand me? *Never.*"

There was silence. Suddenly, Ellen's hand struck her bosom while tears broke her voice. "Ow, sir, I weep for ye, sir! I'm nae blind—I see the pain my visit makes for ye tonight! But it's bindin' on me, Mr. Dallington, tae speak. It's bindin' on me tae ask that if God's grace cannae reconcile the past with our future, then why should we trust that his ways are higher than ours?"

"I don't want your compassion, Ellen; I want your cooperation. You must see that the disclosure of my past would certainly ruin the life and reputation I have striven to rebuild for myself and my two children here in America. It is obvious that I am a successful man in this community, so why not continue to leave me to manage by own affairs?"

"Cassandra begged yer forgiveness, sir, but bitterness is preventin' ye, an' ye're now hurtin' yerself an' yer children, an' will continue tae do so until ye've destroyed yerself an' them. I willnae stand by tae see this happen, sir, an' say naethin'. There is a lost sheep in the wilderness. Priscilla has a twin sister, an' she must be found."

"The other twin is not my responsibility. Cassandra and I agreed to each take a lass. When Cassandra died, the sickly twin, along with Geoffrey's child, naturally went into the custody of the Sisters at the asylum."

"Is Katherine, then, tae be a helpless sacrifice for the sins of her mother?"

"Don't insult me, Ellen. Only the pagans do things like that."

"Then why do ye lay yer life down tae free black folk, an' yet care nae that ye turn yer back on yer own flesh an' blood?"

"That is a different circumstance entirely."

"I see nae difference, sir. Black or white, infant or adult, male or female—God's eyes see their souls—nae their bodies. An' he willnae charge innocents with the crimes of their parents."

"Ellen, I don't know where Katherine is—if she's even alive. The child was so frail and sickly she probably died anyway."

"She's alive, sir."

John cast her a withering glance. "Really?"

"Aye. I know where she is."

"That's impossible."

"She's a Nursing Sister."

He shrugged. "Well, that's not so astonishing." He seized the poker and stabbed the low-burning flames in the hearth until they began to shimmer and turn orange again, leaping up toward him until their heat made him thirst for a glass of cool water. "Her mother was a Roman Catholic if ever I saw one."

"There is a young woman named Sister Kate, sir."

It flashed before him in stark relief—her face—and his throat tightened. The face of the little nun at the hospital. Had he not once mistaken her for Priscilla? Both girls—did they both have green eyes? Did they both have sweeping nut-brown eyelashes? Did they both have contoured narrow jawlines, high cheekbones—delicate upturned noses that appeared to be cast in identical moulds? "There are coincidences, Ellen, in appearances, but your theory is a broken cistern that cannot hold water."

"Then if ye willnae see yer own child, perhaps ye'll mind the illegitimate lass, sir? Geoffrey's child, as ye call her—why have ye flung her at the mercy of an institution ye hate when ye know Geoffrey himself deserted both her an' Cassandra?"

It struck a nerve. "That devil Geoffrey Clayton can look after his own child and go to hell for all I care!" John cried, and swore, and flung down the poker, where it clattered against the brass grate of the firebox. "Ellen, listen to me—whether or not Cassandra failed to perform her end of the bargain regarding the twins has *never* been—and *will* never be—any of my concern. Do you understand me?"

"But Mr. Dallington! Don't ye see what ye're sayin'?"

"What I see is that the woman I loved betrayed me for my one-time friend—the miserable product of their infidelity is not my responsibility!"

"But sir! Would ye have me tae believe that because of a great wrong done ye long ago ye wish to spend the rest of yer life nestin' bitterness an' prejudice against two innocent children?"

"I never said such a thing."

"Then where is yer pity? Mr. Dallington! I know ye're a learned man in the ways of a minister, sir, an' ye've a good mind, an' I respect ye for it. But when I see how ye treat them wee ones the way ye do"—she dabbed her eyes with the edge of her linen apron, shaking her head—"then I say that all that book-learnin' an' memorizin' an' all that theology an' doctrine of grace—it's all for naught if yer heart ain't softened by it!"

Clenching his jaw, John stormed toward the desk, stood over it, and looked at her across the scattered books and papers. "Ellen," he said, "you have not lived my life. You have not known pain as I have, so I advise you to take care who you judge."

"I ain't judgin' ye, Mr. Dallington. By sayin' what I do, I show ye a neighbour's love, for I won't hate ye by sufferin' sin upon ye."

John felt the blood leap in his veins; his face grew hot. "It was Cassandra who sinned against me. She deserved what came to her—no one in their right mind can deny that."

"Ye may chuck yer stones at the poor lass who wronged ye, sir, but when ye judge her without mercy even after she's repented—when ye condemn her own bairn an' yer own for nae sin of theirs—how can ye 'spect our Father in heaven tae forgive ye yer debts when ye willnae forgive these debtors?" For a moment, silence swallowed up the room. "Geoffrey's child was named Collette, sir. I know it, for the Sister at the Magdalene Asylum who told me that Cassandra died also told me the name the mother gave the child."

"And why would that matter to me?"

Ellen looked away; she reached into the pocket of her blue gingham linen dress and withdrew an article concealed in her loose fist. Her eyes streaming with tears, she looked at John and opened her palm to reveal a golden necklace and ornament. Carefully, she draped the glittering necklace across her hand and stretched it toward him as the pendant swayed between her fingers. "This, sir," she said quietly, and a tremor passed over her small frame. "This is why it matters."

The pendant was a small, delicate gold band. A ring. He could not resist the urge to touch it. Reaching out, he brushed his fingertips against the piece. He took the necklace in his hand, looking closer at the ring, turning it over, noticing three scrawling initials engraved into the metal band.

The wind left his body; his heart went still for an instant. It was so long ago… but he could not mistake it. "Where did you find this?" he heard himself say.

"Ye'll nae believe me, sir."

"Tell me, Ellen. Where did you find this ring?" His voice cracked, and he felt her delay would suffocate him.

"Cassandra gave it tae me afore she died. Years later, upon the promise I made tae her, I gave the ring tae her illegitimate daughter, Collette, who received it through the bars of the asylum fence. The lass upstairs, sir—her name is Collette Clayton. An' she claims that she grew up with Sister Kate—Katherine Fletcher, sir—in the Magdalene Asylum in Ireland, an' has had this ring in her possession since childhood."

John's muscles tensed and went still as Ellen's words fell like muffled sounds upon his ear, swirling in his head as though void of reason, making him feel disoriented. He turned his face away. Could it be possible?… The woman upstairs—the illegitimate child? And Sister Kate… Katherine—the daughter he disowned?

His breathing grew quick and heavy; he reached out shakily and placed the pendant on the edge of the desk, then motioned toward the door. “Leave me.”

He did not look at her, for he could not. But he listened to the silk-like clink of the ring and necklace as she picked them up; to her soft footfalls as she moved toward the door; to the swish of her skirts as she slipped through it; to the slight click of the door handle as she pulled it closed behind her; and to the dull sound of her retreating footsteps, measured and controlled, until they died away and all he heard was the tortured, undying voice inside him that screamed for the rule of equity.

Feverishly, he began running his hand again and again over his head, pressing his hair against his skull, wishing he could escape the tombs of memory, thirsting to smoulder the fire scorching his brain, willing to do anything to deaden the crying voices in his ears and cease the stones of bitterness from cutting away at his heart. He walked first to the fire, then to the window, then turned back to the desk, restlessness mounting with every unsuccessful effort to distract himself, robbing him of even physical composure, teaching his soul the agony of a rich man perishing in the flame of his own self-inflicted torment.

— CHAPTER XXIV —

AT DAYBREAK

With reeling brain and dizzying nausea smothering his senses, John staggered forward, seeing nothing but dim, hazy shapes that lurched and swayed in front of him… tasting nothing but the guilt of opium on his tongue.

"The chair! The chair! Where is it?" he gasped, reaching out blindly until his hand bumped against the edge of the desk. He clutched at it, tried to steady himself. Again his mind wandered back across the tide of years, drifting, ghostly and unmoored, toward those craggy rocks and the hard, bitter reef of that deserted shore; again, his feet were on the deck of the clipper *Narcissus*; again, there was a mighty storm; again, the uncontrollable thoughts that surged him up and noosed him on a frightening wave, dangling him above that day—that day long ago when bright, blissful reverie became eternal dusk and heaven and hell met together as rivals fighting for his soul.

A full harvest moon is suspended in the dusky violet sky; there is still some straggling embers of daylight. He approaches the old moss-encrusted stone farmhouse; a rushlight burns in the kitchen window—aye, perhaps feebly, but yet it burns, saying that she thinks of him.

He enters the house an hour earlier than Cassandra is expecting him, for a neighbouring farmer had seen him working alone to stook the hay before rain came and had lent him a kind hand so that he finished before sunset. A kind neighbour, indeed, to help him complete his task that he might go home and be with his wife!

He closes the door—no need to fasten the lock, for it is a God-fearing community.

He kicks off his boots and goes to the kitchen, where cold cheese and ham will certainly be set out on the table for his dinner.

But no—the table is empty.

He recalls that a headache has been ailing Cassandra for the past two days, and the twins have been unusually crabbed. Likely, she is exhausted and has gone to bed early. He rummages through the dark pantry, finds vittles, and eats hastily.

He makes his way up the creaking staircase. He pauses before the door of their bedroom and catches a whiff of his own body odour.

"Sweat," he mutters; she hates the smell. But there is a basin of water and a pitcher in their room, that he might wash.

He puts his hand to the door handle and tries to turn it, but the door won't budge. Puzzled, he tries again but finds it locked from the inside. He taps lightly on the face of the door.

No answer.

He lays his ear against the wooden slabs; he hears only the faint rustle of sheets, and a low moan.

A bad headache, indeed, he concludes. She must have sleepwalked and locked the door on him by accident.

Amused, he smiles and goes back downstairs, then loosens his leather belt and stretches himself out on the old settee. He closes his eyes and drifts off to sleep.

He wakes with a start to the sharp sound of a latch click. He springs from the settee and looks around, squinting against the dim light of a cloudy morning. Rain is pattering on the roof, streaming like tears down the windowpanes. Half-dazed with sleep, he studies the light—it is gloomy, but he can tell that the sun has been up behind those grey clouds for at least an hour.

"Eejit!" he says, cinching up his belt. He has slept in.

The brass buckle is easily notched a hole tighter—a sure sign it is time for breakfast. Then he frowns: why are both babies crying upstairs as though the sky is falling?

He goes to the kitchen, but Cassandra's willowy figure

is not there. Rubbing the back of his neck, he makes for the staircase, and as he passes by the window, he glances out. He catches sight of the dark shape of a man on horseback in the distance, galloping away down the wet slope in the direction of Dublin.

Neighbours have already gone to work, despite the rain.

He continues upstairs and goes to the bedroom. The babies can howl two minutes longer while he checks on Cassandra. He puts his hand to the door latch, half-expecting it won't open again. But the door does open, and he steps into the chamber.

There is Cassandra, asleep in their bed. Their white sheets and peach-and-navy wedding quilt are rumpled about her figure. Her shapely arms are thrown up over her head, resting gracefully amidst a garden of tangled flaxen hair that shimmers across the feather pillows like the rays of the morning sun. She is his sleeping goddess, waiting for him.

He walks over to her side of the bed and gazes upon her flushed sweet countenance. He feels safe and whole in her presence. She is an angel sent from God, and he will love and cherish her forever, no matter the future. Bending forward, he kisses her lips repeatedly.

"I love you," he whispers.

Cassandra's eyes flutter open. Her gaze fixes upon him, and then her face grows white with shock.

"Johnny?"

Tension steals into his limbs. At first, he says nothing. He doesn't know how to begin, and the babies are bawling in the other room, making the moment seem strange, unearthly.

Cassandra sits bolt upright, her half-matted tresses flying wildly about her face and tumbling over her shoulders and down her back. "I, I'm sorry I didn't get your breakfast, Johnny." Her eyes have a blank look in them, and her voice shudders, as though she is about to burst into tears.

"Forget my breakfast." John shrugs, unable to identify the sense of foreboding closing over him as he takes in her dishevelled appearance. "Priscilla and Katherine need you for theirs."

"Oh yes, of course, the twins…" she murmurs hurriedly, almost defensively. She tumbles out of the bed, her partly open chemise hanging loose like a cloud about her soft body.

As she hastily yanks on her cherry gingham dress, John looks casually around the room, and that's when he sees it, lying on the floor at the foot of their bed—a man's white kid glove.

Before he can make a move to reach for it, Cassandra bends down and snatches it. Her gold wedding band sparkles on her tiny finger as she attempts to conceal the glove in the gaping bodice of her dress, fumbling with the small buttons, finding no success.

John scowls. "What is that?"

"N-nothing. 'Tis nothing, really," she falters, evidently terrified.

"Nothing?" he repeats harshly, not making a single move.

Her white face grows whiter still, until it seems almost transparent. Her full lips are extracted of every drop of colour as her gaze darts across the floor. "Please, Johnny… forgive me…"

She says no more, but her face becomes strangely, horribly contorted. Her hands reach out to him but freeze mid-air. The glove falls from her bodice, landing on the floor between them.

"Och! Johnny! Johnny! Johnny!" she shrieks, casting herself at his feet, her convulsive sobs drowning out the screams of the babies.

There is no more feeling in him now; only fear that paralyzes it. Words mean nothing. He hears a harsh, unnatural pounding in his ears as his pulse elevates; his mind throbs with the horror that possesses him as he dares to question his wife's fidelity.

He hunkers down and reaches for the glove. It is a gentleman's glove, velvety to the touch—an expensive brand made in France—and he recognizes it. The dark figure on horseback flashes across his mind; the sharp click of the latch sounds in his ear, and he feels like vomiting.

"Not… Geoffrey?" he says.

He moves to the window now and looks out—the glass is surging with muddy water now, and he sees nothing through it, for he is conscious now of nothing except the disgusting truth that smears his eyes with red and reeks in his senses like the stench of a rotting carcass.

That was the feeling he had lived with ever since. The pain he suffered then was the pain that justified the suffering of others… the suffering of Cassandra, the suffering of her children, the suffering of the Rebels his bullets had ripped through. If he could not see vengeance taken against Geoffrey, or inflict it himself, it had not happened. The anger had made him deal out physical wrath against a dumb, unfeeling wall of wood. Unforgiveness—was it the itching, oozing, spreading boils that grew and ruptured now on all his thoughts and actions, infecting everything his life touched, maddening him to seek a life of spiritual nakedness among the tombs?

Leper and lunatic—was he both?

John sank into the desk chair, wanting to weep but instead choking on despair. He shoved the pile of books and notes aside, disgusted by the sight of them, and looked at his hand—the only hand he had left. It had put Cassandra's ring on her finger and caressed her beautiful hair; it had touched the button noses of his sweet children; it had written endlessly on Protestant doctrine and patience and faith and had instructed prodigals. But that hand had also pulled back countless rifle triggers, made countless wives widows, made innocent children orphans.

And it had stoned the adulteress that even the scribes and Pharisees had not dared to touch.

"Can a fountain send forth at the same place sweet water and bitter?"

What mercy had saved such a disgusting stump of flesh? It would have been better to have lost his right arm, to have started life over with his left—better to have been all this time as illiterate as Private Gunderson than to have known the treasures of wisdom and knowledge and then turn from them with a two-faced heart. He was a living contradiction of the very faith he had preached but failed to live; and his conscience, bound for years, was now let loose to torment him.

A tortured cry broke from his lips.

"It is too much—too much for me!" he cried aloud, conflict smiting and raging against his emotions. "How can I forget? How? Forget her, and the love we shared together—the sacred love that joined us in one flesh before God? No, I cannot forget—I never will, but how could *she* have forgotten? And betrayed me? Cassandra—my wife!—she *betrayed* me for another man! In adultery—rejecting me as her husband! How? How could she do it? My own sweet, innocent Cassandra? And with him—*with Clayton*!" He seethed with fury, hatred burning his stomach, scorching his brain.

Tears stung his eyes and streamed down his face, and he tasted of their salt. He could not forgive—he knew not how. Though he should turn himself into a heathen, he could not flee the idolatry, for still he loved her—still his soul desired her more passionately than ever. He had loved her and believed her God's child—yea, even his own salvation. And there was Clayton—a serpent, poisoning her with the kisses of his forked tongue—and she had believed him. Oh God! Why had she believed him?

Stooping forward, twisting with agony, he slid his hand into his pocket and took out the opium tin, set it on the desk, looked long and steadily at it. There was no more pain in his arm, but this would deaden the other kind of pain.

His gaze darted. Priscilla's eyes—there, calmly looking back at him from the miniature. Taking the picture case, he turned it face down. She did not need to watch.

His hand went to the tin, opened the lid, took a pill, put it on his tongue. First, a pang of guilt; then, a rush of pleasure, of euphoria. It was relief, though it was still darkness, though he could still feel it.

He reached across the top of the desk until his fingers touched the open page of his notebook. On those pages were scribbled his sermon notes, his scripture references, his quotations from Calvin's writings, and his own intellectual reasoning and debate that had taken so many tedious hours to compile. And the pen that copied them? Was it not smeared with fingerprints of white paint and opium that told of the leprosy the hand could never hide? Someone's eyes might look upon that pen—alas, they might discern those fingerprints that reeked. What then? Would not a bird of the air tell the guilt of his double mind if the voice of his presence did not cry out, "*Unclean! Unclean!*"?

Slowly, his hand closed over the papers, tearing them away from the binding, crushing them in his fist. What right had he to preach righteousness and Biblical principles to a congregation when idolatry and pride and secret addiction had made simple truth and brotherly love strangers to his soul? He saw again his bloodstained hands riddled with wood splinters. He saw again Cassandra's gaping bodice, saw again the white kid glove that fell from it—and he saw himself pulling on that leprous hand to conceal the stains and scars that ripped up his own.

"The man I cursed… is he the man I have become? O God—can it be me?"

Page after page of laboured writing he yanked from the notebook and crunched into a tight ball; and then, wrenching himself into a standing position, he hurled it against the opposite wall, where it slid to the floor and landed amidst a forgotten heap of filthy, blood-crusted rags.

Those rags and his own righteousness were equals. And he was the lost son, grovelling with the swine.

He stood there a moment, silent, stunned. How could he be in his right mind when the past ate him from the inside and he took God's vengeance in his own hands?

Feeling mastered him. There was no more euphoria. Only black horror and the madness of demons feasting on his brain as the unclean flesh that it was.

Outraged emotion unleashed; it raked his body with sobs he could not control. "O Father in heaven!" he cried as his knees hit the floor and his head stooped low over his heaving chest. "All thy waves and thy billows are gone over me!"

— CHAPTER XXV —

MARCHING ON

Washington
April 15, 1865

"Da President's bin shot, suh."

A sudden scudding of chair legs across the office floor and a rustle and rattle and scattering of papers and ink pots mingled with the clattering of rain on the rooftop as the doctor bolted from his chair and exclaimed, "Lincoln—shot?" His face turned white. "Sam, where did you hear that?"

Kate's pen stopped, suspended in her fingers as she looked up from the letter she was writing. Sam stood in the open doorway, bare-headed, dripping with rain, his tattered boulder hat in one hand and the morning's newspaper in the other.

"Sure as I is a'standin' here, Docta, I is sure." There was a stifled sob as his brows drew together.

"Where?"

"Ford's, them says. Ford's Theatre—late last night." Sam resorted to wringing the limp brim of his hat as he spoke. "After da shot dey brought him 'cross Tenth Street to da Peterson's Boardin' House 'cause a theatre ain't no fit place for a man like Mista Lincoln to die. Poor Missus Lincoln, she done gone near crazy dem is sayin,' and Mista Lincoln, he gone died early dis mornin'. Dat was why dem church bells was ringin' before—'cause dey was bringin' Mista Lincoln back to da Big House. It's here in da paper, suh." Sam held out his copy of the *Washington Evening Star.*

In two strides Dr. Hall reached Sam and snatched the paper from him, scanning the front page.

"ASSASSINATION OF THE PRESIDENT—son of a gun..." Dr. Hall slapped the paper with the back of his hand. "Right on the front page, bold and black. Lying politicians and priests—the mitred tyrant finally made his entrance, eh? Just as he liked it, and even used a veritable player to make the exit of our hero. Mark my words, though—someone's going to hang for this crime."

Kate pressed her lips together and drew her feet more closely beneath the chair.

Sam was weeping now, wiping his eyes as he repeated, "He's dead... one of da best-loved men in da land... One of da best-loved men in da land... Our world needed him, Docta—our world needed him bad!"

"I know," returned the doctor. "A controversy and a saint at once. Lincoln will be mourned by millions."

"Dey was celebratin' da victory and da end o' da war, I guess, with goin' to dat play dere, but poor Mista Lincoln, he gets dat crazy actor's bullet in his head. I guess dat Booth fella, after he fired da shot, he stabbed Major Rathbone, den jump ten feet off dat box dere and onto da stage, waving' a dirk in his hand and cussin' at da president jest likes da devil hisself."

"Hmm, I believe it, Sam, but it's more than that, even. Chiniquy saw it before any of us did—he warned Lincoln, too, because he knew Rome considered Lincoln's brilliant court defence of Chiniquy as being unforgiveable in the eyes of his would-be assassins.

"God bless the old priest—that man will do to Romanism what John Newton did to the African slave trade, mark my words. It's a wonder Chiniquy's Wilberforce in Lincoln lasted *this* long." Dr. Hall shook his head and went to the door, seizing his hat and coat. "The Vatican will cheer tonight. Our rail-splitter saw the Stars and Stripes flown over Fort Sumter, but the Jesuits made sure he'd pay for this free republic with his own blood." The doctor swore and then punched his arm through his coat sleeve. "Even if the Pope had used his necromancy to summon Emperor Nero's legions to join the modern Confederacy, it couldn't have shocked Lincoln's republic the same way this treason has." He was about to don his hat but then looked at it suddenly and flung it aside. "No day for hats," he said, then tucked the newspaper under his arm and turned to Kate. "I'll be back later. Finish that letter for me, will you? It's for the War Department." He turned to Sam. "We're heading down to Harvey's to get the lowdown. Come on."

Sam nodded and stepped outside, followed by the doctor, who marched through the door and slammed it, the windows rattling in sympathy and rain lashing against the panes as he left his conjectures to vex the air with questions.

Five weeks passed. Spring breathed a fresh glow into the May landscape and chased cleansing breezes through the tumultuous city, fanning the paradoxes of celebration and mourning that thrilled the city with winds of dissatisfaction and change. The Union mourned Abraham Lincoln, ordaining his vice president, Andrew Johnson, in his place; and all the world seemed to watch, and wonder, and weep for centuries over the loss of the honest man who had become the president.

Eleven o' clock on a Friday morning, Kate sat alone in the office. The blast of cannon shot, the tramp of marching bands, and the noise of voices wildly singing "Yankee Doodle" and "Red, White and Blue" clashed in the streets outside the hospital. The noise barged into the open window on a stray draft of wind, ruffling the written page before her, reminding her to sign it.

It was only a brief letter. One for the Mother Superior. It was on behalf of the Sisters and Father Andrew, relating through Kate's handwriting their anticipated return to Ireland.

Kate dipped the pen into the ink pot, drew the nib across the lip of the jar to stop the drip, and applied the ebon tip to the page. "Two weeks… just two more weeks," she said, and in one brisk motion flourished her signature across the bottom of the page.

Bustling sounded outside the door.

"Mercy! But all that *noise* out there!" came a sudden exclamation, and Sister Bernice entered the office, her face flushed red as an apple. "How you can work with that hubbub going on out there, Sister Kate, is a mystery to me!" To the window she went and looked out into the street. "They say it's a majority government," she commented. "He's a decent man, this President Johnson, it appears," she added, and pulled the shutters closed.

"I don't mind the fresh air," Kate said. She stroked the address on the envelope before snatching up another leaf of stationary to begin a second missive.

Sallying to the desk, Sister Bernice sat down at it and took up her pair of spectacles. "Ah," she said, "I see you have completed your letter to the Mother Superior at St. Agnes? When does your ship sail?"

"Early next week."

"Well, we certainly shall miss you. And," she added in a lower tone, "I daresay none so much as Dr. Hall."

Kate put her lips together, wetted them instinctively. Somehow her pen increased its pace along the page. Yet her eyes saw nothing of letters and words. They saw his face—only his face. The face her eyes fled from but always yearned to look on.

"The doctor shall simply have to find another nurse to assist him," she said.

"It may be difficult for him. He seems to have grown quite attached to you."

Kate went on writing. A Sister she was, and a Sister she would stay. A man's sentiments meant nothing to her.

"Will you be happy to return to Ireland, Sister Kate?"

"Yes, I… I…" She cleared her throat. "Of course I will be."

Sister Bernice tipped her head back and peered through the wire rims of her round spectacles. "But…" She paused doubtfully. "You are not so certain?"

"Oh no, it's not that," Kate corrected with a short, hasty laugh. "I am certain—truly."

"I understand you are a candidate for final vows?"

"Indeed I am."

Sister Bernice thoughtfully nodded her approval. "It is a precious sacrifice, for you possess remarkable gifts—ones that cannot be easily hidden behind a habit and a veil."

Kate's pen halted its course along the page, and she turned to look at her. "What do you mean?"

Sister Bernice shrugged modestly; but a certain leaning forward, a certain looking deeply into Kate's eyes made Kate's heart stand still. "The struggle against forbidden love, my dear, is not an uncommon one, even for a nun."

Kate felt her pulse quicken, felt the sting of longing and the barbs of mortification as they flogged her conscience for her lack of inner strength.

Forbidden love. Her heart bled because of it.

Through a mist of conflicted tears, she felt a hand laid across her arm, pressing it with a warmth that seemed maternal.

"It will be a beautiful ceremony, my dear, and I know you will be faithful in the spiritual union, just as you have been faithful here, with us."

With a sense of relief, Kate glanced up to find Sister Bernice smiling kindly upon her. "Thank you," she said, mustering a return smile.

Just then Dr. Hall burst into the room.

"Doctor? Is anything the matter?" asked Sister Bernice.

The doctor was breathless, but a ruddy streak across his high cheekbones told of exultation. "He's a jailbird."

"Jailbird?" said Sister Bernice. "Who, Doctor?"

"Jeff Davis—under lock and key in Fort Munroe."

Sister Bernice calmly adjusted her spectacles. "On what charges?"

"Treason." He carved his fingers through his hair.

Kate noted—as she had noted for the last several weeks—that his hair was uncommonly clean and meticulously combed and pomaded, and that his moustache and sideburns were neatly trimmed with the usual stubble of cheek and jawline shaved smooth.

"Wouldn't surprise me," he went on, "if our Nebuchadnezzar started growing hair like eagles' feathers and nails like birds' claws. Pope Pius should weave him a crown of thorns now, too, just to assure him he did the right thing."

The doctor strode to the desk, stood directly in front of Kate, and leaned forward as he planted both hands on the desk and scanned the mountain of documents. Partly expecting to smell the rank odours of body sweat and cigar smoke on his person, she was surprised to notice that they were replaced by the delicate scent of lavender and musk. Her eyes wandered to his hands. They appeared clean from recent washing, and the veins pulsed an indigo river through sands of milk and a wood of dusky-brown hair.

"Booth's dead, too. You know that, right?"

Kate looked up to find the doctor staring down at her. Provoking heat rose in her cheeks, and she looked away as she said quickly, "Yes, Doctor, I already knew that."

"Yankee boys shot him down in Garrett's barn." He pushed himself away from the desk and crossed his arms over his chest. "Once the trial's over a public hanging is certain. Don't be shocked if a woman dangles with the men this time," he added grimly.

"A woman?" gasped Sister Bernice, her hand at her mouth.

"Mary Surratt owned the house where Booth and Harold stopped for whiskey the night of the assassination. There's hard proof she was in on the plot."

"But to hang a *woman*?" said Sister Bernice. "How cruel that would be!"

"Cruel? Compare it to the living death those unfortunate 'fallen women' are forced to endure in Europe's workhouses and asylums—perhaps ask yourself which is preferable: the inevitable punishment for committing adultery, or murder."

"But I have heard Mrs. Surratt pleads innocent—does she not?"

"Certainly Mary Surratt pleads innocent." The doctor half-laughed. "She's Roman Catholic. And according to Rome's theology, she *is* innocent—now. You see, the poor woman's soul is more than redeemable through confession to her priest, never mind that her crime was premeditated. Lincoln was Rome's enemy—even its apostate, as the false accusations go—so if Mary Surratt was required to commit sin for the greater good of defending the Mother Church, then the priest's absolution can certainly do away with the very existence of her crime." At such times as this the doctor might generally have produced a cigar, but Kate had not once seen him smoking since their interview together in the office.

"It's no secret," he went on, "that before the assassination, Roman Catholics and Jesuits made Surratt's boarding house their stomping ground. So did Booth, who was a zealous apostle of Rome and a pauper who thought to rake in a few greenbacks by doing the Pope a favour. Mark me—that knave was groomed for the job."

Sister Bernice and Kate exchanged a secret, apprehensive glance, then continued with the letters.

Their disapproving silence only seemed to invigorate the doctor, and he continued, as though resuming a lecture. "This five-year war wasn't just a political debate—or a debate against African slavery. It's a religious debate, and one that's going a whole continental deeper than the fight for the emancipation of the blacks—frankly, it's a fight for the emancipation of the white man enslaved by the tyranny of popery. What? You don't believe me, eh? Ah, I see—" He nodded, cutting himself short, then paused as though to rethink his response. "Don't waste your breath. Sin will be its slave's best bloodhound." He reached in front of Kate and snatched one of the missives—the one for Mother Cecelia—and scanned it in moody silence. "John Surratt will find that out soon enough, too," he said absently, and his eyebrows flickered up, and he looked over the top of the envelope as though the former subject still nagged him. "He's another conspirator on the loose, hightailed it to some priests' hideout in Canada. But his conscience will hound him whether he makes it to the ice rim of Antarctica or follows the stubborn needle of the compass to the North Pole and gets sucked into the vortex." He threw the missive aside, looked at Kate, and said, "Thank her personally for me when you're back home, Sister Kate—the venerable matron of the mother house, I mean—for sending you here."

He strode to the window. "Why in tarnation are these shutters closed? It's a sunny day." He unlatched the shutters and threw them open. "There! Enjoy some fresh air!" he exclaimed, his hands going to his hips, where they rested lightly as he surveyed the muddy, bustling streets. "Even though they think they've won, Rome has just succeeded in making yet another martyr to be cherished by millions—Lincoln's funeral train from here to Springfield was hard proof of that."

"You speak your opinions very harshly, Doctor," said Sister Bernice. "If you would be so kind, at least in our presence, I would beg you to refrain from expressing your contentious sentiments."

Dr. Hall shrugged. "Why? It's a known fact," he said, turning to look at her. "Shell-shocked people the world over are heartbroken over Lincoln's death. What else can a man say when practically the only foreign condolence *not* received over our president's death has been from the Pope?"

"We cannot answer to these things, Doctor," returned Sister Bernice, firmly depositing a stamped envelope on the pile. "We are here to serve. Not to criticize."

"Life's just a nice little game of scotch-hop, then, eh?" He rubbed his hands together and glowered out the window. "The scandals of Mystery Babylon! Who knows it? I'll be danged if Charles Chiniquy won't pick up his pen and write an epic to expose the fifty years he spent in the gilded lair. Next enters Tennyson's 'federation of the world' where the twin dreams of Rome and Rothchild are recognized when

> *'the common sense of most shall hold a fretful realm in awe,*
> *And the kindly earth shall slumber, lapt in universal law.'*

A lovely description, isn't it, to imply the new order of the ages? I'm sure the Pope will make no bones in granting absolutions to the infamous banking family on account of their bloated coffers."

With a disapproving sniff, Sister Bernice reached for her notebook and quietly began to scrawl in the hospital's large record-keeping book. Dr. Hall inhaled a steamy breath and watched, tapping his foot impatiently.

Kate eyed the pile of letters. It was decently high—high enough for her to make a reasonable errand out of them and excuse herself from the tension in the office. She rose from the desk and gathered the letters into a bundle in her arms.

"Please excuse me," she said. "I will take a walk down to the post office." Pinching her lips together, she crossed the floor and passed out the door, ignoring the doctor when he asked if the heat did not agree with her.

She hastened down the hall, out the front door, and onto the noisy, crowded boardwalk. The rumble of the streets was not loud enough to drown out the sound of his voice; the storm of sights and the rush of people was not sufficient to distract her mind from secretly dwelling on his face, his hands. So she increased her pace. But how could she outrun the thoughts that moved faster than her feet?

Reaching the centre of the city at the northwest convergences of Seventh and Eighth Streets and E and F Streets, she came upon the three-story-high Greek Revival structure of Robert Mills, which occupied the entire block and showcased glittering marble, an imposing façade, Corinthian columns and pilasters, and lintels of peaked intricacies above long windows that looked down into muddy streets from the proud pinnacles of the second story. Bounding up the expansive flight of steps, she stepped into the echoing, barrel-vaulted passageway and directed herself to the counter where the postman stood. One by one she selected each letter and handed it to the postman. But by the time the bundle had dissipated, it struck her that there was one missing.

"But… the one for St. Agnes Mercy Convent—where is that letter?"

"Eh? What's that?" said the postman, protruding his lip with a scowl while he inspected the address of the final envelope.

"A letter—one bound for Ireland is missing. If you can wait…" She dove her hands into the deep pockets of her habit, but both pockets were empty. She glanced at the floor, at the lineup of people assembled behind her.

"Everything all right, miss?" The postman lightly touched the right tip of his sandy waxed moustache.

"Uh, well, it seems I misplaced a letter, sir. When does the post go out?"

"Mail coach goes out at noon today—that's in twenty minutes."

With a firm nod to the postman, Kate turned around, ducked through the growing crowd, and dashed out into the hot sun. She ran across the street, dodging carriages and men on horseback, retracing her steps as her eyes roved the wide muddy streets and dilapidated boardwalks, seeking the missing letter. Yet her hands were still empty when she reached the hospital. Scurrying up the flights of stairs, she threw open the front door and went directly to the office. It was empty, and as she entered the room, she caught sight of the lost envelope lying on the floor beneath the desk.

"Ah, there! And still fifteen minutes to get back." She snatched the envelope from the dusty floor and brushed it against the skirt of her habit.

"Sister Kate, there is someone here to speak with you." Sister Bernice was in the doorway.

"Please," said Kate, "tell whoever it is that I cannot possibly see them right now. Somehow this letter to the Mother Superior fell out, and now I must—" A quick movement in the hall outside the office caught her eye. It was a young woman dressed in a straw poke bonnet and an attractive yellow twill dress trimmed with white lace and pink silk florets.

"It is Miss Priscilla Dallington." Sister Bernice stepped away from the door to allow the visitor to enter.

Recollections surged through Kate's mind, dizzying her.

The young woman was removing a crocheted ivory glove from her slender hand; now she was extending that hand to Kate; now she was smiling. "How do you do, Sister Kate? I believe we have met before."

Ignoring the proffered hand, Kate stammered out, "Why— Yes." She deliberately clasped her own hands behind her back while the letter twitched nervously between her fingers. "I do believe I have seen you before."

The slender hand went down and the crocheted glove was drawn back on, but the smile warmed. "Sister Kate, may I ask if you would be so kind as to step outside for a moment?" She looked askance at Sister Bernice and lowered her voice as she added, "My visit is most urgent, but I wish to speak to you alone, if I may?"

Kate, conscious that the fifteen precious minutes were now likely reduced to twelve, brushed past Sister Bernice and said, "Yes, you may speak to me in the hallway—but it must be quick."

Once out of the office Kate stood mute in the corridor with her hands still behind her back.

Miss Dallington began. "I know this visit must seem strange to you, but I am here on behalf of a very ill woman. Bedridden first with depression and now with fever, her situation is most desperate. She begs a visit from you. Sister Kate…" She paused and looked more deeply at Kate—did she know the thoughts that galloped through Kate's brain? "…you know her."

Kate's heart lurched suddenly; the letter twitched nervously again, but she squeezed her lips together, unmoving, resolved that shock would not penetrate her studied mien, for somehow she already knew that the woman was Collette.

"The Father Confessor is the one this woman ought to see," she said. Her voice sounded strained and unnatural in her own ear. "Besides, I do not have time today—there is a letter here"—she held it out in front of her—"and I must—"

But Miss Dallington interrupted her. "Sister Kate, Miss Clayton has asked to see *you*, not the Father Confessor."

Kate gnawed her bottom lip and shifted, hiding tears by looking away, ashamed for the emotion that would batter her reasonable argument. "Why?" One arm escaped to dash the tears from her cheeks. "Why does Collette want to see me?"

"She loves you. You are her sister—her friend."

If blood could come from a stone, it seemed then that it did, for it felt to Kate as though her heart cracked and bled the tears that her body had never fully spilled. Then a partial laugh escaped through the stubborn flow of tears. "She still cares?"

"She contracted typhoid fever after working at the hospital. Depression, though, has been the greater enemy. But even delirium and unconsciousness cannot dissipate the prayers she offers for you." She touched Kate's arm. "Sister Kate, I believe your heart knows what to do."

Kate stiffened, fumbling with the letter, bringing one hand to her hot brow, shaking her head again and again. Oh! Not her heart! Her heart did not know what to do—certainly it did not! It was the priest who would know what to do! Yes—Father Andrew, of course. She must first ask his advice—ask his permission, receive his blessing, just as she did in all other things. But where was he to be found? Was he in the halls? Was he in the wards? Was he in the streets? Was he sleeping? How could she find him quickly, and know what he would say?

"No—no!" Kate faltered as she wept. "I cannot visit her! Not today, not tomorrow—not ever!"

"But why, Sister Kate? Why can you not? Please—you must have a reason!"

"It's because the priest— I mean, he is not here, you see, and I do not know what to do, but *he* will—the priest will know what to do. He will tell me, but he is not here—in fact I do not know where he is, and I certainly have no time to look for him now, for the mail coach will be leaving in less than ten minutes, and my letter must be on it so the Mother Superior will receive the news in time. Don't you see how I must hurry, Miss Dallington—don't you see?"

"But there is Collette! What about her, Sister Kate? You do not need to wait for the priest to decide for you—why cannot you decide for yourself?"

"I know what he'd say already!" Kate cried, pressing the letter with one hand against her side, taking it in both hands, turning it over and over and over again. "Collette's influence will ruin me—it will ruin me, you see! Infect my soul and breed incurable disease! Yes, I know he would say that; I know he would!"

Miss Dallington's face flushed. "But Sister Kate," she exclaimed, "how can you know that? Collette is a kind woman—she will not ruin you! She is bedridden and only wishes to see you—she is ill! Don't you understand? Surely no person with any compassion will turn their face away from the cries of the sick or condemn those who visit them!"

Kate clutched the letter and paced up and down the hall. Oh, that Sister Bernice would call her back into the office! Why would not someone come down the hall immediately and interrupt the interlude? Where was Father Andrew when she needed him? Where, even, was Dr. Hall?

"Compassion… Compassion, yes… compassion," Kate repeated to herself. "That is true, yes, that is true. And I am a nurse, and I visit sick patients. That is what I do, surely there is no sin in that—no terrible consequence I must fear if I only show a compassionate heart to the sick…"

"Sister Kate?"

Miss Dallington was touching her elbow, drawing her attention, holding out an embroidered handkerchief, looking at her with pleading eyes.

"Where is Miss Clayton staying?" Kate heard herself say as her hand reached out and took the handkerchief and wiped the tears from her eyes.

"At my family's home, not far from here. I have a carriage that will take us there."

"I shall inform the head nurse of my absence," Kate said, returning the handkerchief. "Wait for me at the front door."

She walked past Miss Dallington and went to the office. As she entered, Sister Bernice looked up with knitted brows.

"Sister Bernice, I must step out for a while. Would you please excuse me?"

"Of course," she said. "Is everything fine, my dear? You are just taking the letter down to the post office, then?"

Kate showed the letter, then securely tucked it away in her pocket. "Yes—yes to both," she said somewhat stiffly. The answer would suffice. She would be fine, and the post office was on the way to Miss Dallington's house, and she would mail it on their way there.

Kate marched to the front doors and stepped out of the cool, dim atmosphere of the hospital. The afternoon sunlight flooded her body, drying the tears. There was Miss Dallington, standing on the boardwalk, next to a light carriage drawn by a team of beautiful bays. Those horses would belong to Sergeant Dallington… The thought suddenly pricked her. It was Sergeant Dallington's house that she was going to—his very house, was it not? What if he saw her there, and tried to argue with her again, and mock her, and tell her to hate him?

"This way, Sister Kate, come." Miss Dallington was beckoning her down the steps.

Kate went, blindly. She reached the side of the boardwalk. The carriage door was being opened by someone.

"Thank you, Thomas," Miss Dallington was saying.

"But I cannot be gone long," said Kate, stepping up into the vehicle behind Miss Dallington and hearing someone close the door behind them. "And you must promise to drive by the post office on our way out of town, for I must still mail my letter, you see."

And the carriage pulled away from the boardwalk.

— CHAPTER XXVI —

DALLINGTON HOUSE

As they drew near the General Post Office building, the dull chime of a church bell tolled the noon hour. From the carriage window, Kate saw the mail coach and its draft horses baking in the glare of the hot sun—dingy and insignificant creatures beneath the gorgeous and towering proportions of sophisticated architecture.

"Whoa-da!" the carriage driver bellowed.

Kate stood and braced herself against the inside wall as the carriage came to a halt. She threw the door open and dashed out into the dusty street, making for the expanse of steps; but as she did so, the sudden interruption of a large object in front of her brought her into a collision.

"What in Sam Hill?" exclaimed a gruff, frustrated voice.

"Oh! Excuse me, sir. Pardon me, sir! I'm so sorry, sir!" she exclaimed as her letter took wings and made an arc above her head while her eyes met the fierce gaze of a short, burly man with a massive mailbag slung over his shoulder.

"Sorry you are, miss!" the man grumbled, hoisting his mailbag along the foothill of his hunched back.

"I have one more letter for you, sir," Kate said, scrambling to snatch the envelope from where it had fallen along the gutter. "Would you take it for me, please, sir?" she added, daring to smile winningly.

"Already late, I am, miss," the mailman said, pushing past her with merciless haste. "Two minutes past noon already. Sorry, miss, but if you're late, you're late—that's your kettle of fish."

"But sir—*please*!" she said, close on his heels as he lumbered to the side of the mail coach. "Sir?... My letter is urgent, and I would consider it most kind of you to do me a favour and take it with you!" She advertised the missive to his red nose as his mailbag slid down his thick body and landed on the earth with a thud.

He straightened up, rooted his stubby hands into the thick furrows on the small of his back, and peered at her. She did not flinch, and neither did the letter. He looked at it, and the peer turned to a scowl. He looked at her, and the scowl turned to a grin.

"Only since you're wearing that habit, miss." He bent forward and rolled back the top of the mailbag. "Give it here," he said, holding out a thick hand with thick, wiggling fingers.

Kate handed it to him and smiled again. "Thank you, sir, I am much obliged."

The mailman grunted as he deposited the letter into his bag and rolled it back up. "Don't mention it." He hoisted the bag into the coach.

Kate lifted her chin and returned to the carriage. The letter to the Mother Superior was sent: there would be no turning back. She stepped up into the vehicle and found her seat. Miss Dallington instructed the driver to continue, and they were once again jolting through the streets of Washington.

"Have you seen the Capitol building up close since it was recently finished, Sister Kate?" asked Miss Dallington as they passed by the glittering edifice boasting the completed cast-iron dome.

"I have seen it many times," said Kate, for she had often walked this way and marvelled at the structure during the chance evenings outdoors when hospital workloads allowed her the pleasure. "There was once an army encampment inside the unfinished building."

"Yes, I heard so, too. And now Thomas Crawford's mysterious Statue of Freedom has been enshrined on the dome—it is over nineteen feet high—see there?"

Yes, Kate saw it—she had often seen it. Atop the massive white dome with her feet set upon a bronze globe towered the bronze statue of Armed Freedom. She was facing east atop her lofty pinnacle dazzled by the sun. Long hair fell down her back; an eagle head and feathers morphed into the shape of her Roman-style helmet, which was girdled about the crown with nine pentagram stars. Her dazzling skirt and robe blended strangely into a Grecian toga with the dress of a Native American. A sheathed sword rested in her right hand, and in her left a laurel wreath and a thirteen-striped shield.

"It is a strange statue, is it not?" said Miss Dallington, straining to glimpse it as they passed by.

"Strange, yes," returned Kate absently. "Stunning also—worthy, I'm sure, of its thirty-five-gun salute and the dozen forts of guns that answered when it was installed two Decembers ago." But she could still hear Dr. Hall's grumblings that Masonic fraternity was creeping into their capitol like the Black Death and that it would feed uneducated mobs the counterfeit liberties engendered through Babylon's mystery religions. She could still recite the lecture he had given more than once to the men in the Third Ward. Armed Freedom, he had said, might be considered the solar-spiritual offspring of obelisk and dome; he claimed that, as an infant, she narrowly escaped being topped by a Phrygian cap like Santa Claus. She was endowed most generously with ecumenical personalities—including Minerva, Indian Princess, and Francis Bacon's beloved goddess Pallas Athena—and she consummated her reign over the District of Columbia the way the Roman goddess Libertas did following the second Punic War. Coincidentally—and without shame—she plagiarized ancient paganism by facing the rising sun, and with the obedience of a corpse confirmed NOVUS ORDO SECLORUM by her symbolic thirteen-letter motto E PLURIBUS UNUM.

"Do you read Latin?" asked Miss Dallington suddenly.

"I know the translation," Kate responded, recalling Dr. Hall's oft-repeated phrase. "It means, 'Out of many, one.'"

One day, before an operation several weeks previous, she had ventured to argue with him. "Perhaps Crawford, in his design," she had said, "had meant to represent the Blessed Virgin Mary, as in the Column of the Immaculate Conception at the Vatican?"

The doctor had burst into laughter and, to her embarrassment, praised her wit.

"Perhaps? Perhaps!" he had said, and his fingers had rolled a corner of his moustache. "Well then—since we are on the subject—let us critically observe, Sister Kate, that the Immaculate

Conception is mounted on the Corinthian column that formerly belonged to the lost statue of the goddess Minerva; and then let us conjecture, if you will—on account of that wonderful coincidence—that the Armed Freedom of Columbia and the Blessed Virgin of the Vatican are perhaps *twins*—just perhaps? They are, of course, both decorated by star-crowns and wreaths and their feet both rest upon their own bronze globe, don't they now?" He had rolled up his sleeves then and washed his hands and arms in the basin of water. And then she had passed him a towel, and he had dried his hands as he remarked that Jeff Davis would know every detail she could imagine, since he was the patron of the enterprise and had ordered the mould for the goddess directly from Rome itself.

By now they had journeyed out of the city and were going northeast through the quiet countryside. After passing numberless dilapidated homes and farmyards—standing evidence of the ravages of war—the carriage at last turned off the main road and entered into the sun-dappled shade of a long avenue lined with tall maple and beech trees. The heavy branches spread a glossy green canopy over the driveway and seemed to wave welcome to the carriage as it passed beneath them. It ascended a gentle slope and came in view of the house, then passed through a set of green gates. A pot of yellow flowers was there. They were like daffodils… perhaps they were daffodils…

The carriage pulled around the circular drive. In a patch of ground behind the wicket gate, poppies waved a crimson tide beside a violet sea of cornflowers. The front and sides of the house were swaddled in a blanket of ivy that reached to the topmost story. To the west, an apple orchard blossomed snow-flowers as a robin sang a song among them.

There was a shining pond several yards away from the house. A bustling crowd of noisy fowl clustered together as they hurried toward it.

"Ah, they are ducks," Kate remarked as loud quacking, flapping wings, and the pitter-patter of webbed feet accelerated with the approach of the carriage.

"Indeed!" Miss Dallington laughed as she watched them. "Ducks suffer a sort of humorous trepidation when startled in any degree"—there was a sudden dash of the flock, a crescendo of the chorus, and an immense splash of water—"and as you can see, they find imagined safety in the shelter of their pond."

The carriage pulled up to the wicket gate. Along the fence line dozens of blotchy pickets slanted sideways; some lay on the ground, trampled. A partially shattered windowpane stared out from an upper story; a few shutters hung limply from rusty hinges. A selection of maimed cots littered a large rectangular patch of short dead grass on the front lawn.

"There's much improvement needed, to be sure," said Miss Dallington, standing up as she waited for the driver to open the carriage door. "Before the field hospital was stationed here, everything was neat as a pin."

Thanking the driver, Miss Dallington stepped down into the lane. Kate followed. Somewhere a rooster crowed and a cow mooed languidly, as though welcoming them.

"Our milk cow, Daisy, is back from Maryland now—saved from the looters. And my brother Peter attends the chickens down at the barn—see?" She pointed eastward along a descending hillside splashed with a flock of red chickens to where a faded chestnut-coloured wood barn with a gambrel roof stood in the shade of two or three maples. Just then, the loud barking of a dog drew their notice.

"Ah, Cap!" cried Miss Dallington as a black-and-white border collie bounded toward them, head lifted, ears pricked, tail wagging so as to almost lift his rear from the ground. "He's gentle, don't worry," she said as the dog sniffed Kate's hand and seemed to smile at her with his tail.

Kate glanced around the yard. Despite the ruin left by war, the home was free and the air fresh and sweet-scented, so different from the close, oppressed atmosphere of the hospital. The harsh noise of city streets—the incessant rumblings, rattlings, and janglings of army wagons and omnibuses and ambulances; the dash of mud spattering; the feverish clatter of horses' hooves over boardwalk; soldiers shouting, men crying, women weeping—all was gone now, like a dream, and in their place only a deep, quenching serenity.

"This way, Sister Kate."

Miss Dallington led her up a stone pathway framed with green shrubbery and violet hydrangeas. The smells of parsley, sage, rosemary, and thyme wafted to Kate's nostrils, and she glanced down to see that the skirt of her habit was brushing against those same herbs, releasing their delicate fragrance into the air.

They passed beneath an arbour laced by red roses and green vines, beyond which was a faded red door with a burnished brass knocker and handle. Miss Dallington opened it and stepped across the threshold, inviting Kate in. The dark-brown wood wall panelling above the wainscotting of the entryway was decorated at tasteful intervals with a portrait or two, accented by several stunning mountainous landscape paintings.

"Papa loves Albert Bernstadt's work, as you can see," Miss Dallington remarked as she removed her floral-sprigged hat and placed it on a nearby bureau. "Come, this way," she said, and made her way toward a narrow flight of stairs ascending into an upper story.

They mounted the stairs, which creaked and groaned almost intelligibly with each footfall upon them. Holding loosely to the scuffed mahogany railing, Kate scanned the walls and ceiling and the upper hall, where shafts of afternoon sunshine gushed through a gable window at the top of the staircase and washed the stairwell with light.

Now they were upstairs, in a hallway that hosted several closed doors. Miss Dallington led her to the last one. "This is Collette's room," she said, and opened the door.

The fogs of fear and tears together blinded Kate's vision as she entered the room.

Was she doing the unthinkable… the forbidden?

"Ah, bless ye, Miss Dallington!... Oh! Sister Kate! How good of ye to come! Come in, come in!"

The Scottish accent of the speaker came from a plump little woman with silver-stranded, russet-coloured hair. She was bustling forward, setting aside a bundle of yarn and knitting needles while her vacated rocking chair swayed vigorously back and forth on its smooth crescent legs. No sooner had the little woman reached them than she was embracing them with almost suffocating affection.

"Sister Kate, this is Ellen," said Miss Dallington as the little woman dabbed her eyes with the corner of her apron. "Ellen is a midwife and has been our family's nurse ever since I was a little girl, when we lived in Ireland."

Kate started. "Ireland? You lived there?"

"Till I was about two years old, yes. Then my father immigrated with my mother. Ellen came with us. But come, Sister Kate," she continued, ushering Kate toward the bed.

Collette reclined, asleep, it appeared, in a nest of white linens and feather pillows, bathed by the bright afternoon sun streaming in through the white gable window. How content, how restful, how beautiful she looked there! Yes, her face was thinner and flushed with fever, but it was happier, even in slumber. The lips and cheeks and polished forehead smiled and said in a spirit of perfect unison: *"I found it… I found what I was seeking! Come and see!"*

And her golden hair—long, and thick, and beautiful, spread in deep layers across the pillow. It had grown back.

"We'll leave ye now," whispered Ellen, and she and Miss Dallington withdrew.

Kate heard the door latch click, their footsteps die away down the hall and steps. How, suddenly, was she alone now?… Alone with Collette?

Motionless, Kate calmly studied Collette's face. She saw the ring. It glittered on her bosom, almost speaking. A general stirring beneath the coverlets, then a deep inhaling, announced Collette's waking; her exquisitely shaped eyebrows slanted and her eyes fluttered open.

"Katie… Katie?" Here voice both smiled and trembled. She blinked twice, slowly. "Is it…? Is it… *you*?"

A breath of fresh wind stirred the gauzy curtains at the open window. Tears bleared Kate's vision as she leaned forward and brushed her fingertips along the side of Collette's face.

"Yes." Her voice quavered. "Collette, it is me… Katie."

Collette's lips parted; a sigh escaped—were those tears? "Oh, Katie… Katie… thank you! Thank you!" she repeated, grasping Kate's hand first to her chest and then to her lips and then to her cheek.

Kate bit her lower lip against a wave of emotion; and the years rolled back, and made them children once again, and brought them back to the drafty old orphanage room. "I heard you were unwell," she said.

"They sent for you? Yes, I asked them to. I couldn't bear the thought of your leaving without seeing you one last time… Please, you will sit down, and stay awhile?"

Kate sat down on the edge of a chair next to the bed.

"Will you tell me how you are doing, Kate? It's been so long since we spoke."

In an instant Kate was back in the landing of the hospital stairwell. Collette was before her, her face sunken, haggard, desperate. In her sorrow and need, Kate had turned her away. It was the last time they had seen each other.

"I'm sorry I… I did not come sooner," Kate managed to say, wishing that somehow she might explain the regret that ate out her stomach—explain the release she needed from the cruel unforgiveness that tormented her worse than she had meant to torment Collette.

"Do not feel guilty, Kate. I forgave you long ago. Please know that. And now I wish for you to forgive me, for I was once very harsh and unkind toward you."

Tears gathered in Kate's throat. She could not swallow them; she could not blink away their evidence.

Collette must have seen, for she went on. "When I left the convent, I had no love in my heart. I was reckless, and angry at God, driven to madness by the questions I could find no answers for. That you strove to know God and please him, I neither understood nor respected. I loathed the institution to which you were devoted, and that loathing manifested my cruelty toward you.

"But there was more about you, Kate. More I did not realize. You were afraid, I think. Very much afraid. Afraid in the same way I was afraid—that God might not see you. That he might not care about you after all, or give you peace for the labour of your soul. Kate, will you please forgive me for the way I despised you?"

Kate was crying, holding a kerchief to her nose, muffling the sound of her sobs. "I forgive you… of course I forgive you;

thank you for understanding… I didn't know you did… in this way. But oh for shame!" she exclaimed with embarrassment, raking the damp handkerchief repeatedly across her wet cheeks and making an effort to sit upright in her chair. "What a sight I am—crying and whimpering like a silly little child!"

"But children are honest, Kate—like you are."

Kate wiped her nose repeatedly. "Me, honest?" she said, stifling a short laugh. "If anyone has been honest, it is you, Collette—despite your harshness, at least you were blunt."

"There is a time for bluntness, to be sure," Collette returned with a smile, "though an untamed tongue is no virtue. My pride bred self-loathing, which nearly ended in my suicide."

There was the dark cell again, and the flickering candle, and the groan, and the knotted bedsheets—the hard knot at Collette's throat. All rushed back. And so did the swelling Potomac at midnight, when it had invited her to plunge herself beneath its black waves and be swallowed up into a realm where the demons that feasted on her mind would finish her at last, leaving her carcass still and silent on the cold bank of the river. "No one can live in a body and mind that devours itself," she said.

Collette's eyes fixed on her. "You know the feeling?"

"In my own way, I suppose." Kate stood abruptly and walked to the open window, looking out along the green sward and snowy orchard. "You imagined my tears came from an honest heart before, Collette; but I never could make my heart honest." She exhaled, took the smooth rosary beads in her fingers—turned them over in her hand, looked at them. Every day and every night she had used those beads, striving through their intercession to be free of the burden of guilt her conscience could never release. Those large, round, burnished black beads, so long venerated by her and by an unknown number of Mercy Sisters before her—they were as familiar as breathing.

"Kate, I want to ask you something. May I?"

Kate nodded.

"Do you know that you are a child of God?"

Kate let the beads fall to her side and looked down at her hands—her skinny, skinny hands that were red and chapped. Her whole body was like that—red and chapped and skinny all over. "Not a child anymore, I'm afraid," she remarked. "Children are beautiful and innocent. I am not beautiful like a child, and I am certainly not innocent. I suppose, though, that the Father Confessor calls me that—'My child, my child,' he says—if that is what you mean."

"It is not what I mean," said Collette solemnly. "I mean you are *God's* child. Not the Father Confessor's."

"What is the difference?"

"The Father Confessor is not God."

Abruptly, Kate turned and looked at Collette, who was smiling a half smile as she looked back at her. "We have had these conversations before, I believe," she said, shaking her head in partial disbelief at Collette's tailored audacity. "Are you inclined to argue the subjects we have long since exhausted?"

"Religious opinions, yes—we have discussed them," Collette said with a nod, "but love is different than religion, and we have not discussed that."

"Love?" Kate said with a short exclamation.

"Yes, would you tell me what it means to you?"

"Well... Perhaps for certain people it means certain things; I do not know, really," said Kate, shrugging, thinking suddenly of Dr. Hall, "but in my poor perception of what I *perceive* love to be... well, it could be selfish... it could be adultery. It could be unrequited. But turned God-ward, it is holy—likely the highest expression of human goodness. What is it to you?"

"Frankly, I believe that love is more about God loving us than us loving God," said Collette. "You see, even though we were conceived in sin, God still loved us."

"I hadn't thought of that." Kate laughed lightly and squirmed. Indeed, she had not.

"He has been watching over you, Kate, ever since then."

"I, I know that," Kate lied. But it was too hasty of a lie, and she quickly regretted it, for Collette became quiet—too quiet. Peacefully quiet... Did she know? Kate squirmed again and fixed her jaw, waiting for her companion to break the silence.

"Every person has a vulnerable part about them that is deeper than consciousness," said Collette after a lapse had expired. "A need lives there—a need to know in our heart and mind the things we cannot see with our eyes. It drives us forward, though we fear its exposure, and we choose one of two paths in our effort to satisfy it. In my old life, I sought to satiate my need by becoming the object of a man's lust. You likely wonder, Katie, what became of me then? Come, sit down again; listen, and I will tell you."

— CHAPTER XXVII —

COLLETTE'S STORY

"When I arrived in Paris," Collette began as Kate regained her seat, "I sold myself to a charming middle-aged Frenchman by the name of André Dimon. I used to be a carefree girl, believing myself strong and capable. But such confidence betrayed me and led me into a terrible, soul-sickening moment where I became the victim of stolen innocence.

"André promised me everything. Desperate and impatient, I willingly became his *idée fixe*. That other foolish girls had been snared by the same techniques he exercised on my ignorance did not once occur to me, and I became the one upon which, I believe, his diabolic spell was brought to complete perfection." She pressed her lips together and a painful look crossed her face.

"Stolen waters are sweet, but laced with poison," she went on. "Not six months later and André found a new obsession—an opera singer. I fought to maintain his temperamental fascination but discovered that my embarrassing tactics were awkward and inept beside the artful seductions wielded by the black-haired, scarlet-lipped woman of the stage. Shame grappled my conscience; guilt controlled my actions; despair drove my mind to madness. And still somehow, through it all, André kept me shackled to the will of his own selfish and despicable pursuits.

"Two years passed. I knew no passion save the passion for death, for the demons of suicide were many and my passive mind had become their plaything. Then there came another girl—her name was Charity—who claimed André's suit. I shuddered when I saw my reflection in her. For a short time he left me, and I watched from a distance as he repeated with disgusting exactness the same slow, deliberate, flawlessly accurate cycle he had performed on me. He came back later, wanting me again. In that time I became pregnant and gave birth to a beautiful baby boy—you have seen William, Kate?"

Kate nodded, remembering the little boy hiding behind his mother's skirts at the hospital. "I have," she said.

"I love my son, very much. But André did not share my sentiments. He scorned and shamed and mocked me, and said that he, a prominent businessman, was too closely occupied with his thriving business affairs to have anything to do with the responsibility of raising a son. He determined to take my William away from me—to send him to a nearby abbey to be raised by the convent nuns. I refused. He threatened to murder my child, so I ran away.

"For two years I worked to support Willie and myself, but my shame followed me. Everywhere I went, I inquired about my mother's ring and the Clayton family name. I heard there were Claytons in Lancashire, so I went to England for a time. Still, I found nothing substantial in my search for my father. Two years later I returned to Ireland, hoping, at least, that I might find you. That is when I met the Dallingtons.

"I wandered the countryside outside Dublin for weeks, scouring every convent and orphanage I knew of. You were nowhere to be found. After hearing rumours that you were serving as a war nurse, I decided to sail to America—that is when Priscilla received word that her father was ill, so she accompanied me, and we came to Washington together. My work at the hospital was terminated by my illness, and since then Priscilla and Ellen have cared for me and my son. They left me a Bible"—she motioned to the cherry-wood table where it lay—"and when I could, I read it, and for the first time in my life I heard the voice of Jesus tell me I was forgiven."

Kate twisted her fingers in her lap. "It is merely a book, Collette—you cannot actually *hear* him speak."

"How do you know?"

"The writing—it is difficult to understand."

"Have you read it yourself?"

Kate stopped, swallowed hard, and shook her head.

"Then how shall you know if it is difficult to understand?"

"Collette, it is a voice in your head, that is all—fleeting and unreliable."

"More like a rock, I would say—solid and steadfast. I am the one who is fleeting and unreliable."

Kate could sit still no longer; she stood up. "Collette," she began, then drew breath, steadying the trembling of her nerves. "I do not understand this… this Jacobinical view of Christ that you explain; it is strange to me—but never mind that now. What I do know is that you asked me to forgive you, and you went through the trouble of detailing what you perceive to be virtues in me. But it is I who must ask forgiveness…" It was no use now: the tears would come again, despite her resistance. "I know I have sinned… I hated you because you were honest and unafraid, yet still I judged you weak and foolish. I condemned you when you came to the hospital. I cut off all your beautiful long hair," she said, weeping suddenly, pressing her hand to her wet eyes. "I am so sorry… so sorry, Collette! Did you know it was me who did it? Did you suspect? I thought the ugly haircut would force you to stay—but it did not, and… I cannot forgive myself."

A hand pressed her arm. "I forgive you, Kate."

Kate choked back a sob and began to shake her head from side to side. "Collette, you may not think it when you look at me, but every day since you left the convent I have striven for perfection and still I feel desperately unacceptable." She trembled and averted her face to hide her burning cheeks as her gaunt shoulders curved inward with the weight of self-reproach. She shuddered as she remembered the day of her First Communion, and the repetitious pomp of the Mass, and her sacrilege of the Eucharist that had left her heart trembling with the fear that she was utterly unworthy, guilty of desecrating the body and blood of the Lord. "I envy you, Collette. I envy you your confidence—your peace of mind. You speak of forgiveness without penance—without judgment—but I cannot imagine that."

Again the gentle hand pressed her arm. "Christ will justify you, Kate—if you let him."

"A simple, mental conclusion, Collette." Kate pressed her

damp palm against her forehead. If only she could crawl out of her brain—escape the scorching fires of thought burning within. But she could not. Pacing rapidly across the floor, she exclaimed, "I must know for myself. I must *see* for myself—with my own eyes and my own mind—like I see this!" She impatiently grasped her rosary and shook it in front of Collette. "It is the way I am, the way I have always been—" The trembling of her lips interrupted her voice, and she stopped.

"Trust in Jesus, Kate. He will help you see clearly."

"But my mind does not know what that means!" she burst out, pressing her palms against her hot temples. "*Trust*—what does that mean? I want assurance, assurance that my soul will rest in eternity and not burn in everlasting torment—words in a book are feeble, Collette! Yes, hopelessly feeble! I want stillness in my mind—in my heart. I want peace! I have wanted peace all my life, and I have done everything in my power to find it, but do you think I have? Me: a Religious Sister of Mercy, who has striven and hungered and bled to know God—who has *expected* to know him and *thought* that she did; me, above anyone else, should know what peace feels like, and yet I do not! I positively do not!"

"Then, Kate, if you have not found peace in the convent, why are you going back?"

"For others, Collette! For others! Don't you know that? To serve others—to serve my family through my life's intercession to God on their behalf!"

Fervour seemed suddenly to fire Collette's eyes. "Katie, listen to me: your responsibility is toward God for your *own* soul." On a sudden burst of impulse, she grasped for the book on the table, flipped it open, and scanned the pages till she came to a certain passage. "Here it is—right here, in plain words. Listen." She began to read: "'Wherefore he—meaning Christ—is able also to save them to the uttermost that come unto God by him, seeing he ever liveth to make intercession for them.' Do you hear that, Kate? The Son of God himself is the intercessor—not you! He can save you from sin, from guilt, from everything you fear; he can save you from yourself, if you let him—but you must first believe that he can!"

Collette's cheeks streamed with tears; it seemed that in her eagerness she might rise from her sickbed and run toward Kate. "Take this book, Katie—I want you to have it," she said, holding it out, trembling with feeling as she waited for Kate to take it. "I beg you to read it—just read it, and see what happens… please?"

Kate cleared her throat as she remembered the lashing rebuke she had once dealt Collette for reading the Bible. "I won't understand it," she said bluntly, staring at the book suspended in the air in front of her.

"God gave you a mind, Kate!" Collette exclaimed, her tone nettled. "He also gave you free will—and with those two things you can *ask* God to help you understand—and he *will* help you understand, Katie! I know he will! Now, here, come." She motioned for Kate to come forward, and when Kate did, she pushed the book into her hand. "There!" she said, sitting back with a sharp exhale. "And you needn't tell anyone you have it, either, if you fear discovery. It is just a book." She paused and punctuated her meaning with a sharp glance. "*A book.*"

Bewildered, Kate nodded dumbly. At that same moment the click of a doorknob interrupted them, and they both looked around to see the door open by degrees and announce a visitor.

"William? Oh, hello darling. Well, look—aren't you charming!"

A little boy entered. His shoulders were draped in a great wool overcoat, its sleeves shoved up his pudgy arms to allow a set of dimpled hands to appear. The tall beaver top hat on his delicately moulded head resembled a blackened, overgrown stovepipe, and it had been forced down around his brow, causing golden ringlets to fringe his face and his ears to bend outward like two pieces of rubber. A well-used stethoscope dangled from his neck, and projecting from the breast pocket of his overcoat were the swirled red-and-white tips of two peppermint candy sticks.

"Hello, Mama!" The little boy marched up to the bedside and thrust the stethoscope's ear tips into his ears, brandished the bell in his right hand, and applied the diaphragm to the centre of Collette's forehead. "Please shush, Mama," he instructed in an important whisper, holding the index finger of his other hand over his pink lips. "I'm *listening*!"

Four or five seconds passed while the child's concentrated gaze roved from one corner of the room to the other and up along the ceiling until they returned to Collette's face, accompanied by a triumphant smile that sparkled across his countenance as he removed the diaphragm from the forehead of his patient and extracted the ear tips.

"You're gonna get *all* better, Mama!" he reported. "Now! Would you like a peppermint from Dr. Hall?" Grinning, he withdrew one of the candy sticks and flourished it before Collette.

"Why, thank you, my darling! That is most thoughtful of you. Do you have one for Miss Kate as well?"

The child looked at Kate, and as he did, her bony hands locked themselves together as she struggled to maintain a pleasant expression in front of him to disguise the sudden feeling of confusion that came over her when she realized how much she would actually love to have a child of her own.

William seemed about to speak, but then a knock sounded at the door, and Kate felt herself breathe more easily as their attention was drawn to the entrance.

"Come in," said Collette pleasantly.

The door opened, and Ellen entered. "The doctor's here tae see ye, Miss Clayton."

A familiar step in the hall, a familiar fluttering in her stomach, and Kate looked up to see Dr. Hall standing in the doorway.

"Welcome, Doctor," said Collette.

"Good afternoon, ladies—William." With a courteous smile Dr. Hall nodded and strode to the bed. His black leather medical bag was held in one hand and his hat in the other. He had looked at Kate, but no special mark of recognition or surprise had crossed his face upon seeing her. "And how has my patient fared since my last visit?" he continued easily, directing his attention to Collette.

"Somewhat tired, but better," Collette returned.

"I already checked her, Dr. Hall!" William exclaimed as he stepped boldly forward, sticking out his chest, throwing back his shoulders, and lifting his chin in an attitude of jubilation.

"You did, did you?" Dr. Hall's eyebrows wiggled with suppressed laughter.

"Yes sir! My mama is gonna get *all better*!"

"Well then, little man, let us take a look, shall we?" With a playful laugh, he patted William on the shoulder, then laid down his hat and turned to examine Collette.

Kate watched him, and a strange feeling stole over her. His manner was businesslike, his touch appropriately skilled and tender. He took Collette's temperature, felt her pulse, made several detailed inquiries as to any variables in her condition since his last visit.

She saw flecks of grey at his temples that disturbed the raven of his hair—they told that he was a conscientious man who met the needs of others before his own. She saw his hands—there was kindness and skill in them, which rendered them suddenly attractive. The ring finger of his left hand… there was no wedding band on it.

But why did she notice that now?

The lines there, in his forehead—they had not existed when she first met him, but somehow they softened his countenance. And his eyes when he laughed—they were beautiful, weren't they?

When he finished the examination, Dr. Hall packed his tools back into his medical bag and straightened up. A tug on his sleeve made him turn.

William was on tiptoe, looking up at him. "Well?" he whispered.

Dr. Hall hunkered down next to William and placed his hand on the boy's shoulder and leaned close to his ear. "Well, Master Clayton, let me tell you, I think you're pretty darn right—your mother's a strong woman with a good constitution, and she is getting all better."

William applauded.

"And you know what else, Master Clayton? You'll make a mighty fine doctor someday." With a wink, he clapped William on the back and straightened up again as he addressed Ellen. "Miss Kelly, continue to administer the medicine. I'll be back again tomorrow to check in on her."

A "Blessed by the Lord God Almighty!" was uttered by the older woman as she raised her palms upward. "An' thank ye very much, Doctor! Ye've been so good tae us, we cannae thank ye enough. God bless ye, sir!"

"'Tis a pleasure. Good day to you, ladies. Good day to you, Master Clayton." Smiling as he took his hat, the doctor turned to leave, but an exclamation from William brought him to a halt.

"Miss Kate—here! Would you like a peppermint from Dr. Hall?"

With William's extricated peppermint stick fanning her face insistently and the attention of all eyes turned in her direction, Kate could hardly think for surprise. "Why… oh—" she faltered awkwardly, swallowing hard as she hesitated. Surely Dr. Hall would be laughing at her now, remembering the times she had refused his proffered candy stick. But it was no use now being stubborn on account of her pride. William was just a child, and she would take his peppermint no matter what the doctor might think of her, or how he might laugh.

"Thank you, William." She held out her hand determinedly, allowing her mouth to soften into a smile. "That is very kind of you."

William's grin widened as she took the candy in her hand; he waited for her to try it—he would not look away till she did—and at last she tasted it.

"Mmm, it is good," she said, though she felt like an idiot—but what did it matter now? She had made William happy, and he was giggling at her, his pudgy hands covering his cherry mouth, his shoulders lifting, his eyes dancing as he cast a mischievous glance in the direction of the doctor, who still stood on the threshold.

Kate glanced in the same direction, but at that instant the doctor turned abruptly away—did he smother his own secret grin?—and then he was gone. She heard his firm, quick footsteps passing along the corridor, accompanied by his best whistled version of "Battle Hymn of the Republic."

And Kate did not trouble herself to suppress a laugh of her own.

— CHAPTER XXVIII —

AT SEA

sudden wave dashed up against the side of the steamship, and the fine sea spray stung Kate's eyes and burned her lips, leaving its briny taste on her tongue.

The late-morning sun was brilliant, glancing off the gently cresting waves made by the hull of the steamship as it cut through the waters. Only a few fleecy clouds sailed overhead, sallied forth by a gusty west wind that sped their course eastward across the Atlantic. The swelling waters, shimmering and transparent, stretched in every direction as far as Kate's gaze could reach, blending indistinctly with the distant azure rim of the sky. Beyond, whitecaps jumped like shining horses reaching into the dome of the sapphire zenith, where, just the night before, a million flickering stars had lay scattered like diamonds.

Oh, she loved being out at sea—loved the sensation of being tossed on a peak of waves and then plunged momentarily into a valley of waters, loved the thrill of the wind rushing into her face and fluttering her veil—what would it feel like to have her veil off and the wind rushing through her hair? And to swim like that dolphin—yes, over there! A dolphin! Oh, and another one! Twins dancing in the waves together, their smooth wet bodies glistening in the sunlight! To dive and splash and play as they did in those wonderful waves, to feel the cool of the water running over her and through her fingers and toes and hair, cleansing and energizing at once—wouldn't it be a dream?

Her mind wandered back to her first voyage. Vexed and confused, she had not loved it then—indeed, she had resented it. But this day was new—wasn't it? Although it was true she was still alone. No father or mother mourned her departure;

no boyish sweetheart waited to welcome her back to the shores of her green island home. She had wished for him; indeed, she had, but it was not to be—not for Sister Kate. She was going home… Back to Ireland. Back to the convent. Back to her ceremony of final vows and her Heavenly Bridegroom.

Other passengers mulled about the ship's deck, some of them alone as they paused at the railing to take in the ocean view, others conversing in small knots of three or four. The company of Sisters and Father Andrew were not then up on deck—Kate had shared in their companionship for most of the morning and partaken of the morning Sacrament, then taken her leave, bringing the Bible in her pocket.

The steamship darted forward over the glittering watery expanse, releasing itself into the free, uncharted air as though it were a bird taking flight. Kate leaned against the railing, watching the gem-like tract of sea and sky together and wondering what might have happened if she had not accepted the calling to serve in the Washington hospital? What if she had never left the convent?

It had not been her will to obey, yet she had. But did a greater power than the Church of Rome send her all those miles across the ocean to serve on another continent? Did a greater power than government, and even a greater emancipation, influence the course of the war that caused a Washington surgeon to beg the service of the Sisters of Mercy—and the coincidence that she should be among them? Had a higher will than man's interceded on her behalf to bring her to where she was today?

It was evident that she had served well and had eased much suffering, and for that she felt privileged, almost content. Indeed, she would not wish it otherwise. Yet still, if she had never stepped across the threshold of that Washington hospital, certainly someone else would have filled her place…

But Jack Gunderson would have died in the arms of another nurse—perhaps he would have died alone; her ears would never have heard Sam's singing; Sergeant Dallington would never have mistaken her for his daughter; she would never have seen Collette again; Dr. Hall would have found someone else to make his favourite.

Or would he?

Amidst the tapestry of coincidences, was it possible to recognize God's will over whims of chance? And now, returning to St. Agnes, how could she know that what she imagined to be God's will for her now was not—actually—her own?

Kate reached into her pocket and took out the Bible, then opened it to the one hundred and thirty-ninth Psalm. The pages fluttered and rustled; she held them down with two fingers and read aloud: "O Lord, thou hast searched me, and known me. Thou knowest my downsitting and mine uprising, thou understandest my thought afar off…"

The wind took her words, and she looked up.

A lone white-breasted seagull flew overhead, uttering its piercing cry—they were not far from land now. The bird circled again and again, then, stretching out its neck, it made one mighty swoop downward while its grey-mantled wings navigated toward the surging, folding emerald waters until its body plunged beneath them. Seconds later it emerged, floating like driftwood on the swaying tide, a glistening fish snapped between its shining yellow beak. Minutes passed. The bird happily enjoyed its noon repast. And Kate looked on, marvelling.

The seagull was free. Free to soar. Free to go wherever its will desired. Free to follow whatever wind of fancy might come its way.

Or was it, truly?

What was free will to the birds—or did they even have it? What was law to them? Were they servants to God's decree, bound by instinct to an absolute authority—an absolute truth that had instituted the laws of nature, which they obeyed without any thought of rebellion?

"There was once a nest of six little sparrows in an apple tree…" she whispered. "One day five of them had flown away; one had been left. That little sparrow was lonely, but still it sang with the sunrise and ate the worms its mother brought him. A little orphan girl prayed to God for that sparrow—prayed that its wings might grow strong so it could fly away, too…"

God cared about the sparrows, she knew that now; and he had heard her prayer, for the next day, the bird had soared away, happy and free.

"But what is it that distinguishes me from birds and dumb beasts? Indeed, from a senseless machine?" Kate returned the Bible to her pocket.

She grasped the damp railing and leaned forward, eager for Ireland's Cliffs of Moher to appear like natural spires in the distance. "It will be any moment now," she said, breathing deeply, filling her lungs with the fresh sea air.

And what of creation? The sun had risen upon that day in accordance with a law outside of itself. The moon had not resented its going down; it was content to obey the command it had reverenced for thousands of years—a command that kept all creation in harmony. The west wind blew perhaps unpredictably, but not independently—not defiantly.

It seemed that the speech of nature was eternally responding to God in a sort of faith, or belief, within which was hidden a sacred rest that caused the earth to become, for man, an inspiration toward acceptance of divine will. For if neither sun nor moon nor wind obeyed the laws that governed them, who would deny that such disobedience would inevitably send earth and firmament spinning into chaos? Was it possible that an infinite God could grasp those invisible billows in his fists and send them forth like messengers at his own speed and bidding?

And then, amongst it all, was the independent man.

Was there a law for him by which he might find the same contentment that creation enjoyed—freedom from himself, and satisfaction for his needs? When one observed the loss of paradise and immortality suffered by Adam and Even in the Garden of Eden, it seemed incumbent to ask whether man's choice to eat the forbidden fruit—and, verily, every choice of man thereafter—was either a silly whim or an unseen universe upon which time itself did hang irrevocably.

Because of one man's choice to sin in Eden, was all mankind now doomed to reap eternal defeat? Or did there exist somewhere an arm of redemption whereby he might regain his lost immortality?

Perhaps the fruit of the knowledge of good and evil now presented itself to mankind day and night in innumerable instances… Perhaps the life and time of every human on earth was a private test of individual loyalty to learn by actions if the Lord was his God, or the Serpent… Perhaps the forked tongue of lust and doubt still sought to poison the minds of men, seducing them to make themselves as gods who turned evil hearts from the living God to sow their seeds of unbelief and eat the fruit thereof…

Who had caused the irreversible sequences of time and choice to exist that such a test of loyalty might be legitimately enacted? Who was Sovereign—God or man? Who could speak a word, and create a world?

"But who *is* God?" she said.

That her life should appear at last so determinable, so perfectly predictable without variance of any sort, ought to have been one of her chief sources of comfort—but somehow, at that moment, it was not. She still longed for intimacy; she yearned to feel complete, to know more; she required something deeper to satisfy the insatiable need of her soul. And the reality that she did not have it caused her heart to chill with loneliness.

"How shall I hear his voice?" said Kate, weeping.

The seagull flew away. The steamboat sailed on. And softly, tenderly, Kate heard a whisper in her ear, asking,

"Are you not of more value than many sparrows?"

— CHAPTER XXIX —

THE RING

From a branch in the beech tree overhead, whose leaves still sparkled with droplets of morning dew, the song of a red-breasted robin accompanied the steady pulse of tamed saddle leather and the muffled rhythm of Skipper's hooves along the soft, reddish dirt road as John rode the gelding up the gravel drive toward the farmhouse. The morning's hard gallop through bright-green fields and misty dells at sunrise had left his horse foaming, his powerful frame surging with energy.

But neither bodily exertion nor mental exhaustion could settle John's mind. He ate the opium—it seduced him with the necessity he now felt for it and could not resist, though the secret practice seared his conscience—and he could no longer deny that he was growing so blind and deaf that not only had nature lost its beauty but his own family had lost his interest while he took another, and another, and another piece from the battered old tin. There was no longer joy in the robin's song; no longer diamonds in the droplets of morning dew; no longer warm sun in the stainless summer sky; no longer a thrill in his morning gallops; no longer camaraderie even with his horse. Everyone was a stranger—the world was a stranger, and he was a stranger to himself.

As they made their way up the road, taking time to cool down from the recent exertion, the gelding's velvet-tipped ears pricked forward. John followed the horse's line of sight until his own gaze rested on a female figure emerging from the vine-veiled front door of the house. Priscilla's nut-brown hair, wide-skirted calico morning dress, and lace-trimmed peach apron were unmistakable.

"Good morning, Papa!"

He raised his arm and waved, then watched as she ambled lightly along the winding garden path through the herb and flower beds, plucking a stem here and a blossom there. Aye, his lovely and carefree Priscilla—Priscilla, who knew nothing, who was as innocent as she was lovely and happy. His little girl who would soon be married to her sweetheart.

"Aye, Paul," he said to himself, contemplating the suit of the young man. Paul had returned from the war not only physically unscathed but with flying colours attesting to his faithful service and stout bravery on the battlefield. Not long after his return, he had requested a private meeting with John in which he humbly declared his love for John's virtuous daughter, sharing his cherished hope that, in little less than a year, he expected to have his house built and the sufficient means required by his prospective father-in-law to support a young wife and a growing family. Pleased and honoured by the integrity displayed by the young suitor, John watched with pride as the engagement between the two lovers was made public and plans began to form for a wedding the following spring.

A second figure emerged from the doorway, a woven willow basket swaying on her arm as she followed Priscilla's footpath through the garden. Collette Clayton—yes, that lovely smile and that crown of golden glory massed on her queenly head had also belonged to another.

The mournful heaviness—the guilt—greeted him again, the way it had greeted him for all those long, agonized weeks—months—since Ellen had confronted him. Tasks could not silence its presence. Could not deaden its influence. The days only got longer, and the tasks more grinding, and the temporary distractions he had used to excuse a full confession more frustrating, until hours turned to days, and days turned to weeks, and weeks turned to months, and months turned to years, and he finally realized, by the end of them, that only a day had gone by.

He reached for the tin. He opened it. He put another piece in his mouth, for the pain was bad now.

"God in heaven," he said as Skipper approached the hitching rail in front of the house, "if you wish me to speak, then give me a sign. I won't speak it until you give me a sign—a strong, clear one. Something I cannot miss." He swung his leg behind the saddle and dismounted, then wrapped the reins twice around the circular rail. He patted Skipper's damp, thick-muscled neck. "Aye, old boy—I can do it all now, with one arm."

Priscilla's voice ascended from the garden path as she chatted merrily with Collette. "My roses and marigolds are over there in the corner near the Mayday tree. Roses and marigolds were our mother's favourite flowers, so I like to keep care of them myself in memory of her. Ellen, of course, tends the herb garden. Each herb is created into almost any remedy imaginable. Ellen is a regular nurse. And now—see over that way—that is the vegetable garden. It is tended by Ellen and I. Peter helps when he is not milking the cow or collecting the eggs or mucking the barn or chopping kindling—oh, his kindling, he used to be quite negligent about it! But now it is quite the other way, since he has his own hatchet now, which Papa gave him, and it has prompted him to be much more responsible."

"It must be wonderful to live in this way," said Collette, "so free from the constraints of city streets, never hedged in by stone enclosures. My senses want to drink in every smell, relish every texture, absorb every sound of this place, it is so beautiful. Priscilla, do you know? It is nearly two months since I have enjoyed a walk out of doors… and today feels like heaven to me. It is perfect."

John looked in Priscilla's direction, and she smiled brightly at him. "Papa! Did you have a pleasant ride this morning? I saw you leave at six o'clock—that is very early for a ride."

He received her customary morning embrace. "I did, Prissy, thank you. Good morning, Miss Clayton." He offered Collette a nod. She offered a courteous smile.

The savoury aromas of fresh cornbread and brewing coffee and the sound of eggs sizzling in a frypan were coming from the open kitchen window, the prelude to an inevitable breakfast announcement. John made a move toward the front door. "Shall we go in now, ladies?"

"Yes!" Priscilla cheered. "Ellen will have her famous farmhouse morning spread for us."

John opened the door for the ladies to enter first and then followed behind them. From the breakfast parlour came an original combination of boisterous shouts, the clattering of wood across the floor, intermittent laughter, and—a groan of agony?

"What's going on?" John said, removing his boots and hat in the entryway. "Is that the boys?"

All three hastened down the hall, passing by the kitchen, where Ellen was bent over the hot stove.

"Thank ye, ye're in!" exclaimed Ellen, her face shining and red. "I near sent Peter out tae fetch ye in time for prayer, but he's rowdier'n a Rebel with the yell, an' since ye're here, let's sit down an' eat afore the Scotch eggs get cold."

A tremendous bang ushered from the parlour.

"What drama do they have going in there?" John said, heading in the offending direction.

Ellen continued her rant as she followed him down the hall. "Ow! Energy—where those lads get it from I cannae mind! Ye best get in there, Mr. Dallington, for they've been tearin' up an' down the house like wildcats… Prissy, fetch the cornbread when ye come, lass… I said 'Sit down, laddies, an' wait for yer breakfast,' but ye think they would mind me now? Ow!"

John entered the room. A terrific crashing welcomed him. There was William, standing on one of the chairs overlooking the breakfast table, where an array of plates, pots, and platters full of steaming food was spread out. An angular hat constructed of old newspapers decorated his curly yellow head, complemented by a conspicuous black patch that covered his right eye and a stubby wooden sword that he brandished above his head as he shouted a lisped version of "Arr, *mate*!" over the limp figure of Peter, who was sprawled out on the floor alongside the table, his arms and legs jerking and twitching grotesquely as groans mimicking a tortured sufferer ushered from his lips.

"Hmm, amusing," said John. "A veritable battlefield, it appears."

Collette gasped and rushed to her son's side. "Oh, Willie!" she cried, looking anxiously at both boys in turn. "Whatever have you done to poor Peter?"

William's eyes widened as he looked at his mother, his expression of scowling pirate transformed to that of endearing child as he cried out, "Oh, Mama! Mama! You're finally feeling better, Mama! You're finally feeling better! I"—he hooted with excitement—"am"—bounded nimbly from the chair—"so"—and landed softly on the floor—"glad!" He tossed his wooden sword aside, where it clattered noisily across the floor as he threw himself headlong into the abundance of his mother's skirts.

"Oh, Willie! Willie!" Collette crouched down to his level as though about to rebuke him, but she failed, instead nestling his head against her bosom.

A moment passed. John watched closely. Lifting the boy's dimpled chin with her finger, Collette looked into his beaming face and a queer expression burst over her countenance—an expression that seemed to be faltering between frowning and smiling and laughing outright.

Aye—that look. He had seen it before. Cassandra had shown the same expression once when dealing with the one-and-a-half-year-old twins. She had, of course, meant to scold them for playing and squealing so loudly and disturbing John in his study—but she had been too weak to do it. And when John had barged out into the hall to find out why the twins were giggling so loudly and disturbing him?... Well, that night, when he lay beside her in their bed and had asked her why she hadn't paddled them, she had answered, *"Johnny, forgive me—for how can I punish them when they are merely being children?"*

"Why, Peter! What are you boys doing in here?" Priscilla had just entered, both her hands mittened as she held the hot pan of steaming cornbread. A warning glare fixed on her brother. "You know you are *not* supposed to be roughhousing in the breakfast parlour—you have been told so repeatedly!"

Peter sprang up from the floor. He swept back his hair and straightened his shirt collar sheepishly, then, like a meek convict standing before his judge, stood mute before his sister as though she were the only person in the room. John watched, his eyebrows raising, wondering for a moment if she, too, would weaken; but as he waited, noting that the stern look on her face did not falter, he highly doubted that she would. She was serious, and Peter knew it.

"Well!" Ellen concluded. "Do let's eat afore the Scotch eggs *an'* the coffee turn cold!"

"Yeah, let's eat!" William cried. "I'm so hungry, Mama, I could eat a whole *elephant*!"

Collette laughed. It was a merry laugh. It reminded him of someone. Then she straightened up, placing William on his feet, and as the boy unwound his arms from her neck, John saw a necklace flash at her throat and catch on one of his lace cuff buttons. Jerking his arms down, William dashed away, and as he did, the necklace fell to the floor at Collette's feet, unnoticed by her as she sailed to the table.

Readying to point the loss out to her, John moved forward and was about to speak, but before the words left his mouth he saw that the piece was not merely a necklace.

His heart bounded in his chest. How could he mistake it? He glanced around. Everyone was bustling to their places. He alone had noticed it.

All at once his senses grew dull. All faces seemed turned to him, but his vision was unfocused and he could not see their eyes. He walked to his seat at the head of the table and sat down; still, his eyes sought the ring glittering on the burgundy wool carpet.

But his family was waiting for him to say the blessing. Bowing his head, he mumbled grace over the repast without knowing what he said; he dished and passed the food without seeing it; he poured his coffee without smelling it, ate his eggs and cornbread without tasting them. All his senses were being drawn toward the ring sparkling on the carpet, calling him to reach for it, summoning him like a sign he could not deny.

Like the sign he had prayed for.

"Papa, will you not finish your coffee?"

John started. Priscilla was standing at his elbow, her arms full of dirty dishes ready to be transported to the kitchen sink. Had they finished eating already? The chime of the clock answered: Yes, it was nine o'clock.

He shifted forward in his chair and waved his hand at his still half-full cup of black coffee. "Uh, no—no, darling. No more coffee for me now, thank you."

Priscilla smiled, then took his cup and sallied out of the room, followed by Collette and Ellen, their arms laden with empty dishes as their voices chattered merrily down the hall.

"C'mon, Willie! Let's go capture the enemy ship!" Peter sprang from the table.

William followed him. "Yeah! Let's get 'em!"

A hazy cloud tore past him. Ah—the boys? It dashed from the parlour. The front door creaked open and slammed shut; distracted fowl quaked loudly outside.

Why was he alone in the parlour now? Had everyone gone away? How his eyes wandered now—yes, wandered back into the past, wandered back to all the guilt that he carried, wandered back to the ring glittering on the carpet. He pushed himself away from the table. He stood up. He walked over to the ring, hunkered down, reached out, and touched it. Aye, a most familiar piece. He picked it up and turned it over in his fingers. Morning light glanced off the band. It was a gold band—it was engraved on the inside. He had engraved it himself.

Footsteps sounded in the hall. He looked up. Collette stood in the doorway. Her gaze darted to his hand, then instinctively she put her hands to her bosom, feeling for the something that was not there.

"Oh, excuse me, Mr. Dallington…" She cleared her throat delicately. "But that belongs to me."

Yes, worry edged her voice. He hesitated, his brows knitting together. "Where did you get this?" he said at last. His voice sounded hollow.

"It was given to me, sir."

John rose slowly, still holding the ring between his fingers. "Who, uh—" He cleared his throat. He was an eejit. "Who gave it to you?"

"It was my mother's wedding ring. A certain woman gave it to me through the bars of the fence when I lived at the asylum."

"Cassandra gave it tae me afore she died. Years later, upon the promise I made tae her, I gave the ring tae her illegitimate daughter, Collette, who received it through the bars of the asylum fence."

Ellen's voice.

His mouth grew dry; the muscles in his face grew rigid as

he fought back the glaze stinging his eyes. Collette was that child. "Your mother gave it to her, to give to you?" he repeated mechanically as his hand began to tremble.

"Papa, what is it?"

Priscilla's voice—she was standing motionless in the doorway, looking straight at him.

"How can ye 'spect our Father in heaven tae forgive ye yer debts if ye willnae forgive yer debtors?"

Memory grappled with him. The dark billows rolled, the breakers surged fiercely, the weight of his sin fell upon him—mighty waves crashing against the rocks of his bitter reef. He could neither answer nor lift his eyes. They were locked upon the ring. He was back at Fisher's Hill, lying helpless on the field. Cannons and gunfire rumbled and blazed, bullets whistled over his head like swarms of angry hornets, cries of tortured men rang in his ears with sickening exactness as he watched their mangled bodies writhe in an infernal sludge of human gore.

"Give me just one chance to make it right," he had prayed then. And God had heard his cries and granted him mercy. Yet now, as his daughter stood before him in all her youth and innocence, believing him to be something that he was not, he knew it would have been easier if he had died on the field that day; for she was a little one, and he had offended her.

Weakness came over him; he was sweating. He shook his head; the millstone was heavy. "Prissy, you can have no idea." His eyes went to Collette. He would not run—he would not. "Miss Clayton," he said quietly, "I knew your mother."

Collette stared back at him. "You… You knew my mother?" she said, and her mouth dropped open.

"Papa?" Priscilla stepped forward as she looked from him to Collette to the ring, and back to him again.

Ireland… his boyhood… Geoffrey… Cassandra—their debts and his, they all stood as real and equal as if those twenty years had been but a day. God saw and knew all. His eyes sought the depths. His ears heard the cries.

How could John Dallington have ever thought that he would escape the judgment of God?

— CHAPTER XXX —

THE CONFESSION

The room was drowned in a prolonged silence. At last John lifted his aching face. His hand, cold and damp, still held the ring on the necklace, and in his distractedness he had resorted to rotating it over and over between his stiffened fingers. He halted, clutched the ring in his sweaty palm, and, with one concentrated effort, mustered himself together and forced his lips to move.

"Miss Clayton," he said, "I scarce know the words to speak this to you. But…" He swallowed. "Your mother was my wife."

Collette's eyes blanked and widened at once. "Your… *wife*?"

He held the necklace out to her. "Yes."

She took it and stood there, looking eager. "All my life I have been searching for the man who gave this ring to her. Are you…?" She partly whispered, partly gasped the words. "Are you my… my…?"

"No… No, I am not. I…" John looked down and shifted on his feet as his debts stared him in the face. "I once knew him, though."

"What?... Do you— Do you know where he is, sir?"

Icy drips trickled down his chest, over his ribs. Breathing was more difficult now. Bitterness was a stinking tide; he forced it back. Vengeance belonged to God, not John. "No, I do not," he said.

Collette stared at him, her eyes asking more questions than he had answers for. He plunged his hand into the pocket of his trousers, withdrew the tin, walked to the table, and cast it down there while the opiate pills rattled inside… rattled loudly, telling secrets to the air.

"Miss Clayton, your father was the friend of my youth,"

he said, turning from the table. "And the partner in my wife's adultery."

"*Papa?*" Priscilla's voice was an unearthly echo in the room.

"Prissy…" His heart struck repeatedly hard and fast against his body. The terror in her eyes terrified his conscience. "Mary Dallington was my second wife."

A single blue vein pulsed visibly beneath the skin of her left milk-white temple. "But… Why… did you… not…?"

"Tell you?" Impatience crescendoed his tone, and he paused to check himself. "Prissy, my past is a bitter one. It is not one I wished you to know."

"But"—her words came in fractured accents as her hand pressed repeatedly against her breastbone—"all this time I haven't known… my own… mother?"

Aye, yes—how his debts weighed heavily against her; his answer had the power to estrange her from him forever. But if the dogs came and licked his sores today, it would be better than to lift his eyes from the torments of hell tomorrow. "Priscilla," he said, "I divorced your mother." The words crashed from his lips.

She gaped back at him from among the ruins, her lips silently repeating the terrible word.

"Her name," he said, "was Cassandra. And she bore Geoffrey Clayton's child."

The silence moaned in agony; the walls pressed against them. In painful suspense John watched Priscilla's fair brow eclipse with a look of absence that made him shudder.

"Papa," she said in a thin, wavering voice, "please… Tell me where… my mother is. Please, Papa?"

John's restless limbs goaded him to cross the room, stuff his hand into his trouser pocket, feel for the tin that was not there, and in agony to plant himself before the bay window that faced out over the sunbathed orchard. Aye. There was nothing hid that would not be known.

A long, breathless minute; a silent look at the floor; a sight. And he began:

"Your mother was the most beautiful creature in the world. I fell in love with her the first day I saw her. She was sweet, tender, innocent. Just like you, Prissy… just like you." He paused, remembering. "Her eyes were like violets. Large, soft… deep as the ocean, just like—" But he stopped short as the words slashed from his mouth, scraping away the diseased flesh covering his heart. It hurt. But he must go on.

He cleared his throat of thickness. "My pa," he said, "was a staunch Presbyterian minister from England who moved to Ireland to establish his own parish and join the Orangemen before he married my mother, Brigitta Walsh, a fiery Irishwoman with no fortune. Pa's view on marriage was that if a young man could not maintain celibacy until he was mature enough to govern himself perfectly as well as provide a reliable and substantial income for a family, then he had no business to even think on a lass. His opinion passed to me, requiring that I not marry before twenty-five. In the meantime I was to devote my energies to farming. Any spare time was to be devoted to the study of mathematics, history, and theology, of which he was very fond.

"I resigned myself to my pa's dictum resolutely enough. But then the disease came. Ma and Pa died… and I met Cassandra Fletcher when I was eighteen years old. My friend, Geoffrey Clayton, suggested that I marry her. I shoved his suggestion aside, resolved never to marry into a Roman Catholic family, and determined to stay true to the wishes of my deceased father.

"After two years Augusta left home and moved to England with her lover. I remained in Ireland, planning to shortly assume the role of minister in the local parish in place of my late father. Marriage was the last thing on my mind—until Geoffrey returned from a holiday and mocked my celibate state, then reminded me of Cassandra. I asked for her hand in marriage only two weeks before my twentieth birthday. On our wedding day I gave her a ring…" John glanced down at his feet. "That one, actually"—he looked over at the ring in Collette's hand—"the one you're holding… the engravings on the inside of the band are her initials, you can see them." He glanced at Collette's face. It was flushed, but she neither moved nor spoke, only looked upon him with eyes wide, full of feeling.

"Our marital happiness seemed doomed from the first," he went on. "First, Cassandra's mother and sister died of famine, and her father and the remains of the Fletcher family immigrated to America—I do not know where. But worst of all misfortune was Geoffrey, whose lust was bent upon my wife the moment she and I sealed our vows at the altar. He became a frequent guest in our home, and it was not long before his casual visits became an almost daily routine."

He fidgeted with the lining of his trouser pocket. "A year went by. Twin daughters were born to us. Cassandra was a glowing mother and adored them both. Ellen was our housemaid even then, and skilled in midwifery. She assisted Cassandra's delivery and continued to live with us as our daughters' nanny, staying in the baby's room—you know, Prissy… where the cradles are.

"Seven months elapsed. Geoff's visits continued. But since he always had a different girl hanging on his arm—the next one always prettier than the last—I never thought he would cast his greedy eyes on mine. But he did. And his snare was deadly." John stopped as his chest constricted and his voice grew hoarse. "Ellen— She wasn't there when it happened. She was in Dublin, visiting an invalid sister. When she returned home and learned of the affair, she was devastated. Neither of us once doubted that it was my best friend who had locked my bedroom door and spent the night in my bed with my wife."

His jaw clenched hard and contracted repeatedly; his eyes burned. They were likely red, and Priscilla would likely notice. This time, though, she would know why.

"For weeks, I lived outside and slept in the barn. I never saw Geoffrey again. No one in the village or surrounding area knew where he had gone. I vowed that if I ever found him, I would kill him. Cassandra repented and pleaded forgiveness. Ellen never tried to defend Cassandra's weakness, but she did beg me to be merciful to her, believing that her repentance was sincere. But within a week I had issued Cassandra a bill of divorcement.

"Ellen wept. Cassandra was pregnant, she said, and needed mercy, and so did the child. But I would not forgive the debt. Bitterness and resentment devoured me. My fury at the knowledge that the two people closest to me had betrayed me sent my judgment into a disastrous plummet. I had been an inadequate husband, and the realization tortured me. Cassandra was lost, and so was God. Love had become a confusing and maddening contradiction.

"We each took a twin. I chose the eldest—the strongest, and my favourite. The younger twin, Katherine, was a pale little thing, weak from the start. Still, Cassandra received and loved the child, her willingness exposing my lack of compassion. The fact that she was pregnant with Geoffrey's child only maddened me further, and in my spite I arranged to have Cassandra and her little Katherine sent to the place where fallen women and their children are sent—the Magdalene Asylum, run by the Sisters of Mercy. Into their custody I gave all responsibility for the younger twin, affirming that neither Cassandra nor I would carry any responsibility for the other twin, and neither of the girls would know of the other's existence. The past was locked behind the gates of an asylum fence, I argued, and it would stay there." He paused, looked down, pressed his lips together.

"Shortly afterward I became engaged to a young widow named Mary Skyler," he said, lifting his face again. "Mary was an independent young woman, strict and sensible, the only daughter of a well-to-do family. She had been widowed after only three months of marriage to a wealthy elderly gentleman, and from him she had inherited a generous fortune. When I met her at a church function, she was eager to marry again, and I was impatient to find a mother for my daughter. It was a marriage forged more out of necessity than affection. My first wife had died, I told her, leaving me with one daughter. She learned of none of my secrets—if she had, I am convinced she would never have married me. Later, we immigrated to the United States and settled in Virginia." He paused, and a weighty silence hung in the air. "Since then I have learned from Ellen that Cassandra died in the asylum while giving birth to an illegitimate baby girl."

Chins quivering, eyes awash, faces ashen with shock and awe, Collette and Priscilla looked back at him.

Finally Priscilla's mouth opened. "Papa?" she whispered. "That baby girl… Papa? Ellen knew all along—that she, she was Collette?"

A nod sufficed. Another moment and he heard her broken voice say, "And the twins, too… Papa… I was one of them, wasn't I?"

Long, measured breathing could not steady the quaking he felt within. His chest hitched as he said quietly, "Yes, you were."

Then he heard a sob. A rustle of skirts. He looked over. Priscilla sat on a chair, her shoulders slumped forward and quivering, both hands pressed against her mouth, her eyelids compressed.

Collette's gaze was on him and Priscilla by turns. He could feel its strength, but he could not meet it.

She was weeping, too.

"The woman… the woman with the red hair," she was saying. "The woman outside the gates of the asylum—who gave me my mother's wedding ring… it was Ellen! It was Ellen!"

Time seemed to cease its measured course in a pause that felt eternal. What to do, what to say, how to act, John knew not; he could only stand rooted where he was, chained without, conflicted within, desperate for the forgiveness he knew he did not deserve.

Priscilla raised her face. "Why, Papa?" Her glazed eyes were red-rimmed and swollen, her cheeks watered with tears, her words broken by sobs of conflicted feeling. "I have… two… sisters…. then? And all my life… I have… believed a… a *lie*?"

Over and again he had attempted to prepare himself to answer the inevitable question; but every mustered sentence, every thought-out explanation he had imagined before now seemed stilted and contrived. Now, as he stood facing her, hollowed-out and powerless, he knew she was right. He had lied to her. And what a magnificent lie it had been.

"I was afraid," he began, unable to meet her eyes. "Afraid of the shame. Priscilla, I wanted to… to shield you."

"From truth, Papa?" She stared blankly at him. "You wanted to shield me from the *truth*?"

Somehow, her gentle words flogged him. What could he say? Inside every man there was a hidden truth about himself that could only be reconciled in God's perfect timing.

"Priscilla," he said and turned, at last forcing himself to seek her insistent, steadfast look. But his gaze weakened and he glanced at his hand, where a blue vein strained and pulsed against the flesh. "I do not deserve your forgiveness, but I am—" He faltered with sudden tears of remorse. "I am asking you if you can give it to me?"

No sound rustled the waveless atmosphere of the room. John braced himself. She could reject him now, if she wanted to.

Priscilla rose to her feet. She glided forward. Her face—was there resentment in it? Was there bitterness? Was there spite? He looked for anger but did not find it. Her manner—it could have jabbed him for all the truth he had withheld from her, but no—it was soft, and meek, and gentle. She was a lady as much as she was his daughter, and she reached out and took his cold, trembling hand in hers.

Aye, she was looking down at his hand now—his scarred hand… turning the palm down, searching the raised white scars that permanently disfigured his knuckles and told of the pain. She met his eyes. "Papa," she said, "it is a part of life, you once told me—the pain, I mean. Every man feels it, and every man must live through it. Either it will soften him, or it will embitter him. It is his own choice. You once told me that the sovereignty of God can turn evil for good when we put our trust in Christ's mercy and redemptive power." Her tears bathed his hand as she lifted it to her face and cradled it against her cheek; and he felt his heart melt like wax before the warm closeness of a flame.

Now she was embracing him, clinging to him like a little child afraid of the dark. "Papa, I forgive you… and *I love you still!*" She was weeping, at first gradually and then violently. Her slender frame trembled in his arms, her sobs muffled against his shoulder, mingling with his, the only vibration that penetrated the stillness. Some minutes elapsed; he knew not how many, before he gently released her, and she stepped back, dabbing her eyes, turning to look at Collette.

John looked at her, too. "Miss Clayton?" he said hoarsely.

She was watching them with eyes moist and red. Alone, she stood motionless in the centre of the room. Was she pained by the sting of longing? He had despised her as an unborn infant, and he knew he could expect from her nothing less than the pain his unsatisfied revenge had inflicted upon her. The revenge he had meant for Geoffrey Clayton.

"Miss Clayton," he said again, glancing at the floor and back to her as he moved toward her. "Years ago I failed to show compassion to you in the time of your helplessness. I despised, and offended you, before you knew who I was." A tremor interrupted his voice; he hardly trusted himself to go on. "May I… have… the—" He cleared his throat loudly as he lifted his chin to beat back the mighty sob that arrested him and sent the tears streaming down his face. "Collette… a helpless child—I cast you away. Forgive me." He stopped. Her ocean-deep eyes were glistening. Her shoulders were trembling. She was crying. "May I now… have the opportunity… to make it right with you? I want—very much—to welcome you into my household. As my—" He reached out his hand toward her, wiped the tears from her face. "As my own daughter."

Collette drew in a quick, steadying breath. "It is, sir…" she began, and faltered, then began again, tears trembling in her eyes. "It is what I have always dreamed of." Her voice broke between a laugh and a sob, but her face shone, and she nodded and stepped forward, giving her hand to him, embracing him.

Many minutes were sacred footsteps that came and passed and died away in a voiceless calm. Collette, wiping away the tears of joy streaming down her face, broke the silence when she exclaimed laughingly and tearfully at once, "And William—oh! My dear little boy! He will have a grandpapa!"

Aye. John smiled—the lad, so full of life and energy, would be a bright light in his home.

Priscilla was watching. "Collette?" She stretched out her hand. "The Lord knew how I always wanted a sister"—she smiled and wept and laughed, and smiled again—"and look—he sent you! He did—I know he sent you!"

John watched Collette's face quiver until tears burst forth

with a smile like the dawn. "Oh, dear God in heaven! Thank you, yes, thank you! Thank you! Thank you, dear God!"

They stood yet at arm's-length, gazing into each other's faces, Priscilla's dream of sisterly love fulfilled in that moment. Gradually they came together and held each other in a long, fond embrace, each sister's joyful tears mingling with those of the other.

"Can it be— Can it be possible?" Collette wept. "This joy! Oh! I can hardly believe it! But it is happening! It's true! It's true!" she said again and again. "And God's mercy is everlasting!"

When at last they released one another, Collette, her face fair and shining, looked upon the ring and chain still held in her palm. Then she lifted her eyes, wiped the tears aside, and focused on John.

"Mr. Dallington," she began, "I cannot thank you enough for your and your family's great kindness toward me and my son. My heart has never been so full. It overflows with gratitude to God and to you for what has happened here today—I have never known a happier, sweeter day in all my life, God knows it. But…" She glanced down for an instant, then refocused her gaze upon him. John sensed he knew the current of her thoughts as she said, "Somehow I feel—" She faltered again, then drew breath, and went on with collected resolve. "I feel that the joy is nearly complete, but it is not yet, because there is one person missing it… Mr. Dallington, there is still the other daughter, is there not?"

She was goading him on, gently but insistently.

"Yes, Papa, where is—" Priscilla stopped as the new name formed on her tongue. "Katherine?"

"I know her," said Collette abruptly. "Her last name—it is Fletcher. I knew it when you mentioned it, Mr. Dallington; it is an obvious connection to me now. I grew up with this girl—in the Magdalene Asylum. She preferred to be called Kate. She became a Sister of Mercy."

John shifted on his feet. "Darling," he began, but Priscilla interjected.

"A, a what—a *nun*?" Priscilla's delicate brows came together as she looked vacantly at him. "A nun… Kate? Oh…" Shakily, she reached out and grasped the back of the chair next to her and, as though the muscles had fled her body, collapsed into it. Then, raising her hand to cover her heart, she sat there, voiceless, as her eyes strayed from the floor, to wall, to window, to rest in a patch of bright sky above the apple tree where shafts of light glistened on fluttering leaves. At last her mouth opened and her tongue loosed. "Sister Kate—Collette's friend from the hospital. Yes… Why, yes, of course," she said, breathless. "My sister—my twin?… Oh! I have a twin sister—and I know her? Sister Kate?... It must be… It must be her, yes, certainly it must… Oh, dear God!" Both hands flew to her face. First, she covered her mouth, then wiped her gushing eyes, then dashed the back of her hand beneath her moist nose. "My twin… my twin… my twin sister?" she repeated, "*That* Sister Kate? Yes—*that* Sister Kate," she assured herself. "*She… is my… twin sister!*" Priscilla bolted to her feet, clasping her hands to her bosom. "Papa! Kate is just as much your daughter as I am," she burst out with eyes brimming, with irresistible pleading. "It is not too late. It is not! It is not too late, Papa—you must go to her!"

It was the dreaded response he had waited for. Heaven knew he had nothing by which he might justify or argue his position. He had wronged Kate despicably. He had robbed her, cheated her, sold her as a slave into Egypt to make her priceless heart the victim of his disgusting self-pity. Now, he could neither swim against the powerful tide of his late confession nor smoulder the voice of his own conscience that forced his pride to surrender. Everything that was just, and fair, and right pointed in one direction, and one direction only. And as he saw clearly the glaring hypocrisy of his situation, saw the insanity of his selfishness and realized the cruelty of his judgments against those closest to him, his soul stood still in terror. He knew the good that must be done now. Therefore, it would be more than callous to refuse Priscilla's request—to him it would be sin.

Rapid footsteps drew him from his thoughts. Collette was advancing to the table, her hand reaching for a pencil and a paper; she was scribbling hastily across the page; now straightening up. "Kate is about to take her final vows—vows which will subject her to things you would not believe if I told you. But if you knew, Mr. Dallington, you would move heaven and earth to go to her. Now here"—she held the paper out to him—"the location of the convent of St. Agnes, where you will certainly find her. And take this with you," she added suddenly, placing the ring and chain in his hand along with the paper and closing his fingers firmly around them. "Kate will know it."

Though partly receiving, partly resisting, John took the items. Collette withdrew from the room. Priscilla followed softly. The door closed, and he was left alone.

He opened his fingers; the ring gleamed in his palm. The finely engraved initials—they were so familiar as he fitted his fingertip along the inside edge, feeling the tiny grooves. Cassandra had loved the ring, had tenderly kissed him for it.

Cassandra—how he had worshipped her and left his heart kneeling at her shrine! He, who despised patriotism because it hugged the shores of idolatry; he, who had abhorred idols—he had committed sacrilege.

"Cassandra! My idol! My idol!" he cried at last, shaking his head as his voice swelled on a wave of passion. "Was I no better than a heathen for such idolatry of flesh and blood? Such making for myself another god before the Lord? Did I scorn to break the second commandment but then break the first, and by that grasp the tables of stone in my own two hands, and cast them down, and break them all?"

This stony heart that throbbed within him—this heart that had broken one commandment—it verily had broken all, for he had worshipped her—a woman. Loved her above God himself. And like as his idol of humanity had fallen, and died, even so had he.

A rich man could live—in hell. He had. Rich in unforgiveness, rich in pride, rich in offences against the poor in spirit, the depths of the sea were a more fitting place for him to drown than standing in a pulpit, drowning himself in hypocrisy.

For look at the little child—look at Katherine! She stood before him now, in all her self-possessed regality, her unspoken sadness, her mournful grace. He remembered…

Once, long ago in a hospital, she had seen him when he was an hungred, and she had given him meat; he had been thirsty, and she had given him drink; he had been a stranger, and she had taken him in; naked, and she had clothed him; sick, and she had visited him; in prison—the prison of his mind—and she had come unto him.

How filthy and stinking his feet had been! But she had not thought twice to wash them. How he had been her enemy! Yet, she had loved him as a neighbour. And for all her kindness, what had he done?

He had mocked her.

"Oh, Kate, my daughter! My daughter, Kate!" he broke out at last, walking blindly to a chair and collapsing into it as the coals heaped heavily upon his head. When he had been himself one of the least of these, the little, unassuming Sister—his own child—had become the blessed of the heavenly Father.

He cast the paper and ring aside and they clattered across the tabletop, colliding with the rejected opium tin. He cursed himself, for he had shown no mercy. The hypocrite had respected one daughter but despised the other; adultery may not have been his crime, but a murderous heart was, for he had hated his wife, despised their children, scorned the forgiveness she had asked for, and rejected them all in bitterness because he imagined himself to be better. No man could see the heap of wreckage within. But God did. No man's ears must hear the confession of his mouth. But God's must. Indeed, neither John, nor John's life—however perfect—could take away his sin, or intercede for it, or atone for it. If one point of the law could be broken and all other points broken with it, then it had been done by him—by the very man he had tried to conceal behind this deceptive façade of flesh; and now, guilty and tormented, worthy to be judged as mercilessly as he had judged his debtors, his soul asked how the unmerciful servant could pay to God all that was due?

"O heavenly Father, you are the witness to the sins I have committed against my family!" He pushed himself up on the arms of the chair, struggled to his feet. He stood shakily, but his knees grew weak, and he staggered beneath his own weight as he grappled for the back of the chair to lean himself against. Jairus had run, had fallen at the Master's feet, had besought him to lay healing hands on his dying daughter. But he, John? He had done nothing.

"I abandoned them—I sought vengeance, I sought to punish my wife, and I did that through condemning her and two innocent children to a life of confusion and misery! My crimes have warped my judgment! They have motivated partiality and lies toward the innocent! They have turned themselves against me now, and take occasion by the law, and slay me—what have I done? What have I done?" He gasped, tears quavering in his voice, breaking over his cheeks. "I am loathed and despised by myself, O God! I cannot tolerate the person I have become—for sin has deceived me, and I have obeyed it, and served it, in all its lusts! And now, O God, there is nothing—absolutely nothing—that I can offer to my children for the pain they have suffered because of my actions. But somehow—" His words broke off. He pressed his hand to his wet lips, his contracted brow, and pinched the bridge of his nose between his thumb and forefinger, pressing them inward to his eyes. But it could not stem the flow of tears. "I want her home—I want Kate home! I want to be—" He choked on emotion. "O God! I want to be there for her—be her strong protector, as I should have been long ago—but now… it is too late!"

Crushed by the granite of remorse, the sense of extreme hopelessness, he fell to his knees by the chair, utterly overcome; covering his head with his hand, he bowed himself low, humbly preparing to receive the blow of punishment his sins had incurred. "O heavenly Father, I have come to the end of myself! Forgive me—forgive this wretched man for his sins!"

Minutes passed as he sat slumped over in a motionless stupor. Presently, a gust of wind rustled the branches of the apple orchard outside; it whisked through the open window, billowing the white chiffon curtains, and he remembered, in an instant, the words:

My grace is sufficient for thee: for my strength is made perfect in weakness.

He gnashed his teeth and ground his fist into his thigh until his palm burned, his flesh infuriated by the vulnerability within. How could he reject his own flesh and blood and then expect her to forgive him?

He shall turn the heart of the fathers to the children, and the heart of the children to their fathers.

Aye, the words of the prophet Malachi—poetic, indeed, and to come to mind in a moment like this… lovely. But those words—they were not meant for him, surely not. Not for John Dallington, and certainly not for a scheme that was quite obviously pure foolishness. He had stabbed his daughter in the heart, and he would be a blind eejit to ask her to trust him now.

All things are possible to him that believes.

The former doubt crashed back, instantly defective, spoiled. A moment passed; he waited, the breath paused in his lungs. Hyssop dipped in lamb's blood flashed before him: it was ready to strike the lintel and doorposts of his heart—to intercede. There was the angel of death: it was smiting the firstborn of Egypt; it was passing over the houses of the Hebrew slaves in Goshen, for the Lord's eyes were upon those that feared him and believed and would not suffer the destroyer to come in.

It was called mercy. It was for prodigals, and he was one of them.

Through fog-like moisture, he saw the heavy curtain of heaven rent with power by the finger of God; and there was Christ Jesus; there, the mercy seat of heaven; there, the blood of the Lamb that had been spilled at Calvary to wash man's conscience and cast his guilt into the depths of the sea.

"It is my only hope," said John.

His neck bent low in reverence; his heart drew near; it entered through the door of his Father's house, and there his spirit bowed down in worship as the shadow of death passed over. Was it a strong wind that blew now, its heaviness rolling back, like mighty waves of the sea, the heavy span of darkened years to make a way for him?

His feet were planted on dry ground now. In stillness of soul his heart raised itself to God. Something touched it—he felt it! It burned a light within, like a burning coal! A hand that moulded clay—was it moulding him? He looked ahead and saw rejoicing and dancing and heard singing and music.

He saw the wastes rebuilt, the breaches repaired, the paths restored. He saw his children and grandchildren standing beside him, washed in light and glory—and there! There were his three daughters, their faces shining with peace, their smiles hope, their eyes windows of joy to the kingdom of God. They were coming home, taking husbands, building homes, rearing families—his life was being redeemed by the eagerness of a Father who still loved his prodigal son.

"I will go."

He lifted his eyes, seeing light for the first time; cloaked with boldness, he stood upon his feet, filled with power; he moved: it was with the ease of a lame man set free.

Excitement quickened his pulse, thrilling his soul with passion. He rushed to the door, but once at the threshold a thought arrested his progress. Turning, he crossed the room again, back to the dining table. There—across the tabletop—the crumpled slip of paper. And there, beside it, the ring.

He took the ring in his palm, then grasped the paper firmly between his fingers and pressed his lips together.

This time his hand would do the right thing.

Squaring his shoulders, he passed quickly from the room, and the curtains at the open window billowed a second time.

— CHAPTER XXXI —

RETURN TO ST. AGNES

July 1865

Kate inhaled deeply, savouring the fragrant smells of Ireland's damp turf, violets, and salty sea air. The sound of the carriage wheels rolling along the dirt road... the gentle sway of the vehicle... the warm sun flashing through the shading trees of a road that wound and dipped and climbed through cove and grass and cloud and sheep-grazed countryside... and the convent of St. Agnes less than a mile away...

As the vehicle jostled onward, she rested her head back against the hard wall of the carriage. Closing her eyes, she listened. Birds sang a carol on the drifting tide of juniper-scented air; ash trees whispered secrets in the rustling of their leaves; the carriage driver bellowed a gruff "Get on there, Pence and Swallowtail" to his team of hefty draft horses as they pulled the carriage up a gradual incline.

"I am meant for this place," Kate whispered. "They all welcome me back, don't they?"

"Begorra, lass—what's that?" exclaimed Father Andrew from his seat opposite her.

His voice was like a pinch on her arm. Inside the vehicle, it was noisy; and out of the five of them in the carriage, none had spoken since they had stepped off the train that had brought them from Queenstown to Dublin. How had he heard her above such a rumble?

Kate stirred, opening her eyes. Father Andrew's stare piqued her—doubtless, he had read her lips.

"Oh, nothing," she said, lifting her fingers dismissively and turning her face to the window. "I said nothing."

Indeed: she had said nothing to *him*.

Father Andrew sucked his fleshy cheeks inward, making his fleshy lips form the shape of a fish's and his fleshy eyebrows arch as though he disbelieved her. His glance wandered sideways to the two Sisters dozing on either side of him, and he inhaled with a wag of his fleshy head before focusing his fleshy eyes lazily on a vacant patch of wall at the back of the carriage.

The dirt road became a wave as it dipped through hollows and ripples heaved by winter frosts. It twisted and turned, too, like a meandering brook, following alongside moss-encrusted walls of mismatched stones borrowed from great piles of craggy boulders that dotted the landscape at stray intervals.

"Whoa!"

The carriage rolled to a stop at the top of a hill. There were the massive black iron gates, and beyond them the turreted old convent towering like a great shadow against the stainless sky. Though the reds, ambers, and golds of autumn had been replaced by the vibrance of springtime hues, nothing more about St. Agnes had changed since the day she had left it.

The coachman opened the door and the passengers alighted from the carriage. Kate was the last to step down.

"Thank you, driver," she said, grasping her carpet bag.

"Welcome, miss," he said, tipping his hat with a kind grin. He jumped back up into the driver's bench, cracked his whip, and then, with a lurch and a sway and a boisterous rattling, he urged his team forward and away.

Looking toward the gates where Father Andrew and the Sisters were already assembled, Kate noticed two black-robed Sisters waiting on the opposite side of the portal. Yes—the black iron gates—she pondered them: were they changed? They swung open on their massive hinges, groaning as they received each of them back into their confines.

She remembered the daffodils. Were they still there?

Yes, there—right there! In front of her! Yes, all three pots of them, their bright faces smiling up into the clear blue heavens, reflecting the sun in their eagerness to reach it—yes indeed, nothing had changed.

The two Sisters greeted them with studied reserve, then led them up the smooth gravel walk, through the sun-dappled garden that swayed with sweet and spicy fragrances, and to the convent entrance. They came under the shadow of the main archway; they stepped over the threshold.

"Mother Cecelia will be glad to see you, Sister Kate," remarked the Sister who had led the procession to the convent entrance and paused beside it while all passed through.

"As I shall be to see her," returned Kate.

The Sister leaned toward Kate. "Such an interview is in order for you," she returned quietly, "considering your lengthy absence. Mother Cecelia will hear of your experience and examine your readiness to undertake the upcoming ceremony. Each of the other candidates is prepared, Sister; only you she has not seen. Stay with me and I will conduct you to her room."

They entered the long arched corridor. Cool, damp air hung under suppressed lighting. Kate searched the passage; every creak of a door, every echo of the passageways, every particular turn of a stone positioned in the wall was distinctly familiar. She recalled the countless times she had crawled endlessly along those chilly wet stones, scrubbing them one by one till her hands bled and her knees grew raw and her mind and body screamed for rest.

The group of Sisters and Father Andrew dispersed while the Sister silently directed Kate to follow her around a corner. They passed by the kitchen. A lump gathered in Kate's throat as the fragrant smell of fresh baking wafted to her nostrils. Her stomach churned with the old sense of guilt. It smelled delicious, but she had promised herself she would not eat again until the next day.

They came to a dim vaulted hall. An organized procession was coming toward them, led by another black-robed Sister. It was a silent group of girls, all between the ages of about seventeen and twenty. They drew near; Kate's eyes followed them, studying the faces and figures that made up the two perfectly organized rows of six. Each girl wore a short white cambric veil.

Each girl wore a long black habit. Each wore the same expressionless look on her face as the girl behind and before her, and each moved forward in mute symmetry, close to the walls and in perfect step with one another.

"This year's novices," remarked the Sister.

"Yes," said Kate. But how she shuddered to look at them! Somehow "this year's novices" had summoned a vision of corpses to her mind, for she had seen many dead faces since the days when she had walked this bleak, familiar passage.

The line of girls followed their mistress down the corridor and disappeared around the corner.

"This way," said the Sister. They had come to a heavy wooden door. "The office of Mother Cecelia—come in, Sister Kate."

Kate stood still. She remembered the day when she had stood before this door, wondering why she had been called to appear before Mother Cecelia Doyle. She had feared the Mother—she had feared herself. And she had left that door fearing she might never return to it.

But today there was no fear.

The Sister ushered Kate into the office, and they were kindly welcomed by the elderly matron of the establishment. Observing throughout the meeting every action, expression, and response of the woman, purposefully looking for even the slightest alteration of either character or purpose, Kate was relieved to find that, aside from a few deeper lines furrowing her sallow forehead, the older woman had suffered no significant changes. She was still the same person. The same Mother Cecelia, with the same smell, and the same shrivelling smile. Subjected to a list of questions, Kate answered each of them with quick precision and calmness, rendering a swift though undetailed overview of the events she had experienced during her absence. The woman appeared pleased and applauded the faithful service she had rendered, praising the spirit of the Venerable Mother Catherine McAuley that she had exemplified with such correctness. She offered a blessing, and by the end of the afternoon she released Kate from the examination with a new set of personal duties and chores assigned to her, along with the keys to her old cell.

The sun went down; twilight came on. The final evening pilgrimage to the chapel came and went, with every chant, and Sacrament, and benediction presented in unchanged, uninterrupted succession. By nine o' clock, Sisters and novitiates retired silently to their private cells. Holding a lighted candle in her hand, Kate made her way down the dim, echoing passageways toward her chamber. She reached the door; paused for an instant.

Had it been altered? Had another Sister lived in the little room during her absence?

But why was she afraid to discover a change?

Kate compressed her parched lips. She reached into her pocket, withdrew the key, and applied it to the lock; it turned, and the door creaked open. She dropped the key into her pocket, and, entering the cell, she glanced around. The candlelight flickered and danced along the homely, unadorned walls of the room. Like a playful, waif-like ghost, it mocked her fears: the room was exactly the way she had left it. The low, narrow wooden bed was positioned against the right wall. The homespun blanket, pillow, and white sheet were spread out in flawless order with not a wrinkle in sight. The chipped ceramic wash basin and pitcher still stood next to it. The skimpy desk still stood beneath the small window. The self-flagellation whip—even that had not been removed.

Instinctively, her hand went to the leather cincture at her waist; her fingers closed over the metal and wooden crucifix secured inside the leather pouch on the inside of the belt. Tremblingly, she withdrew the relic while her eyes fixed upon the naked figure of the Christ stretched out upon it. Questions crowded her brain; they took her hand and wandered into forbidden ground… she remembered her First Communion, and smelled the incense, and saw the blue smoke envelop the priest as he raised the Eucharist in his hands before the rising sun. She saw a sea of men's faces—men who had been sick in the hospital. Men who had been thin, and white, and lifeless—just like the corpse on the tree.

"Why is he—" She pressed her lips and swallowed hard. "Why is he dead?"

With a shudder she reached out and laid the crucifix on the desk, then brought her hand to her chest and touched her neck repeatedly. She looked at the wedding ring on her finger, and back at the corpse, and again at the ring, and touched the golden band, and twisted it on her finger as a powerful thirst overcame her.

"Am I married to a Heavenly Bridegroom any more than I am married to… to this—"

No!

Her own voice flogged her brain, left an oozing gash—pain that would remind her not to question again. Of course she was married—married to God himself! She had been dressed in white wedding garments! Had walked down the aisle with all the other girls! Had received her wedding ring and vowed to remain a virgin all her life! Any thoughts contradicting *that* belief could do nothing but reveal to her paranoid conscience the full extent of her disobedience.

But then she glanced around the room. "Nothing about this convent has changed," she said. "Nothing. I had presumed that something, or someone, would have changed, but…"

And her hand grasped her stomach as it hardened to a knot. "Am I the one who has changed?"

At the notion her head became thick and clouded, her ears began to ring and plug with fullness. Her chest constricted; her breathing grew rapid. She wished for a mirror that she might look at her face once—only once—to convince herself that, indeed, she was still Kate.

Sister Kate—the Sister of Mercy.

Trembling fingers grasped for the veil on her head. Yes, there it was. The veil. The sacred proof of her identity. Cold fingers crept down her right hip and closed tightly over the large beads of her rosary.

"Quiet!" she said, and shook her head against the dizzying thoughts and questions swarming against her. How silly she was to doubt!

But the candle trembled in her trembling hand, opposing her mental dictates to control it. She walked across the room to prepare for bed, and loathed herself for swaying like a drunkard as she did. She set the candle on the desk. The brass candleholder rattled as it met the hardwood. She swallowed hard, reached up, removed the two pins securing the rectangular wool serge veil on her head, then untied the cords that held the white linen coif at the back of her neck. Next, she removed the pin that held the pique dimity concealing her forehead; next, the pins and ties of the linen guimp that draped her back, shoulders, and bosom. Reaching behind her back, she took hold of the buckle and unfastened the thick black leather cincture.

Her Bible and catechism—there, both of them, still in her pocket. She withdrew the books and laid them on the table.

She unfastened the large hook and eye that held up the train at the back of her serge habit, then the hooks and eyes that ran down the centre front of the nine-pleated bodice past the gathered waistband. With a sudden shaking of her shoulder, her body shed the heavy, itchy garment, and it fell to the floor, a mass of baggage at her feet. Looking long and steadily at it, she recalled how she had sewn every piece with her own hands.

Her eyes drifted up and caught movement—there—in the window in front of her. She stopped and leaned in closer. A reflection: an old, lifeless person, staring back at her from the glass.

Who was it?

The face—it was so thin. The eyes were so dark and sunken, the corners of the lips turned so depressively downward. And the head—it shamed her, shorn and monstrous as it was. Perhaps the hair had grey in it by now—but she could hardly bear to look.

Icy fingertips brushed the pale flesh of one cheek, tracing a narrow contour of the jaw. There was a breathless pause. Her hand fell to her side. She shifted her gaze and looked down at the bare arm, and shuddered. It was as emaciated as a corpse's.

"O God…" she whispered.

She turned from the window. A cold, vacant loneliness, as though of a tomb, swallowed up her soul. She had done it to herself: she had tortured that body and starved it of food the way she had wished to starve out the demons that were eating her from the inside. Now she wanted to weep. But why were her eyes so dry?

Kate could not sleep that night. She lay awake, waiting feverishly for the dawn to come, straining her ears so as not to miss the bell that would summon the Sisters to chapel at quarter past five for the early morning prayers and Sacrament. Her body tossed and turned fitfully upon the bed. Waves of perspiration drenched her body while shaking fingers clutched the rosary and pressed it against her sweaty chest. Her mind revolved with endless thoughts and accusations: She was not holy. She was not true. She was not fit to be the person that she seemed. She did not know who God was; for to her, he was like a piece of cloth, as easy to put on as he was to put off. She did not know his voice, for the voice she had always thought to be his was the voice of a man behind a screen. She did many works, but were they the works of God? She feared something—something she had always feared—but had she ever feared God himself?

She was a lie that walked around in clothes, and the long-awaited ceremony would only mask more terribly the shame she hid inside.

The grey hours of the morning found Kate alone in the chapel, prostrate and motionless on the cold stones before the crucifix.

— CHAPTER XXXII —

THE VOICE

Kate paused in the vaulted corridor where she knelt on the chill, slippery tiles slopping with grey wash water and repeated the words recorded by the prophet John on the Island of Patmos. "And when I saw him, I fell at his feet as dead. And he laid his right hand upon me, saying unto me, Fear not: I am the first and the last: I am he that liveth, and was dead; and, behold, I am alive forevermore, Amen; and have the keys of hell and of death."

When the words had lifted from her tongue, she straightened her back while the sponge in her hand dripped grey water down the red blisters of palm and fingers. Engrossing herself in reading the Bible—diligently, even feverishly at times—she had, for weeks following her return to Ireland, memorized its passages and scribbled notes in the margins, searching the Book of Revelation, the Letter to the Hebrews, and the Epistle to the Romans. She wept with joy over the sublime teachings of the Gospels and the Hebraic poetry of the Psalms. She discovered substance and hope, offered to her by an omniscient God who could speak through the poor, unassuming pattern of the written word.

And then she looked upon her condition, and the crippled state of her will, and she became sick as she realized the vicious cycle that, since childhood, had sent her into continual spirals of self-centredness and fear.

"Alive forevermore," she repeated, and—charged with sudden energy—she dunked the sponge into the bucket of foaming soap and water, splashed the stones, and set again to scrubbing.

When at last the hunger pangs of her skeletal understanding had tasted the words of knowledge and truth through the Bible, she knew she could not blind her eyes nor stop her ears again. An enlightened intellect was now asking with stubborn insistence why such bread had so long been forbidden to her? Why such drink had so long been withholden? And day and night she asked herself whether that dread, daunting spectre of atheism was not hopeless man's independent though erroneous reaction against the enslaved intelligence enforced by tyrannical popery? All her life, she had been taught to punish her intelligence—to squelch it in order to fulfill her vowed obedience to her superiors. But what self-doubt such efforts had engendered! What self-loathing! Was it not better that her mental faculties were now gaining strength, and shifting, and stirring, and with courage mounting the green foothills of independent thought, and that they were taking hold, at last, of that divine gift of free will that had the capacity to steer her onto the narrow pathway of life everlasting?

Somewhere there was a spotless bride—the Lamb's wife—in a city of precious stones. The prophet had written about such a place. Her eyes could not see it, but her heart could. The bride's reflection was in the crystal river descending from God in a place where night, and tears, and sorrow, and crying would be no more forever; and somewhere, in the midst of a glorious throne, were magnificent creatures that rest not day or night, saying, "Holy, holy, holy, Lord God Almighty, which was, and is, and is to come." The kingdom of God that Christ had taught to the thousands who had sought him—she yearned with all her heart to find it.

"His kingdom is not of this world…" she said as she stood at the end of the corridor and looked down the floor of the nave that gleamed with water and the sunshine streaming in from the long narrow window. "It is within you…"

She tossed the sponge into the grey water that splashed and sloshed—and she heard the sound of waves, and winds, and mighty angels, and the coming armies of heaven upon horses. The Revelation of John spoke of such wonders—what jealous hierarchy was it that had sought to blind her eyes and ears by criminalizing her perusal of the apostle's account on Patmos?

Her hands went to her hips; her brow wrinkled. She drew breath, bent down—but her arms and legs felt like lead.

She grasped the rope handle of the wooden pail full of grey water and heaved it up. "A heavy bucket today," she said, suppressing a mild grunt as the rope dug into raw flesh along her palm.

The water in the bucket sloshed and dripped, making a dark wet spot on the skirt of her habit that clung to her thighs as she dragged herself forward. How much longer could she mask the exhaustion of her body? How much longer endure the dull aching of her head, the uncomfortable waves of heat and cold that by turns stifled her senses and reminded her that her belly was cramped from extended fasting?

The chapel bell tolled. Mass was a quarter of an hour away.

Staying close to the wall, she glided down the corridor and deposited the cleaning tools in the laundry room. She unhiked her skirt from its gathered bunch in the side of her leather cincture and unfastened the train, then smoothed the damp, wrinkled folds and felt instinctively for the comforting shape of her Bible filling her pocket.

Rustling robes and footsteps were coming along the hall. Her big sleeves—which were to be fastened onto the black buttons on her shoulders before attending chapel—were still in her cell. She would have to forgo their customary donning this time in favour of punctuality.

In haste, she sallied from the room, falling perfectly in line and blending indistinctly with the flowing, speechless cloud of the dark-robed Sisters as they glided outside and toward the chapel.

All that day the weather had been fitful. Violent winds vied with each other, blowing by turns from the north and west, dashing through the courtyard, bringing with them an unsettled mood that boded a summer thunderstorm and blended with the Gregorian chant echoing from the lofty, web-like masonry of the vaults.

Each footfall demanded a concentrated effort as she forced herself up the three steps that led toward the arched stone doorway. She lifted her eyes; the thick mass of deeply layered stone formed a narrow pointed crescent that reached to the height of three men and framed the massive, ornately carved oak door that was girded by heavy iron bands.

For an instant—only an instant—Kate paused there, scanning the entrance as a sudden thought occurred to her. If she could, would she turn from that door—would she turn, and instead run barefoot along the warm sandy banks of wild seascapes and up aisles of green pastures above which jagged cliffs crowned lofty mountains to kiss the stone of sapphire…

If Sister Kate could do such a thing, would she?

~

Very slowly, as though in a dream, she lowers her head and passes beneath the towering stone archway and into the nave.

"Kate, I'm hungry—so hungry… Do ya hear me?"

Collette's voice echoes through the vaulted ceiling overhead as it echoes through the lonely recesses of her mind.

"Yes… Collette," she whispers, and tears start to her eyes, and she clutches her empty stomach. "I, too, am hungry… So hungry…"

Very slowly she walks down the aisle toward her pew, passing the glinting glass windows stained by the green and blue and scarlet pictures of people she does not know and the marble statues with unfeeling limbs enshrined in the fish-shaped vaults along the wall. Though the voices in her head would convince her eyes of the beauty of the chapel, her ears will not heed them. Perhaps, as Dr. Hall had asserted, the Roman Empire never fell—perhaps it was merely renamed? Perhaps it was true that popes replaced Roman emperors… perhaps it was true that these cold saints are but the old Empire's pagan deities, whose shameful nakedness is concealed by painted robes and halos?

"I see no simplicity… no life of Christ in this place," she says under her breath, and she kneels in the pew as the priest ascends toward the altar.

Perhaps these endless chants are but the *requiem aeternam deo*, sung, as it were, to declare that this convent—this stony chapel—is nothing more than a painted, incensed sepulchre that commemorates the perpetual death of a god…

Upon the altar stand six tall thick white candles, flickering eerily through the gloom. The flaring tapers may once have lured her with magnetic mysticism, but tonight they seem no more significant than the stubby, stinking, drip-lined tallow candle sputtering in her room.

Her eyes rove the scene. There is the Eucharist exposed in the monstrance. She has been told to worship at the foot of the Most Blessed Sacrament, told that it constitutes the body, blood, soul, and divinity of Christ—told that she must reverence it with her entire being. She has been told that it will feed her—weekly, daily. But today her eyes look upon the wafer-god and question if the feeble flour disc clamped inside a piece of metal can truly give her life? What good is the perpetual sacrifice doing for her now? She has never missed a day of partaking of the Sacrament, yet the hunger is there still—and so, too, is the pride that finds cruel pleasure in her flesh's ability to dry up her bones with famine.

But if she goes to the Father Confessor and confesses the vice to him, the act only digs her soul a deeper grave. It will taunt her with false peace. It will haunt her with self-doubt. It will shroud her in disgrace that will never go away though the man might hear her and say he forgives her and then give to her ten thousand acts of penance in one day.

Her guilt—has it grown somehow routine?

Her eyes have wandered from the altar now. She forces them back. The Mass is enacting before her. Now the priest in his flowing white and gold garments is gliding toward the bowl of holy water. Now he is dipping his hands into it, now he is washing them, now he is drying them with a spotless white towel as he prepares to consecrate the sacrifice.

A chill creeps over her, and she almost gasps. She sees Jesus before the judgment seat of Pilate. She hears the cries of the Jews. She feels the blood-guiltiness of their own curse upon them in that moment as the mob cries out to crucify the Messiah. She sees the Roman governor dipping his hands in the bowl of water, and washing them, and drying them with a spotless white towel.

"Pilate washed his hands..." she whispers as her heart beats wildly against her bosom, pounding and racing in her ears, leaving her vision blurred and stinging with hot tears.

But is the dark cloud of Sisters going up now? Up to the

altar to receive the Sacrament? To receive what they all have vowed to believe is the "good god"?

She can hardly make them out, for everything has become a moving mass of shadows and shapes that crowd and sway in front of her. Her senses have always told her that the Eucharist is nothing but a pitiful little wafer.

She wipes away her tears. She peers ahead. Yes. There they are—the dark shapes of all the women, young and old, swarming and kneeling before the priest as he places the wafer on their tongues.

Her belly twists and churns. "I will not go!" she cries in a desperate whisper, her fingers fastening and knuckling hard to the edges of her seat. "*My God is not a wafer-god!*"

The long line of women file back, supposedly satiated—but how can it be true? They enter their pews in silence. She is an alien among them. Somehow, the ceremony continues.

The priest is reaching for the golden chalice, and lifting it above his head, and chanting Latin as he lowers it again, and brings it to his lips, and drinks deeply of the bloody cup just as he did at her First Communion. And the crucifix looks on, its emaciated dark outline a sad and ghastly sight revealed through the shadows of coming twilight. Her gaze drifts to the pyramid in the altar—at the monster's eye within. The eye glares at her as though jealous of the victim pinned behind it.

She looks closer. She remembers the questions she asked as a child. Her temples throb; she presses them. Her stomach knots; she grasps it. Her lips tremble and part; she bites her tongue to cease the cry they utter.

Jesus is not there!

The solemn voices of the chant resume. The priest concludes the rites and benedictions. The congregation is released. All flow like a tide in dumb, noiseless procession back down along the nave, and beneath the archway, and out into the courtyard where the wind is howling.

And Kate remains behind, unnoticed by the train.

Gales tossed and tore the branches outside the stained-glass windows, whistling and moaning and dashing against the building. Motionless in her pew, Kate sat mute. Her mind was far away… listening to a voice… looking upon a face… remembering Dr. Hall.

"We're all servants to a master."

Had she travelled all this way along the arduous road of religious piety and unrelenting accusation, of self-inflicted physical and mental torture, only to discover that she was condemned already because of her unbelief?

The swelling Potomac flashed before her. She felt the strong arms lift her from the mire, felt the gentle hand wipe the clay and tears from her blistered eyes.

Her voice struggled from the shadows. "There is not a word in my tongue, but lo, O Lord, thou knowest it altogether."

He heard every word she spoke, knew every detail of every thought that passed through her mind. His eyes had watched her since infancy—since conception. He had chosen her in Christ before the foundation of the world—the Bible told her so. The Father Confessor had never done—and never could do—such a marvellous thing.

"My Father is in heaven…" she said, and began to cry. "Christ's house… is it within? Shall I partake of him, if I hold fast, and hope, and believe… in his kingdom, in his Spirit that comforts me… and shall I talk with him? And will he not teach me all things, and bring all things to my remembrance… just as he has promised?"

She sensed the band of gold on her finger; her hand touched the heavy veil on her head and the other clutched the smooth beads of the rosary at her side. These things were her treasures, and yet—could not moth and rust corrupt them? Could not thieves break in and steal? What relic could she touch that she could one day carry with her into eternity?

"Where is my faith?" she said.

Why had she cut and starved and flogged her body as if Christ's own flesh had not been sufficient—as though he had not died at all; as though he had not been the bread given for the life of the world; as though he had not been beaten and scourged, whipped and spit upon and nailed to the cross, his blood spilled on Calvary to declare that *he* was the one High Priest who loved her and forgave her—that he alone was the one worthy to hear her confession and save her from the eternal damnation of hell?

Indeed, had her own flesh not died with his flesh there, on the cross, on that day? And her new life... was it not today, hid with Christ who was seated on the right hand of God?

Her head bent over her chest, and salty tears touched her tongue. "I am the bread of life: he that cometh unto me shall never hunger, and he that believeth on me shall never thirst."

She lifted her face, scanned the stone-crusted room; she drew herself up and stood upon her feet.

"I require a priest," Kate said. "But my Priest will never again be a man."

She walked from the pew. A statue of the Virgin Mary stood in the dim corner. The crucifix shadowed the altar. She saw again the broken body made of stone lashed to the tree and crossbeam. She saw again the heartless faces, the chiselled mouths, the blind eyes, and the deaf ears.

The Father Confessor had told her many things that she had hardly believed as a child. To her he had been God—and because of that, she had feared him, and served him, and believed that he could forgive her sins. But the man had fed her lies—ugly lies—day by day, hour by hour, confession by confession.

"I will no longer seek the living among the dead," she whispered, and turned her back on the sight.

She looked down along the nave—back at the door she had walked through. Her eyes caught sight of the shadow of the ash tree, thrashing its boughs furiously against the blood-red windowpane, trying to get in. She looked back at the crucifix, then lifted her hand that wore the wedding ring. With the other hand she slid the band from her finger.

"I am not a married woman," she said, and set the ring on the edge of the pew.

Her gaze lifted. There was the door. She fixed her eyes on it.

"I am the way, the truth, and the life: no man cometh unto the Father, but by me."

Her feet moved slowly at first, but forward—firmly, steadily, deliberately forward. Three steps, four steps, five—faster now, more eagerly, and she was halfway down the nave, three yards, two, one—there! The door. She set her teeth together, grasped the latch firmly, and threw it open. The wind burst in, flinging the door violently against the back wall. The gust tore wildly through the chapel, roaring down the aisles, dashing against the east wall, lashing the empty pews, extinguishing the tapers, bringing the sacred vessels on the altar clattering to the floor as it howled through the vaults.

Kate stepped across the threshold and into the wind. "I will never leave thee, nor forsake thee."

The sun dipped behind its western border. A heavy bank of gold and crimson clouds was rolling in from the west, a striking contrast against the luminous blue that stood behind it, and the low noise of thunder rumbled in the distance. Another violent gust rushed through the darkened courtyard, rending the branches of the garden's shade trees, swirling dead leaves, dashing the stone facades, snaring Kate's habit and veil and wrapping and twisting them around her face and ankles as she walked forward, forward, into the rushing wind.

Over there!... Just a few yards ahead, the lawn was wide and open, the grass thick and soft and beautiful. Beyond that was the high stone wall—no more a cage to her whose heart was to be made the sanctuary of the living God.

She stopped on the edge of the pavement and looked down at her scuff-marked shoes and remembered the ones she had worn at her First Communion.

"I never did like the shoes," she said suddenly, then shook them off, flung them aside, and walked barefoot through the damp, cool grasses. "He will guide my feet into the way of peace." She lifted her hands to her head and took hold of the veil, feeling for the pins that held it. Oh, the meticulous effort she had taken in arranging that piece of black cloth upon her head that morning! What time it had taken to wash, and iron, and fold those two pleats just right! But it was just a piece of cloth, was it not? It could not save her, nor could it make her clean.

"And ye shall know the truth and the truth shall make you free."

She smiled. She pulled out the pins and tossed them aside. The veil fell off. She removed the ties and pins that held her wimple in place. All fell off, and she cast the items behind her as the mighty wind rushed through her short waves of hair, and her face lifted as she said, "His salvation shall cover my head in the day of battle."

Walking a little farther, her eyes swept across the living sky that swirled and changed above her with mountains of wild white, navy, and granite clouds. She reached an incline on the sward where she could see over the high wall—over there! The light was young and pink! And far, far away upon the distant hillside—a flock of sheep safely nestled in their pasture beneath some sheltering oaks!

A sudden thought occurred to her; her hand went immediately to her side; her fingers closed over the long string of black beads threaded through the pliable ring at her right hip, and she ran her fingers along the burnished wood of the venerated item.

Yes, it had been a heavy chain.

"I promised I would not part with it till the day I died," she said, then grasped the smooth ebony and ivory cross and withdrew it from the cincture along with the string of beads. "Except a man be born again, he cannot see the kingdom of God." She threw the rosary away from her: the beads and ebony seemed to clink together as they fell into the wet grass, becoming the pile of stones that the priest could never throw at her again.

She took hold of the crucifix secured in the small inner pouch of her cincture. She extracted it from its usual place and looked at it, as she had looked at it on the night of her return to St. Agnes. It was the scene of an old memory. An old life.

An old Kate.

She cast the piece of carved wood and metal aside. Past religious cloth, and Latin prayers, and wooden beads, there was her conscience—her soul: it stood naked and open before the eyes of God, as much in need of Christ's sanctification as the soul of any common harlot, or atheist, or notorious tobacco chewer.

She threw her arms open to the heavens as a crack of thunder shattered the sky overhead. Rain broke from the mighty clouds and poured down in torrents, plunging down her head and neck and shoulders, washing her, streaming down her face with the tears that flowed from her eyes as a smile burst across her face—oh, how sweet it was to smile! To smile and be free!

"I am a child of God!" she shouted, filled with joy and laughing merrily as the rain drenched her body. "I will dwell in his house *today* and *forever*! And of tomorrow"—she began dancing and twirling and splashing through the clear puddles gathering everywhere about the rain-sodden turf—"the little lambs of the flock and the birds of the air and the flowers of the field—they don't worry about tomorrow, and why should I? I may have nothing at all, but Jesus loves me! He sees me, and he cares! His hand leads me, and holds me, and perfects me, and fills up my heart with his love!"

Her gaze swept the lawns and garden and the towering turrets and frowning facades and the high stone walls that had kept her captive for so long. God was not keeping her in—she had chosen to stay. God had not told her to starve her body—she had starved herself. God had not demanded she wear a veil and a habit, nor had he been punishing her for her mother's sin—she had believed a lie. God was love, and he had come to cleanse her and give her life.

"I will put my laws into their hearts, and in their minds will I write them; and their sins and iniquities will I remember no more."

Impulse seized her, and she gathered up her soaking skirt and dashed down the grassy sward and onto the groomed pathway until she reached the iron gates. Panting for breath, she stretched out her hands and tightly grasped the bars. They rattled loudly. She pressed her face against cold iron and looked upward as the rain poured down. "Out there—yes! And through these gates!" she cried with delight as her heart leapt within her. Did she hear a faint squeal of rusty hinges, a long empty echoing sound as though the old gates were giving way beneath her hands?

"Yes! Outside—romping those hills! Swimming in that ocean! Climbing up those mountains where dreams like clouds will crown the peaks and wash them all in sunshine! That is where the little sparrow will be free!"

Another gust of wind billowed through the garden and shook the wet branches and flowers and foliage, sprinkling crystal droplets all around, raising the fragrance of dewy grasses and roses and damp earth to burst the air with sweetness. Then soon the storm stilled, the wind silenced, the rain fell softly in the open fields, and a voice on the wind said,

"Behold, I make all things new."

— CHAPTER XXXIII —

THE MISTS FADE OUT FOREVER

A silvery fog wends its way through the humid valley and in and out of a dark, silent woodland tinged with hues of saffron and gold. The moist scent of wet grass and dampened sod float on the air, a grateful sigh. It smells to John like freshly mown hay from his boyhood.

The air is getting cooler now; he has been riding since the afternoon. The shadows from the solitary tall oak trees studding the fields and the dry stone walls hedging the roadside are all lengthening. As he passes a small homestead, he scans the yard and garden. There is an old barn and chicken coop. He hears the languid lowing of a cow, the dull tinkling of a brass bell, the contented clucking of hens as they roost for the night. Beyond, a herd of some fifty sheep dot the gently sloping hillside as they shelter beneath some oak trees. A gentle bleat, and an answer, are heard. All of it is familiar. His own family's homestead is not many miles from here. Far distant is the open sea; he imagines he can still hear its low, unceasing murmur. He had stood on the coast that day, just as he had done as a young man; his eyes had swept over the breakers that crashed and foamed against the jagged rocks below, pulsed by a steady, universal heartbeat unchanged by time. The ocean beckoned him. Aye, it drew him like a magnet. It always had.

Twilight deepens; the moon glimmers; the stars shine their pale light over a world wrapped in tranquil silence. John spurs his horse to a brisk trot up the slope and along the winding road—it is a very old road. The passing rainstorm has watered the regular potholes and left condensation dripping from the brim of his black beaver hat. It is running down the sleeves of his oilskin overcoat, under which his clothes sop like a wet sponge. His high Wellington boots are muddy and damp inside. But it matters not, for he is almost there.

He reaches the crest of a hill and reins in his mount. There he waits. He looks beyond the pink evening light and distinguishes what seems to be a mirage. The sky over there is murky, but he sees that it is an enclosure, for there are two black iron gates. It is the convent of St. Agnes looming, dumb and dreary, on a distant rise. There are vacant turrets rising from a gaunt body of stone that stretches itself along the high place like a corpse upon an altar, insensible.

His heart quickens. He swings down from the saddle and tests the girth. It is snug.

"We'll walk a pace, old boy," he says to the horse.

He grips the reins and leads the animal off the road and along the summit of the green slope—the leather is clammy in his palm, but more with sweat than rain. He hears the soft tread of his feet passing through the thick grasses… the steady *swish-swish* of his horse's hooves that jingle drops of rain from the heavy stems… the squeak of moist leather… the occasional whisper of wind that rustles the wet leaves of the trees. But John's legs are trembling. He stops, and his horse stops with him. The animal lowers its muzzle, sniffs the grass, eats. A second look at the black gates—John tenses; his jaw twitches, and he takes in a steadying breath, swallows hard. He feels his chest, the left side, over his heart. The ring is there—there in his vest pocket. Cassandra's wedding ring. The ring that Kate would know. He lifts his hand and removes his hat, then raises his face to the heavens.

"His strength is made perfect in weakness."

His eyes wander again across the speechless mass of stone facades dominating the horizon, staring out from the distance. He strains his eyes and peers through the mist and dusk, tears dimming his vision worse than any mist or dusk could do. And then, for the second time, his life flashes before him, but it is different now. Once, long ago, on a different ship, he had been a Jonah, staggering blindly along the starboard deck of a clipper, drenched in rain and salt and tears. But not today. Whose prayer went up to God to make it so? Whose voice had lifted itself and cried against the storm to entreat the mighty hand of God to move this mountain?

"O God," he whispers, "give me that faith."

Vivid with contrast and colour, shadowed by pain and regret, the old life passes away like a vapour. He is no longer a wanderer in a painting on the wall, nor a soldier bleeding to death on a distant battlefield; neither is he maimed any longer. He has died, and is rising again, with new life brimming in his spirit; and when he returns on the next ship, she will be with him.

He puts on his hat; he fits his foot in the stirrup; he swings into the saddle and holds the reins loosely in his palm, pausing for a moment as he looks for a third time at the black iron gates.

Is that movement, behind the bars, that he catches sight of in the distance? Yes, there—there! A silhouette… a silhouette moving about, natural and free, along the slope of the green sward… is it a waif-lass?

And then, as though from somewhere deep within himself, he listens, and waits, and hears at last the voice in his spirit say:

"These things saith he that is holy, he that is true, he that hath the key of David, he that openeth, and no man shutteth; and shutteth, and no man openeth; I know thy works; behold, I have set before thee an open door, and no man can shut it."

THE END

ACKNOWLEDGMENTS

I am indebted to many individuals and sources in my quest for historical accuracy and spiritual insight in this novel. In addition to the personal testimonies I have had the privilege to both hear and witness, there are many other testators of the faith and followers of the gospel—past and present—who may be gratefully acknowledged by saying that, without the inspiration of their remarkable testimonies, this book could not have been written.

Deepest thanks goes to my family for their prayers, advice, and support, and especially to my parents, Bob and Linette Biegel—you always believed in me, and always believed this book was possible, even when I didn't. I love you.

A heartfelt thank you to my amazing book-production team: evaluation and manuscript editor and mentor Tanis Nessler of ReVision Editing; historian, mentor, and evaluation editor Susan Raby-Dunne; and book designer Dean Pickup of Canada Book Design. Each of you has given generously of your insight, suggestions, talent, and support, and I am sincerely grateful to you.

And above all I wish to thank my heavenly Father for his great love and miracle of redemption, of which this story has endeavoured to make a small testimony: "Unto him that loved us, and washed us from our sins in his own blood… to him be glory and dominion for ever. Amen." Revelation 1:5-6

ABOUT THE AUTHOR

Brooklyn lives in the rugged and inspiring climes of Northern Alberta, Canada. She holds an Associate Diploma in Violin Performance from the Royal Conservatory of Music (ARCT) and maintains a thriving violin and speech arts studio at her home east of the Rocky Mountains. She loves bicycling in bare feet, foraging for herbs, and eating dark chocolate. *Through These Dark Gates* is her debut novel.

Please visit Brooklyn online at *www.atthebrooksbend.ca*

Instagram: *atthebrooksbend*

Facebook Page: *www.facebook.com/brooklynbiegel*

YouTube: *Four Seasons North–Biegel Family*
and *Biegel Family Music*

Four Seasons North: *www.fourseasonsnorth.com*

SELECTED BIBLIOGRAPHY

This work of fiction was birthed out of a lifelong interest in the history of the Roman Catholic religion, nursing, and immigration to the Americas—my own family heritage is intimately connected to all three subjects. Because of the vast number of informational resources I have consulted for the duration of a project that has spanned nearly eight years, it would be next to impossible for me to compile an exhaustive list of every work referenced pertaining to the subjects explored throughout this story. However, I have provided a selected bibliography of works that have been particularly helpful to me and which I have—either in full or in part—conferred with and recommend for further personal research.

Alberino, Timothy, Stephen Quayle. *True Legends: The Documentary Film Series*. Episode 2, "The UnHoly See." DVD. N.p.: GenSix Productions, Released 2016.

Alberino, Timothy, Stephen Quayle. *True Legends: The Documentary Film Series*. Episode 3, "Holocaust of Giants." DVD. N.p.: GenSix Productions, Released 2017.

Alcott, Louisa May. *Hospital Sketches: An Army Nurse's True Account of Her Experiences During the Civil War*. New York: Fireworks Press, 2015. First published 1863 by James Redpath

Bible Manuscript Society (website). "1382 Wycliffe Bible." https://biblemanuscriptsociety.com/Bible-resources/English-Bible-History/Wycliffe-Bible

Billings, J. D. *Hardtack and Coffee or The Unwritten Story of Army Life*. Boston: George M. Smith & Co., 1887.

Chiniquy, Charles. *Fifty Years in the Church of Rome*. Edited by Gerald E. Greene. New York: Fleming H. Revell Company, 1886.

Chiniquy, Charles. *The Priest, the Woman, and the Confessional*. New York: Fleming H. Revell Company, 1880.

Eleftheriou-Smith, Loulla-Mae. "Italian Convent 'Forced Nuns to Self-Flagellate and Write Vows in Blood' Former Nun Claims." *Independent* (UK). January 5, 2016. https://www.independent.co.uk/news/world/europe/italian-convent-forced-nuns-to-self-flagellate-eat-out-of-date-food-and-write-vows-in-blood-former-a6797176.html

Elliott, Charlotte. "Just as I Am Without One Plea." *The Invalid's Hymn Book*. 2nd ed. Dublin: John Robertson, 1841. https://www.hymnologyarchive.com/just-as-i-am

Faust, Drew Gilpin. *This Republic of Suffering: Death and the American Civil War.* New York: Vintage Books, A Division of Random House, 2009.

Fryd, Vivien Green. "Thomas Crawford, Statue of Freedom, 1855-63." Picturing United States History (website). American Social History Project Centre for Media and Learning. https://picturinghistory.gc.cuny.edu/thomas-crawford-statue-of-freedom-1855-63/

Gerard, Philip. "During the War, Sisters of Mercy Provide Medical Attention: Nuns from the North Travel South to Nurse the Sick and Comfort the Dying." *Our State* 4, no. 9 (August 25, 2014). https://www.ourstate.com/sisters-mercy/

Hoeck, Kenneth M. "The Jesuit Connection to the Assassination of Abraham Lincoln." Truthontheweb.org (November 1999). http://www.truthontheweb.org/abe.htm

Howe, Julia Ward. "The Battle Hymn of the Republic." *The Atlantic*, February 1862. https://www.theatlantic.com/magazine/archive/1862/02/the-battle-hymn-of-the-republic/308052/

Jesus-is-lord.com. "The Testimony of Charlotte Wells." https://www.jesus-is-lord.com/charlot1.htm

Leech, Margaret. *Reveille in Washington 1860-1865*. New York: New York Review of Books, 2011. First published 1941 by Garden City Publishing.

Lincoln, Abraham. "Early Speeches of Abraham Lincoln 1830-1860." Internet Archives (website). https://archive.org/stream/earlyspeechesofanotlinc/earlyspeechesofanotlinc_djvu.txt

Longfellow, Henry Wadsworth. "The Wreck of the Hesperus." *Poems of Henry Wadsworth Longfellow*. New York: Thomas Y. Crowell, 1901.

Luther's Small Catechism with Explanation. St. Louis, MO: Concordia Publishing House, 1986.

MacDowell, Michael. "Catholic Nuns an Inspiration Through History." The News-Press (August 3, 2017). https://www.news-press.com/story/opinion/contributors/2017/08/03/catholic-nuns-inspiration-throughout-history/535760001/

More, Hannah. "Slavery, a poem." Eighteenth-Century Poetry Archive (website). https://www.eighteenthcenturypoetry.org/works/o4179-w0010.shtml

Mullaly, Larry. "First Communion." *Faith Patterns: Catholic Belief in Contemporary Society* (blog). May 1, 2015. https://www.faithpatterns.com/2015/05/01/first-communion/

Nee, Watchman. *The Spiritual Man*. New York: Christian Fellowship Publishers, 1977.

Newton, John. "Amazing Grace." *The New Church* Hymnal. Newbury Park, CA: Lexicon Music, 1976.

Nietzsche, Friedrich. "The Parable of the Madman." *The History Guide: Lectures on Twentieth Century Europe* (blog). April 13, 2012. http://www.historyguide.org/europe/madman.html

Nightingale, Florence. *Florence Nightingale to her Nurses: A Selection from Miss Nightingale's Addresses to Probationers and Nurses of the Nightingale School at St. Thomas's Hospital*. London: Macmillan, 1914.

Noyales, Jonathan A. "Battle of Fisher's Hill." American Battlefield Trust (website). https://www.battlefields.org/learn/articles/battle-fishers-hill.

O'Loughlin, Ed. "Ireland's Last Magdalene Laundry: 'They Should Knock It to the Ground.'" *The Irish Times*, January 16, 2018. https://www.irishtimes.com/news/social-affairs/ireland-s-last-magdalene-laundry-they-should-knock-it-to-the-ground-1.3358058

O' Loughlin, Ed. "These Women Survived Ireland's Magdalene Laundries: They're Ready to Talk." *The New York Times*, June 6, 2018. https://www.nytimes.com/2018/06/06/world/europe/magdalene-laundry-reunion-ireland.html

Pinto, Christian J. *Secret Mysteries of America's Beginnings*. Volume 1, "The New Atlantis." Documentary Film. N.p.: Antiquities Research Films. Presented by Exploration Films. Released 2006 Available on DVD and YouTube. https://www.youtube.com/watch?v=tzKqVtu6C5s

Pinto, Christian J. *Secret Mysteries of America's Beginnings*. Volume 2, "Riddles in Stone: The Secret Architecture of Washington D.C." Documentary Film. N.p.: Antiquities Research Films. Presented by Exploration Films. Released 2007. Available on DVD and YouTube. https://www.youtube.com/watch?v=oaEKBBsncng

Quayle, Stephen, and Thomas R. Horn. *Unearthing the Lost World of the Cloudeaters: Compelling Evidence of the Incursions of Giants, Their Extraordinary Technology, and Imminent Return*. Crane, MO: Defender Publishing, 2017

Schnoebelen, William. "What's So Good About Good Friday?" With One Accord Ministries (website). 2016. https://www.withoneaccord.org/assets/images/freedownloads/Good%20Friday.pdf

Shakespeare, William. "As You Like It." *The Works of William Shakespeare Gathered into One Volume*. The Shakespeare Head Press Edition. Oxford: Oxford University Press, 1938. See Act II, Scene VII, "All the world's a stage."

Shakespeare, William. "Hamlet." *The Works of William Shakespeare Gathered into One Volume*. The Shakespeare Head Press Edition. Oxford: Oxford University Press, 1938. See Act I, Scene III, "To thine own self be true."

Stearns, Amanda Akin. *The Lady Nurse of Ward E*. New York: Baker & Taylor, 1909.

Stowe, Harriet Beecher. *Uncle Tom's* Cabin. New York: Modern Library, 2001.

Thomsen, Emily. "Where's the Evidence that the Sabbath was Changed?" *Sabbath Truth* (blog). 2003. https://www.sabbathtruth.com/free-resources/article-library/id/916/catholic-church-admits-they-made-the-change

Tennyson, Alfred Lord. UNPA Campaign (website) "Locksley Hall" https://www.unpacampaign.org/es/1341/tennyson-alfred-statement/

Toplady, Augustus Montague. "Rock of Ages." *The Gospel Magazine,* October 1776. https://hymnstudiesblog.wordpress.com/2008/10/20/quotrock-of-agesquot/comment-page-1/?unapproved=14750&moderation-hash=8da368d49013162dd01e926ee9736da2#comment-14750

Tuberville, Henry. *An Abridgment of the Christian Doctrine: With Proofs of Scripture on Points Controverted.* New York: John Doyle, 1833. https://books.google.ca/books?id=2SkPAAAAIAAJ&printsec=frontcover&source=gbs_ge_summary_r&cad=0#v=onepage&q&f=false

Vieth, Walter J. *Total Onslaught Series: The Islamic Connection.* Videotaped lecture, filmed live on location. Blaine, WA: Amazing Discoveries, Copyright 2004. Available on YouTube. https://www.youtube.com/watch?v=j3MnkVg8xGo

Ward, Andrew. *The Slaves' War: The Civil War in the Words of Former Slaves.* Boston: Houghton Mifflin Harcourt, 2009.

Webb, Robert L. "The Waldenses and the Bible." Landmark Independent Baptist Church (website). https://www.libcfl.com/articles/waldbib.htm

West, John G. *Human Zoos: America's Forgotten History of Scientific Racism.* Documentary Film. Directed by John G. West. Music composed by: Donnie Alan. Screenplay by John G. West. Cinematography by Jesse Eastman, Keith Pennock. Edited by John G. West, Rachel Adams. Seattle, WA: Discovery Institute, 2018. Available on YouTube. https://www.youtube.com/watch?v=nY6Zrol5QEk

Wikipedia. "Jefferson Davis: Imprisonment." Wikipedia's "Jefferson Davis" entry. Last modified March 29, 2022, 13:50, https://en.wikipedia.org/wiki/Jefferson_Davis#Imprisonment

Wylie, J. A. *History of the Waldenses.* United Kingdom: Cassell, Petter, Galpin & Co., 1888. https://www.google.ca/books/edition/History_of_the_Waldenses/TA7UDwAAQBAJ?hl=en&gbpv=1